POWER GAME

PROF CROFT BOOK 6

BRAD MAGNARELLA

Copyright © 2018 by Brad Magnarella

All rights reserved.

No part of this book may be reproduced in any form or by any electronic or mechanical means, including information storage and retrieval systems, without written permission from the author, except for the use of brief quotations in a book review.

Cover image by Damonza.com

bradmagnarella.com

THE PROF CROFT SERIES

PREQUELS
Book of Souls
Siren Call

MAIN SERIES
Demon Moon
Blood Deal
Purge City
Death Mage
Black Luck
Power Game
Druid Bond
Night Rune
Shadow Duel
Shadow Deep
Godly Wars
Angel Doom

SPIN-OFFS
Croft & Tabby
Croft & Wesson

MORE COMING!

1

Palming a drink holder with four cups, I turned from the coffee bar and made my way past tables crowded with students, a few I recognized from Midtown College, and men and women in business wear. From a corner couch, the vampire hunters watched my approach. Maybe not the best place for our meeting.

"Black eye with four extra shots of espresso," I said, lifting out a tall cup and placing it on the coffee table in front of Blade. Without waiting for it to cool, the rail-thin punk rocker with a scythe of pink hair took a swallow and shrugged.

"Kind of weak," she said.

"I'll ask for cardiac-arrest strength next time." I lifted out another cup. "Jumbo raspberry mocha freezer with whip."

Bullet raised a meaty finger, and I handed it to him. He wasted no time sucking half of it down, his tattooed face seeming to collapse toward the straw.

I stared for a moment. "Easy there, big guy."

"He's addicted to brain freeze," Blade explained.

Bullet winced sharply, then shuddered in a kind of ecstasy,

causing the bandolier of shotgun shells that crisscrossed his large torso to rattle.

Oookay, I thought.

"And a chamomile tea, one bag." I passed Dr. Z his drink.

"Proper." The young black man sporting green hair and shiny leathers with slots for his sai swords blew through the tea's steam and relaxed back into the couch. Blade's and Bullet's weapons—a katana sword and shotgun, respectively—leaned beside them, within easy reach.

"That leaves my Colombian dark roast," I said, twisting it from the holder. I adjusted the cane I'd slid through my belt as I took a seat next to Dr. Z and looked over the three hunters.

I'd met them a couple years earlier when I—or more accurately, Thelonious—crashed their apartment concert in the East Village. I'd woken up the next morning with the mother of all hangovers and in Blade's bed. Nothing had happened, she said, except that I'd made a complete ass of myself. Pretty standard when my incubus came calling.

I didn't discover that Blade and her punk-rocking crew moonlighted as vampire hunters until months later when Vega and I were tracking the mayor's half-vampire, half-werewolf stepdaughter. The three were more skillful than I would have guessed, sparing us from Arnaud's blood slaves at one point. That they were still hunting—and still alive—spoke volumes.

"Clock's ticking," Blade said.

"Right, right." I had been the one to call the meeting. With the Order still repairing the rips around our world, I hadn't known who else to turn to. I leaned forward, propping my forearm on my knees. "I have a job for you."

"We're listening," Blade said. Though none of the hunters carried formal titles, she seemed to have taken on the role of leader.

"You remember Arnaud Thorne, CEO of Chillington Capital, right?"

"The vampire you blew up downtown? That whole shit show cost us a lot of business."

"Hey," Dr. Z said to her, "fewer vamps and spawn means more time to jam. Our sets are tighter than ever."

"Bigger crowds too," Bullet put in through a mouthful of his freeze.

Blade made a face as if their points were hardly consolation and took another swallow of rocket fuel.

"Then you'll be happy to hear Arnaud could be back," I growled.

"Back?" Blade perked up. "In the city?"

"Right now, it's more a hunch than anything," I said, feeling the chronic knot that had formed in my stomach two months earlier starting to tighten again. "When I 'blew up' Arnaud, he was attached to a shadow fiend. I'm worried he used that to his advantage in the Below and became something demonic."

"He survived the Pits?" Bullet asked, taking a break from his noisy slurping. "Whoa."

"A demon attacked Yankee Stadium in the fall, and this ring stopped him." I angled my fist toward them so they could see the silver ingot with the rearing dragon. "It holds an enchantment that only works against vampires bonded by the Brasov Pact, an age-old agreement between their kind and mine. Arnaud falls into that category. Plus, the demon took a ... well, an unusual interest in me."

I remembered the demon's interrogation of Thelonious, something my incubus companion still hadn't recovered from and maybe never would. I was happy to no longer be serving as his joyride, but if I had to choose between Thelonious and whatever Arnaud had in mind for me, I'd go with the big fellow.

"And you two have history," Blade said.

I grunted a laugh. "Yeah, just a little."

"If the ring stopped him, what's the problem?" Dr. Z asked. He was sitting with one leg crossed over the other, holding his tea with a pinky extended. He could have been at a garden party discussing someone's problematic pool man.

"The ring blew the demon from his host," I replied, "but I'm concerned that some of his essence came through."

I thought about the hole Arianna had described in the host's body, as if a large grub had squirmed from his core. She had found no trace of whatever had emerged, suggesting the being couldn't sustain itself up here. But my gut was of a different opinion. I'd been researching the hell out of demon germ ever since.

"If he *did* come through," I continued, "he would have been weak. Really weak. His priority would have been feeding. Small animals first. Assuming he survived that phase, he'd have moved on to higher life forms."

Blade raised a stud-lined eyebrow. "Humans?"

"Maybe," I replied. "If not now, then soon."

"And you want us to find this thing that may or may not exist," Dr. Z said.

"Right now, I just want you to keep your eyes and ears open. If Arnaud is back in the city, he won't look like he did. Not yet anyway. He'll be smaller, grayer. He may even appear a little amphibious. And you're right—he might not be here at all. But if he is, we need to nail him while he's weak." I stopped myself from hammering the coffee table for emphasis, but it was everything to me. "Put him down for good."

"Will this be different than hunting a vampire?" Blade asked. "'Cause if so, it's not really our expertise."

"According to what I've learned, it shouldn't be much different. At this stage, he's susceptible to silver through the heart, decapitation, cremation—the standard vampire-slaying tactics."

Blade gave me a look that said I didn't need to tell her their job.

"Anyway," I continued, "his vampiric powers will be limited. His demonic powers even more so. That doesn't mean you should take him lightly, though."

Blade's lips pursed as she took in what I was saying. "Can you give us a minute?" she asked.

"Yeah, sure."

I stood and, retreating out of earshot, watched the three hunters huddle over their drinks.

I wasn't entirely comfortable handing off the job to a group who might not take the threat as seriously as I did. But after hunting Arnaud for more than two months—often at the expense of my teaching and wizarding duties, not to mention my training with Gretchen—it was time to outsource. And whom better to outsource to than this trio of hunters who knew the city and its undead creatures as well as anyone.

After a minute, Blade jerked her head to tell me I could come back.

"Here's what we've decided," she said as I took my seat. "Two K a week for the hunt, and that starts on day one. We don't do partials. Thirty for a kill."

"Thousand?" I exclaimed.

"It's normally twenty," Blade said with a smirk. "But since the quarry's part demon…"

I crunched the numbers in my head. Between the Order and my tenured professorship at Midtown College, I did well, but I wasn't exactly sitting on a mountain of cash. "How negotiable are your rates?"

Blade shrugged a shoulder. "Like Bullet said, we're getting pretty good audiences now, more bookings. And without the occupational hazards of hunting."

I looked at Bullet and Dr. Z, but they returned poker faces.

Blade was the boss, and she was basically saying they could walk away, no skin off their backs. I dragged a hand through my hair.

"How about this?" I said. "Let's just start with the hunt. If you get a lead or find him, tell me."

"So, *don't* kill him?" Blade asked.

"Not for thirty thousand I don't have."

"If we destroy him in self-defense, you're still on the hook," she pointed out.

"As long as it's in self-defense." But it wasn't like I could prove they *hadn't* acted in self-defense.

"Then that's two thousand for week one," she said.

Blade had informed me over the phone that they dealt in cash only, so I'd arrived prepared. I pulled a bank envelope from my inside coat pocket and walked my fingers through the sheaf of hundreds until I'd counted out the amount. Blade checked my math before stuffing the thick billfold into her front pocket.

"What's the best way to reach you?" she asked.

"The number I called from. It forwards to my cell when I'm not home." I held up my new flip phone proudly. It had taken considerable work and practice, but a neutralizing spell coupled with some subtle changes to my casting technique, and I could actually handle something with a circuit board now.

Blade looked from the phone back to me, completely unimpressed.

"You do realize the rest of the world has moved on?" Dr. Z asked.

Muttering that it was different for wizards, I returned the phone to my pocket. Outdated or not, the flip phone was a big step for me.

"All right, Everson," Blade said, setting her finished drink down. "We're on it."

How she wasn't bouncing off the walls from the toxic dose of caffeine, I couldn't begin to understand. As she stood and slid her sword into the scabbard on her back, I eyed the bulk of bills in her pocket.

"Hey, don't take this the wrong way," I said, "but how will I know you're actually working on finding him and not, you know, screwing around on your instruments?"

"Because we trade on our reputation," Blade said as the others retrieved their weapons. "If you're paying, we're hunting. And if he's out there, we'll find him."

"Truth," Dr. Z said.

"And you'll call me," I reminded them.

"And we'll call you," Blade said.

"Immediately," I stressed.

Eyes hooding with impatience, Blade turned away. I joined the end of their line as the three hunters filed from the coffee shop. Our armed procession drew a few disconcerted stares, which is why I preferred places like Two Story Coffee to this Midtown chain, but it had been more convenient to meet here.

By the time we stepped onto the sidewalk, the street lights were blinking to life. Their amber halos pushed against the cold, cloudy dusk moving over the city. I shuddered and cinched my trench coat. I didn't know if it was the coming winter or my magic talking to me, but I felt a premonition of death.

Bullet pistoned his elbow into my side. "Hey, we're gonna grab some pizza. Wanna come with?"

Blade patted the pocket with my payment. "It's on us."

The gem in my watch began to pulse red as my cane kicked to life. "Ah, no can do. I'm being summoned."

"To what?" Bullet asked.

"My work."

2

"*Vigore!*"

I ducked and charged into the wake of my force invocation, splinters and door parts blasting off my shield. Beyond was a one-room efficiency. I absorbed the vital info at a glance: an open spell book, two casting circles, and one whimpering young man moments from learning that amateur conjuring had consequences.

But the nasty being holding him by the shirt was no shallow nether creature. It was too large, its shape too humanoid. A cracked surface of black magma covered its body, fire licking from the fissures.

Demon?

When the creature's horn-ringed head jerked around, I braced for Arnaud, even though I sensed it wasn't him. The creature's face was gargoyle-like and grotesque. Red pupils smoldered in a pair of dark pits. Slitted nostrils opened and closed in a fiery wheeze.

"Is that wizard I smell?"

He sounded nothing like Arnaud either.

"Full-blooded," I replied. "Must be your lucky day."

I flicked my sword and spoke an invocation. The force flashed across the room, landing across the demon's face with a sharp slap. Flames burst up on impact. *Need to keep this joker's attention on me until I can get the conjurer to safety.*

I was preparing an invocation to shield the young man, but the demon released him. The conjurer thudded to the floor and began kicking himself backwards while slapping out the flames on his hooded sweatshirt.

"Help me!" he gasped.

With a pair of invocations, I shoved the conjurer into the bathroom and sealed the door behind him. "Stay in there!" I shouted.

The demon, who had been cupping the place where I'd smacked him, rose to his full height. Shards of plaster fell as the tips of his horns gouged the low ceiling. Yeah, *definitely* not a shallow nether creature.

"Why waste effort on a puny mortal when I can feast on wizard?" he asked. Smoke broke around his cloven feet as he stalked toward me. His horns left tracks in the ceiling. "It's as if Satan himself delivered you."

"Yeah, I doubt that," I said.

The force invocation that ripped down the length of my sword slammed the demon into the far wall, throwing up a pluming cloud of smoke. Hanging pots clattered to the floor of a nearby kitchenette.

But as the foul cloud broke apart, the pinned demon was grinning.

He spoke his own Word, an evil one, and flames burst over the doorway.

"Really? You're barring my escape?" I asked, incredulous.

"I can already taste you," he said, licking his lips with a charred tongue.

"Taste this."

The creature choked on a gargle as I pinned him harder. I was dealing with an arrogant low-level demon, one small enough to have wormed his way through the various rips between our worlds, biding his time until he could hitch a ride on an amateur summoning through the final layer. That's what certain arcane spell books plus a city humming with potent ley energy could accomplish in this day and age.

The smart play was to put him down hard and fast and then alert the Order. You didn't screw around with demons, even low-level ones. But I wanted some info first. Maybe the demon was a blessing in disguise.

"I'm looking for someone," I said, stalking toward him, my trench coat batting with the power radiating off me. "Cooperate, and I'll simply cast you down to the Pits. Give me crap, and I'll reduce you to ashes." So six of one, half a dozen of the other.

The demon laughed derisively. "You lack the power to banish me. You're not even bearing anything holy."

"Oh, no?"

Black magma fell to the floor as I thrust my sword into his gut and shouted a new Word. The grooves of the blade's topmost rune began to glow. Holy light enveloped the demon, causing him to shriek.

My father had embedded the blade with nine enchantments designed to unlock as my abilities grew and I could handle their power. I had recently unlocked *numero uno*: a banishing enchantment. No more recitation of Latin texts required.

"Stop!" the demon screamed as his fissures opened over his body. "I beg you!"

I backed off a little. "Are you going to play nice?"

He answered with another evil Word. Fire flashed around my shield as the entire room exploded in infernal flames. I winced against the heat, uncapped a vial of ice crystals in my pocket, and swung it in an arc, shouting, *"Ghiaccio!"*

As the frost invocation reduced the flames to smoke, I pushed more power through the rune. Inside the burst of holy light, the demon screamed. "Yes, yes, all right, I'll tell you what you want! I'll tell you!"

"A year ago, a vampire was cast into the Pits," I said. "He had a shadow fiend with him. Do you know what became of the vampire?" The demon continued to shriek and writhe as I held him over the brink of banishment.

"Yes, yes, I know!" he cried. "I know!"

You couldn't trust anything out of a demon's mouth, especially one under duress. "First, tell me the vampire's name," I said.

"Samael! It was Samael!"

"Wrong."

"Lestat?"

"Enjoy your return trip to Hell."

The power I'd been holding back stormed through me. Holy light exploded from the rune, eviscerating the demon and his final cries. When the light receded back into the blade, the demon was gone.

Disappointed at the lack of info, I resheathed the sword into my staff. It had been a long shot—demons numbered in the millions and they swam in different infernal soups—but this demon hadn't known shit. It was going to be up to me and the vampire hunters to determine what, if anything, had become of Arnaud.

"Is it gone?" came a muffled voice.

With a Word, I released the locking spell on the bathroom door. The door cracked open, and the conjurer peered out. He'd drawn his hood over his head and pulled the strings tight, as though for extra protection.

"Yeah, it's all clear."

He shuffled over in a pair of jeans whose cuffs flopped

around his dirty socks. He was a little younger than I'd first thought, the cheeks cinched by his drawn hood featuring patches of acne. "I—I didn't think it would work," he stammered. Fingering the burn holes in his sweatshirt, he stared around his singed apartment.

"What's your name?" I asked.

He blinked over at me. "Nathan."

I picked up the spell book and flipped through it. The black cover was made of fake leather, and the spells inside had been typed in modern English. By the layout and host of errors, it looked like a shoddy self-publishing job.

I examined the spells more closely. Most read like recipes and recitations that someone had thought up on a whim. *Eye of newt, toe of frog,* that sort of thing. But the one Nathan had used was real enough. Not only that, it had been sufficient to summon a demon. A low-level one, granted, but that shouldn't have happened. I'd already given Nathan a thorough scanning, and he didn't possess an ounce of magic-user blood.

The conjuring spell was in a small section in the very back that was different from the rest of the book. The spells weren't typed, but handwritten in a smoky script. The intro to the section instructed the user to "HOLD THE PAGES OVER FIRE TO REVEAL THEIR POWER."

I looked more closely at the script. It had been rendered in some sort of enchanted ink—invisible until burned.

"Where did you get this?" I asked Nathan.

"I, uh, I ordered it."

"From where?"

He stumbled over to a gaming table heaped with manuals, modules, painted statuettes, and piles of notes. Some of the loose pages were still smoldering from the demon fire, but Nathan didn't seem to notice. He was too busy digging for something.

I glanced around the unit. Hand drawings of fantasy subjects —mages with glowing hands, dwarfs hefting giant axes, and a lot of muscled men in war skirts sporting broadswords—were tacked to the walls. Drawings that no doubt explained his interest in the spell book. A moment later, Nathan emerged from the gaming table with a magazine.

"In here," he said.

I caught the magazine's title before he flipped to the back: *Dragon Master: A Guide to All Things Gaming and Magic.*

"See?" He thrust the magazine toward me, an ink-stained finger indicating a box in the classified section advertising a "REAL SPELL BOOK!"—for $25 plus shipping and handling. The only identifying info was a P.O. box in New Jersey to which the money order was to be sent. There wasn't even a phone number.

"Do you know who the author is?" I asked, taking the magazine from him. That information wasn't in the spell book.

Nathan wiped his nose with the back of a hand. "Nuh-uh."

"Does anyone else in your circle of friends own these books?"

Nathan's head shook again, but his gaze had wandered down to my cane.

"You—you're the real thing, aren't you?" he said. "I mean, a real wizard?"

"Don't worry about what I am." I added the magazine to the spell book I'd already slipped into my satchel. "You're just lucky to be alive. That was an honest-to-God demon you called up. If I had gotten here a second later, you'd be extra well done, and we wouldn't be having this conversation."

"Dude..." he said in wonderment.

I pushed power into my wizard's voice until it shook. "You're not to attempt another spell ever again. Do you understand me?"

Nathan's eyes snapped to mine and he nodded vigorously. "Yes, Mr. Wizard."

That's where I usually left things, but I handed him a card with my number on it.

"If you encounter any more of these books, I want you to call me right away."

The Order would get to the bottom of whoever was distributing the powerful conjuring spells and why, but it was my job to contain the fallout in the meantime. At least in the greater New York area. When Nathan realized I was walking out, he shuffled after me.

"Hey, wait! You're leaving?"

"Yeah, I'm late for something."

"Can't you stay for another few minutes? You know, just in case it comes back?"

I paused in the doorway and turned. Nathan looked at me expectantly, fingers tugging on the crispy strings of his sweatshirt.

"You wouldn't happen to know of any flower shops nearby?" I asked.

3

I swore under my breath as I knocked on the door. *Of all the damned nights to be late.* After informing the Order of the demon conjuring, I hadn't even had time to shower or put on fresh clothes, and I smelled like a burnt piece of toast.

I peered down at the bouquet of flowers I'd bought from the street-corner vendor Nathan had recommended. The arrangement had looked pretty sad on the cart, and in the light of the front porch, it looked even more pathetic. I was about to chuck the flowers into the bushes when the front door shot open.

Vega's son appeared, his round eyes shining with excitement. "Mr. Croft!"

"Hey, Tony," I said, ruffling his hair. Sweat plastered his curly bangs to his forehead, and my hand came back damp. A group of kids grunted and shouted inside, but I couldn't see beyond the foyer from my angle.

"Is your mom here?"

I craned my neck in search of an adult. This was my first time meeting Vega's four brothers, and though Vega had given me every assurance they were cool, I was wary of what I was walking into. If she were *my* younger sister, I'd want to know who she was getting serious with, and there were four of them.

"C'mon," Tony said, grabbing my cane hand and pulling me inside.

The modest house in the Bronx had been their father's. Following his shooting death, Ricki's older brothers had pooled their resources and taken over the subsidized mortgage. Thanks to the Crash, the three oldest still lived here, along with their families. I had time to glance over a pile of kicked-off sneakers—how many of them *did* live here?—before Tony yanked me from the foyer and past a room where his cousins were engaged in what looked like a rugby match with a foam football.

At the end of a short hallway, I missed a step down to the living room and stumbled into the midst of Ricki's family. Their spirited conversation ended abruptly and faces turned toward me.

"Mr. Croft's here!" Tony announced, then abandoned me at a sprint to rejoin his cousins.

Gee, thanks, kid. With an uncomfortable chuckle, I got my footing and looked around the room. The half dozen or so adults were seated on couches and chairs in the casual manner of a family get-together, drinks and bowls of chips scattered around them. A smoky fire crackled in a small hearth.

When I didn't spot Vega, I gave a lame wave.

"Hi there," I said. "I'm, ah, Ricki's friend." Which I was convinced they heard as, *I'm the guy sleeping with your sister.*

"Everson," a man said from the couch nearest me. He was big and bald with a sweet smile that pushed his cheeks up to a pair of sleepy eyes. It was the kind of face you appreciated immediately in situations as these. I recognized him from the photos in Vega's apartment as her oldest brother.

"You must be Diego," I said, extending my hand.

He clasped it warmly in both of his. "Yeah, but everyone calls me Teddy."

"Short for Theodore?" I asked, wondering if Diego was a middle name.

"No," a lean man in white athletic warmups sitting beside him said. "Short for Teddy Bear. I mean, just look at that mug. Don't it make you wanna do this?" He reached over and grabbed a wad of Teddy's cheek.

That got the room laughing. Teddy pushed his hand away with a mellow chuckle.

"Alejandro?" I asked the lean man, which would make him Ricki's second oldest brother. Before he could answer, though, another character, whose muscular build had left him neckless, spoke up.

"Naw, that's Weaks, short for weakling."

Weaks chucked a couch pillow at him. "Yeah, and Gabe over there is 'the Rock,' but only 'cause he calls himself that."

"Man, I earned that name at the gym," the Rock protested.

"Just do what the rest of us do, Everson," Weaks said. "Call him 'Dumb as a Rock.' He'll answer to that too."

The Rock, who was third oldest, sprang past the coffee table and put Weaks in a headlock. Weaks countered with a series of soft shots to the Rock's stomach.

While they went at it, Teddy introduced me to the three women in the room, their wives. They greeted me with strong hugs and forbearing smiles, telling me to pay no attention to "the boys." Teddy's wife accepted the flowers—which suddenly didn't seem so lame—and invited me to sit down as she headed to the kitchen to put my gift in water.

I sidled over to where the Rock had been sitting, leaning back as he took Weaks to the floor. Teddy chuckled and shook his head. *Those two,* he was saying.

I couldn't help but smile. This was nothing like the grilling

I'd been dreading. Everyone was carrying on as if I were just another member of the household. I knew right then that we were all going to get along just—

"I'm Carlos."

"Jesus!" I cried, wheeling in surprise. He had been sitting silently in my blind spot.

It took me a moment to place him. Carlos was the youngest of the brothers, just a year older than Vega. A practicing attorney, he was the only brother who could afford to live alone. The other brothers alternated between whatever work they could find and unemployment. Vega often referred to Carlos as the "smart one," and it was clear she looked up to him.

Carlos stood from a wooden chair, coming almost to my height, and gripped my hand solidly. Unlike his brothers, he was dressed formally: white button-down shirt and brown vest. A neat beard accented his jaw. Though there were hints of Vega in the others, his resemblance to her was the most striking. From behind a pair of glasses, his critical eyes were a dead ringer for Vega's during our early, adversarial days.

"So, no nickname?" I asked.

"No," he answered without humor.

"We tried to give him one," Weaks said from the floor, "but nothing took."

"Yeah," the Rock put in. "Pencil Neck. Poindexter. Dweeb. He passed on all of them."

"I wonder why," I said, sliding Carlos a smile.

But Vega's brother only seemed to stiffen at my attempted friendliness.

"What about Ricki?" I asked to get the subject off him, which was making *me* uncomfortable. "What do you guys call her?"

"Don't you dare get them started."

Vega entered from the kitchen, drying her hands with a towel. She was wearing her midnight hair down over a gray turtleneck sweater and looked incredible. A host of simmering smells wafted in after her. She gave me a kiss and slipped an arm around my waist. I could feel Carlos watching us.

"So, I see you've met the Zoo Crew," she said.

"Oh, c'mon," I said with a wave. "They're nice."

"See there," the Rock called from the floor. "Even your boyfriend has our backs."

Vega shook her head in exasperation. "And you wondered why it took me a year to bring him over here. Get off the floor and let Alejandro up," she snapped. "And wash your hands while you're at it. We're eating in five."

The two brothers complied with playful mutters and hung heads.

Teddy turned to me, a twinkle in his sleepy eyes. "Miss Bossy Pants."

"Huh?"

"That's what we called her."

Vega chucked her towel at him, a perfect throw that bloomed over Teddy's face and covered it completely. The towel shook with muffled laughter, and soon everyone joined in.

Everyone except for Carlos.

DINNER WAS SERVED IN THE FAMILY DINING ROOM, WHERE TABLES of various lengths and heights had been pushed together and covered with a pair of mismatched tablecloths. We took our seats on an equally motley arrangement of chairs, the kids squeezing in between us with plates of hotdogs and potato chips.

I caught Vega eyeing me for my reaction as she sat beside me. I winked and rubbed the curve of her low back. The idea of introducing me to her family had no doubt been as anxiety-producing for her as it had been for me, but save for the odd vibe from Carlos, I couldn't have felt more at home.

Vega smiled back.

"Yo, Carlos!" she called past me. Her older brother by a year was entering the dining room behind the last of the kids. "Over here." She waved and pointed to the empty setting directly opposite me.

Wonderful.

"I've been wanting you two to talk," Vega said as Carlos lowered himself down in front of me. Above her smile, Vega's eyes shone with pride. I felt my own lips locking into something between a grin and a grimace. "Carlos practices full time, but he's in academics too. He teaches a course at Guffin Law School."

"Yeah?" I said. "What do you teach?"

"Contracts."

"Wow, that's..." I had nothing. "That's really interesting."

"I've told you about Everson," Vega said. "He's a professor in the history department at Midtown College. Ten years?"

"Yeah, just about." My normal MO was to tack on a self-deprecating joke, but I couldn't come up with squat. Carlos's presence seemed to sap even the potential for humor from the atmosphere.

"How about you?" I asked. "Been in the classroom long?"

Instead of answering, he said, "Mythology and lore, huh?"

I nodded, surprised he had known or remembered. "That's right."

I waited for some sort of follow up, but Carlos only took a large bowl of yellow rice and roasted pork from the center of the table and began spooning the traditional Puerto Rican dish onto his plate.

Vega shook my knee as if her brother and I were getting along famously and turned to a sister-in-law on her other side.

Crap. I slid my gaze to the right, hoping to pull someone else onto Carlos's and my shrinking island of conversation. A little girl at the end of the table stared back at me, her mouth ringed in ketchup.

"Good hotdog?" I asked.

"Ricki told me about your other work," Carlos said.

I looked back at him. Vega had never mentioned sharing my wizarding life with her family. "Oh, yeah?" I said, accepting the dish he extended toward me. This line of conversation could go several ways, and none felt promising. Carlos didn't strike me as a believer in the arcane. I busied myself with loading my plate.

"How's that going?" he asked.

"Oh, you know. It's going."

"Working on anything currently?"

This wasn't idle chit-chat. Carlos was steering toward something.

"There's always a job of some kind or another," I replied vaguely. "You know how it goes."

"I don't, actually. Not when it comes to exactly what it is you do."

He was regarding me with those critical eyes. I glanced over at the little girl with the ketchup mouth. She was still staring up at me, chewing methodically. "Well, it—it's complicated," I stammered. "Maybe I can explain it some other time."

"I understand Ricki nearly walked into an ambush this summer."

And there it was. He was referring to the trap Damien—or Arnaud, possibly—had set to draw attention from Yankee Stadium, where he'd tried to claim 50,000 souls. Had he succeeded, there was no telling the size and strength of demon we'd be facing. Certainly nothing like the riffraff I'd banished an hour earlier.

"One that killed your partner," Carlos added.

"Yeah, Pierce Dalton," I said. "Ricki was well back when it happened," I added to reassure him, but my words came out sounding defensive, maybe because of the critical way he was staring me down now.

"Her job is dangerous enough."

"I won't let anything happen to her," I replied a little too quickly.

He glanced over at Vega, but she was still in conversation with her sister-in-law, the two of them talking over some jabbering girl cousins. "It doesn't sound like you have much control over that," Carlos said. "If anything, it sounds like you're making her job more dangerous than it already is."

My pulse ramped up at the insinuation that I was intentionally throwing hazard his sister's way. "Look, it's not by design. It's just that her work in Homicide and mine happen to overlap."

"Funny. Before you showed up, I don't remember her being shot at point-blank range, getting into gunfights at the mayor's mansion, or being napalmed in Central Park. Not to mention nearly walking into that exploding building."

"She *wasn't* napalmed—we got out in time." God, talk about a terrible retort. Setting my fork down, I leaned forward and lowered my voice. "All right, man, what's the point of this? What are you wanting me to say?"

"I just want to make sure you understand our concern."

Our? I thought.

I looked around the table, but the other three brothers weren't paying us a lick of attention. Weaks tossed a potato chip into the air and caught it with his lips, to the delight of the kids around him. His wife smacked his shoulder.

Yeah, our, *my ass,* I thought.

"If it were just Ricki, fine," Carlos went on. "She's a grown woman. But it's not just her, is it?"

His gaze shifted to the other end of the table. Vega's son

smiled and waved at us. I raised my own hand and forced a grin. When I looked back at Carlos, his eyes bore into mine.

"Now do you see my point?" he said.

"Nothing's going to happen to him, either."

"Can you promise that?"

4

"So, what did you and my brother talk about?" Vega asked. When she looked over at me from behind the steering wheel, her eyes shone in a way that told me we'd just shared in something especially close to her heart.

"Oh, you know," I said, shifting in my seat. "This and that."

We were barreling down Ninth Avenue in her sedan, street signs flashing past in descending order as we made our way toward my West Village apartment. Tony was staying over at the house with his cousins, which meant Vega and I had the rest of the night to ourselves—something we'd been taking more advantage of lately.

But while my intro to her family seemed to be having an aphrodisiac effect on Vega, I was having flashbacks of my encounter with Carlos. Talk about a mood-killer. And now she wanted to talk about it.

"I'm serious," Vega said. "I've been dying for you two to meet."

"A little warning would have been nice."

The skin between her eyes creased. "About what?"

"Well, for starters that you told him about my other life."

"Everson, the man reads like half a dozen papers a day. He already knew about your role in the mayor's eradication program. He also knew we worked together. I just filled in the blanks."

"So, what does he think?"

"About you being a wizard?" She shrugged. "He was skeptical, but that's how he is about everything. He knows I'm the same way, so when I told him I could one hundred percent attest to your abilities, he went with it."

"He went with it," I echoed.

"Is that what you talked about?"

"Not ... exactly."

I shifted again. I hated being evasive, but what was the alternative? Saying that the brother she admired most had given me a stern talking to? I didn't want to make Vega feel like she had to choose sides.

"Then what?" she pressed.

"Well, his concern for you," I said, which was half true.

Vega shot me a sarcastic look. "I think he already knows I work in Homicide."

"Yeah, and he feels that your involvement with me increases the risk. *Work* involvement," I clarified. But Carlos hadn't really said whether he meant work, personal, or both.

"He brought that up at dinner?" Vega asked, a cloud moving across her face.

Great. Exactly what I *hadn't* wanted to happen. "He's your brother, Ricki. He's just looking out for you." Was I actually taking up for the guy?

"Still." The gleam left Vega's hardening eyes.

"Just think about it from his—" I started to say.

My phone rang, cutting off the rest of the sentence. I pulled the device from my pocket. Even after the earlier demon encounter, the neutralizing spell continued to hum around the phone, protecting its sensitive circuitry. The caller was Blade. I held up a finger to tell Vega we'd get back to our conversation. I didn't want to leave it there.

"What's up?" I asked into the open phone.

"We might have something," Blade said.

My heart contracted into a fist. "Talk to me."

"After our meeting, I put out the word. We have a network of informants keeping eyes on some of the grittiest spots in the city. The kinds of places bloodsuckers who want to keep a low profile often go to feed. Anyway, a creature was spotted about ten minutes ago that matched the description of your friend."

"Where?" I asked, digging for my notepad.

"East River Park near Sixth. There's that Container City down there."

I stopped digging. "Yeah, I know the place."

Vega wrinkled her brow to ask what was going on.

"Can you hold on a sec?" I said to Blade.

"Sure."

I muted the phone. "I might have a job," I said, my heart still beating through the words. *Was* this Arnaud? "Could you veer over to FDR Drive and drop me off at East Sixth? I'll meet you back at my apartment."

"Container City?" Vega shook her head. "There's no way I'm leaving you down there by yourself."

"Ricki, it's too dangerous."

"Are you my brother now? Even if you handle whatever's down there, you're going to have to navigate the city's worst projects to get out. You remember Ferguson Towers, right?"

A cruel bang went off in my memory—the sound of a drug lord shooting Vega at point-blank range. Something Carlos had been sure to include in his list of indictments against me. Watching Vega go down in the rain that night was the first time I'd realized I had more than professional feelings for her.

"And since when does someone call you about a breach?" she demanded. She looked down at my cane, which I'd set across my thighs. "That thing should be going spazoid."

"Because it's not that kind of creature," I said. "It might be … Arnaud."

Vega swore under her breath as she popped her siren lights and sped up.

"Ricki…"

"When were you going to tell me?"

"When I knew for sure."

"He kidnapped my son," she snapped, as if I needed any reminding.

"Which is exactly why I don't want you back on his radar."

"I have protection," she said, tapping the center of her chest, where my grandfather's coin pendant rested. "I'm also packing enough silver to reduce that fucker to a pulp."

I thought about Carlos's and my talk, wondering now what had bothered me more: what he said, or how closely it matched my own anxieties. Despite my improving abilities, I couldn't guarantee Vega's safety. Or Tony's. Towards the end of dinner, I'd slipped outside to place wards on all of the doors and windows.

"Anyway, we're a team," she said.

My phone's small display lit up to remind me Blade was still holding. I unmuted the device.

"Sorry about that," I said to Blade.

"Did you take a newspaper in there with you?"

I ignored the bathroom jab. "Anything else I need to know?"

"He was spotted at the edge of the old track, moving south."

Headed straight for the containers, I thought grimly.

"Do you want backup?" Blade asked.

I glanced over at Vega. She was right about her offense and defense—they were potent. And if I could trust my research, it was still too early for Arnaud to have recovered his preternatural speed and strength, not to mention his casting powers.

Still ... Blade and the hunters were only a few blocks away. And suddenly thirty thousand to end Arnaud for good didn't seem an unreasonable asking price.

"Remain on standby," I told Blade.

Vega raised her eyebrows at me in question.

"My partner and I are going in."

Vega parked on East Sixth, and we took off over a pedestrian bridge that spanned FDR Drive. Like so many of the city's parks, the one hugging the East River had fallen into decay after the Crash. Its cleanup and restoration weren't political priorities either, considering the park's location: in the shadows of the housing projects Vega had mentioned. Indeed, most of East River Park's inhabitants were castoffs from said projects.

Through the dark trees ahead, I caught the first glints of streetlights off metal. One of the city's nods to the park's refugees had been to drop a load of old shipping containers for use as shelters. As we descended the bridge, I caught a strong waft of human funk. At the end of every month, an armed sanitation team went through Container City and collected the dead. It smelled like they'd missed October.

Vega and I slowed, my protective shields crackling around us.

"How many containers?" I whispered.

"More than thirty in the entire park. Maybe a dozen or so in this section."

I had already tried tracking Arnaud using hunting spells, but nothing had responded to them, not even items that had belonged to the vampire. If he *was* back, his essence must have been fundamentally altered.

Finding him would mean getting actual eyes on him.

"The creature was spotted coming down from that way," I whispered to Vega, gesturing to our left. "I'm thinking we start where the path bisects this section here and then work our way north." As a demon germ, sustenance was everything right now. Meaning he would be looking for an easy meal.

"Are we breaching the containers?" Vega asked.

I grimaced at the thought. "Only if we have to. Right now, we're looking for anyone who might have been caught out after dark." Even in their sorry states, the citizens of Container City knew to lock themselves in at night.

We made our way quietly through the trees toward the first containers. The service pistol Vega clasped in both hands held a full mag of silver-laced ammo. I had pulled my cane into sword and staff, arcane power humming around both.

Shouts and deranged cries rang from inside the nearest containers but nothing that sounded like an attack in progress. We wove our way past them. Cold wind gusted off the East River, clacking the trees around us. But the prickling wave that passed through me was warm, like a whisper. Part of my training with Gretchen involved learning to listen to my magic, and it had just spoken.

We were being watched.

I locked eyes with Vega and made a small rotating signal with a finger. Trees, containers, and darkness slid past my field of vision as we each turned in opposite directions, weapons readied. I thought I caught something creeping just outside my peripheral vision, but when I jerked my head, it vanished.

"Shield your eyes," I whispered.

When Vega brought a hand to her face, I thrust up my staff and bellowed, *"Illuminare!"*

A ball of light spun into being and shot above the trees, blowing open the night. As the ball hovered, great sparks rained down through the branches and swelled into their own luminescent orbs.

Nowhere to hide.

Without warning, a creature spat and scrambled from behind a thick tree.

Shots exploded from Vega's weapon. The creature was stooped like an old man, its gray, vein-mapped body glistening in the light of my invocation. Bark burst and bullets caromed after the creature as it darted from tree to tree. I summoned a barrier but was too slow to stop it. The creature fled past it, disappearing around the corner of a container.

Dammit! I thought, taking off.

"Stay in the light," I called to Vega. "It might double back."

"Where are you going?"

"To head it off!"

I broke toward the other end of the container the creature had ducked behind and cut around the corner. I glimpsed the creature's back as it disappeared behind yet another container. It didn't look remotely vampiric. *Was* this Arnaud?

"Vigore!" I called, swinging my sword toward the ground.

In a burst of leaves and dirt, the force invocation cratered the ground and shot me skyward. I landed on top of a container with a hollow clang, setting off a commotion inside. Ahead of me, the creature was scrambling through the maze of containers toward the water's edge. As it paused to crane its neck around, its bulbous eyes found mine. A sickly yellow magic began to radiate from them.

I thrust my grandfather's ring forward. *"Balaur!"*

The ring tightened around my finger before releasing an explosive force. The creature leapt into a slot canyon between two containers, but not before the force from the ring found it.

The creature screamed as white fire flashed across its trailing leg.

I recognized the power: it had originated from the enchantment of the Brasov Pact. Meaning the creature *was* Arnaud. And I'd just crippled the son of a bitch.

Now to finish him.

With another invocation, I propelled myself through the air to the next container. Arnaud was in full flight, scrambling on three of his four appendages toward the water. I chased along the tops of the container, tracking Arnaud with my fist, shouting the word that gave lethal force and direction to the Brasov Pact.

Pulse after pulse slammed into the containers as Arnaud continued to thrust himself behind and around them.

By the fifth blast, though, I felt the enchantment flagging.

I swore at myself. *You're being too undisciplined, dammit.*

Arnaud cut between two final containers, his way to the water clear.

"*Vigore!*" I shouted.

The force invocation rammed the ends of the containers together, blocking his passage. I dropped down to the ground and raced toward him. He began climbing a rusted container, his injured right leg hanging beneath him. With a spoken invocation, a shield flashed into being above him.

"End of the line!" I called.

He peered back at me, fear in his bulbous eyes, but it was way too early to celebrate. Silver through the heart would stun him, decapitation or cremation—ideally both—would kill him. Vials of dragon sand jostled beside an iron amulet in one of my coat pockets, but the manifestation of fire was hard to control, and I couldn't risk superheating the containers.

Instead, I shouted a force invocation and opened my sword hand. The blade shot from my grip toward the center of Arnaud's upper back, just left of his knotted vertebrae. But before the blade could hit and cleave his demonic heart, Arnaud wriggled into a hole in the side of the container, rust breaking off around his disappearing body. My sword clanged from the metal siding as screams erupted from inside.

"Ricki!" I called. "He's inside a container!"

I covered the shipping container with a shield to prevent Arnaud's escape, then scooped up the sword and launched myself over the enormous box. The items in my coat rattled as I came to a jarring landing at the container's doors. I sent up a light ball as a signal to Vega, then wasted no time blasting the container's lock with an invocation.

Arnaud might have been trapped, but there were innocents with him.

With the lock destroyed, the right side of the giant door clanged loose and began to lurch out. The rusted hinges protested with a shriek to rival those coming from inside. I was preparing to thrust my shielded body through the narrow space when the door blew open the rest of the way and a pale, naked creature with wild eyes appeared.

To this point, I'd only seen Arnaud from a distance. Up close he looked like a nightmare.

His skin was sore-riddled and sagging. Parts of him actually appeared to be rotting away. He shambled from the container's smoky pools of firelight, a mouth of broken teeth opening as he descended on me.

With a grunt, I thrust my sword through his stomach and swung him away from the container. He came off the blade and landed hard against the ground.

"Nice to see you again too," I said. "Unfortunately, the reunion is going to be brief."

Grandpa's ring tightened around my finger, telling me the enchantment had recharged. I aimed the ring at Arnaud as he struggled up. The vampire-demon wasn't going to survive this one, not at point-blank range.

"*Balaur!*" I shouted.

Nothing moved from the ring.

I dispelled my shield and pushed more power into the Word, but the ring didn't so much as flex. Arnaud was up now and staggering toward me. I drove the sword forward. With a dull crunch, the tip of the blade broke through his sternum and became buried in his heart. Foul gray fluid burst from his chest.

But the blow didn't have the paralyzing effect it should have.

With a crazy smile, Arnaud shot out a slick hand and seized my throat.

I gagged as a rank smell of death flooded my nostrils.

5

For reasons unknown, the ring had crapped out, died on my finger. And now, with Arnaud's hands around my throat, I couldn't speak to invoke. Tensing my neck against the constricting force, I twisted the sword that pierced his chest. More gray fluid spilled out and spattered around our feet. The silver-lined blade was skewering his heart. That alone should have been enough to paralyze the son of a bitch.

His eyes rolled crazily as laughter shook his naked body.

Though I could feel demonic magic swimming sickly around him, he didn't look like a demon germ. Hell, he didn't even look like a vampire. Not that his precise classification mattered at the moment.

The fucker was trying to bite me.

His broken teeth clacked again as he struggled to pull me nearer. Gargling, I jerked the blade from his chest and managed to work it up against his throat. Tears sprang from my eyes as Arnaud redoubled his grip. By see-sawing the sword back and forth, I managed to cleave the blade into the putrid flesh at his neck. He moaned, and his fingers began to slip.

Blam! Blam! Blam!

Fluid and gobs of foulness pelted my face. Arnaud's hands fell from my neck, and he staggered backwards in a drunken dance. Where his head had been was a pulpy stump. He dropped to the ground in a heap.

"You all right?" Vega asked, lowering her weapon.

"Yeah," I replied hoarsely, wiping the tears from my eyes. "Thanks."

As I invoked to get the creature's filth off me, Vega peered past me to where Arnaud's body lay. "So, is he finished?"

"I'm going to incinerate him to be sure."

I had already thumbed the cap off the dragon sand, but I paused before covering his body in the ultra-combustible granules. My magic was talking to me again, and I didn't like what it was suggesting. I summoned shields around Vega and me and spun toward the shipping container.

"Is he still inside?" I shouted at the host of scared and grimy faces peering out.

Heads shook and a few fingers pointed toward the water. I sprinted to where the East River lapped the concrete wall below and cast out a ball of light. The invocation blazed brilliantly, but I couldn't see anything across the span of choppy waters.

I spat out a curse.

Vega arrived beside me. "What's going on?"

"Arnaud outsmarted me," I muttered.

Vega looked from the headless body behind us to the vast expanse of water. The ball of light I'd cast moments before faded, returning the river to inky darkness. "Then who did I just take down?" she asked nervously.

I sighed. "A zombie."

"A zombie?"

In my mind, I cycled through the chase—the pulse-pounding sequence that had begun with the prickling sense someone was watching us and ended with Vega blowing the head from my attacker.

Only the watcher and the attacker had been two different creatures.

"When Arnaud climbed into the container, he found a body," I explained. "Dead a week or so from the smell of him. In fact, his fellow container people had probably already stripped him of his clothes. Arnaud animated the body and sent it out the door. While the zombie and I were dancing a tango, he slipped away."

I watched the muscles around Vega's jaw harden.

"Yeah," I agreed.

She pulled out her phone and called NYPD dispatch. Peppering her rapid speech with codes, she gave a description of Arnaud and ordered a perimeter as well as an aerial search of the East River and both shores. I made my own call to the Order, filling Claudius in and asking that he have Arianna contact me immediately.

I hung up before the old man could start babbling.

BACK AT THE CONTAINERS, AN INTERVIEW WITH THE MORE coherent of the container inhabitants confirmed what I'd guessed about Arnaud's actions. He'd come in, grabbed a dead body—"Franklin" was the man's name—sent him out, and then slipped away himself. Fortunately, he hadn't claimed any living victims while inside. That was small consolation, though.

As the first NYPD choppers arrived over the East River, their spotlights sweeping the waters, Vega put away her phone.

"They'll let me know if they spot anyone," she said.

I nodded vaguely, knowing in my gut that Arnaud had gotten away.

"Hey." Vega's hand slipped into mine and gave a firm squeeze. "We'll find him."

I nodded. He was faster than I thought he would be, more resourceful. More powerful too. I mean, hell, he'd channeled enough demonic magic to animate a corpse. He shouldn't have been that far along, dammit.

"Why don't you go stay with Tony tonight?" I said. "I'll hang out here."

I expected another argument, but Vega was thinking along the same lines, apparently. My grandfather's coin pendant, which currently hung from Vega's neck, would shield anyone inside its aura from Arnaud's aggression. And right now, she and I both wanted Tony inside that aura.

I escorted Vega back over the pedestrian bridge.

"I'll have them contact you if they spot anything," she said, climbing into her car.

"And I'll be searching Arnaud's path of flight, see if I can find anything to cast from."

"Keep me updated. And *call* if you need anything," she stressed. "I'll have a car give you a ride home." I caught the door before she could close it.

"Hey, ah, would you mind not telling your brother what happened tonight?"

Vega smirked at my joke that wasn't entirely a joke. "We'll keep it between us."

"Miss Bossy Pants, huh?"

"Don't you dare start."

As our smiles straightened, I stooped down and kissed her. "I love you," I whispered, which was me saying I wouldn't let anything happen to her or her son. But in place of whatever Vega said back, her brother's critical voice echoed in my head.

Can you promise that?

Or was the voice my own?

As I'd predicted, the police search didn't turn up Arnaud. Farther north, they found a floating body. A jugular bite coupled with the recentness of the woman's death suggested Arnaud had found his meal after all.

I fared no better back at Container City. I searched exhaustively around the container where the pulse from Grandpa's ring had lit up Arnaud's right leg, but if the demon had dropped any matter, it had already sublimated. Neither could I locate any kind of trail on the astral or ethereal planes.

At midnight, I checked my phone. No return calls from the Order. I dialed the officers Vega had placed on standby and had them drop me off at Gretchen's place.

The large, handsome townhouse just south of Midtown had belonged to Pierce Dalton, the magic-user I'd worked with briefly before his demise. Through some arrangement with the Order, Gretchen had taken it over, and that's where we had been holding our irregular training sessions. Though my teacher still acted as though she barely tolerated me, I knew better. She had helped me foil Arnaud's attack on Yankee Stadium by ensuring I had everything I needed. I was betting she would help me now.

I climbed the stone steps and banged the heavy brass knocker against the door. As I waited for her to answer, I shifted to my wizard's senses. Multidimensional bands of magic hummed around the house like a giant magnetic field. For someone who looked so disorganized on the surface, Gretchen had her defensive shit together. She'd been teaching me to improve my own wards, lessons I'd put to use on Vega's apartment as well as my own. So far nothing had breached them.

Yet, the Carlos voice inside me added.

I was about to knock again when a grumbling sounded on the door's other side.

Bolts popped and the door yawned open. But instead of a large woman with a savage case of bedhead, I was looking down at a creature in a bathrobe with squash-colored eyes and a menacing exhibit of sharp teeth.

"Whad'ya want?" the goblin barked.

I jerked my sword from my cane. "Who the hell are you?"

His eyes crossed toward the point of my blade, which now hovered inches from his face. Goblins were nasty little creatures. Vega and I had encountered an army of them in Central Park during Mayor Lowder's eradication campaign and barely escaped with our lives. A few dozen police officers hadn't been so lucky.

The goblin's eyes returned to mine, entirely unconcerned. "Make your move, tough guy."

When lines of energy wavered between us, I realized Gretchen's defenses were protecting him. There was no way a lowly goblin had gotten inside unless Gretchen had intended it, meaning he was a guest of some kind. What kind, I couldn't begin to guess ... and wasn't sure I wanted to. Eyeing the creature's cotton bathrobe, I lowered my sword slowly.

"Where's Gretchen?" I demanded.

"Not here."

"Can you be a little more specific?"

He crossed a pair of tattooed forearms and leaned against the doorframe. "I could."

I wanted to reach through the ward and shake the four-foot creature by the lapels of his robe. But knowing I wouldn't get that far before Gretchen's wards put me in a world of hurt, I took a calming breath.

"I'm Everson Croft, her student. I need to talk to her about something important."

The goblin pulled a pack of cigarettes from a breast pocket, shook one out, and took his time lighting it with a match.

Goblins were notoriously bad tempered, prone to violence at the drop of a hat. But this one's aggression seemed more passive. He blew a contrail of smoke from the side of his scarred mouth and studied a talon.

"Look, I'm sorry for pulling my sword on you," I said. "I've just never seen you here before, and—"

"I'm a goblin?"

"I wasn't going to say that."

"You wouldn't be the first."

"It was just a shock, that's all."

"Oh, look, a goblin," he deadpanned. "Must be up to no good."

In fact, goblins rarely were, but I kept the thought to myself. "More like, oh, look, a stranger in my teacher's house."

He flicked the butt with a thumb to drop the ash. "Gretchen's never mentioned me?"

Though his deep, barking voice didn't lend itself to nuance, I thought I sensed a hint of disappointment. "Well, like I said, she's my teacher. We don't really get into each other's personal stuff."

The goblin gave a vague nod as if that explained something. He dropped the barely-smoked cigarette to the floor and crushed it out with a bare heel. "She's in Faerie," he said. "I'm looking after the place."

So that explained it, though I was having trouble picturing a creature built for war collecting her mail and watering the geraniums.

"Do you have a way of getting in touch with her?" I asked.

"Gretchen?" He gave a snort. "Said she'd be back in a few days, which could mean anything."

True enough. "Well, if you hear from her before then, could you ask her to call me?"

"I can ask." His tired look suggested he and Gretchen had history.

"Hey, I didn't catch your name," I said.

"That's 'cause I didn't toss it."

Thinking the goblin was going to leave it there, I turned to go.

"It's Bree-Yark," he said.

"Thanks, Bree-Yark. Sorry for getting you out of bed."

"I was already up. Don't sleep so well in your world."

Not knowing how to respond, and with too much already on my mind, I bid him goodnight. When I was halfway down the sidewalk, he called after me.

"Hey, you wanna come inside? Watch a movie or something?"

I looked back. The creature cut a lonely silhouette in the doorway of the huge house.

"I would, but I'm in the middle of something important."

"You and everyone else," he muttered, and slammed the door.

I shook my head. *Talk about moody.*

When I reached the sidewalk, I paused to organize my thoughts. With the Gretchen option out—for now, anyway—I decided to head down to Blade's place in the East Village to debrief her and the other hunters on my encounter with Arnaud. I was also going to tell them I was good with the thirty-thousand-dollar bounty. I'd underestimated Arnaud's strength and savvy. His animation of the dead man had probably taken every last reserve of power he'd amassed, but given time, those kinds of demonic feats were going to cost him little to nothing.

The more scopes we could put on him, the better.

Because Blade's place wasn't far, I flipped my coat collar up against the cold wind and set out on foot. If I saw a cab en route,

I would flag it down. I'd only gone a few blocks when a warm prickling passed through me.

My magic was talking again, telling me I was being watched.

Heart thumping, I hardened the protective field around me and unlocked my sword from my staff.

Please, let this be another crack at Arnaud.

The watcher was to my left and behind me, just out of sight. I could feel him tailing me now, following soundlessly. He was accompanied by a shadowy whisper of magic. Demonic? Hard to tell.

I took two more steps and spun.

"Entrapolarle!" I bellowed.

With a flash, a spherical shield crackled into being around my pursuer. When the light dimmed, something was batting up and down the shield's inside in a mad flurry of dark feathers. I shrank its confinement until the creature was pinned. It blinked out at me from an obsidian black eye and released a ragged caw.

A raven?

A bolt slammed into my back and threw me to the ground.

Christ, what now?

6

The demonic creature that had once been the vampire Arnaud slipped from the East River, dragging his right leg behind him. Wincing, he craned his neck around. Off to the south, helicopters circled. He had passed beneath them, keeping to the river's garbage-strewn bottom, where their searchlights were reduced to murky specters.

With a sneer, he pulled himself to a large tree above the island's shore and disappeared among its roots. He had burrowed the tunnel when he was newly returned to the world —and smaller. Now the rocky earth squeezed and gouged his sides. He cursed as he arrived in the lair he'd clawed out.

"Wasn't supposed to return here," he hissed.

After two months of feeding on the island's pathetic creatures, he had grown. His senses had sharpened. Just a week before, the first gaslight of promised demon magic flickered inside him. That's what he'd been waiting for—a sign he was ready to move onto humans, to assimilate their potent life forces.

His plan had been to infiltrate the human dregs around the city's periphery where he could move unnoticed, even as the dead grew in number. He knew the city's politics too well, for they were the politics of all great cities. Broken and penniless earned you no true sympathy, much less an autopsy. The bodies would disappear into the city morgue along with the others. Their blood and souls would grow and transmutate inside him, increasing his power five, tenfold!

He slumped against the damp wall of his cramped, bone-littered lair and peered down at his mangled leg.

That *had* been the plan before the bastard wizard showed up —just as he had two months before—but wielding more power. And that cursed ring. The demon slammed a fist into the wall, creating a small earth slide.

"But how did he find us, Zarko?" he asked. "*How?*"

Arnaud's head servant had perished along with his blood slaves when he himself was cast into the Below. But Arnaud had spent so many centuries talking to him, he found he couldn't quell the habit. If anything, he found it comforting.

But Zarko's memory did little for him now.

"We've been nothing but prudent," Arnaud continued as he seized his right leg in his taloned hands. "Nothing but ... *careful!*"

As he said the last word, he gave a violent wrench. The leg came away with a wet crunch and rip. Biting back a scream, Arnaud shoved the useless appendage aside. Black vapor rose as it began to sublimate. He composed himself and wiped away the messy strings of matter from around his hip socket until he could see the new limb—a scrawny salamander-like leg that would grow and morph into shape.

But it would take blasted time.

"How?" he demanded of Zarko again.

Had Everson Croft tracked him somehow? Impossible. His agonizing passage through the Harkless Rift had changed him, cloaking his nature from all but fellow demons. But what good was the cloaking if Everson showed up every time he ventured out? Was the ring homing in on the pact that connected them? Arnaud shook his head. The agreement at Brasov had explicitly forbade any tracking features in the binding enchantment. The enchantment was to be used for enforcement only.

And that enchantment had hurt him tonight. Indeed, it had very nearly destroyed him a second time.

Arnaud cradled his new leg as though it were an infant. He had been spent and wounded, barely able to pull himself through the water. Were it not for the crazy woman tottering along the shore, he might not have made it back here. Now angry tears stung his eyes at the thought of having to spend more months in this foul hole.

"Why didn't you sever my bond to the cursed pact?" he demanded of Malphas now.

Malphas couldn't hear him, of course. Not without a Dread Council, but Arnaud had no plans to invoke one, or him, ever again. *Just as you didn't plan to come back to this hole*, he reminded himself. *But you do what you must to survive.*

He gnashed his sharp teeth. It would mean humiliation, groveling prostrations, but if Malphas could restore him and sever his bond to the Brasov Pact…

Swearing, Arnaud swept the debris from the ground in front of him. Using the talon of an index finger, he etched Malphas's symbol into the earth, then slashed the same talon across his right wrist. The blood from the crazy woman spilled into the grooves, steam rising as the blood oozed around the symbol and joined up.

Arnaud struggled onto his good knee and forearms until he was bowing before the liquid symbol. The act filled him with bitter hatred. *He* was the one who should be bowed to, not doing the bowing. He swallowed his resentment and from his throat came a guttural sequence that sounded as though he were on the verge of vomiting. In fact, he was speaking the demon Malphas's true name.

The effort was painful, but already the blood in the symbol was bubbling and turning black. Smoke rose, congealing into the form of a dark specter with savage red eyes. A dark, taunting voice uttered Arnaud's true name.

His demonic name.

"Long have I waited to hear from my servant," he said, "my *capable* servant, only to find him hiding in a hole like a shithouse rat." Malphas's laughter was malicious and sent a rake of chills down Arnaud's back.

"Yes, I hadn't the power to summon you until now," he lied.

"Or were you preparing to turn your back on our agreement?"

"No, never! I exist only because Malphas wills it. I serve you and no other—not even myself!"

Arnaud despised the words as they left his mouth, despised Malphas for compelling him to speak them. But it was the game he'd had to play ever since *Croft* had cast him down a year before. He had spent the first days fending off his wretched tormentors—imps and lowly devils who existed only to torture, to break down bodies and minds into grist for their masters. But for the shadow fiend Arnaud had commanded, the vermin would have succeeded.

Instead, he and his fiend ripped them to pieces.

Arnaud spent untold days in a fugue of rage and killing, until the space around them looked and smelled like a charnel house. That tenacity earned him the notice of a higher demon. She plucked him from the rabble and placed him in her service. The six-armed demon Calista was as ambitious as she was grotesque. With his shrewd mind, Arnaud helped her undermine her demon competitors and ascend the teetering hierarchy of that underworld.

But Calista became greedy, challenging a demon well beyond her in power and malice. Arnaud knew this but said nothing, for he saw an opportunity. He betrayed Calista and came under the service of the new demon, Barong.

And so Arnaud negotiated the brutal terrain in this way, serving one master, biding his time, and then betraying that master to serve another, more powerful master, thus ascending the hierarchy himself.

At last he arrived under the service of Malphas, who was one level from a demon lord.

"We had a plan," the demon Malphas said now. "I returned you to the world to claim human souls for my army. I have received no souls."

"Yes, a wizard interfered."

"A *wizard*?"

"A protector of the city. He frustrated our plans. I was only able to claim souls enough to take form in this world, and I praise you for that. Praise you for sending me up and for the infernal magic that grows inside me. But I emerged a pathetic creature, even weaker than the one who is only just now capable of calling you forth. I have been building my strength these past months so that I may serve you, oh great—"

"What happened to your leg?" he snapped.

"I encountered the wizard tonight."

"The wizard again," Malphas scoffed. "Have I overestimated you?"

"My core remains bound to a pact," Arnaud whispered.

"A pact? Speak up!"

Malphas was far too large to emerge into the world, but the Dread Council gave Malphas power over him. Through it, he could hurt Arnaud or recall the forces that sustained him, which would mean certain death.

He could also bestow more power.

"Yes, a pact between wizards and vampires," Arnaud proceeded delicately. "I did not believe it would hold dominion over my new, demon form, but I am ashamed to admit that it does." Though it went against everything inside him, he forced himself to whimper. "I want so much for you, Malphas. I want you to dominate your lowly brethren and take your rightful place among the Lords. I *burn* for it. I know this city. I controlled it once. I can do so again. As your servant, I will send you more souls than you ever dreamed."

Arnaud was sliding into the seductive voice from his vampire days. That power hadn't left him, and he'd found that as long as he was prudent, the voice could sway even demons. Right now, he needed to fill Malphas's head with visions of armies, control, and above all power, for that is what demons craved most.

That was their game.

"But the pact prevents you," Malphas said.

"It *frustrates* me, yes. And could frustrate our plans."

With his forehead to the ground, Arnaud felt Malphas searching him over for the least deception. Demons were ever suspicious of betrayal, and rightfully so, but Arnaud had chosen his demon masters wisely. The most arrogant never truly believed their servants would dare betray *them*, he had learned.

"Why should I not destroy you right now?" Malphas asked.

"I would understand if you did," Arnaud said. "But your faithful servant is in the world now. Why not use me? With this one obstacle removed, I will destroy the wizard and carry out your designs."

In fact, what souls Arnaud claimed, he would use to grow his own power. He didn't care about the Below or its demon lords. Someday, perhaps. Right now, his ambitions revolved around the world he'd once controlled from behind a wall in Lower Manhattan, a world he could *dominate* as a powerful demon.

"You are not the only demon in the world," Malphas hissed.

Arnaud peeked up. He hadn't known this. "No, my liege?"

"Others followed you through the rift that you did nothing to disguise, you fool. Now they are claiming souls for their masters. For my *competitors*. My armies are strong, but the battles are becoming more pitched. All because you cower from a lowly wizard."

"Help me this once," Arnaud pled, "and I will devote myself entirely to your glory."

Malphas fell into a brooding silence. Could the demon sense Arnaud's deception? He would suspect it, of course, but Malphas stood to lose too much by being quick to judgment. A powerful servant in the world? One who could claim souls on his behalf, especially if competitors were already doing the same?

No, he won't jeopardize—

An excruciating claw tore through Arnaud's insides. He screamed and writhed on the ground, certain it was over. The agony! Not even the blast from Everson's ring earlier had induced this level of pain.

But just as suddenly as it had come, it left him.

"The pact is bound to your essence," Malphas said. "I cannot remove it without killing you. Though I am tempted."

Panting, Arnaud realized Malphas hadn't attempted to destroy him, but his connection to the Brasov Pact. He took another moment to catch his breath. *You haven't the power to negate it?* he wanted to demand. *Did I choose poorly?* But one didn't call into question a superior demon's powers—or lack thereof. Not if you valued your existence.

"Then there is nothing that can be done?" Arnaud asked meekly.

"There is something," Malphas shot back.

"Yes, tell me. I'll do anything."

And he meant it. As much as he hated Malphas, the pain he'd just endured put a bright, shimmering point on how much more he hated Everson Croft, for he was the cause of it all. Arnaud would make him suffer before destroying him. And for that reward, Arnaud was willing to endure this temporary shame.

"There was a scepter that belonged to Luther Underwood," Malphas said.

Arnaud repeated the name. He had been a fellow vampire CEO in the Financial District. He had fallen during the battle for downtown Manhattan. Without the benefit of a shadow fiend, he had perished in the Pits of the Below.

"The scepter holds a powerful negating enchantment," Malphas went on. "It will work on your pact."

"So all I have to do is find and bear it?" Arnaud asked, already cycling through the places Luther might have hidden it. During his life as a vampire, Arnaud hadn't been as arrogant as the demons he would betray in death. He understood that his survival depended on trusting no one. At Chillington Capital, he used his blood slaves to spy on the other CEOs. He knew about the secret vault Luther kept in his building's basement level. And yes, he had seen a scepter with a dark stone at its end.

For the first time that night, something like joy flared inside him.

"Thank you, great Malphas," he said through slanted lips.

"A full moon rises soon. I will expect my first delivery then."

"Yes, my liege," Arnaud replied, still smiling, for how was the fool ever going to enforce that?

At the thought, what felt like large hooks tore through Arnaud's torso. He screamed and looked down expecting to find his body skewered and running with the crazy woman's blood. But the hooks were psychic.

An infernal bond, he understood in outrage and alarm.

"What? Did you believe I would take you at your word?" Malphas laughed. "You are too much like me, *faithful* servant. I know your history. I know your appetite for power. I am prepared to grant it, but you will *only* attain that power through me. As my fortunes go, so go yours. Do you see? Through the bond, I will compel you to invoke my council when and where I demand it. And I will demand it *often*."

Arnaud gasped as Malphas gave the hooks a violent tug.

"Y-yes, my liege!" he sputtered.

"Give me your leg."

Arnaud scooted around like a chastised dog until he was offering the nubile limb to the hovering cloud. Angry red eyes glared down at him as if he were a feces-caked rodent. In coils of black flame, infernal energy climbed Arnaud's leg, infusing the limb, filling it out, until it was the same size as his left one. Malphas flung the leg to the ground, and Arnaud quickly pulled it to him. Now a gaseous vitality filled him.

"There," Malphas said when he'd finished. "I have given you everything you require to succeed. Do the work you have pledged me. And never again invoke me from a filthy hole, or I *will* destroy you."

"Y-yes, Malphas," Arnaud replied meekly.

The cloud dissipated, and Arnaud felt Malphas's presence rush from his lair. He looked from where the demon had been to his restored leg. Scowling, he raked his talons through the symbol, creating a mud of blood and earth.

"Stupid brute," he growled.

But he'd worry about his infernal bond to Malphas later. For now, he had an important artifact to recover.

And a wizard to destroy.

7

One moment I'd been standing, reinforcing a light shield around a raven, and in the next I was being blasted into the street.

But even as the asphalt rushed up at me, I remained in control. All in a second, I willed power into my shield and released it in a bright pulse that shoved me from the spot where I'd been about to faceplant. Like coming off a trampoline, I went from horizontal to vertical and quickly gained my footing. The pulse also caught my attacker. Behind me, I heard a woman grunt and stumble backwards.

I spun, thrust my sword, and shouted, *"Vigore!"*

The force invocation blew through the faint incandescence surrounding a slender blonde woman, lifted her from her feet, and flung her into the side of an apartment building. Golden light showered around her on impact, and she collapsed into a weedy strip of lawn. Behind me, the trapped raven cawed again.

Wincing, I brought a hand to my low back. The place where the woman had hit me smoldered, the pain spreading. When I felt my shield begin to sputter, I realized who—or rather, what —I was dealing with.

Fae.

Their magic had an inhibiting effect on mine, and she'd nailed me with a solid dose. Fortunately, Gretchen was an expert in fae magic and had already taught me a couple tricks (even though she had dangled them over my head for two full weeks), including how to make my neutralizing potions even more kickass.

Reaching into my coat, I pulled out a vial and incanted. Small gems sparkled inside the gray suspension, heating it and turning it bright green. I chugged down the bitter-tasting potion and threw the vial aside. As it shattered over the street, my magic stormed back to life. At the same time, though, healing magic was swirling around the woman. I reached into another pocket.

Need to press my advantage.

"Release Jordan!" the fae shouted, raising an arm.

She must have been talking about the bird. Golden light licked from her hand, but I was one step ahead of her. Palming an amulet of cold iron—another of Gretchen's gifts—I aimed it at her and bellowed, *"Attivare!"*

The blue cone that shot from the amulet dissolved the fae's bolt and swallowed her body. The fae withered into the grass, her glamour coming apart to reveal a gangly woman with plain hair and freckles.

Now to find out who you are and why the hell you attacked me.

As I stalked toward her, the raven cawed—too loudly. The damn thing had gotten out of the orb. Before I could pivot, the weeds at my feet writhed over my shielded legs. They twisted and cinched up my body like anacondas.

With a shouted Word, I sent out another pulse from my shield, but the animating magic was stronger than my own. Rather than being blown apart, the weeds only paused before resuming their climb and turning into vines.

I got in two good hacks with my sword before the vines arrested my arms. They pried the amulet from my grip. The blue cone fell from the faerie, and she crawled to safety. Though I'd managed to negate her power, these weren't amateurs. The vines looped around my neck, twisting and cinching like a garrote.

Second time tonight someone's tried to strangle me.

But this time I had a shield protecting my airway, and as long as I could draw breath, I could invoke.

I whispered a low-level force invocation. A vial wriggled from a coat pocket and out of the shield through a seam. Sprouts punched from the vines and tried to grope their way inside, but I closed the seam again, severing their tips. My shield shuddered inside the crushing grip of the plant animation. Fortunately, the animation wasn't particularly intelligent. I watched the vines take the vial into their leafy grasp and crush it apart, spilling dragon sand everywhere. Time to torch the jungle.

"*Fuoco!*" I shouted.

The fireball that exploded from the dragon sand warmed my shielded body and reduced the vines to ashes. Freed, I spun toward my second attacker. He appeared through the smoke as a hooded figure wielding a quarterstaff and bore the same shadowy magic as the bird.

A raven shifter, I realized. *Druid, most likely.*

I had no beef with the druids. None that I knew of, anyway. Regardless, I didn't have time for this shit. I aimed my own staff. Like with the fae girl, I'd drop him first, ask questions when I got around to it.

And since a shield invocation had worked on him once…

I sensed the incoming blow this time and ducked. Good thing. The fist that whooshed above me was almost the size of my head. I found myself eyelevel with a turquoise set of abs you could have cracked a coconut on.

"*Vigore!*" I shouted, driving the opal end of my staff into the center of the six-pack.

A force invocation that would have blown a normal person into next month only sent my latest attacker stumbling back several paces, giving me a good look. A good *gawk*, rather.

The amphibious-looking being stood on webbed feet and stared back at me from black orbs. Beneath a spill of long, dank hair, fins wriggled at his ears. A sharp fin ran down his back to a tail that flicked back and forth on the street.

"A merman?" I asked aloud.

I'd read about the creatures but didn't know they still existed around New York City.

I kept my staff on him while aiming my sword at the druid. The fae had moved such that she was standing behind the druid, her glamour restored. Powerful energy shimmered through the air surrounding them.

"Someone want to tell me what in the hell this is about?" I demanded, my voice trembling from the adrenaline still pumping through me. Did they even know who they were attacking, or was this some sort of mugging gone wrong?

"You challenged *us*," the fae said, then added, "Everson Croft."

Okay, so they did know me. "Yeah, because birdie over there was following me," I shot back.

"Is that a crime?" the merman challenged in a ghetto voice. "To tail you?" Though there were no anatomical features to indicate gender, the merman's voice and side-cocked hip actually suggested mer*maid*. Regardless, the thing had a point.

"Depends on why." I turned back to the druid. "That's your cue, bird boy. Start singing."

The druid drew back his hood by the sides, revealing the face of a black man. He looked to be about my age, maybe a little younger. The street light showed a glistening fade cut. A thin beard traced his jawline. When I picked out a pair of sigil-like tattoos on each temple, I wondered if he was connected to the Black Earth cult I'd faced in Central Park two years earlier. I had barely escaped those psychos with my life.

I cinched my grip on my sword, an invocation ready on my tongue.

"We've come to make you an offer," the druid said in an even voice.

"Oh yeah? And what kind of offer is that?"

"Mutual protection," he replied.

"Protection," I repeated. Judging by their unsmiling faces, the irony completely escaped them. "First, how do you even know me?"

"Not here," the druid said. "There's a place nearby we can talk."

"I wasn't exactly out for a stroll when you bumped into me. I'm headed somewhere. And no offense, but your cousins tried to burn out my eyes a couple of years back. So, yeah, we're either talking here or nowhere."

The three glanced at one another, not sure what to say next, it seemed.

I raised two fingers to my brow in salute. "Sounds like goodnight, then."

"Professor Croft!" a new voice called after I'd turned and gone several paces. "Wait!"

A taxi had pulled up to the corner, and now a young man was getting out. He ran toward me in jeans and a gray puffy jacket, sneakers beating the pavement haphazardly. Something about him looked vaguely familiar. And then I saw his ponytail. In a dizzying spell of cognitive dissonance, I recognized him.

But what in the hell was his connection to these guys?

"Weren't you the acolyte at St. Martin's?" I asked as he arrived in front of me.

"Yeah," the young man panted, nodding his head. "Malachi Wickstrom."

He had been there when the demon lord Sathanas possessed the vicar and tried to break free from the cathedral's hold. In fact, I had briefly suspected the young man of being the one possessed. He'd gone on to help me find the entrance to the ossuary where the demon and I'd had our final showdown. A memory of channeling the cathedral's powerful fount of ley energy shuddered through me.

Now, he offered his hand. His shake was the same dead fish I remembered from back then, but the eyes set in his narrow face had hardened in the two years since. From experience, probably, though they also appeared vaguely haunted.

"I'm the one who told them about you," he said quickly. "Please, just thirty minutes of your time."

"You've got to tell me what this is about."

He glanced over at the other three, then back at me.

"The big demons are coming."

8

We filed into the basement apartment of a nearby townhouse, passing through a curtain of defensive energy that made my incubus grumble. Malachi closed and locked the door behind us. It wasn't just his pleading eyes that had persuaded me to come, or our history at St. Martin's, but my surprise encounter with a demon that very morning.

Still, I remained on guard.

Malachi beckoned me to follow as we crossed the unit's open plan to a large table whose surface was strewn with maps and various texts. Diagrams covered the walls. Whatever was going on, they appeared to be taking it as seriously as cancer. A grimness permeated the apartment, despite being well lit. Everyone sank into chairs around the table except Malachi, who remained standing.

"Please." He gestured to an empty chair.

As I sat, the druid nodded at the shield still humming around me. "That won't be necessary."

"Thanks, but I'm more comfortable with it on."

The fae snickered. "If we'd wanted to take you out, we would have."

"Is that what you told yourself when you were bouncing off that brick wall." I had too much going on to put up with smart-assery.

The mermaid whipped her head around at me. "What did you say to her?"

"C'mon, guys," Malachi intervened. "It was a misunderstanding. Look, Jordan located you, Everson, and called the rest of us. When Seay arrived, she was afraid you were crushing his raven form. She only wanted to neutralize your magic. Jordan then tried to keep you from hurting *her*. That's when Gorgantha showed up and..." He sighed as he looked over at the gargantuan mermaid. "Well, more misunderstanding."

"Yeah, and next time I'll misunderstand him upside his head," Gorgantha said.

You'll have to connect first, I thought, but kept my mouth closed this time.

"Why don't I formally introduce everyone?" Malachi said quickly, resting a hand on the druid's shoulder. The druid had removed his long cloak and was wearing a stylish white shirt and dark jeans shredded at the knees. "This is Jordan Derrow. He represents a group based around Harriman State Park, north of Manhattan. Next to him is Seay Sherard. She's here on behalf of a group of half fae who have chosen to make the city their home."

I looked over at Seay the Fae. Even with her glamour restored, she was clearly pissed I'd flung her into a wall and then hit her with a blast of cold iron, something I was starting to feel a little bad about myself. But what did she expect after knocking me to the street like that? She squinted at me with pursed lips in greeting.

"Last but not least, Gorgantha."

In the light of the apartment, I could see her more clearly. The mermaid was really something to behold. Her size, musculature, the blade-like fins coming off her forearms. This wasn't the stuff of Disney.

"See something green?" she asked me without a hint of irony.

When I realized I'd been staring, I cleared my throat. "No, it's just that I didn't know there were still merfolk in the area."

"Lower Bay," she said.

"Oh yeah?" I pictured the body of water south of Brooklyn and Staten Island. "How many of you are down there?"

Instead of answering, she looked her scaly arms over and muttered something about starting to dry out. When she stood and strode toward a large clawfoot tub in a sunken corner of the unit, a melancholy seemed to come over her. She slid into the water and propped her elbows on the tub's sides.

"And you already know me," Malachi said. "After leaving St. Martin's, I went back to seminary. But the experience with Sathanas left a mark. I became interested in demonology—consumed by it, some of the professors said. I read everything I could on the topic. Traveled to some of the oldest church vaults in the world to search their collections. I was in a monastery on the outskirts of Dublin when I started to have visions."

"What kinds of visions?" I asked.

"Dreams, mostly." A shadow seemed to pass over his eyes. "Great wars, famine, pestilence, death. Billions of lives, Everson."

"You're describing the apocalypse," I said.

"Yeah, but not Four-Horsemen style. This is a demon apocalypse."

"But how?" It was rare enough for a single demon lord, or even a higher demon, to come through. They were too large to enter our world, the energy required too great. Lesser demons might be able to slip through the seams the Order was working furiously to repair, sure—I'd faced that fiery one only hours earlier. But they hadn't the power to pull off the mass devastation Malachi was describing.

"During my research, I came across what are known as Strangers."

"A demon servant who infiltrates a group, twisting that group's beliefs to their demon master's purposes," I recited to save time. "But to kick off an apocalypse, we'd be talking about the beliefs of a massive group, like the entirety of the three major religions, to even have a chance. I'm not seeing that."

"The *how* doesn't matter," Malachi said, irritation tightening his words. He didn't look or sound like he'd been getting a lot of sleep lately. "What matters are the signs. The arrival of the Strangers is one of the first."

"What? You're saying they're here?"

"Damn straight," Gorgantha answered from the tub.

I twisted in my chair so I was facing her.

"You mentioned not knowing my kind was around New York. That's because we haven't been, not since I was a girl." I had a feeling she was jumping the script, but Malachi let her continue. "Our pod lived near the mouth of the Bronx River. That was in the early '80s, back when Grandmaster Flash was spinning in the projects. My friends and I used to sneak off to his block parties." She must have caught my perplexed look because she said, "Our kind blend pretty well with humans when we're young. Now that was *real* hip-hop. The crap they're putting out today?" She waved a webbed hand. "Anyway, for the health of the pod, Gohalo decided to move us up the coast."

"Is that your leader?"

"Yeah, but most of us call him Gramps. He had us hanging around the islands near Maine. Cleaner waters, more fish, fewer people. Good for the pod, I guess, but damn that place was dull. The only thing that kept me sane was a radio I found and stashed on one of the islands. Anyway, things sort of rolled along till this merman showed up. Happens sometimes. Lone merman gets tired of swimming solo and looks to join another pod. This pimp went by the name Finn. Gramps and the old merfolk liked him right off, but he set off my creep detector big time. My friends' too. Merfolk worship a god called Leviathan," she went on.

"Lord of the Deep," I said.

"Yup, and for older merfolk he's as real as this here tub." She slapped its side producing a wet sound. "For the rest of us, he's more a legend, someone to, you know, rah-rah around. This Finn convinced Gramps he'd found Leviathan's trident during his travels and that it had spoken to him. Said it taught him the rituals to access Leviathan's realm and attain immortality. Next thing we know, Finn is holding nightly ceremonies, speaking in a tongue we'd never heard. And there was Gramps at his side. Merfolk started going away on trips. *Retreats*, Finn called them. But when they returned, they weren't themselves. Like they'd been hollowed out."

"Possession," I said.

"Sure looked that way," Gorgantha replied. "The physical changes came on a few days later."

"Physical changes?" I asked.

"They were turning into sea monsters. Fewer of us were going to the ceremonies by this time, even when Gramps made them compulsory. And that's when my friends started to disappear. Only *they* weren't coming back. When I noticed the waters around our caves turning pink with blood—merfolk blood—I knew we had to split. A group of about fifty of us left in the night. Some of the changed merfolk headed us off. Only half of us escaped. Beat it back to the city, but down in Lower Bay this time. There's a reef of junked cars down there. Rank water, but a good hiding spot."

"And you think this Finn was a Stranger?"

"After what Malachi told me, I *know* he's a Stranger.

"Harvesting souls for his master," Malachi put in.

"And who's the master?"

"Presumably a greater demon," he replied. "Like I said, the whys don't matter right now. Only that it's happening."

I turned to Jordan and Seay. "Can I assume something similar is happening in your groups?"

"The possessions, yeah," Seay said, her words still carrying a sour bite. "Only our Stranger isn't showing him or herself. Some of the possessions we've been able to reverse with magic. The others?" She shook her head. "The ones who return describe sitting in a dark room with something evil moving around the shadows."

"You too?" I asked, shifting my gaze to Jordan.

The room went quiet, as if I'd just stepped on something delicate. "Yeah," he replied at last.

When Jordan didn't offer anything more, I turned back to Malachi. "How about in the Church?"

"Nothing yet. The Strangers seem to be targeting smaller groups right now, claiming souls and making vessels of the victims. When their masters have enough power, they might pool their resources and go after the larger groups."

"Demons cooperating?" I made a skeptical face.

"It goes against what I've read too," Malachi admitted. "But—"

"Right, right," I said. "The whys don't matter right now."

I glanced around at the others. If we were looking at a concerted effort from the demons, this was a big deal. So why hadn't the Order said anything?

"Is this only occurring around New York?" I asked.

"Could be happening elsewhere," Malachi said, "but my dreams led me to these three. And to you."

"Why me?"

"Has a Stranger visited your Order?" he asked.

I almost scoffed. A lower demon would have to be suicidal to try to infiltrate their ranks. But not wanting to offend the others by suggesting they were being targeted for their groups' weaknesses, I only shook my head.

"Then there must be another reason," Malachi said reflectively.

"I thought you said he could help us," Seay challenged. "His group's not even under threat."

The druid rested a hand on her forearm. He struck me as the steady one. "Perhaps he still can. Malachi has told us about you, Everson. He described your work in the city. What we're proposing is a mutual defense arrangement. You help us, and when a time of need arises in your work, we'll be there to help you."

"You already have our help," I said. "The original purpose of our line was to defend against demon incursions and their evil spawn. Don't worry about a tit for tat. This falls squarely under our mission statement. I'll put in a call to my Order right now, in fact." I stood. "I'll let you know as soon as I hear back."

At least I'd gotten to the bottom of who these three were and what they'd wanted with me. Now I had to get back to my scheduled program—updating the hunters. But an urgency seemed to take hold in Jordan's eyes.

"We'd like a commitment from you now."

"Right this second?" I looked around. "Can I ask why?"

"Malachi told us about that demon lord you put down," Seay said.

"And if you can handle a demon lord, you can sure as shit deal with these Strangers," Gorgantha added from the tub.

I let out a surprised laugh. "Look, a lot of things came together for that to happen. It was a million to one shot. Even under identical conditions, I'm not sure I could repeat it. The Order is our next step."

"How can we help you?" Jordan asked with the same insistence.

The fact of the matter was I could use any and all assistance in my search for Arnaud, especially from supernaturals, but these three were proposing a quid pro quo: we help you, you help us. And if we *were* dealing with coordination among demons, I couldn't commit to something of that scale without the Order's guidance, if not direct involvement.

Which put us back to square one.

"Look, if you'll just be patient—"

Jordan slammed the table with his fist. "There isn't *time*, dammit!"

All right, so much for bird boy being the steady one.

"What about sanctuary?" Malachi asked me.

"Sanctuary?" I repeated.

"For you and a loved one," he said. "I don't doubt your protections are stout, but I can offer the protection of the Church. As part of the Interfaith Council, we have safehouses throughout the city. Space is limited, but we would be able to hold a spot for you and someone else. The power that protects the safehouses would shield you from even the most determined demon. Or servant."

"And you're offering this in exchange for my commitment?"

But it was the druid who answered. "We're offering it in exchange for your pledge."

Light glimmered over a faint tattoo on the side of his right hand, beneath the thumb. A bonding sigil, I realized. As I glanced around, I saw that they all had them. Even Gorgantha, who's webbed hand was perched on the side of the tub. *So magic binds the pledge-holders.* And judging from how quickly they had rushed to Jordan's defense earlier, powerful magic. Mutual protection, indeed. Once someone committed, there was no backing out.

"But there's a condition," Jordan added. I noticed Malachi's jaw tense. "You have to prove your commitment to our cause before we help you, *including* getting you a spot in one of the safehouses."

All the more reason to consult the Order first.

"Look, as soon as I know something, I'll be in touch," I said.

Gorgantha made an impatient face while Seay swore under her breath. When Jordan opened his mouth again, I braced for another eruption, but he appeared to have composed himself. His eyes shifted past me.

"Malachi, give him our info."

Malachi dug out his wallet and handed me a business card with a name and number.

I accepted it and squinted at the small print. "'The Upholders,'" I read aloud, thinking it sounded like a support group for single fathers. On the backside was a handwritten druidic incantation above a symbol: the bonding spell.

"When you're ready," Jordan said, "speak the words and hold the sigil to your hand."

I put the card in a coat pocket without comment. As I turned to leave, Malachi clasped my hand. But this wasn't the dead fish from earlier. His grip was powerful, charged with traces of the same energy that had coursed through me the night I channeled the power of the cathedral into the demon lord Sathanas.

It made me uncomfortable.

"There's time, but not much," he whispered. "Don't wait until it's too late."

I reclaimed my hand from his grip and walked toward the door.

"You have a role to play," he called after me.

9

I called Claudius en route to the vampire hunters' East Village apartment. The old man who took messages for the Order sounded as harried as ever.

"Is everything all right?" I asked him.

"Yes, yes—I mean no! I haven't heard from the Order in days."

A cold hand wrapped my heart. "Days? Why didn't you tell me that when we talked earlier?"

"Didn't I? Oh, geez, there's so much going on here, Everson. Magic-users are leaving me messages left and right."

"What kind of messages?" I asked with more foreboding.

"Demonic presences, like the one you reported earlier."

Great, so Malachi's dreams and visions weren't delusions.

"And you have no idea where Arianna and the others are?" I asked.

"Well, they've been in the interplanar realms, but at least one of them checks in daily. The last I heard from someone was Tuesday, though. It was, um, let's see..." I heard a shuffle of papers. It continued for the length of time it took me to cross a street. "Yes, Arianna. She said they'd discovered a new breach in the Harkless Rift."

The layers around our world featured their own esoteric geographies. Arianna had given me an updated book with ink-drawn maps that represented them. A little magic, and the maps turned into moving holograms, but even those were hard to make sense of. There were no earthly equivalents, and yet each geographic feature had a name. The Harkless Rift was one of the largest features on the fourth plane.

"And that was the last you heard from anyone?" I asked.

"Yes, and if I can't start clearing this paperwork off my desk, I don't know what I'm going to do. I feel like I'm suffocating, Everson." He began to pant, as if he was on the verge of a full-blown breakdown.

"All right, just stop for a minute. Breathe." But, hell, I was starting to feel short of breath myself. Arnaud, demonic summonings, active spell books, Strangers, mutual protection agreements—this was *not* the time for the senior members of the Order to ghost us. "Is there anyone from the next tier you can contact?" I asked.

"All the upper tiers are in the breaches, Everson. I guess I could be considered next tier, but I … well, my magic's not what it once was. It was highly specialized magic too. I dealt in complex bindings. In fact, I remember this one time—"

"Claudius," I said firmly.

"Yes, yes, sorry. After me, it's magic-users like you. The ones who are leaving all these messages." There was a riffling of papers in the background, and Claudius began breathing hard again.

"What about my trainer?"

"You have a trainer?" I pictured Claudius blinking in confusion.

"Yes, Gretchen Wagonhurst. Spends a lot of time in the faerie realm. Do you have any way to contact her?"

"Let's see…" I heard a desk drawer slide open followed by the mutters of someone in search of something he had no idea how to find.

I looked both ways before crossing another street and entering the East Village. Off to my right, large lattices of steel were rising from the dust and ashes of razed buildings, evidence of the mayor's promised neighborhood redevelopment project. But my route took me left, into the still-crumbling Alphabet City. I kept a watchful eye down the streets and alleyways. Though the eradication program had ended the once-rampant ghoul threat, other horrors continued to lurk at this end of the city.

"Ah-ha!" Claudius exclaimed, making me jump. "I found her! No contact information, though. And there's an agreement that Gretchen's role is strictly for training purposes. She's under no obligation to… Let's see, there's a list that runs for several pages. Shall I read it off?"

"No, thanks."

I already knew her song and dance. She didn't care about humans, magic-users, or the Order and would be perfectly content to spend her golden years in the faerie realm, never having to look at any of us ever again, blah, blah, blah…

But it was talk. She'd help in her own way—if I could find her. Hopefully, she would reach out to her goblin house sitter in the very near future, and he would pass on my message. Though after the way our encounter had ended, I suspected he was more likely to say *screw it*.

I could hear Claudius reading Gretchen's list off to himself. By this time I'd arrived at the vampire hunters' apartment building. I peered up its crumbling facade. Demolition notices plastered the doors and windows on the ground level. I couldn't say I would be sorry to see the building imploded. My memories of the place weren't especially cheery, including the night I'd treated Vega's gunshot wound.

"Claudius, I've gotta go," I said. "Give me a call the second you hear from the Order."

"Oh, okay, Everson. I'm sure it will be soon."

But his voice was verging on panic again.

My meeting with the vampire hunters was brief. I actually caught them rehearsing. After they killed their amps and thumping generator, I filled them in on my encounter, agreed to the thirty thousand dollars for a kill, and told them to be extremely cautious. Contrary to my earlier assessment, Arnaud wielded enough demonic magic to animate a corpse.

Bullet and Dr. Z exchanged nervous looks, but Blade didn't blink. She reassured me her network still had eyes on the city, which *was* reassuring. The second Arnaud showed his demon face, her team would be armed and ready to roll.

I texted Vega on the cab ride back to my apartment.

```
U ok?
```

`Fine here,` she responded seconds later. `Finally got Tony to bed. You?`

```
Sounds like he's already taken care of.
```

```
Smartass. You know what I meant.
```

```
No Arnaud. Hunters looking. Going home.
Sleep.
```

```
What's with the Tarzan speak?
```

I snorted at the joke from her end.

```
Flip phone, I texted back. Have to scroll for
each letter.

Call Jane morning? ;)

Will do. Love you.

Love you too.
```

I closed the phone and gazed out the window. My smile straightened as I imagined Vega and Tony settling down for the night in a house that, despite my wards and Grandpa's pendant, felt far too vulnerable. I even caught my eyes skipping from one dark alley to the next in search of vampire-demons.

In the last two months we had talked about what would happen if Arnaud *had* returned. The uncomfortable but necessary topic of getting Tony out of the city had come up a few times. Most of Vega's family lived in New York and Jersey, but she had a cousin she knew somewhat well out in Texas. Would Tony be safer with them, fifteen hundred miles away? At the end, it always came back to the same conundrum: though our proximity to Tony made him a target, Vega and I were also the best equipped to protect him.

Sighing, I turned from the window. I had texted Vega instead of calling to keep from waking anyone, but it had also saved me from having to share the encounter I'd had with the "Upholders." I would tell her eventually—probably tomorrow morning—but I needed the night to digest what they'd shared.

What they'd offered.

Sanctuary for you and a loved one.

Malachi wasn't exaggerating: the interfaith houses were frigging fortresses, much more so than my wards. And if Arnaud *was* coordinating with other demons, Grandpa's pendant might only do so much. Access to the interfaith houses required permission from a religious authority, but once inside, you were sheltered by the faith of billions and made practically untouchable.

If I can get access for Vega and Tony, at least until the danger passes...

Man, it was tempting. But the price of admission was a commitment to the Upholder's cause *first*—something the bonding spell would enforce. I could literally have Arnaud in my sights and be compelled to aid one of the others. That felt like a deal breaker.

But damn, Gorgantha's swimming abilities alone would have been an asset tonight when Arnaud slipped into the East River. And that was to say nothing of Jordan's and Seay's abilities as druid and fae. Having all three in my corner?

Still, it wasn't up to me. It was up to an Order that had gone radio silent.

Back at my apartment, I shed my coat and hung it on the rack. My watch showed the late hour. If I could get a solid six, I'd be happy.

Though I tried to walk quietly to my bedroom, Tabitha shifted on the divan and squinted over a shoulder. Her green eyes glowed at me through the dimness before closing again.

"Oh," she said. "Thought I smelled a demon."

I sniffed the shoulder of my shirt. Beneath my own sourness, I picked up faint traces of the demon from Nathan's apartment. "You did," I said. "I got into it with one earlier tonight." Two if I counted Arnaud, but we hadn't actually gotten close and personal.

Damn, what I would have given to have that encounter over.

"I hope you're not too tired to fix me something," Tabitha said.

"As long as it isn't anything more complicated than goat's milk."

She let out an aggrieved sigh. "I should probably be used to missing dinner by now."

"Missing dinner?" I walked into the kitchen. "What happened to the rosemary porkchops I left out for you?"

"They hardly made an appetizer."

"It was a stack of four. They weighed almost a pound each."

"Oh, come now, darling. You're exaggerating and you know it."

I wasn't going to get into it with her tonight. "Anything to report?" I asked.

"Do you mean those dreaded *tours*?"

"Tours, visitors, the same thing I mean every time I ask the question." I snapped on the gas flame, adjusted it to medium, then upended the milk above the pot, splashing some over the side. Tabitha watched me with a wry look.

"What's got you in a stir?"

"Just a lot going on," I muttered. "And I was hoping to get some sleep tonight."

"Well, I completely understand you there. I was hoping for the same. But yes, the tours. I did manage to sneak in one before dark."

"You snuck in *one*," I repeated.

The original deal had been a ledge tour every two hours, but she'd worn me down to the point that I was happy now to get half or even a fourth of that. One was pushing it, though, especially with Arnaud out there.

"Do you know how fucking cold it is?" she complained. "I

lost sensation in four of my nipples, and two have only just come back to life."

I winced. "All right, enough of that."

"The swearing or the nipple talk."

"Both. Anything to report, yes or no?"

She sighed.

"What?"

"I can't do this anymore, Everson!" she burst out.

I'd been watching for the milk to steam, but now I looked over sharply. Tabitha usually spoke in a tired, scornful voice that made me want to strangle her. It had been years since her pitch had risen like that.

"What are you talking about?" I asked.

"The tours. The lounging. The constant eating and sleeping. This is no way to live."

I couldn't help myself. "And you're only now coming to that conclusion?"

"I'm serious, darling. I..." She choked on her next word as her great orange body started to heave. Was she crying? Holy crap, she was. "I don't think I can go on like this," she managed between sobs. "Just ... just end me now."

Okay, this was more serious than her usual dramatics.

I turned off the stove and hurried to her side. "Where is all of this coming from?" I asked in confusion.

"Do you want to know why I only did one tour today? Because when I was halfway around the ledge, I found myself staring down at the street and all the cars going past. I caught myself thinking that if your wards and the four-story plummet didn't kill me, the traffic would. And there was a horrible relief in the thought that all I had to do was step off. It's a wonder I made it back inside."

"That is horrible." I waited the appropriate beat. "But I'm still trying to understand why now?"

"Seven years I've been in this body," she went on, "and what do I have to show for it besides this unsightly figure and a permanent depression in the cushion? I'm nothing but a big, hairy waste of space. Not even the idea of a man's soul excites me anymore." She sniffled and wiped the snot running from her nose with the back of a curled paw. "And look at you, a popular professor, a big-shot wizard—you're practically a superhero in this city. Though I don't see it," she added in a burble.

The dig barely registered as I thought back. Had it really been seven years since I'd channeled the succubus into that scrawny kitten in Times Square? Wow, it had been. Which meant Tabitha's cat body was approaching midlife.

A small lightbulb went off.

"Tabitha, listen. I'm no doctor, but if you can't think of anything that might have triggered this change in outlook, then it could very well be hormonal. And that's a good thing," I hastened to add.

"What's good about having the chemistry of a night hag?" she snapped.

"Well, it means it could just be a matter of, you know, bringing things back into balance."

I was dangerously out of my element. And to be dealing with this now of all times...

"Oh, God," Tabitha moaned. "Pills? What's next? Electroshock therapy? A lobotomy?"

"No," I said firmly. "It won't come to that. Look, I'm going to call a vet in the morning. Just don't do anything rash in the meantime, okay?"

I cast a locking spell over the cat door, but then I thought about the blades in the kitchen, the electrical outlets, the ease with which she could fill the bathtub—there were literally a dozen ways Tabitha could hurt herself that didn't involve a four-story fall onto Tenth Street.

"Wait here," I said and climbed the ladder to my lab.

In one of the plastic bins beneath the table, I pulled out a long vial with one of my pre-mades and hurried back down. After activating the potion in the kitchen, I tipped a couple of drops into Tabitha's milk.

"What are you doing?" she asked suspiciously.

I brought the bowl over, set it down, and remained in a crouch so my cat and I were at eye level. "First, I love you," I said.

Her eyes narrowed to their characteristic slits before falling to the milk. "Did you just slip me a roofie?"

"I just added a little pleasure elixir. At this dose, it should act like a relaxant. It's not a cure, but it should clear up the dark thoughts enough to help you sleep tonight. How does that sound?"

She regarded me for another moment before sighing. "Stand back."

With what appeared tremendous effort, Tabitha heaved herself to her paws. I moved away as she thudded to the floor and began lapping up the milk. When she finished, she looked at me and then raised her eyes to the divan. I had a hard time believing she couldn't get back up under her own power, but I lifted her anyway. The potion was already taking effect, reducing her muscles to thick slabs of putty. I arranged her body until it was curled in the general shape of the cushion's depression.

"How's that?" I asked.

A small smile wrinkled the corners of her mouth. "Nice, darling." The words oozed from her like warm honey. A definite improvement. I waited until her eyelids fluttered closed before turning off the lights and heading to my bedroom.

"Oh, and Everson?" she purred.

I paused. "Yeah?"

"I *sort of* love you."

10

That night I was awakened by the sound of my name.

I shoved off the covers and stepped from my bedroom. Out in the main room, Tabitha was asleep on the divan, her side rising and falling in a steady rhythm. A soft light limned everything. I peered around in confusion.

"Everson."

I recognized the voice now. "Arianna?"

The source of the light was a flicker in the center of the room. It swelled until the robed figure of the senior member of the Order took shape. The warm waves pulsing from her reminded me of my mother's emo ball, which made sense. Arianna, who had delivered me in the Refuge, was like a surrogate mother.

But what was she doing here, like this?

Her face took solid shape last. "Can you hear me?" she asked.

Her voice sounded very near and yet somehow very far away.

"Yes," I replied, "where are you?"

"We're in the Harkless Rift."

"Is everything all right?"

"We discovered a fissure in the Rift's blackest depths. We're working to knit it closed, but it's requiring all of our energy. We've been out of communication for several days." For the first time, I picked up the strain in her voice.

"Did you get my messages?" I asked.

"Yes, it's why I've come to your resting mind."

My resting mind?

I looked over at Tabitha. Despite the sound of our conversation and the light swimming over her closed eyes, she hadn't stirred.

I then thought to peer over a shoulder. Beyond my bedroom doorway, I could make out a mound in the bed. Me, I realized, still sleeping. Far easier for Arianna to access my astral consciousness than to project from somewhere as distant as the Harkless Rift to my apartment, especially if energy was at a premium.

"Yes, Everson," she said, picking up my thoughts. "But I cannot maintain the connection for long."

"Sorry, I'm listening."

"Following my last visit, I puzzled over how a demon had come to take form in the world, even if only briefly. I also worried over the ways the demon might have eluded me." She was referring to Arnaud tunneling from the host. "Those questions led us to the Harkless Rift, where we discovered a fissure to the deeper places. It had started out small, probably imperceptibly so, but through the power of the claimed souls, the demon forced it open. There is a particular energy there, one that can conceal a demon's energy. That is how this one escaped our notice. Other demons have come through since."

I thought about the Strangers the Upholders had mentioned. *Was* this the beginning of what Malachi had foreseen?

"How many?" I asked.

"Many hundreds," she responded, sending a chill through

me. "They've turned up at nexuses all over the world, where we've placed magic-users like you. A large number of them came to New York City." Her face turned toward the bay windows. "Here the powerful patterns of ley energy are most conducive to their magic."

"So, you'll be sending a senior member of the Order?"

"When we can, Everson. More demons are trying to force their way through. Hordes of them. The most vital work at the moment is here. We must keep them back while we close the fissure, or the world will be overrun."

"Gretchen, then?" I asked, feeling the first clutches of desperation.

"I've attempted to reach her, but her defenses are up. I will try again."

"A group approached me with an offer to collaborate in the fight against the demons."

"Yes, you mentioned the Upholders in your message," she replied. "But for reasons you've already determined, your first action must not be with them." So, Arianna and I were on the same page about the whole pecking-order thing, them not helping me until I had helped them. "The demons are looking for a being in your world they're calling Sefu."

"Sefu? Who's that?"

"At the moment, little more than a name. But there is power behind the name. You must find and hide Sefu."

"All right. Where is he? Or she?"

Arianna's eyes closed. "The currents are indistinct. The Order is receiving only impressions. Sefu is concealed now, but that will change." She opened her eyes again and looked at me intently. "In the morning you will receive a phone call. Do what that person asks, and it will lead you to Sefu."

And if I still don't find them? I thought to myself.

But we were convening in a dimension of my sleeping mind,

and Arianna heard the words as clearly as if I'd spoken them. "Then a demon will find and possess Sefu and grow exponentially in power. Events will cascade."

I shuddered to think that the demon could be Arnaud.

Maybe I could put more resources into finding and destroying him before—

"No," Arianna interrupted. "You must focus on this single task. All others are secondary right now."

I took a breath and centered myself. "All right, but … alone?"

"You already have a team," she said. "Organize them. Utilize your diverse perceptions."

I was going to ask who exactly she meant, but her light was fading, her form turning gauzy.

"The same magic that speaks to me also speaks to you," she said as she disappeared.

And then everything fell dark.

11

"You said Wall Street and Broad, right?" the cabbie asked, glancing at the rearview mirror.

Though Arnaud's eyes were already hidden in the shadow of the fedora's brim, he lowered them to conceal the glints of yellow in his irises. It had only taken a short walk into Midtown to notice the way people reacted to them. Women paled; men lurched from his path. Unconscious reactions, certainly, their souls correctly perceiving in those sulfurous yellow slivers the infernal depths from which he had risen.

In time, he would display that feature openly, proudly, but for now the word was *discretion*.

"That's correct, young man," Arnaud said, pushing a little vampiric charm into the raspy words.

The cabbie smiled and gazed out his window.

"Is something amusing?" Arnaud asked.

"Today's gonna be a great day. I've just got a feeling about it." The sun cresting the buildings over Brooklyn bathed his face in salmon pink. "That ever happen to you? This sorta gut certainty about how a day's gonna go?"

"Oh, absolutely," Arnaud replied.

"Hey, nice suit," the driver said. "You heading to an interview or something? They say the downtown firms are hiring again."

Arnaud steeled himself at mention of his former dominion before reminding himself he had loftier ambitions than the city's purse strings. "More like an opportunity," he replied with an easy smile.

"You sound confident."

"Do I?"

He had been anything but confident last night.

Even after Malphas had restored his leg and infused him with power, even with the promise of a pact-breaking scepter, Arnaud feared his return to the city. It had been more than a year, after all. He had only recently taken form. He was no longer the vampire who had ruled lower Manhattan, inspiring veneration and fear. Now *he* was the fearful one. A human soul would salve that, he'd decided. With morning nearing, he left his lair for the final time. An urge came over him to collapse the opening to ensure he *couldn't* come back, but Arnaud was not foolish. He was a survivor.

At his island's edge, he scanned the distant shorelines in his sharpening vision.

In the gray dawn, a lone figure walked the park at the southern tip of Roosevelt Island. Alone. Plunging into the cold water, Arnaud raced toward him like a predatory fish.

The short man in a business suit and fedora, cigarette pinched between finger and thumb, never saw the naked, gray creature coming for him. Nor did he hear him leave the water and creep low around the giant slabs of granite that hid the man —and soon Arnaud—from the rest of the still-awakening city.

It wasn't until Arnaud was almost on him that the man seemed to sense danger. He dropped his cigarette and turned, but Arnaud was already around him like a giant spider. The man jerked once as Arnaud's teeth punched into his jugular, the hot release of blood flooding Arnaud's senses. He pulled the sagging body into the deep shadows of a slab and fed quickly, as he had with the woman the night before.

When the blood was exhausted, he went deeper—coaxing, then seizing the man's soul and drawing it into him. As a vampire, he had believed he could consume souls, but he'd been doing little more than scraping off the emotional outer layers. As a demon, he had license to the entire mystical entity, which he could turn into raw power and infernal spells or simply place in bondage. Higher demons, such as Malphas, built armies.

As Arnaud fed, he bristled at the notion of sharing his stake on this man. But curse it all, he needed to remain on good terms with his master until he could kill that connection—perhaps one day kill *him*.

With a scowl, Arnaud released the soul and funneled it through the umbilicus that connected him to Malphas. *There,* he thought bitterly, *you have the fool for your army, where he'll last a minute, if he's lucky.*

Whether or not it was Arnaud's imagination, the hooks that tethered him seemed to relax slightly. That was something. The meal of blood had strengthened him too. And he had appropriate attire now to wear into the city.

Arnaud peeled off the man's clothes and dressed in the shadows of the granite slab. To his right stood a monument with a former president's quote on the four human freedoms for which this particular park had been named.

"'The fourth is freedom from fear,'" Arnaud read aloud and snorted.

He dragged the man's drained body to the park's edge and dumped it into the river.

The cabbie released a hearty sigh, returning Arnaud to his present surroundings. "Yeah, gonna be a great day."

A slow smile crept over the vampire-demon's face.

"I'm beginning to agree," he said.

Arnaud paid the driver from the dead man's wallet and then stood on Wall Street for a moment to get his bearings.

In the year he had been away, the place had changed. The wall on Liberty Street that had protected him and his fellow vampires from the mortal rabble was now gone, removed. For a dizzying moment, Arnaud felt vulnerable, especially on street level. He'd become accustomed to viewing his domain from ninety stories up, controlling the movement in and out.

Now, everything seemed chaos: the rattle of jackhammers where pockets of reconstruction remained; the constant revving of engines and the racket of car horns; humans bustling around him with their stupid, bovine faces. Assailed by the confusion, Arnaud was tempted to pull his hat off and put the fear of God into them!

"In time, Zarko," he whispered, the promise calming him.

Luther Underhill's former building was a half block away, and he walked there quickly, head down. He moved with a wide-legged gait, his form not developed to the point that he could remain comfortably upright. But while crawling on all fours was fine for the island, he was in the world of humans now.

Inside the building, he made a line for the reception desk.

A young man seated behind a computer raised his head. "Can I help you?"

"Yes, kind sir." He had to strain to be congenial. "I require an elevator card to access the L2 level."

"Your name?" the receptionist asked, his fingers poised over his keyboard.

Arnaud took a moment to size the man up. He was slim, his chestnut hair gelled in a tousle. Not a look Arnaud cared for, but there was something in the young man's eyes—just enough turquoise to set him apart. Yes, in the old days Arnaud might have expended energy to seduce the young man and add him to his collection of blood slaves. Now, he was just someone to manipulate.

"You won't find me in your system ... Ronald," Arnaud said, reading the man's name tag. "Or do you prefer Ronnie?"

"Well, the L2 level is a restricted area, and all permissions are stored—"

"I'm afraid we're not hearing one another," Arnaud interrupted, tapping the counter with a wrinkled gray finger. He pushed a little more suggestion into his voice, reaching deeper into the young man's mind. "You won't find me in your system because I *am* the system, young Ronnie. I am *all* systems. Do you follow me?"

"I'm ... Well, I'm not sure I do..."

When Ronald lifted his gaze, Arnaud traced out a series of designs on the counter to distract from his yellow eyes.

"Yes," Arnaud whispered. "Everything flows from me."

"So..." Ronald said, watching his finger. "*You* give the permissions?"

"That is precisely so, Ronnie."

A change came over the receptionist's eyes as if it all made sense now.

"The access card?" Arnaud prompted.

The young man nodded and unlocked a drawer beside his left knee. A moment later, he held out a white card with a metallic strip on the back. As Arnaud accepted the card, he caressed the back of Ronald's hand—a gesture he couldn't resist

—and smiled as a small shudder passed through the young man.

"Good day, Ronnie," he said. "Perhaps I'll see you again."

"I—I'd like that," the young man replied, though Arnaud could see he had no idea why.

As Arnaud walked toward the elevator, he reflected on how the power to seduce remained seductive to him. It had fallen in the hierarchy of importance, yes, but that it was still there filled him with a pleasant nostalgia. Vestiges of his old self remained in his new form, demonic or not, alchemized or not. And the one vestige that presently encumbered him—his connection to the Brasov Pact—was about to be negated once and for all.

At the elevators, he remained back from the people until he could be assured a car to himself. Inside, he held the card to a metallic pad, waited for an indicator light above it to turn from red to green, and then pressed the button for the bottommost floor. When he arrived, he navigated the corridors from memory. The closed rooms he passed were mostly storage spaces for the building's various tenants.

At the end of a corridor, he listened before pulling open a locked door with such force that the bolt fell to pieces at his feet. His eagerness had overcome him. The room, another storage space, was empty by all appearances.

"But we know better, Zarko."

At the rear wall, he depressed a power outlet, worked his fingers into the slot, and pulled. The wall slid to one side on hidden tracks, revealing a vault door. Clever, but Luther had been a fool to share the location with his blood slaves. Now, infernal magic seeped from Arnaud's fingers and slipped into the vault's dial. Clicks sounded as it began to turn, one way and then the other. The sound of the lock's release was sudden and satisfying.

Stale, cool air wafted past Arnaud as he opened the heavy

vault door, his confidence surging now. He could already picture the look on Croft's face when that whelp of a wizard tried to cast through his grandfather's ring and nothing happened. His lady friend, the detective, would lose her protection too. Oh yes, he'd felt the bite of the pact coming off her last night, preventing him from going near her.

Now it would be no deterrence at—

His smile fractured as he peered into the darkness. Something was wrong. Containers lay open, their contents either missing or scattered. The damned vault had already been looted!

But how, Zarko? By whom?

He wondered whether Luther had come here prior to the war for downtown Manhattan. Like most elder vampires, he had amassed a collection of valuable artifacts over the millennia. Perhaps he'd come in search of a weapon. But Arnaud remembered that day. Luther had gone into battle with an enchanted broadsword and a ring of protection, items he'd kept in his armory. Little in here would have been practical for battle.

Arnaud searched through what remained. When he found no scepter among the rubbish, demonic anger flashed hot inside him. He thrust a hand forward, releasing a wave of infernal energy that sent the containers and spent items crashing into the back of the vault. The noise rang around him, but he was too furious to care.

Damn this world! Damn it all!

From the moment he had returned, forces had conspired against him. Now he was weak, dependent on Malphas, and vulnerable to Everson Croft. Without the scepter, it was only a matter of time before he was cast back to the Below. Once there, Malphas would have him brutalized and ground to dust for his failure.

"Which is why you must recover the scepter," a voice whispered.

Arnaud whipped his head around, his anger suspended. "Zarko, is that you?"

"Find the one who has taken the scepter, and you will find the scepter."

He was hearing the words as if his faithful servant were standing beside him, breathing them into his ear. It didn't matter to Arnaud that he was alone or that the words were likely drifting from his own mind. They infused him with a wild joy. He had spoken to Zarko often since returning to the world, but this was the first time his servant had answered.

"'Find the one who has taken the scepter,'" Arnaud repeated slowly, "'and you will find the scepter.'"

He paced the vault deliberately now, nostrils drawing in the air. The scent was old, but unmistakable. Humans had been inside. More than one. Could the order of magic-users have found the vault and cleaned it out?

Perhaps, but Arnaud sensed no magic save remnants from some enchanted items.

"What say you, Zarko?" he asked. But his former blood slave fell silent now.

It suddenly occurred to Arnaud that Luther's restored blood slaves, the ones young enough to have survived the transformation back to human, might have informed the authorities about the vault. Then why hadn't *everything* been collected and catalogued? Why had he found it closed and locked?

At that moment, something on the floor caught his eye. Arnaud knelt and peered over a scatter of dull granules. When he touched it, the infernal magic running through his finger guttered for a moment.

Gray salt, he realized, cleaning his fingers on a pant leg.

It was of a kind used to store magical items for transport in the Middle Ages.

"Looters," he hissed.

He was considering the implications when two pairs of approaching footsteps sounded in the corridor. By their crisp cadence he guessed security, no doubt coming to investigate the racket he had made earlier. Lights turned on. The footsteps slowed as they neared the door to the room—the door whose bolt lay in pieces on the floor.

He picked up the whisper of a woman's voice.

"Hello?" a man called a moment later. "Is someone in there?"

"Why, yes, just me," Arnaud replied. "Please, do come in."

The man peeked around the corner. Arnaud had moved to the front of the vault where he stood now, his hands out to the sides to show they were empty.

The man entered, his service pistol drawn. The woman came in beside him. Their uniforms of black pants and white shirts looked cheap, and the man's collar was starting to yellow. Distasteful, Arnaud thought. Not nearly as dignified as the tailored suits he'd dressed his blood slaves in.

"Do you have a reason to be down here?" the man asked.

"I'm searching for something," Arnaud answered as pleasantly as his raspy voice would allow. "Something very important."

"And what's that?" the woman demanded.

"Well, since you ask, perhaps you can assist in my search."

The security guards glanced at one another. When the man reached for his walkie-talkie, Arnaud raised a hand. Why he had toyed with them, he didn't know. But he'd enjoyed it. Only now did he slip power into his voice.

"Oh, there's no reason to involve anyone else," he said.

The man's hand hovered uncertainly over his walkie-talkie before relaxing. His stupid face softened.

"Why, you're all the help I require," Arnaud said.

"What can we do?" the woman asked, but without the prior note of challenge.

"You, sweetheart, can wait for us there while your partner joins me in the vault."

"Me?" the man asked. His eyes were working hard now to focus.

Arnaud grinned, already retreating. "That is correct, big boy."

He stepped backwards until he was in full darkness, still grinning as the security guard holstered his sidearm and lumbered after him. He would not share this soul with Malphas. It would belong to him.

From the back of the vault, Arnaud released his mental hold over the man just long enough to savor the inrush of confusion and fear: *Why am I following this strange man into the dark where I can't see him? Why is my weapon no longer drawn?*

And then Arnaud was sinking his teeth into the man's throat. The victim's pulsating lifeforce rushed inside him. Arnaud stroked the back of the man's head as he fed on blood and soul. Minutes later, he released his throat with a wet gasp. The nearly-drained man moaned weakly. Arnaud hadn't killed him. That hadn't been the plan.

"Now," he whispered into the man's ear, "I would like to bring you into my service. Ah, but with your consent, of course."

The man moaned again.

"Was that a *yes*?" Arnaud asked in a taunting voice. "I believe it was."

The city was too large to track down the looter's scent himself, he thought as he sliced his wrist with a talon, sending up a crude oil of demon essence. His new blood slaves would perform that duty for him.

"Everything all right in there?" the other security guard called.

"Right as rain," Arnaud replied, dribbling the dark fluid over the man's neck. The demon essence gathered and then slipped, worm-like, into the deep puncture wounds left by Arnaud's canines. The transformation wouldn't take long.

In the meantime...

"Say, sweetheart?" Arnaud called toward the opening. "A little help in here?"

12

The brassy ring of the telephone shattered my deep sleep. I opened my eyes to a bedroom just beginning to glow with sunlight. The hands of my bedside clock pointed to 7:50. When the phone rang a second time, Arianna's words returned to me in a rush. This was the call that was supposed to direct my next move.

I jumped out of bed and rushed toward the kitchen, cycling through all the people it could be. Vega? Gretchen? Budge?

"Hello?" I answered.

But I didn't recognize the woman's voice. "Is this Everson Croft?"

"Who's this?"

"You're needed at the Centre Hotel. Do you know the location?"

"Yeah, but can I ask what this is about?"

"Room B-6, basement level."

"What's this about?" I repeated more firmly.

"A conjuring."

A second voice entered in the background, this one distinctly male.

The woman lowered her voice to a whisper. "Only you can stop it."

"Who *is* this?"

But the caller had disconnected. I made sure she was really gone before returning the phone to the cradle, my mind tense with suspicion. Arianna's words had been clear: do what the person asked, and I would find Sefu. But was I supposed to run blindly to a hotel basement on an anonymous caller's say-so? This could be Arnaud, or any number of the recently arrived demons, laying a trap.

I checked my watch. Not flashing. My cane was resting quietly in the bedroom where I'd left it. If there was a conjuring in progress, one or both would have alerted me by now. There were exceptions to that rule, of course...

Oh screw it, I thought and rushed to get ready.

I was heading for the door, trench coat clinking with spell implements and potions, when Tabitha let out a noisy yawn. Crap, I'd almost forgotten about her. She smacked her mouth and looked over at me with puffy eyes.

"How are you feeling?" I asked.

"About as crappy as the taste your potion left in my mouth."

A mild hangover was one aftereffect of the elixir.

"But you slept all right?" I asked.

"I suppose," she allowed with a sigh. "But nothing's changed. I'm just going to spend another pointless day of my pointless life in the same apartment on the same pointless cushion." She peered around blandly.

I can't leave her here by herself.

I dragged a hand through my hair and gripped my neck, not believing what I was about to do. In the closet, I found what I was looking for on a hook behind my winter coats. Tabitha caught me approaching her, one of my hands behind my back.

I pounced.

"Ow!" she cried. "What in the hell are you doing?"

I'd already slipped the harness over one front paw, and now I struggled as she pulled the other paw to her chest. But I finally got it through, jerking my hand back before she could bite it. With an uttered invocation, I cinched the harness, which just fit around her girth, and secured the fasteners.

"You're coming with me," I said, picking up the leash from the floor.

She hissed and spit before words came out. "Take this infernal thing off me!"

I'd bought the harness at a pet shop in our second year together. I thought it would be a safe way to take Tabitha outdoors for some exercise, but she'd never shown any interest. Five years and thirty pounds later, she looked like an orange pom-pom someone had bound in the middle. Under different circumstances, watching her try to retract her head through the harness would have been comical.

"Until I can get ahold of a vet, I'm not leaving you here alone."

She stopped struggling long enough to glare at me. "I'm *fine*."

"No, you're not. Now c'mon."

When I gave the leash a gentle tug, Tabitha changed tactics and made herself dead weight. There wasn't time for this. I spoke an invocation, and a shield of light crackled around her. The energy made her hair stand on end.

"You can either come under your own power, or I'm carrying you."

As a quasi-demonic being, she reacted poorly to my brand of magic, and I knew that. As I started to lift her, she pinned her ears back and scratched furiously at the inside of the orb, sending a cascade of sparks tumbling down around her hind feet. It was the most I'd seen her exert herself in years. Within moments, she was exhausted.

"Fine," she moaned miserably. "Set me down."

I placed her on the floor and dissolved the shield. Her hair settled as she got her footing. She took a few staggering steps toward the door, stopped suddenly, and looped the leash around her neck.

"What the—?" I cast a pulse that knocked the noose free.

Tabitha winced and shook her paw. "Won't even allow a girl a dignified end."

"There's nothing dignified about self-strangulation," I said irritably. Plus, the way she had attempted it would have been physically impossible. I kept that to myself for fear it would motivate her to prove me wrong.

"If you really loved me, you'd let me go," she said.

"And if you really loved *me*, you'd let me help you."

"Sure, use my drug-addled words from last night against me." She glanced around the apartment. I could feel the clock ticking on the conjuring as I tried to anticipate Tabitha's next move. *Was* I going to have to carry her?

But she surprised me by rising and sauntering toward the door.

"Can't be much worse out there than it is in here," she muttered.

It could be a lot worse, actually. But I kept that to myself too.

FIFTEEN MINUTES LATER, A CAB DROPPED US OFF IN FRONT OF THE Centre Hotel in Midtown. I forced myself to walk at Tabitha's pace, which was only slightly faster than glacial. Though I was tempted, dragging her would have been a mistake. That she was walking at all, not to mention still tolerating being harnessed, was a small miracle.

"And who are you supposed to be?" the doorman asked when we arrived at the large glass doors.

"I'm sorry?" I said.

"The coat? The cat?"

Tabitha and I looked at each other. "I don't know what you're talking about," I said.

The bald man gave me a sly grin as he opened the door. "Sure you don't. Registration won't start till nine, but it'll be in the lobby there."

Tabitha followed me inside, and I immediately began looking for the elevators.

"What was *that* all about?" she asked in annoyance.

I started to tell her I had no idea when I noticed a handful of people in the lobby in costumes. A couple of convincing female zombies milled around near a party of drunken pirates. I spotted the elevators just as a door dinged open and a guy in full military gear with a blue wolf mask strolled out.

"I think someone missed the memo that Halloween was last month," I muttered.

I was coaxing Tabitha toward the elevators when a hand fell on my shoulder. I spun to find a middle-aged man dressed head to toe as Captain America. If not for the healthy bulge above his belt, he might have pulled it off.

He broke into a huge smile. "Ha-haa! I love it!"

"Love what?" I snapped.

"John Constantine, right?"

I played dumb as I kept walking. "Who?"

He hustled to keep up, the shield strapped to his arm pumping back and forth. "C'mon, man. Snarky wizard in a trench coat?" His smile faltered as he looked down at Tabitha. "I don't remember him having a fat cat, though."

"You're one to talk, pork chop," Tabitha muttered.

Captain America didn't hear her, though. His eyebrows were

working furiously as he tried to peg my *costume*. "Dresden, then? But his cat's gray."

"Look, I've gotta go."

Even Tabitha seemed in a hurry to get away from him.

Panting, Captain America began to lose ground. "Slim?" he called after me. "Verus?"

I made it to the elevator, tugging Tabitha in after me, just as the door slid closed. I hit the B button for the basement level. "What's with these people?" I breathed as the elevator started to descend. "It's like you can't cast spells in a long coat unless you're trying to cop someone's brand."

"They're *mortals*," Tabitha said, as if that explained everything.

The elevator slowed to a stop, and the door opened. I'd filled Tabitha in on our way here, but the fact was, I had no idea what we were walking into. The air around us hardened as I invoked a shield.

Time to put my game face on.

"Keep your eyes open for a room B-6," I said.

By the concrete walls and black wheel marks up and down the corridor, it looked like we'd arrived on a storage level. I listened, but all I could hear was the mechanics of the elevators at our backs. My watch and cane had yet to alert me to any conjurings. Thinking trap again, I sniffed the air for the sickly-sweet scent of demon before realizing I had a living, breathing detector sitting on her haunches beside me.

"Hey, can you tell if any demons are in the area?" I whispered.

"So is that all I'm good for now?"

"You were the one who said you wanted purpose."

"A demon-sniffer wasn't what I had in mind."

I shook my head. "You know what? Forget it."

"Well, if you're going to go full bitch..." Tabitha raised her nose to the air and gave a weak sniff. "How do you want me to indicate a positive? Fall to my forearms and start whining like an idiot dog?"

"Or you could just tell me."

"No."

"No, what?"

"No demons."

That was a lot of words to get to a negative reading, but I wasn't going to belabor the point. "All right, it looks like B-6 is down this way." I started to lead before stopping. Holding her leash wasn't going to work. "Can you sit still a minute?"

"What are you doing?"

I unhooked the leash from her harness, threaded it through a loop on the side of my trench coat and then through the handle before fastening it again. "Just needed to free up my hands," I said, separating my cane into sword and staff.

"Afraid I'm going to run away?"

"Among other things."

"Well, I'm not. I haven't the ambition this morning."

I peeked back at her, not sure whether that suggested an improvement or worsening of her condition. "Well, if you get tired, give me a little warning," I said. The last thing I needed was for her to decide to become dead weight again, especially mid fight—or flight. That would give new meaning to the expression *the old ball and chain*, which was exactly what this was starting to feel like.

Tabitha breathed something I didn't pick up, but she kept pace behind me.

Room B-6 was closed and locked. I pressed my ear to the door but couldn't hear anything above the faint chuff and vibration of the heating system. Aiming my cane at the lock, I spoke an invocation. In the next moment, I was being slammed into the rear wall of the corridor. My shield absorbed the brunt of the shock, but the force left me stunned. I sat where I'd landed, blinking until my surroundings returned to focus.

Tabitha looked at me blandly, the leash to her harness sufficiently long that she hadn't gone along for the ride.

"Did you not see the ward?" she asked.

I trained my focus on the door. She was right. The ward was subtle but there.

"A heads-up would've been nice," I muttered, pushing myself to my feet. I focused on the ward. What kind of magic had constructed it, I couldn't say. Conventional? Demon? Fae? Whatever the case, it suggested the anonymous caller hadn't been putting me on. "Anything else you'd like to tell me?"

"You're going to need to neutralize it," Tabitha said.

"Yeah, thanks."

Pulling in my breath, I explored toward the ward with my magic. It was basic, though—no additional traps. It wasn't even especially strong. I'd just happened to blunder right into it. I rubbed my right elbow. If this ever got back to Gretchen, she'd have a field day. Fortunately, Tabitha was even more put off by her than I was.

"Disfare," I said, pushing power into the Word.

The soft lines of the ward wavered and came apart in a burst of foreign energy. I checked to ensure there was no more subtle magic at work before hitting the lock with another force invocation. This time, the door flew open.

In the center of the room, a pair of lizard-like creatures rose from their haunches. Smoke curled from their flaring nostrils.

Wonderful, I thought. *Fire breathers.*

13

"Stay behind me," I said to Tabitha.

"Don't worry," she replied.

The lizards regarded me with cocked heads. They looked like Komodos, only nastier. Here and there, blossoms of black singe marks adorned the walls. The creatures had indeed been conjured—from where, I wasn't sure yet, but they were standing in a pair of complex casting circles on the floor, and I could feel a distinct current of nether energy around them. So why in the hell hadn't the Order's wards alerted me?

The lizards stepped from their circles and belched in tandem. Twin waves of fire broke around my shield.

"Hot, *hot!*" Tabitha cried.

With a Word, I enclosed Lizard One in a light shield while thrusting my sword toward the other. The force invocation flipped it onto its back. I stepped on its squirming throat and drove my blade through its chest.

"Disfare!" I called.

The lizard shook before erupting in gouts of fire.

I turned back to Lizard One, whose clawed feet were struggling against its confinement. Another burst of flames erupted from its mouth only to hit the inside of the shield I'd manifested and engulf its scaly black body. The creature was apparently immune to its own heat.

I pushed more power into the confining shield, reducing it until the compressive forces overwhelmed the energy holding the lizard together. The creature broke apart in flames that were quickly snuffed out.

I released the shield and dropped the smoking residue to the floor. When I opened my wizard's senses, I detected no active magic—only the spent energy that had given the lizards form. As quickly as it had begun, it was over.

"Are you all right?" I asked Tabitha.

"Overheating, but I'll survive." She walked up to my side with her tongue out and surveyed the room. "What *were* those monstrosities?"

"Are you sure they weren't demonic?"

"What? You don't trust my nose?"

"Arianna warned me about a demon breach, and those weren't your typical nether creatures." I pictured the bug-like forms I was more accustomed to putting down. That right there told me I wasn't dealing with an amateur. But then I thought of Nathan, who'd somehow managed to conjure a fire demon with a mail-order spell book.

"Well, they weren't from my realm," Tabitha said defensively.

I paused my thoughts for a moment to see if my magic had anything to say. If it did, though, it wasn't loud enough for me to hear. I took my phone from my pocket, accessed the camera feature, and snapped a picture of the casting circles. Though familiar in some respects, they were very foreign in others.

I sent a copy of the image to Claudius.

Tabitha twitched her tail impatiently. "Can we go home now?"

"No," I said, scanning the room again. I was looking for

anything I might be able to cast from to track the conjurer. I wasn't going to chance a reveal spell on the circles themselves. Who knew what kinds of traps the symbols hid. But my scan of the rest of the room turned up no obvious evidence.

"*Now* can we go home?" Tabitha whined.

"No," I repeated.

"Why not?"

"For one, there's someone in the hotel casting magic that I strongly suspect isn't in the service of good. And two, finding that person is supposed to help us find Sefu—ideally before the demons do."

Tabitha moaned.

"What?"

"I've seen the way you work. If this were a book, you'd run around like an insufferable fool for three-quarters of the thing, enduring one beating after another, before your showdown with the big, scary monster. Which you barely manage to overcome. And you think *I* want to be a party to that nonsense?"

"It's not going to be like that."

"How do you know?"

The honest answer was I didn't. I had an unknown conjurer who had summoned from an unknown place for unknown reasons. But I was thinking about what Arianna had said last night about my team.

Utilize their diverse perceptions.

I flipped my phone open again.

"Who are you calling?" Tabitha asked.

"Some friends."

"And I'm supposed to, what, stay tethered to you like a babbling toddler?"

"I'm going to need everyone on deck," I said, pointing at her. "And that includes *you*."

"Fuck," she moaned.

With Vega's help, I was able to secure a small conference room in the hotel for our team meeting. She was the first to arrive, decked out in her professional attire: black suit and blouse, detective badge glinting at her belt beside her holstered sidearm. I'd filled her in on the events over the phone. Vega had had some info for me too. Apparently, the Centre Hotel was the site of a full-blown sci-fi/fantasy convention, which explained the costumes.

Epic Con, it was called. Yeah, I rolled my eyes hard on that one too.

I'd heard about it in the past, but only peripherally. Founded in 2000, Epic Con had just been starting to compete with its peers in the con world before the Crash put it out of business. An attempt to revive it two years before had lost the organizers money. But with major sponsors agreeing to subsidize ticket prices and hotel rooms this year, they decided to give it another go. Attendance was expected to exceed ten thousand, which was a major win in this day and age. And with the hotel and several nearby booked solid for the weekend, it was considered a score for the city as well.

I rose to meet Vega, who was unshouldering an NYPD duffel bag onto the table.

"Thanks for coming right away," I said.

We shared a quick kiss. From her chair, Tabitha made a noise of disgust.

Vega flashed my cat a fake smile. "Nice to see you too."

"She's not super excited about being here," I whispered.

"Really," Vega deadpanned.

"Hey, how did it go last night?"

"Fine." I picked up the subtle tension in Vega's voice. "Quiet."

"And Tony?"

"Still sleeping. I decided to have him stay inside at my brothers' instead of going to school."

"Probably a good idea," I admitted. "I'll try to get up there to reinforce the wards."

I thought about Arnaud, still at large, before my mind turned to the card Malachi had given me the night before. Though I was carrying the card in my shirt pocket, I still hadn't told Vega about our meeting. A few spoken syllables, a brand-new bonding sigil on my hand, and she wouldn't have to worry about her son ever again.

Watching her concerned eyes now, it was tempting as hell.

"I made a few calls on the way here," she said. "We tried to ID your anonymous caller, but they're on a burner phone."

"Figures," I said. "Would have been too easy."

"Also, no cameras on the basement level. I have an officer going through the elevator footage, but so far it doesn't show anyone but staff accessing the floor. The perp probably used the stairs."

Or used a glamour to look like staff, I thought. That was the problem with not knowing the nature of magic at work.

"I got ahold of a list of con attendees that Hoffman's going to cross check against the crime databases," Vega continued, "but that'll take a while."

"Because of the length of the list or Hoffman?"

Vega shot me a look that said, *Don't get me started.* "There's no one named Sefu on it, anyway." She began to scroll and tap her phone. "Here, let me go ahead and send you a copy."

"No, no!" I cried, causing Vega to look up sharply. "It's just that my phone can't handle anything that size. It'll show up as a broken image. Same with group texts. And then I get charged fifty cents, or something ridiculous."

"Relax," she said, putting her phone away. "I'm not sending it."

My face flushed with shame. "So, how many officers are covering the con?"

"About a hundred. I described what you encountered in the basement, and they've been instructed to keep their eyes open but not to engage anything they don't understand. They know you and I are here with a team. I have permission to pull officers from their detail, should we need them."

"Good," I said. "Could come in handy for crowd control."

"Why not just cancel this ridiculous thing?" Tabitha asked.

Though Tabitha was looking for any excuse to go home now, I had considered the same question. There were a few reasons at this stage *not* to cancel the convention. One, we didn't know yet whether this was an isolated conjuring or part of a larger pattern. And two, scattering the con and its participants would mean not only losing the conjurer, but this Sefu I'd been sent to protect, assuming he or she was here. And if the consequences of the demons getting to them were as dire as Arianna had predicted, then I needed to find Sefu first.

Vega cocked an eyebrow at me.

"Look, we will if we have to," I said.

The last thing I needed was Vega and my cat teaming up against me. Fortunately, neither one pressed the issue. Tabitha looked at the empty chairs around the conference table irritably.

"Where is this *team* of yours anyway?"

"Well, we're three so far," I replied. "The other two should be here any minute." I turned to Vega. "In the meantime, I'm wondering if you could have the department take a look at something else."

"What is it?"

"That conjurer I mentioned last night? He had a spell book in his apartment that helped him call up a decent-sized demon. I didn't detect any magic in it, but until we know where the thing came from, better to be safe. He claims to have ordered the book from a magazine."

I made a sign in the air, and a small hole opened to a parallel plane. It was a device Gretchen had taught me for storing items I didn't want to have to lug around everywhere. The catch was that the items had to be inert—the plane wasn't stable enough to hold magical items or combustible material, like gunpowder—and space was limited to roughly what could fit inside a small locker at the gym. My *cubbyhole*, I called it.

I reached inside and pulled out the magazine from Nathan's apartment, turned to the classified section, and pointed to the ad. Vega had seen me summon the cubbyhole enough times that the novelty had worn off. She took the magazine from me and squinted at the small print.

"And you want to know who placed the ad," she said.

"Exactly."

"Think it's the same person who called up the things here?"

"Not necessarily." I signed the cubbyhole closed. "I mean, a convention like this *would* seem to attract the type of person who sells spell books, but it's still a long shot. I'll just feel better having a lead on whoever authored the spells."

Vega flipped the magazine to the cover. "I'll have someone run a reverse P.O. box check and also contact the magazine. One or both should net us a name."

"Excellent."

While Vega made the call, I pulled potions and spell implements from my pockets and spread them over the table. I'd left in such a hurry, I hadn't properly organized them. Tabitha watched, a curled paw propping her cheek.

"Doing all right?" I asked her.

She gave me a withering look that told me to go bone myself. I still needed to contact a vet, though I was already dreading bringing Tabitha in for an exam. The last time had been a disaster. I repacked everything into my pockets in a better semblance of order, finishing as Vega ended her call.

"I've got someone working on it," she said. "Any updates on Arnaud?"

The edge in her voice set off my defensive alarms until I reminded myself she was only worried for Tony. Once more, I thought of the card I'd slipped into my shirt pocket that morning. Arianna had said that my first action shouldn't be with the Upholders—and under the circumstances, I completely agreed—but the bonding agreement could be the boy's ticket to safety.

Now seemed a good time to explain the offer, but the door to the conference room opened.

Vega and I turned to find a police officer showing in Mae Johnson, the "nether whisperer" who had helped me at Yankee Stadium earlier in the fall. The large, elderly woman smiled broadly as she swayed toward me. She had been using a walker for arthritis in her hips and low back, but a couple healing sessions from yours truly, and the eroded, inflamed joints had repaired enough to tolerate her generous upper body without the external support. She'd even slimmed down some, the extra exercise no doubt helping. She was sporting a fresh perm whose color matched her gleaming white tennis shoes.

"So good to see you, Mae," I said, standing.

I kissed her cheek as I took her pet carrier and set it on the table. Beyond the wire mesh door, a small lobster-like creature snapped its claws and wriggled the tendrils around its mouth in either greeting or annoyance; I couldn't tell.

I stooped down. "Hey, Buster."

The nether creature released a pleasant enough-sounding squeal, but I knew better than to try to scratch his head.

"I got here as soon as I could," Mae said, huffing slightly and pushing her thick glasses up from the sides.

I straightened. "Thanks for coming. You've already met Detective Vega."

"Sure have. How are you, sweetie?"

"Fine, Mae." A trace of anxiety remained in Vega's voice, but I doubted anyone else noticed. "How about you?"

Mae waved a hand. "Oh, don't get an old lady started. Unless you want to hear about aches, pains, sleeping problems, hearing problems, digestive complaints, and relatives who never call. Or call too much." She'd been glancing around the conference room, and now her eyes stopped on Tabitha. "And who's this?"

"Oh, that's—"

"Everson's hormonally depleted sack of shit," my cat answered.

"She also goes by Tabitha," I said.

Mae pressed a hand to her chest, eyes wide. "She *talks*?"

"And you have a lobster with tentacles for lips," Tabitha snapped. "Don't act so surprised."

"There's a succubus in that body," I explained, to which Mae nodded. She had studied enough magic on her own to understand what that meant. Her expression told me she also knew to drop the subject.

I pulled a chair back for Mae and scooted it in as she sat.

On the phone, I'd only told her I needed her help with an assignment. I was preparing now to give her the details when the door opened again and the same officer appeared. This time, he was escorting what looked like a ten-year-old boy in a brown bomber jacket, wool cap pulled down to a scarf that wrapped most of his face.

"Thanks," I said, as the officer retreated and closed the door. "Well, we're all here."

Everyone watched the newcomer as he unwound the scarf from his head. A squat nose appeared, followed by a jutting jaw.

When the last of the scarf came free, he blinked his squash-colored eyes.

"This is Bree-Yark," I announced.

He strode forward, arms akimbo, as if he already owned the room.

"Hope no one's got a problem with a goblin," he said.

14

When I'd called Bree-Yark, I wasn't sure I would be able to convince him to come, but he was anxious to get out of Gretchen's house. His exact words were, "I'm dying over here, buddy." Vega and Mae introduced themselves, and he kissed their hands in turn. To the women's credit, neither flinched.

Tabitha watched him through slitted eyes from across the table. I braced for her to say something cutting, but she held her tongue. Fortunately, Bree-Yark didn't appear remotely interested in her.

He draped his scarf over the back of a chair, hitched up his dark, bootcut jeans, which were already rolled up at the cuffs, and hefted himself onto the seat. At his height, his steel-toed work boots came a good foot short of the floor. Buster skittered excitedly in his cage, but Bree-Yark didn't seem interested in him either. The goblin laced his thick fingers on the table and peered up at me.

"Someone going to tell me exactly what this clam bake is about?"

"Yeah, first thanks for coming." I looked around the table. "That goes for everyone."

"Not all of us were given a choice," Tabitha remarked.

I ignored her. "Somewhere in this hotel there's a conjurer or conjurers. We need to find them ASAP. The problem is, I'm not detecting any magic. I can't even tell what kind of magic they're using." That stung to admit, but the facts were the facts. I'd never encountered quite this brand of magic before.

"That's why I called you," I continued, "for your perceptual abilities. I'll go around the table and introduce everyone. Bree-Yark here is from the faerie realm. He can detect fae energies, including a range of magics."

I'd ascertained this info over the phone, and Bree-Yark nodded now.

"Served in the goblin army for almost eighty years," he told the room. "The recruiting officers didn't lie—ransacking and pillaging gets you around. Marched to one end of Faerie and back probably a half dozen times. Crossed the Mirther Range, the Frost Plains. And the Fae Wilds?" He grunted. "They don't call them that for nothing. You see a lot of wild shit, pardon my French," he said, glancing over at Mae and Vega.

"Yeah, so if the conjurer is using a brand of fae magic, he'll know," I interjected, having learned the hard way on the phone that Bree-Yark could be hard to derail once he got going. "Mae Johnson's specialty is nether creatures. Not only can she sense them, but they respond to her commands. She helped quash a major attack on Yankee Stadium this past October."

The lizards I'd faced this morning had shown nether qualities. If more popped up, I was counting on Mae to detect them. Having her here to control them until I could put them down would be a further help.

"I was a practicing veterinarian too," Mae put in importantly. "Thirty years."

Holy crap, how had I forgotten that? I could have *her* take a look at Tabitha.

"Vet, huh?" Bree-Yark grunted. "Any recommendations for keeping these trim?" He splayed his black talons toward Mae. "They're getting too tough for scissors, and you should see the ones on my toes. Thick as railroad spikes."

"Oh, honey, you're gonna need guillotine clippers, extra-large. I should have a pair in a closet back at the apartment."

I raised my voice, as much to get myself back on track as my new teammates. "Last but not least in the sensing department is Tabitha. She'll be able to alert us if anything demonic is afoot."

"Oh, really," Tabitha said.

While waiting for Vega and the others to arrive, I'd gathered some conference programs. I distributed them now, even placing one in front of Tabitha so she'd feel a part of the team. She made a point of not looking at it.

"This has information on Epic Con," I said, "including a schedule of events and a detailed map of the hotel. Most of the conference is taking place on the first four floors. I want to start with a walkthrough to get a feel for the place. Eyes, ears, and senses on high alert. See what we can pick up. Detective Vega will help coordinate."

She responded to the cue by reaching into her duffel bag and producing a handful of communication devices. "Does everyone know how to use a radio and earpiece?" she asked. "If not, it's pretty simple. This goes in your ear, and this clips to your pants." As she went over the controls on the small black boxes, I looked around the table. I studied the contrasting faces of Vega, Mae, Bree-Yark, and Tabitha, realizing it would be my first time heading a team. A bolt of anxiety shot through me.

Relax, man, I told myself. *You'll do fine.*

But the stakes felt really damned high. It didn't help that I had just missed a possible lead to Sefu. If I'd only gotten to the basement fifteen minutes earlier. I checked my phone to make sure the anonymous caller hadn't tried me again, but there were no messages or call records.

Once Vega had us all hooked up, I said, "All right, team. Let's move out."

I stood, seized my cane, and uttered a small invocation to make my trench coat billow like someone you'd want leading you.

Fake it till you make it, right?

My earpiece crackled loudly. An instant later something exploded at my hip. Startled, I batted the radio unit to the floor as if it were a rat that had crawled up my side. As I watched the unit flicker and burp smoke, I realized I'd forgotten to encase the damned thing in a neutralizing spell.

Bree-Yark jumped up and began stomping the unit with a work boot.

While Mae and Buster exclaimed, I turned to Vega, who was frowning.

"Hey, uh, you wouldn't happen to have any spares?" I asked.

Behind me, Tabitha snorted a laugh. "Now *that* was worth coming out for."

BY THE TIME WE STEPPED OFF THE ELEVATOR ONTO THE FOURTH floor, I'd mostly regained my composure, even with Tabitha continuing to grin. At least I'd brightened her mood.

Vega had suggested we start at the uppermost level of the con and move down—a "top to bottom," she called it. By the map on the program, we were entering an area devoted to gaming. Sure enough, clusters of attendees—many in costumes—sat around tables spread with cards, landscape boards, metal figurines, and loads of funny-shaped dice. An elbow shot into my hip, nearly smashing a potion.

"Ever play?"

I looked down to find that Bree-Yark had sidled up to me. Though he'd left his scarf in our meeting room, he'd put his wool hat back on, so at least his goblin ears were covered. Not that it would have mattered much in here. I followed his cocked head to where a group of young adults in medieval-looking garb were pitched in a game of D&D. One was disputing a failed saving throw.

"Yeah, back in high school," I replied distractedly.

"It doesn't take a very friendly view of goblins," Bree-Yark said thinly.

"Well, I only played a couple times. The Dungeon Master was kind of a dick."

"Bet you killed goblins, though."

"I honestly don't remember. Look, are you picking up anything?"

He glanced around the gaming area and shrugged. "Just a lot of hostility toward my kind. And don't get me started on the goblins in Shadowrun. Diseased mutants?"

I turned to Mae. "How about you?"

Though she was scanning the open floor space, I could see her eyes lingering on the attendees' costumes. When a woman strode past in what amounted to a few strategically placed cups of latex joined by fishing line, Mae *tsk*ed. From inside his carrier, Buster mimicked the sound.

"You say people pay money to come here and do this?" Mae asked.

"I guess," I said.

"But why ever on Earth?"

Even though I was trying to focus on the energetic currents and auras imbuing the space for anything magical, I caught my professor's mind mulling the question. "Probably goes back to ancient practices of totemism and hero worship. Acting out hidden aspects of yourself, getting to be someone you're not. These cons are just the modern expression. Plus, there are the social-bonding aspects."

"If you say so," Mae said, looking unconvinced.

"Ridiculous, if you ask me," Tabitha remarked from behind us. "I mean, who *chooses* to be a cat?" Her eyes followed a trio of attendees in bulky feline costumes—*furries,* I'd heard them called.

"Notice how no one's dressed as a goblin?" Bree-Yark said.

"What about him?" Mae asked, pointing.

"That's a gremlin," Bree-Yark growled.

As we left the gaming area and entered a section being set up for celebrity photo ops, I waved everyone over to an empty table. "All right, listen. I get that this is an unusual setting with a lot to look at, but we need to filter out the distractions and—"

Off to my right, a woman squealed. "Ohmygod! I love you, James Mardsten!"

I craned my neck around. *James Mardsten's here?*

"Everson," Vega snapped.

I returned my attention to my teammates. "Right. We have to focus, or we run the very real risk of missing something important. Do we need to take another walk through the gaming area?"

"No to the more walking," Tabitha replied.

"I didn't pick up anything, Everson," Mae said.

"Me neither," Bree-Yark grunted.

"Okay, that makes four of us." I checked my phone again, then scanned our surroundings. Was the person who called me here too? I cocked an inner ear to my magic, but I wasn't getting that "being watched" feeling.

Vega, who had been listening into her earpiece, spoke up. "A team of officers completed their search of the basement.

Nothing to report. They're moving on to the closed rooms and closets on the upper floors."

"Anything happening in the con?" I asked.

"One creep was arrested for inappropriate grabbing. Otherwise, just a couple confiscations of sharpened weapons."

Upon finishing our tour of the fourth floor, we rode down to the third and emerged into what looked like an open market. Vendor stalls stretched from one end of a large hall to the other.

The four of us spread out, each taking a different aisle. I moved past impressive displays of art, leatherworks, and handmade accessories. Trailing on her harness, Tabitha hissed at anyone who smiled down at her or, God forbid, showed an inclination to pet her. She swiped her claws at one determined woman.

"How's demon watch going?" I asked.

"The only demons are these idiot humans," she snapped back.

"Be nice."

At the far end of the vendor area, the floor narrowed to a corridor dubbed "Author's Alley." Stanchions steered book-clutching fans to their favorite writers. I recognized several of the names: Logsdon, Massey, Sanchez, Silvers.

Up ahead, an author sporting a salt-and-pepper comb back finished signing a book, closed it with a flourish, and tossed it to a lone fan who looked suspiciously like his mother. When he glanced my way, there was a mad, almost maniacal, gleam in his eyes that unnerved the hell out of me. Something about it screamed *God complex*. The author grinned and shot us with a pair of finger pistols.

"Case in point," Tabitha muttered.

I smiled tightly at this Brad Magnarella and hurried on.

Beyond Author Alley, the floor opened again to a room with

a smaller collection of vendors specializing in armor and weapons. As Vega and Mae joined us, I peered around.

"What happened to Bree-Yark?"

At that moment, I heard shouting and what sounded like a rack of chainmail crashing to the floor. The barking voice that rose above the scrum was unmistakably goblin. Crap.

I scooped up Tabitha and arrived at a run to find Bree-Yark straddling the chest of a man dressed as a robot. Gold-painted cogs and gears flew as Bree-Yark rained blows down on his head. A semi-circle of conference-goers formed around the combatants.

"House elf?" Bree-Yark barked savagely. "I'll show you a house elf!"

He reached over, grabbed a fallen dagger, and held it to the robot's throat. The tip was blunt and there were no sharp edges, but it was still solid enough to do damage, especially in the grip of a goblin.

"Whoa, whoa, whoa!" I cried, shoving through the crowd in time to grab Bree-Yark's wrist.

Vega joined me, and we managed to pull him off the robot. The plastic shell around the robot's head had cracked open, and a groggy pair of eyes stared out. But even as we dragged Bree-Yark backwards, he continued trying to land shots with his work boots.

"Do you want me to haul you in?" Vega shouted.

Only when the robot's friends had helped him up and ushered him away did Bree-Yark calm down enough to drop the knife. A group of NYPD officers ran up, but Vega shook her head to tell them we had it under control. They eyed Bree-Yark for a moment before dispersing. The goblin's breaths blasted from his nostrils for several more cycles before he raised a hand to show us we could release his arms.

He straightened his wool hat, which had gone askew. "Punk called me a house elf."

"Yeah, because he thought you were in costume," I said. "Something similar happened to me earlier, but I didn't start throwing punches, for crissake. C'mon, man. What did I say earlier about focusing?"

Bree-Yark grunted.

Mae had arrived and, ever the mother, set Buster's carrier down to begin cleaning up the mess.

"Here, let me do that," Bree-Yark said in what sounded like embarrassment.

While they worked together, I turned to Vega and in a lowered voice said, "I'm starting to think calling them here was a mistake."

"At least you're asking for help now."

I felt my brow crease in question. "What do you mean?"

"You have a habit of taking on too much yourself. And no offense, but that's when things typically go to shit. One person—or wizard—can only shoulder so much." Though she was using her firm voice, her eyes were soft and personable. She shifted them to Bree-Yark and Mae. "Even this is an improvement for you."

"Yeah, well, I hope you're right."

But her assurance gave me confidence. It had taken a lot of mental back and forth before pulling the trigger on hiring the vampire hunters. As a result, I had eyes watching the city for Arnaud and three silver-armed pros who could finish the job. And now here I was with a team attuned to various preternatural frequencies, not to mention backed up by a hundred NYPD officers. And if push came to serious shove, I had the Upholders and the power of the interfaith community at my beck and call.

Maybe.

Vega must have seen a change come over my face. "What is it?" she asked.

I considered whether now was the time to tell her about the offer of sanctuary. But at that moment, Bree-Yark straightened suddenly and peered across the room, his vertical pupils narrowing to slits.

I followed his gaze. "Something up?"

"See that group checking out the wands?" he asked in a low voice.

A second later, I saw who he meant. A pair of young men and a woman were milling around a display. But something about them seemed at odds with the other con-goers, and it wasn't just that they weren't in costume. It was in their unnatural movements and expressions, the moonlike glow of their hair. And something about their casual designer outfits seemed just a little too well put together.

"They're lunar fae," he said.

15

I squinted, but the three were too far away for me to discern any magic.

"Sure they're fae?" I asked.

"Yeah, their magic's subtle and they're using glamours," Bree-Yark said, "but I'd recognize their kind anywhere."

I moved forward until I was behind the righted rack of chainmail. Vega came up to my other side. Though I'd never encountered one, I recalled from my readings that lunar fae were mischievous and vindictive. Didn't like humans much, either. When the female fae turned, a lanyard with a badge swung from her neck.

"Attendees?" I said in surprise. "What in the world are they doing at Epic Con? They already live in a fantasy world."

"Maybe they're just curious," Mae replied.

"Not likely," Bree-Yark said. "If they're here, it's for a specific purpose."

"Are they dangerous?" Vega asked.

"Can be," Bree-Yark grunted.

"And they can conjure, right?" I asked, still pulling up info from my memory bank.

"Don't know about these three, but some can," Bree-Yark said. "Use their magic to pluck creatures out of a realm that intersects with the Fae Wilds. Nighttime creatures, usually," he added with a scowl.

"As in a pair of fire breathing lizards?" I asked.

"Never ran into anything like that myself, but it doesn't mean they're not out there. Like I said, lot of wild shit in that part of Faerie." He quickly looked over at Mae and Vega and raised a hand in apology.

I pulled out my flip phone and accessed the photo of the casting circles. I hadn't thought of showing it to Bree-Yark before, but he was proving to be more knowledgeable than I would have guessed.

"Does this look like a lunar casting symbol?"

The thick skin of Bree-Yark's face furrowed as he studied it. "I honestly couldn't tell you. I might be able to sense magic, but it's not really my thing. I'm more into engineering. Hey, ever see that show *Megastructures*?"

"No," I said, returning my phone to my pocket and my attention to the fae.

"Want me to keep an eye on them?" he asked.

"After what you did to Mr. Roboto? No, thanks."

"Look, his remark caught me off guard, all right? It touched a nerve. I'm good now."

The lunar fae were a lead I wanted to follow, but there were still two floors of con to cover. Having Bree-Yark take that job *would* be a big help. I glanced over at Vega, who shrugged as if to tell me it was my call.

I looked back at Bree-Yark. "House elf," I said.

His right hand tensed as if preparing to ball into a fist, but he caught himself and shook his arms loose. "See there? Nobody's gonna trigger me with that one again. Did I pass?"

He'd realized I was testing him. "I suppose, but you're strictly on watch," I said. "No engagement. And keep us updated. In fact, I'm going to have Mae go with you." I turned to her. "Is that all right?"

"Well, sure. If it's all right with him."

I expected Bree-Yark to argue, but he bowed slightly and offered her the crook of his arm. "Fair lady?"

For a thuggish-looking goblin, he had a way of turning on the charm. Mae let out a surprised giggle and accepted his elbow. When he turned to lead her away, I got Mae's attention and used two fingers to make the *keep an eye on him* gesture.

She nodded in a way that told me she knew her role.

"So, second floor?" Vega asked.

"Yeah, there's actually a presentation I want to catch." I shook my folded program open and held it so we could both see the schedule. I moved my finger past sessions titled *Demon Lords Revisited*, *Werewolf-Vampire Hybrids: Fearsome Fact or Cheap Fiction?*, and *Ghoul-Slaying in the Digital Age*, until I found the one I was looking for.

"Here," I said, giving it a tap.

"Confessions of a Modern Day Magic-User," she read.

"Sounds hokey, but if the presenter has honest-to-goodness magical abilities, then we might have another lead."

Vega, Tabitha, and I arrived to find the conference room packed. We managed to grab two seats together near the back. With more people still entering, I could see this was going to be a standing-room-only session. Maybe we did have something.

"Am I supposed to lie on the floor like an animal?" Tabitha asked from my feet.

In the bustle and din of the room, no one else heard her, but I motioned for her to keep it down anyway. "Now might be a good time for a nap," I whispered. "There's space under my chair."

She made a pouty face, which told me what she wanted.

I sighed. "Fine, but keep your claws sheathed."

I lifted her onto my lap. Tabitha spent the next minute rearranging herself—and my legs—until she'd attained a form roughly the size and shape of a car tire. "A neck rub would be nice," she said.

"You're pushing it."

"I'm depressed, remember?"

I consented just to keep her quiet. Within moments, she was purring like a small motor. A woman beside me—dressed, appropriately enough, as Catwoman—tilted her head in adoration and began to reach over with her gold-painted claws, but I warned her back with a stern shake of my head.

"Ringworm," I whispered.

Catwoman grimaced and shrank away. By now the room was dimming, highlighting the stage in front. A tall man with long, graying hair and a two-day stubble stood behind a podium. His faded black shirt read THE ONLY GOOD GOBLIN IS A DEAD ONE. Good thing Bree-Yark wasn't with us.

But was this the "modern-day magic-user"? I wondered.

"All right, everyone," he said in one of those aging stoner voices as he signaled for quiet. The room settled. "First and foremost, welcome to the return of Epic Con!" he shouted, punctuating the greeting with a fist pump.

Being the first session of the day, the costumed crowd answered with a predictable onslaught of enthusiasm. The response had an intoxicating effect on the speaker, apparently. A huge smile stretched his face. He began pacing the stage with long thrusts of his legs, throwing up more fist pumps. This went on for a full minute.

"I'm Stan the Man," he said into his head mic, "and you're all awesome, awesome, *awesome!*"

An even more raucous wave than the first rolled in. Vega nudged my arm and pointed to the second page of her program. Stan Burke was one of the conference organizers. I gave her a thumb's up for the info.

"We've got a really special treat for you," Stan said as he and the noise finally settled back down. "For the first time ever at Epic Con we have a bonafide magic-user ready to razzle and dazzle you with his mad, mystical skillzzz. So put your hands, hooves, paws and claws together, and welcome the great Brian Lutz!"

I telescoped my neck as a round ginger-haired man in a red robe stood from the front row, lumbered up, and took Stan's place on stage. Though his chubby face and short arms made him look boyish, I pegged him to be in his forties. From behind a pair of glasses, mouse-like eyes skittered over the audience. His mouth, framed in a goatee the same color as his hair, worked itself into a tense line.

I'd already opened my wizard's senses but couldn't discern anything magical around him. And if he was planning to do a stage act, he was sorely hurting for any kind of theatrical presence. He looked more like an accountant preparing to read from an actuarial table.

"Is he just going to stand there?" Vega whispered.

"I'm still trying to figure out how he's so popular," I whispered back.

Whereas Stan had taken the energy of the audience and converted it into pacing and fist pumps, Brian just seemed to be stewing in it. Even so, I caught myself leaning forward. There was something a little magnetic about the man. Or maybe it was just the anticipation of him crashing and burning, which seemed more and more inevitable.

When Brian's cheeks started to tremble, I thought he was going to burst into tears.

Without warning, his face clenched. With the wave of a robed hand, he shouted, "Silence!"

There was a strange power in his thin voice, and the room obeyed immediately. I thought I caught a smile twitch at the corner of his mouth as he adjusted the microphone on his headset. He clasped his hands behind his back and began a slow stroll of the stage.

"My story is common enough among wizards, I suppose," he said with the appropriate amount of modesty. "I never knew my parents. I came up in a foster family, though I say the word *family* with no small amount of irony. They were anything but. They derived sadistic pleasure in denying me the basic joys of childhood that I'm sure most of you took for granted: friends, toys and books, a reasonable amount of computer time..." *A bedroom that wasn't a closet beneath the stairs,* I thought with an eyeroll. I may not have been sensing any magic, but my bullshit detector was rattling off the charts.

"All for being different," he continued. He stopped and thrust up a finger. "But everything changed on my eleventh birthday..."

"All right," I said to Vega. "We can go now."

She nodded and stood from her seat. When I lifted Tabitha to place her on the floor, she snorted awake and gouged her claws into my knees.

"Hey! Ow!" I cried.

There was a collective rustling as heads and costumed bodies turned. Keeping my own head low, I gripped Tabitha's paw and tried to unhook her from my pants, but she was caught fast. "Let *go.*" I hissed.

"I can't. I'm snagged."

When a disgruntled murmur rippled through the crowd, I

realized Brian had stopped talking. I peered up to find him glaring across the audience at me.

"Sorry," I said, showing a hand.

Tabitha's claws finally popped free, and I set her down and joined Vega in the aisle.

"Well, if it isn't Mr. Croft," Brian said.

I wheeled in surprise. He knew me?

"The wizard *hero*," he added in a contemptuous tone.

He must have recognized me from the coverage of the eradication campaign the year before. As more murmurs went up, I looked around nervously. The last thing I wanted was for whoever had conjured the lizards to know I was here. That could make them a lot more careful, harder to track down.

"Actually, I'm supposed to be John—I mean, Harry—" I struggled to come up with one of the wizards the guy dressed as Captain America had called me earlier, but under the weight of the room's collective attention, the names all collided in my mind.

"Everson Croft," Brian said, grinning now. He turned to the crowd. "For those who don't know, this is the stooge the mayor used in his campaign for reelection. The so-called *magic-user*. Note my use of irony again."

My cheeks smoldered as chuckles sounded, but I shook my head and continued to follow Vega.

"What's wrong?" Brian shouted at my back. "Don't like being called out by an actual wizard?"

Maybe it was the stress of Arnaud lurking out there or being assigned the task of finding an unknown person before the demons did and without the Order's help, or maybe it was just the thought of the sacrifices I'd made to help protect posers like this guy, but my anger got the better of me and I spun to face him.

So much for my little talk with Bree-Yark about controlling ourselves.

"Whoa-ho-ho," Brian chuckled. "I think I just got someone's attention."

"Relax, man," I called back. "It's just a con. How about enjoying your dress up and letting the rest of us enjoy ours."

A few *oohs* went up.

Brian flinched slightly, and the humor drained from his face.

He took a deep breath that swelled his belly and released it slowly. "Dress up? You believe this to be dress up?" He gestured to his robe, where a crest of some sort had been sewn poorly onto the left breast. "I'd planned a demonstration for the audience, but how about a challenge instead? Would you like to see that?" he asked the crowd. "The talents of a true wizard pitted against those of a phony's?"

The crowd's response was overwhelmingly positive. I even picked up some jeers directed at me.

Vega tugged my sleeve. *"C'mon,"* her lowered voice sounded in my earpiece. *"We've got more convention space to search."*

I nodded. "Yeah."

But as I started to turn from Brian, I picked up something in my wizard's senses. The image was subtle, nearly imperceptible, but a dark electrical energy appeared to be crackling throughout the crowd, fed, it seemed, by their enthusiasm. Maybe it was coincidence, but every time Brian inhaled, it shifted toward the front of the room. It didn't appear to be magic, not exactly, but still…

The crowd grew louder as they observed my hesitation.

"Is that a *yes*?" Brian asked them, his breaths deepening.

Vega tugged my sleeve again. "What in the world are you doing?"

"I need to see something," I said, handing her Tabitha's leash.

The crowd broke into loud cheers as I made my way up the aisle toward the stage. Brian watched my approach, a confident smile stretching his goatee. As I arrived in front of him, he extended his chubby right hand. His grip was damp but firm.

"Now there's a good sport," he said, continuing to squeeze. His eyes peered into mine for a long moment, sweat glistening across his brow, before they fell to my cane. His gaze was much more intense than it had appeared from across the room. "Is that your famous casting implement?" Before I could answer, he drew a slender wooden wand from his robe and held it up. "Well, this is mine."

He showed it to the audience to more cheers.

I discerned nothing magical in the wood or in the runes he'd scratched along the side with what appeared to have been a dull knife. "We'll make this a classic duel," he said. "Five paces, turn and fire."

His eyes flicked to my right. When I glanced over, I saw he'd come with a small entourage. A block of about twenty people in identical red robes sat off to the left.

Brian took me by the shoulders and spun me until I was turned away from him. A moment later, his warm back was heaving and falling against mine, and yeah, it felt as gross as it sounds. I tried to create a little separation, but he seemed determined that we remain in contact.

"So, should I pretend to go down or you?" I asked over the shoulder away from the audience.

His upper back tensed. "Oh, you won't need to pretend anything. I'm going to drop you like a stench cow."

"I have no idea what that is."

He snorted derisively. "You wouldn't."

I wasn't sensing any magic in him up close, and from my new position, I seemed to have lost sight of the crowd's energy I'd picked up earlier—if it had even existed in the first place. And yet Brian's confidence bothered me. He was either delusional or, like Mae, he possessed an ability I couldn't observe.

"Can you count for us?" he asked the audience.

"One...!" they shouted. When Brian separated from my back, I realized he'd taken his first step. I quickly did the same. The only way to know whether he had any magic to his name was to see what happened at "five."

"Two...!" the audience continued. *"Three...! Four...!"*

I gripped my cane and invoked a low-level shield just in case.

"Five!"

When I pivoted on my right foot, I saw he'd turned a half step early. He thrust his wand toward me and shouted a nonsensical word: *"Kon-a-rahk!"*

Instinctively, I braced for impact. But nothing collided into me.

He gave his wand another hard thrust. *"Kon-a-rahk!"* he repeated, this time sending bits of spittle flying from his lips.

A few chuckles rose from the crowd.

When he attempted to blast me a third time—and I went absolutely nowhere—the laughter spread. Brian glanced at his wand, then at his entourage. A look of outrage came over his face. He then fixed his eyes on mine.

"You're supposed to go *down*," he said.

"I thought we weren't playing pretend."

I couldn't resist saying that loud enough for the crowd to hear, which infuriated him even more. But why was he acting so surprised? He stalked toward me, hands clenching into doughy fists. Okay, I wasn't going to fight this guy.

I whispered a minor force invocation. The skirt of his robe wrapped his legs, and he pitched forward. The murmurs of laughter gathered into a surprised burst as he went down.

Brian caught himself against the stage floor, the impact snapping his wand. One end went flying into the crowd, prompting more laughter. Several members of the audience, probably those who had come to see *actual* magic, got up to leave with mutters and shakes of their heads.

Brian's eyes turned desperate. Straightening his glasses, he heaved himself to his knees. "Wait!" he cried. "Watch!"

He jabbed his wand toward me again before realizing he was only holding the handle.

Meanwhile, the exodus grew in volume. "Go back to Hogwarts!" someone shouted.

As I looked down at Brian, I started to feel sorry for him. Especially when someone threw the end of his wand back on stage and it bounced off his head. By all appearances, he was an enthusiast who had taken the role-playing a little too far.

I extended a hand down to help him up. "Hey, everyone has an off day."

Brian glared at my hand, then up at me. "Not today," he said through clenched teeth.

And then his entourage was moving past me, shouldering me out of the way. They were men and women ranging from teenaged to what looked like forties and even fifties. A couple of them stooped to help Brian back to his feet. I picked up an exchange of harsh whispers before Brian spun and marched from the stage. The rest of the group fell in behind him as he shoved his way past the departing attendees.

"All riiight," Stan Burke said, rushing back up to the stage. "Let's hear it for Brian Lutz!"

The smattering of applause was overtaken by boos and some shouted obscenities.

Stan looked from the emptying room to me and mumbled, "Tough crowd."

Vega was waiting when I came off the stage.

"Well, that was entertaining," Tabitha remarked from the end of her leash.

"You were wondering about the turnout?" Vega said. She showed me a short description of the session in the back of the program. Beneath a few sentences of empty boasts and promises, an asterisked line read:

* At the conclusion of the session, attendees will receive a ticket for a free drink in the Copper Lounge.

I raised my eyes to the back of the room. At a table, a woman in a red robe was handing out tickets to the remaining few who had even bothered to line up. Most of the attendees had simply left in disgust.

"So, I guess we can safely cross him off the list, huh?" Vega said.

"He's no magic-user," I replied. "But he seemed so damned convinced he was going to blast me out of my shoes."

At that moment Stan Burke walked past.

"Hey," I said, catching his arm. "What do you know about this Brian Lutz?"

Stan shrugged. "Not much except that his session was a bust."

"Then why did you vouch for him?" Vega asked.

"He paid extra for an intro from an organizer, so that's what he got. Hey, don't look at me like that. If we didn't generate dollars wherever we could, Epic Con wasn't gonna happen. And if that meant whoring ourselves out..." He gave another shrug.

"So you don't know him?" I asked to be sure.

"Never heard of him."

"All right, thanks."

As Stan strode away, I turned to Vega. "I think I'd like a background check on Brian anyway. There was an energy I may or may not have picked up. Plus, my magic seems to be nodding its head a little now." I was also curious how someone like that had managed to attract a following. More inducements, or something else?

"I'm on it," Vega said, already pulling out her phone.

As she spoke to the appropriate department, we made a circuit of the rest of the floor, which held the main conference rooms. I even poked my head into a few of the sessions.

When Vega finished her call, we toured the first floor. But after thirty minutes, I wasn't seeing anything besides a growing number of costumed attendees, and neither was Tabitha. I decided it was time to switch with Bree-Yark and Mae, have them do a tour of the lower levels to see what they could pick up. Maybe there were more fae around.

"How's it going up there?" I radioed.

"We were just about to call you," Mae replied.

"What's up? Something with the fae?"

"No, I've still got eyeballs on them," Bree-Yark said. *"They're checking out the video games now."*

"It's Buster," Mae replied. *"We passed a room up here a moment ago, and he started squealing and carrying on. Didn't stop until we were past it. When I backed up, he started right in again. Door's locked, but I believe he's reacting to something in there. You might want to come up and have a look."*

"All right, stay back from the door," I said, my heart rate picking up. "We'll be right there."

16

"There it is," Mae said as we arrived. The door she was pointing to was one of those mysterious doors you often see in large hotels, nothing to indicate where it leads, barely more than a feature of the wall itself.

"Officers claimed to have searched all the rooms on the convention floors," Vega said, but I could hear her doubt. Her troubled eyes dropped to the pet carrier in Mae's grip. It shook as Buster squealed and snapped his claws toward the hotel door, even though we were a good twenty feet back. The little guy was picking up something all right.

I looked down at Tabitha.

"It's not demonic," she said before I could ask.

"Where's Bree-Yark?" I asked, glancing around.

"The fae started moving again," Mae said, "so he followed."

I would've felt better if someone were chaperoning him, but I wanted Vega and Mae here as backup.

The officers Vega had radioed began to arrive. While she filled them in, I secured Tabitha's leash to the leg of a table. She was thinking about protesting—I could see it on her face—but this meant she'd get a break from walking. She settled for a discontented grunt before retreating beneath the table where no one would see her. As I straightened again and eyed the door, Mae clutched Buster's carrier nervously.

"Be careful, baby," she said to me.

A shield crackled to life around me as I approached the door and opened my senses to any magical wards or energies. I wasn't going to make the same mistake as downstairs. But I didn't pick up anything this time.

When I reached the door, I tried the knob. Locked, like Mae had said. The hotel would have a key, of course, but the less people I had to involve, the better. I eyed the bolt. My normal MO would have been to nail it with a force invocation and burst in—element of surprise and all—but with so many people on the floor, I didn't want to inadvertently release something.

Fortunately, I'd come prepared.

I tucked my cane under an arm and pulled a potion from my pocket. Unlike the other vials, a brush was built into this one's cap. I whispered an incantation. One by one, the tiny crystals inside the potion ignited, turning the liquid a luminescent silver.

I drew out the brush and began painting a small circle beside the doorknob. Within moments, I could see the layer of door just beneath the surface. To the untrained eye, it would have looked as if the glittering liquid were eating through the door, but the spell was actually a form of remote viewing. It was just that the viewing worked across inches, not miles—and for someone at my level, even that little bit required a good amount of potion.

I was nearing the bottom of the vial when the viewing potion finally "broke" through the door, and I was peering into the room beyond. It appeared to be a storage space for spare tables and chairs, which were folded and stacked against the far wall. A light source just outside my angle of sight cast everything in an eerie electric glow. As I leaned in to dab on the last of the potion, a large yellow eye appeared opposite mine.

"Christ!" I shouted, and shoved myself backwards.

"Something in there?" Vega asked into my earpiece.

As suddenly as it had appeared, the eye disappeared from the viewing portal. Even though I'd only glimpsed the eye for a moment, its horizontal pupil suggested amphibian. Whatever it belonged to was frigging huge. Heart pounding, I secured the door with a shield invocation.

"Yeah. We're going to need to clear the floor."

"How about the conference and hotel?" Vega asked.

I thought about it, but evacuating the floor was going to be challenging enough.

"Let's wait and see what we're dealing with," I replied, easing back to the hole.

Vega went quiet, then came back on a moment later. *"Okay. They're clearing the floor."*

I angled my head trying to get a better look into the room. The remote viewing was a one-way spell, so the creature hadn't seen me. More likely it had picked up the sound of the brush strokes. I peered over a shoulder. Already, officers were herding vendors and attendees away from our area.

Need to tilt this encounter further in my favor, I thought, *and with the least risk to the attendees.*

I seized the edge of the rubber seal that ran along the bottom of the door and, with the help of a force invocation, ripped it aside. I then produced another potion, pouring it along the line where the rubber strip had been. As I spoke the activating words, a pink mist drifted up. With another invocation, I pushed the sleeping spell beneath the door.

Through the small viewing portal that continued to waver in place, I watched pink smoke gush into the room. Any moment now, I expected to hear the thud and rattle of something enormous toppling. But when the sleeping potion thinned and there had still been no response, I became nervous.

Maybe it slid quietly to the floor?

The door banged open, and a gargantuan form stood in the mist.

Or not.

I shouted and thrust my sword forward. The force invocation nailed the creature in the chest—and broke apart. The creature didn't so much as wobble. It ducked beneath the doorframe and through the mist. In the next moment, I found myself peering up at something I'd never seen.

The thick, muscled body looked ogre-ish—which would have suggested faerie realm—but its head resembled a frog's. Warts and random thorns protruded from its mottled skin. But there was nothing random about the hooked claws that extended from the back of its fists like the tines of a garden rake.

The hell are you supposed to be?

My sleeping potion hadn't affected the frog-beast, and it had just walked through my force invocation as if it were a light breeze.

With squelching sounds, the creature's eyes rotated in different directions. Before it could get a fix on me, or anyone at my back, I invoked through my staff. Light crackled into a dome around the creature, but the shield felt shaky.

Jaw clenching, I pulled more ambient energy from the room and channeled it into the shield. I strained to close it like a fist, to overcome the forces holding the creature together like with the lizard in the basement. But something in the creature was pushing back.

Its dull, frog-like eyes took in the crackling light around it. Almost faster than I could follow, it lashed out an arm. The claws crashed through the shield as if it were made of breakaway glass. Sparks rained over the carpeted floor. I staggered from the sudden release of energy, spots flashing in my vision.

Thing's resistant to magic, I realized. *Or at least my magic.*

The frog-beast leapt forward, this time lashing its hooks toward my head. I threw my sword up and myself down. The metal blade clanged off a hook. I hit the floor hard. I was eye level with the thing's right foot, a webbed splay with gelatinous toe-pods the size of softballs. Gritting my teeth, I drove the blade into the meat of its calf.

Gathering energy to disperse it, I shouted, *"Dis—!"*

Releasing an ungodly guttural sound that was somewhere between a croak and a scream, the frog-beast swatted the blade aside. The energy I'd pulled in broke apart as my sword clanged away. Knowing the next blow would be aimed at me, I thrust myself back with a force invocation. The frog-beast's hooks gouged into the floor where I'd been and came up with two ragged strips of carpet.

"You stop that ridiculousness right this second!" I turned to find Mae stalking forward, the sleeves of her jacket pushed up, an honest-to-God look of anger in her eyes. "You might be ugly, but you don't have to act a damned fool!"

I gained my feet and whispered another invocation to return my flung-off sword to my grip. The frog-beast was fixated on Mae now. It blinked its eyes and slowly lowered its arm with the strips of carpet hanging from the hooks. Mae must have sensed nether energy in the creature, but would her natural ability hold sway over something this powerful?

I showed her a hand to say she'd come close enough. Mae stopped and placed her fists on her hips. Behind her, Buster squealed from his carrier.

"Now, sit down!" Mae ordered.

This would be the test. If she could lull the frog-beast into docility, I could drive my blade into it from behind and channel enough energy to send the monstrosity back to wherever it had come from. But the creature only stared at her.

"I said, *sit,*" Mae repeated.

When its knees started to bend, I thought we had it. But they were flexing to leap. I threw up a shield just in time. The frog-beast crashed through it in a brilliant cascade of sparks, but that modicum of resistance prevented it from reaching Mae.

Gunshots sounded, and the creature staggered back. I turned to find Vega firing from a wide-legged stance. A pair of pale-faced officers on either side of her joined in. I doubted their standard rounds were having much effect, but thick smoke corkscrewed from the impacts of Vega's silver bullets.

"Its eyes!" I called. "Aim for its eyes!"

Vega adjusted her aim. The frog-beast's right eye blew out. It released a croak-scream and flailed its arms. A moment later, the left eye failed in a burst of black goo. In one long croak, the creature flopped into a drunken series of pirouettes, the hooks on the backs of its fists swiping blindly.

I signaled for Vega to hold fire while I edged closer. I bounced on my toes, looking for an opening. I could already see the yellow orbs of its eyes reforming, the pupils migrating back into place.

On its next turn, the creature's hooks whistled inches from my face. I lunged. My blade broke through the skin of its low back with a wet sound and plunged to the hilt. The frog-beast threw its head back in its most horrid scream yet, then jerked its body from side to side, trying to force me—and the blade—off of it.

Holding fast, I gathered all the energy I could, straining until the ley lines themselves began to bend. Power thrummed through my casting prism, my body. Though my capacity had grown, I was pushing the limits of what I could handle.

But I can't afford to come up short...

When spots began to dance across my vision, I bellowed, *"Disfare!"*

The discharge of energy felt like a bomb going off. I stumbled backwards as an oily black fountain erupted into the air. I gained my footing to find that the creature hadn't been dispersed, but blown through the middle. To one side, its legs flopped as if trying to stand independently of each other. Off to the other side, arms jerked from its severed torso, while its mouth released a weak series of croaks.

"Stay back," I warned the others.

But the creature's two halves were melting, turning to vapor. Though I hadn't dispersed the forces holding the entire creature together, the discharge of energy had disrupted them enough, apparently.

I quickly pulled out the vial that had contained the sleeping potion, scooped up some of the creature's oily discharge, and capped it so that the vial was airtight. I even cast a small invocation to ensure nothing escaped. If I could determine where the creature had come from, I would have a better sense of our conjurer. I would also be better prepared the next time a frog-beast or something like it showed up.

"You all right?" Vega asked, coming up beside me.

"Yeah." I slid the vial into a pocket. "Nice shooting."

"You didn't do so bad yourself." She watched the still-dissolving creature warily. Though it had stopped croaking, its legs continued to twitch. "What in the hell was that?"

"Don't know yet, but it was resistant to my magic."

"That's not good."

"No," I agreed.

"Wouldn't listen to me, either," Mae said, joining us.

Vega slid a fresh mag into her weapon. "At least we know silver hurts it."

I nodded. Silver had the power to damage manifested form

and slow its regeneration. Good to know the creature hadn't been resistant to that too.

Vega turned to the officers behind us and pointed out the panoramic security cameras studding the ceiling. The officers nodded and moved off to review the hotel footage for anyone entering the room the creature had appeared from.

Vega cocked her head toward the room. "Shall we?"

"Yeah," I said, even though I wasn't sure what I would do if another one were back there. I was completely spent—so much so that if Thelonious had been in any shape, he'd be tearing through the conference right now, going absolutely bonkers at all of the idealized expressions of the female form.

"My baby's still excited," Mae said of Buster. "I'm going to get him a soda to calm him down."

"Be sure to thank him for alerting us to the creature," I said. I didn't even want to think what would've happened had the frog-beast emerged onto the crowded floor and we hadn't been there. With its size, speed, and frigging meat hooks, there was no telling how many attendees it would have skewered before we arrived.

"Oh, and can you join up with Bree-Yark when you finish?" I added, still not comfortable with the temperamental goblin doing recon on his own.

"Way ahead of you," Mae said, smiling and bouncing an eyebrow.

As she waddled away, I looked at Vega. "Wait, does she have a thing for—?"

"Not now," Vega said, and tugged me toward the room.

I led the way, sword in hand. Vega followed, aiming her weapon into the room's corners. The storage space was empty. In the center, someone had drawn a symbol much like the ones I'd seen in the basement. Though I was tempted, it was still too risky to attempt a reveal spell.

"This must be how the perp is moving."

I raised my head to find Vega standing in a doorway in the back of the room. An electric sign above it—the one whose light I'd seen through the viewing portal—read EXIT.

"The corridor leads to a staircase," Vega said. "I'm betting it connects every level."

I joined her, and we accessed the staircase. A little exploration didn't turn up any clues, but it confirmed her suspicions. The staircase ran the vertical length of the hotel, top to bottom. As we returned to the conjuring room, I said, "The perp did their homework. No cameras back here or in the stairwell."

"There could be for the access points, though," Vega pointed out.

"Yeah, but all the conjurer would have to do is disable the camera over the one he or she is using."

"Which might point to what floor they're staying on," Vega said. "I'll have the team check to see if any cameras are dark."

As Vega communicated the request, I hunkered at the edge of the circle to examine it more closely. An anomaly on its far side caught my attention. I rose and walked around for a better look.

Vega ended her call. "What is it?" she asked.

"The casting circles in the basement were intact. But do you see this break in the circle? Looks like the result of a timing sigil, set to activate sometime after the creature was summoned. It broke the circle. Someone *meant* for that thing to get out." Probably also explained why the door hadn't been warded.

"So you think the perp intended to target the conference?" she asked.

"Looks that way," I replied with a sigh. "Which means it's time to shut it down."

Damn. That was going to mean losing the caster and this Sefu, who I was beginning to suspect were one and the same.

But I wasn't going to place ten thousand lives at risk. Though we had managed to foil the conjurer this time, we still had no idea who they were or what their end game was.

Vega squeezed my shoulder.

"It's the right call."

17

As Vega and I emerged back onto the cleared-out third floor, I said, "Would you mind if I took a quick look around the neighborhood?"

"Shouldn't you be asking me that?" Tabitha said, emerging from under the table where I'd left her.

"What for?" Vega asked as I began undoing Tabitha's leash.

"Well, *I'm* the one who has to go with him," Tabitha said.

"She's talking to me." I turned back to Vega. "When that frog thing came into the world, it discharged an energy. The wards that triangulate for this area should have picked it up and alerted me, but I got nothing. Just like with the lizards earlier. The conjurer's being careful. I'm starting to wonder if they didn't disable more than a camera."

"You think they took out a ward?"

"A quick check will tell me."

"Go ahead," she said. "I'll break the news to the organizers and help with the evacuation."

The last thing I wanted was to leave Vega here, but with working wards, we could get a major jump on the perp. As it stood now, we could only react. "I won't be long. If anything else turns up, clear out first, let me know second."

"Be safe yourself," she said.

As the cab pulled up to the site of the first ward, I shook Tabitha awake. She looked over at me and closed her eyes again.

"C'mon," I urged, opening the door.

"I'll stay in—"

I clamped a hand over her mouth and coughed. The cabbie's eyebrows furrowed in the rearview mirror. "Did your cat just speak?" he asked in a thick accent.

"No," I said, without elaborating. "Hey, could you keep the meter running? I'll just be a few minutes."

Still covering Tabitha's mouth, I hefted her from the car and set her on the sidewalk. Tabitha hissed when I removed my hand. "If you're going to have him wait, why can't I stay in the cab? It's fucking frigid out here."

"Because I saw the way you looked at him when we got in," I replied.

Tabitha scowled and averted her eyes. "I didn't look at him in any way."

"If I didn't know better, I'd say someone's rediscovering her appetite."

"Well, you *don't*. And even if that were true, it's only because you haven't fed me since last night."

"We'll grab something on the way back."

"Sure, after we walk to one end of the city and back."

Distracted by our exchange, Tabitha had been trudging along beside me as I weaved through pedestrian traffic, everyone either on a phone or in too much of a hurry to notice our conversation. In Tabitha's defense, the wind blowing down Madison Avenue was stinging cold. The late-morning sun showed as a smudge beyond a thick ceiling of gray clouds, suggesting it would remain like this all day, maybe even snow.

I stopped in front of a green wooden door in the side of a building.

"Well, look at that," I said, pulling out my keychain. "We must be to one end of the city already." I grinned at Tabitha and inserted an odd-shaped key into the lock. The door opened with a creak. Beyond, a short flight of steps descended into darkness.

Tabitha peered past my legs. "What *is* this place?"

"An early pump station," I said. "The Order has a ward here."

"It smells horrid."

I couldn't argue with her there. It was also underground, which I cared for even less. I cast a ball of light ahead of us and closed and sealed the door behind us. Though my magic was coming back online, I still felt shaky. I'd expended a ton of power against the frog-beast.

Tabitha and I descended the steps until we were standing in a room snaked through with elephantine plumbing and lined with bolted-down tanks in various states of corrosion. I examined the dust-covered floor, but there were no signs anyone had been down here recently.

"Over here," I said, already feeling the humming ward.

I led Tabitha to the back wall, where an elaborate sigil had been etched into the stone. Vast amounts of energy, invisible to human eyes, coursed through it. Placed at the intersections of major currents of ley energy, the ward grid was originally the work of Chicory, later revealed to be Lich. He employed the system as much to detect intrusions from the nether places as to spy on fellow magic-users. Following Lich's death, the Order in exile cleaned the wards of his influence and updated them.

"I don't like it," Tabitha stated flatly.

When I looked down, I saw her hair poofing out in reaction to the energy. I'm not sure she knew it was happening. I shifted fully to my wizard's senses until I could see the fibers of ley coursing through the ward, could see the ward itself collecting and interpreting ambient energy for blocks and then communicating that information through lines to the adjacent wards. The ward seemed to take a brief interest in Tabitha's and my proximity before something in the network's central brain informed it we were harmless.

In any case, it hadn't been tampered with, as far as I could tell.

"Well, everything here seems to be working," I said.

"Good, can we eat now?"

"Yeah, after we check out the other two."

"There are *two* more?"

"You say it as if I'd told you there were twenty or thirty."

Tabitha's expression changed suddenly. "Everson, demon."

"What?"

"Demon!"

I wheeled as a bald man in a suit charged toward us, a pipe in his grip.

"Protezione!" I shouted.

The shield crackled into shape around us an instant before the pipe descended. Sparks rained over us on impact. Though our protection held, I felt the superhuman blow down to my bones. My next spoken invocation had become a reflex by now: *"Respingere!"*

Energy pulsed from the shield, knocking the demon back several feet and sending the pipe clanging across the room.

Have to keep him on his heels.

I reached into a pocket and jerked out a glass vial of holy water.

"*Vigore!*" I shouted. The force invocation snatched the vial from my upturned hand and slung it like a bullet. The vial exploded against the demon's chest. He screamed as the blessed water tore bloody holes in his skin.

"Where did he even come from?" Tabitha asked, hustling to keep me between her and the demon. I remembered seeing the man on the street now, the one person not conforming to the flow of human traffic. I should have recognized the break in the pattern. Should have paid closer attention.

Just finish him, I urged.

With my depleted power, I only had a few more invocations in me before I was tapped. I summoned another force invocation, this one meant to pull him into my drawn sword. But the demon dove behind the thick bend in a pipe. My force grabbed the steam trailing from his wounded body and sent it back at me in a humid gust.

"Wait!" the demon hissed. "I've come to make an offer."

"Oh, is that what you call trying to brain me with a pipe?"

"A *protection* offer."

"Even funnier." I craned my neck in search of him.

It was clear he was moving, darting silently from cover to cover. That coupled with the pump house's odd acoustics was making him hard to pinpoint.

"What kind of protection?" I asked to keep him talking.

"Protection from me, for one," he said. "But I'm not the only demon here. Perhaps you've heard—there are others. I can ensure they don't harm you. Or your loved ones," he added with what sounded like a grin.

I stiffened at the insinuation.

"One, I don't make deals with demons," I said. "And two, you don't have that kind of power." Still peering past my humming shield, I began stepping around, trying to get a better look behind the network of pipes.

"I don't have the power *yet*," the demon said, his honesty surprising me. "That's where your side of the agreement comes in."

"I can't wait to hear it."

"Tell me where Sefu is," he hissed.

I played dumb. "I don't know what that is."

"You move in the same circles."

"And what circles would those be?"

"*Magical* ones."

That's why the demon had attacked, I realized. He'd wanted to possess me long enough to discover what I knew about this Sefu. I could either keep playing dumb, or I could try to tease out more info from the demon.

"How did you learn about Sefu?" I asked.

"So you *do* know." He chuckled. "Sefu's arrival is the hottest news on the street."

Arrival?

"So, here's my offer," he went on. "A demon *will* find Sefu. A demon *will* make Sefu their host. And that will become the portal by which the demon's master enters your world."

I remembered Arianna's warning about events escalating.

"Do you know that for a fact, or is this more news from the street?" I asked.

"And once the demon master enters your world," he continued, "that master will become *unstoppable*."

"Well, I'm not seeing where that helps me."

Still moving behind the pipes, the demon chuckled. "If the master in question is *mine*, I'll ensure you're compensated for your assistance. As I said, protection for you and your loved ones. You'll get no such offer from the others. You'll never need to worry about them again, in fact. My master will smite them from existence."

Two protection offers in twenty-four hours. How often did that happen?

But mention of the other demons shook me, even if what this one was describing sounded nothing like cooperation. And if they also had the idea I knew something about Sefu, I could be looking at a lot of company. As dangerous as Arnaud was, these demons appeared to be further along too, already possessing hosts.

"How did you even find me?" I asked, trying to sound casual.

The demon laughed again, the wheezy sound whistling in and out of him. "I can't tell you *all* my secrets," he replied. "Let's just say I have connections."

Thelonious? I wondered.

"Remember, Everson, a demon's pact is binding. Once we exchange our words, it will be so."

What he neglected to mention was that demons were notorious for exploiting loopholes.

"Well?" he prompted.

I could feel the demon watching me from the darkness, muscles tensed, waiting for an opening to make another attempt on my body and soul. If I agreed to the pact, all the better for him, but he wasn't counting on it.

Like me, he was buying time to recover.

Tabitha tugged my pant leg. When I looked down, I was surprised to find her indicating the back wall with her eyes. And here I'd thought the demon had been making his way to our left. I gave her a subtle nod. I continued to move to the left, pretending now that I had no idea where he was.

"Well, there's a lot to think about," I said.

"Take your time." His voice still seemed to be coming from elsewhere.

I began aligning my mind with the ward, establishing a

connection to it. When I felt the demon creep in front of it, I whispered a Word. Energy discharged in a crackling boom. I wheeled to find the shrieking demon being blasted from the ward and rocketing toward me. I drove my sword forward, impaling him through the gut.

"Disfare!" I shouted.

The topmost sigil on my blade glowed white. The demon's essence blasted from his host in a screaming wave of black energy that quickly dispersed. A successful banishment. Healing energy collapsed around the blade as I drew it from the man's body, sealing his wound again. He fell onto his back and lay perfectly still.

Tabitha walked up and nudged his leg with a paw. "Is he dead?"

It was a good question. I'd never used the blade to banish a demon from a human host. Gretchen had assured me the enchantment would spare the human in question, and because my father had designed the blade, I believed her. But now my heart began to pound sickly. *Had* I killed him? I was about to kneel beside the man when he heaved himself upright.

"Holy shit!" he gasped.

Relief poured through me. "You're all right," I said, reaching toward him.

He looked from my hand holding his shoulder to my other hand clasping the sword. He patted his stomach. Though his white shirt was torn where the blade had penetrated, there was no blood.

"Y-you ran me through," he stammered.

"But you're all right," I said with more confidence. He wouldn't be sitting up, much less talking, if the wound hadn't healed. "Just give yourself a minute, take some deep breaths, and I'll try to explain—"

"You ran me through," he repeated.

"Do you want a trophy or something?" Tabitha muttered. "We heard you the first time."

The man looked over at her, then at the ball of light crackling overhead. With a cry, he scrambled to his feet and bolted blindly. Fortunately, it was in the direction of the staircase. The demon had already dispersed the locking spell, so I opened the door with a force invocation. A dull square of light fell inside the pump house. The man oriented toward it and seconds later, his loafers were slapping up the steps.

I would've liked to have asked what he remembered about the possession—it might have shed some light on how the demon had been operating—but the man was in no condition. Anyway, what was he going to tell someone who'd just buried a sword in his gut?

I turned to Tabitha. "Thanks for the heads-up."

"Well, I would've hated to see your brains all over the place. Especially if any ended up on me."

I peered around, paranoid now that there was a demon behind every corner. "I'm really going to need you to keep your eyes peeled," I told her. "You heard what he said—there are more of them, and they're all after Sefu. If this demon thought I had an in with Sefu, others could have the same idea."

"You give servant demons far too much credit."

"I don't think I've been giving them credit enough."

I thought about how this one had tracked me down. If his master had suspected Sefu of being in the city, he could have searched until he'd found a demon bonded to a magic-user in the area—Thelonious. The demon master could then have tapped into our bond and directed his servant to me, wrongly assuming I would know something about Sefu simply on the "birds of a feather" principle. Had this been a unique case? Or were other demon masters making the same assumption?

No way to know, which meant I had to assume they were.

"I'm serious, Tabitha. If a demon so much as sneezes, I want to know."

"Okay, fine," she said irritably. "God, you're as dramatic as the man who just left here. Now can we get the other two wards over with so I can eat?"

18

I did the whole head-swivel thing as we visited the next two wards. Even Tabitha seemed to be on heightened alert, though she took pains not to show it. We didn't encounter any demons, however, and the wards appeared to be functioning as they should, no signs anyone had tampered with them. The conjurer at the con, who I had to believe now was Sefu, was concealing their magic in some other way.

On our final walk back to the cab, I veered toward a hotdog stand. Tabitha planted her paws and leaned back, making the harness push the hair up around her neck until she looked like a lion. "No," she said.

"Oh, c'mon. It's just something to fill our stomachs."

"Well, what about that place." She nodded at a bistro across the street. "That looks nice."

"It's a sit-down restaurant. There's no time." I tried to pull her toward the stand, but she lowered her center of gravity even more and yowled in protest. That earned me a few angry looks from obvious cat lovers. "Look, it's this or nothing," I hissed.

I must have sounded serious because Tabitha relented with a loud sigh.

"At least order extra onion so I don't have to taste the intestine."

"Sure, you can have all the onion you want. Hey, how are you feeling?"

"I'd feel better if I wasn't about to gag on a footlong."

"I'm serious. Mae's a veterinarian, you know."

Tabitha let out an aggrieved sigh.

"What? She might be able to help."

"That would be so awkward, darling, us being acquaintances now. And you know how I feel about awkwardness."

"She wouldn't have to touch you or anything. I could just, you know, describe your symptoms."

Tabitha shook her head. "Still too personal."

"I won't tell her it's you. I'll … I'll say it's my neighbor's cat."

"Oh God, darling. Could you be any more obvious?"

"Well, what do you want me to tell her?" I asked in exasperation.

"Can we eat first and talk about this afterwards?"

Back in the cab, I fed Tabitha her hotdogs out of sight of the driver. Despite her earlier gripes, she ate voraciously, looking disappointed when she'd finished the three I'd bought her. I gave her mine to keep her quiet.

While she ate, I called Vega.

"How's it going?" I asked.

"No more monsters," she said. "And no more freak-outs from Buster."

"Thank God." The relief unbunched the muscles in my shoulders. I'd been convinced something was going to happen in my absence.

"How about on your end?" she asked.

"We're on our way back. The wards are working as designed, so it's not them. We did have a run-in with a demon. We're fine,"

I added quickly. "The demon's been banished, but it looks like the hellion crew is serious about finding Sefu."

"Does that change anything?" she asked.

"Besides heightening the urgency? Not really, but I want to try to cloak my connection with Thelonious. I think that's how the demon tracked me. And the last thing we need right now is more demons showing up."

"You can do that?"

"Yeah, I think so. It's just going to take a little time. How's the evacuation going?"

She hesitated. "It hit a snag."

"A snag?"

"I'll fill you in when you get here."

"How are Mae and Bree-Yark doing?"

"Mae's fine—she's with me—but we haven't been able to bring Bree-Yark up on the radio. Mae was the last one to see him. That was when he left to tail the fae."

Great. I hoped Bree-Yark hadn't gotten into trouble again, but I was also worried something had happened to him. The reputation of the lunar fae aside, one of them could be Sefu. That would explain why the wards—and I—hadn't detected their magic. And if Sefu was conjuring frog-beasts and fire-breathing lizards, Bree-Yark was going to have his hands full if he became the target of the same magic.

"He managed to survive eighty years in a goblin army," I said, as much to reassure myself. "I'm sure he'll turn up. I'll call you when I get there."

"This is as close as I can go," the cabbie said as I put my phone away.

I looked up to find us stopped in front of a police barricade. At the other end of the block, a procession was moving down the street. I recognized the convention-goers by their costumes. I wasn't sure what Vega meant by "a snag" because it looked like the evacuation was underway, complete with police escort.

I paid the cabbie a small fortune for the hour plus he'd driven us around, and Tabitha and I made our way toward the evacuation. Remembering how pumped Stan the Man had been that morning, I caught myself feeling a little bad for the guy, as well as for the attendees who had put so much time and thought into their costumes. Epic Con had been a big deal to them, one of those events they'd probably been anticipating all year. Like with most things, it only took one jerk to spoil the fun.

When I arrived at the far street, the attendees appeared to be handling it well. Rows of men and women dressed as futuristic troops marched in lockstep, while behind them, a gaggle of Smurfs skipped along, tossing flower pedals and waving to the crowds gathered along the sidewalk. When I saw a float approaching—something about a Strange Brigade—I realized I wasn't witnessing an evacuation, but a planned procession.

I pulled out my program, and there it was: the "Noon Parade." Epic Con was going full steam ahead, as if nothing had happened. Swearing, I began hurrying along the route in the reverse direction, toward the hotel.

"Would you slow down?" Tabitha complained. "The hotdogs are climbing up my throat."

But I couldn't slow down. I was having flashbacks to Yankee Stadium and the 50,000 fans who had been trapped inside.

"We're almost there," I told her.

That was when I noticed a group in familiar red robes coming toward us as part of the procession. Brian Lutz, who was the only one with his hood down, led the formation with his taped-together wand and a look of high arrogance. Two others flanked him, one wearing what looked like a medieval gauntlet adorned with metallic feathers, which he held in a fist across his chest. The other wore a headdress, which glinted in the recesses of her hood. The crests on their breasts bore dragons, the different colors indicative of rank, I guessed. Brian's was gold. I scanned the entire group as a precaution, but no magic jumped out.

When Brian looked over, I hunkered my head down—I didn't want to be challenged to another duel—but he didn't notice me. He pushed his chest out and kept walking as though everyone were looking at him and they were all his underlings.

Whatever gets you off, pal.

Their procession was almost past me when a trailing member of the red-robed brigade broke away and pushed an envelope into my hand. By the young man's brown crest and position at the back, I pegged him as a bottom-runger. I caught a glimpse of his face before he turned and ran back to the others. His eyes had appeared vacant, as if from a lifetime of computer-gaming. They'd flickered oddly too.

"Hey!" I called after him, but he didn't turn.

I hastily opened the envelope and pulled out a sheet of printed paper.

THE MILITARY FEDERATION OF THE DRAGON
(MEMBERSHIP BY INVITATION ONLY!)

OPEN YOUR EYES! LOOK AROUND YOU! THE AGE OF HUMANS HAS DELIVERED NOTHING BUT GREED, CORRUPTION, DUPLICITY, AND HEARTACHE. WE HAVE BECOME A SICKNESS ON EARTH!

NOW GAZE BACK THROUGH THE MISTS OF TIME TO THE LUCERO MILLENNIUM, A GOLDEN AGE GOVERNED BY DRAGONS—MOST NOTABLY, DRAGE THE WISE.

DRAGE RULED WITH ULTIMATE WISDOM, POWER, AND JUSTICE. INDEED, HE WAS THE PUREST EXPRESSION OF LEADERSHIP THIS

World has ever known. The King of All, He would be sickened to see how thoroughly Humankind now mocks and defiles his Legacy.

But rejoice! His Return has been foretold! He will rise to cleanse the Earth in Fire. He will commence the Red Era—a New Dawn. A Second Golden Age will follow.

Until then, we will defend His Memory and honor His Spirit.

We are the Military Federation of the Dragon.

If nothing else, the manifesto explained the fantastical, if not fanatical, ideas behind Brian's schtick. It was probably what had brought his group together, despite the ridiculous name. But why had his minion given it to me? I peered back inside the envelope. At the bottom sat a red ticket. It was good for a free drink.

I sighed.

Like at the morning's session, they were trying to grow their congregation. Stuffing everything into a coat pocket, I continued along the sidewalk until we reached the front of the hotel. The same doorman from that morning spotted me. He said something into a walkie-talkie and then gave me an apologetic look.

"Sorry," he said, lowering the walkie-talkie. "Can't let you back in."

"Huh? I'm working with the police."

"Not anymore," he said.

"What are you talking about? Ask them." I gestured to the officers just beyond the doors. They would have recognized me, but they appeared to be making a point of avoiding eye contact. The doorman didn't even glance back at them.

"Like I said, sorry. It's not my call."

I was going to ask him whose it was, when Stan Burke appeared past the officers and burst outside. The conference organizer looked nothing like the cool cat from that morning. His face was red, lean arms bowed out to the sides in a way that made him appear vaguely threatening. The wind thrashed his long gray hair.

"Get the hell out of here!" he shouted. "I don't want you within a thousand feet of my convention!"

It wasn't hard to figure out what this was about. "Why?" I asked. "Because you'd rather see your attendees slaughtered?"

"Because you're trying to ruin it!"

His tenor rose to a screech, drawing attention from nearby parade viewers.

"Listen to me," I said in a lowered voice. "You're on the hook for a lot of money. I get it. But you have security issues. Shut down the con for us to deal with them, and maybe you can reopen it before the end of the weekend."

Stan stopped in front of me. Though built like a scarecrow, he had me by a couple inches. He glared down his beaklike nose at me. "I'm not shutting anything down. Oh, I heard what brought you here—an 'anonymous call.'" He air-quoted the words. "You don't think I know about you? You don't think I know the things you can do? Invocations, spell work, *conjurings*? And, wow, you show up at my convention and just happen to encounter conjured creatures. What are the chances? Oh, and look, now we have to shut it down! Did one of the other cons put you up to this?"

"No," I shot back, an angry heat working its way up my neck.

"Or was it the *fae*?"

"The fae?"

"Are you working for them?" He punctuated the question with a finger-jab to my chest.

I could put up with a lot from people, but having my personal space invaded? Unh-uh. I was preparing to shove him back with an invocation, when his shirt collar drew taut across his throat. He gargled, eyes bugging out, and in the next moment, he was being slammed onto his back. Bree-Yark planted a work boot on his chest and cocked his fist.

"No one manhandles my teammate," he barked.

"It's all right," I said. "C'mon, remember what we talked about. Let him up."

Bree-Yark grunted as if he was going to relent, but then his eyes fell to Stan's "THE ONLY GOOD GOBLIN IS A DEAD ONE" T-shirt. I watched the anger on his face go from simmering to atomic. "Oh yeah? We'll see about that!"

"Protezione," I whispered.

A protective shield manifested over Stan. He blinked through it at the goblin fist that had stopped inches from his face. I followed up with a force invocation to pull Bree-Yark back, then grabbed him by the collar of his bomber jacket.

"That's enough," I said sternly.

Stan scrambled to his feet as officers emerged from the hotel and came between us.

"You saw him!" Stan screamed. "He assaulted me! I want them both out of here!"

"Go up a couple more octaves, why don't you," Tabitha said, flattening her ears in annoyance.

Bree-Yark struggled in my grip, but my invocation held him fast. Fortunately, Vega emerged from behind the officers. "It's all right," she said to them. "I'll handle this. Stan, go back inside." The organizer glared at us for another moment before joining the officers as they returned through the doors.

"And change your stinking shirt!" Bree-Yark shouted after him.

"I'm guessing this is the 'snag' you mentioned?" I said to Vega.

"Yeah, and he's got the chief of police coming down on his side. The man's obviously connected. I'm working on it."

"I can put a call into Budge," I said, already pulling out my phone.

"I already tried. The mayor's at some sort of conference in Europe."

"So I can't go in?" I asked incredulously as I put the phone away.

"Not without a replay of what just happened," she said. "And Stan has a temporary restraining order on you. Technically, you're supposed to stay a thousand feet from the hotel."

"You're kidding."

"Like I said, I'm working on it. I'll get you back in."

I looked down at Bree-Yark. Though he continued to glare at the door Stan had reentered through, he'd stopped struggling. "What happened to you?" I asked, releasing him. "You disappeared on us."

"Yeah, I think those fae bastards made me. They led me outside, then gave me the slip. Oh, and this stopped working." He pulled his radio from a jacket pocket.

As Vega swapped his for hers—she would get another one—I thought about what Stan had said, suggesting that the fae had put me up to closing the con. Did they have history? I wondered now if the lunar fae had planned to plant creatures throughout the conference to terrorize the attendees. Is that why they'd been hanging around the third floor?

"Any idea where they went?" I asked Bree-Yark.

He looked around and shrugged. "Could be anywhere. I'm not feeling them out here, though."

Which probably meant they were back inside. I peered through the glass doors. Attendees not partaking in the parade continued to mill around. They were probably even being allowed back onto the third floor, too.

Shit, I spat to myself.

I didn't want Vega staying inside, but she was the only one in law enforcement who understood the danger and could take over. Plus, she was armed with silver ammo. She had cold iron ones too, if needed.

Still, I wanted some early warning for her.

"How does Mae feel about staying with you?" I asked Vega.

"She refused to evacuate when no one else was, so I'd say she's fine with it."

I spotted Mae now through the glass. She smiled as if she knew what we were talking about and held up Buster's carrier. I could see his tendrils wriggling through the mesh door. I gave them both a thumb's up.

Bree-Yark waved at her.

"All right," I said to Vega, already thinking of how I could use the time to our advantage. "If you and Mae cover the con, Bree-Yark can give me a lift back to my apartment. I'm going to try a spell to cloak my bond to Thelonious. There are also a couple things I want to grab. Any other updates?"

"No one was seen entering the room where the frog thing was, but a couple of cameras are out on the tenth floor. Cameras that just happen to monitor the approach to the stairwell we checked out earlier. And guess who's staying on the tenth?"

"Who?"

"Brian Lutz."

The head of the Military Federation of the Dragon, I thought.

"He just passed us going that way," I said. "Anything come up on his background?"

"No word yet."

I still refused to believe someone like Brian could channel magic, but I couldn't stop thinking about his visible shock when the duel hadn't gone his way. Not to mention the way the crowd's energy had shifted toward him. Throw in the defunct cameras on his floor, the manifesto, and the fact he had followers...

"Hey," I said to Vega. "I'd also like to know who's in his group. They call themselves the *Military Federation of the Dragon*. They may have indicated that affiliation somewhere on their registration."

I watched Vega repeat the name to herself as she inputted the info into her phone, but the longer I stood there, the more paranoid I was getting that demons were watching too. "All right, I should get going."

"There's something else you need to know," Vega said.

When I looked back, her expression had turned grave.

"Police pulled a body from the East River this morning, near Roosevelt Island. The vic was a middle-aged male. They found twin puncture wounds in the neck, and his body was drained of blood. Also, his suit was missing."

Roosevelt Island was upriver from Container City. The missing suit suggested a certain vampire-demon was now in the city. Though Vega didn't say Arnaud's name, I could read it on her face plain as day.

"I'll check on Tony while I'm out," I told her.

19

I studied the casting circle I'd created in my laboratory, eyes poring over each line and sigil to ensure I'd accounted for every potential form of attack. Accessing my connection to Thelonious was going to leave me vulnerable, and I didn't want anything crawling inside me, especially if demons *were* scaling the bond.

Finally satisfied, I stepped into the circle, shoes off, and lowered myself into a cross-legged position. I tried to clear my mind. Easier said than done when the events of the day were zipping around my skull like motorcycles in a Globe of Death.

On the way here, I'd called the vampire hunters. When Blade answered, I updated her on the body in the East River. She'd actually investigated the scene after picking up the report on her police scanner—telling me she was taking the job seriously—but Arnaud was long gone. Vega had been able to obtain a description of the outfit the victim had been wearing when he'd left the house that morning, and I shared that with Blade. She said she'd let her network know. I hung up with the sinking feeling we were losing more ground to Arnaud.

I'd also called the Order, but not even Claudius answered

this time. A part of me feared that the situation in the Harkless Rift had taken a bad turn. Now wasn't the time to dwell on either call, though. I needed to focus.

As I deepened my breaths, my worried thoughts slowed down and began to fade.

I was almost in my trance when Tabitha snapped at Bree-Yark downstairs. The goblin barked something back.

Oh, for the love of...

They were preparing lunch—"a *real* one," Tabitha had said, loud enough for me to overhear—but from the current sounds of it, the two had yet to agree on the menu. Bree-Yark was pushing for shepherd's pie and greens while Tabitha was standing her ground on pan-seared veal steaks and no greens.

A pan clattered to the floor.

"Guys!" I shouted. "I need some quiet up here!"

When their bickering continued, I swore and cast a pair of light shields over my ears. The muting effect was immediate. Within moments, I found myself settling back into my focused state, and then trancing out.

"THAT YOU, YOUNG BLOOD?" A SLOW, RUMBLY VOICE CALLED.

I'd only meant to access the connection to my bond with Thelonious, but a look around told me I'd ended up in his realm. It was dull and lonely like the last time I'd been here, the throbbing bass note that vibrated through the creamy space barely able to hold a beat.

I found the corpulent form of Thelonious reclined on what seemed a large, soft chair. Though everything was indistinct to me in his realm, I felt like I was visiting an old man in a nursing home.

"Yeah, it's Everson," I said, moving toward him. "How are you?"

"Not well. Still broken."

"From Arnaud's visit?"

"Never did catch the cat's name," he replied.

That Thelonious was still in this shape a year after Arnaud's interrogation suggested just how powerful Arnaud had grown in the demonic realm. I shuddered to think what would happen if he ever attained that kind of power in our world.

"Have a seat, young blood," Thelonious said. "Take a load off."

I was about to explain that I hadn't intended to come, but an idea occurred to me. Anything I cast on our bond was going to be tenuous at best, not to mention temporary. But if I could convince Thelonious to release me entirely, there would be no bond, period. Which meant no way for the demons to locate me.

I lowered myself beside my incubus until it felt like I was sitting on a liquid cushion. We sat in silence for a moment, his deep breaths rumbling in and out, but it wasn't the sexy purr of yesteryear. This sounded like a faulty motor, one that could fail at any moment.

"Must get lonely down here," I said.

His breathing became a sad chuckle. "That's the thing about power, young blood. When you have it, everyone wants a piece of you. Gets to where you have to start turning them away. When you lose it, they can't run the other direction fast enough. It's like a disfiguring disease they might contract."

"If it's any consolation, that's true of my world too."

"What's happening up there these days?" he asked with a note of nostalgia. "Haven't been able to travel lately."

"Honestly, nothing good. The demon who visited you broke through a couple months ago. He arrived weak, but his passage left a hole that hundreds of lesser demons followed him through. We're trying to send them back."

"Demons from the Pits?" he asked.

"Sounds that way."

Thelonious shook his head ruefully. "All the worldly pleasures to be had, and they're going to waste it fighting each other —just you watch. Everything's a power game to them. Never take time to savor anything. Me? I'm a connoisseur of the sensual." He looked around his barren domain. "At least I was."

"They seem to be in a contest to reach a being called Sefu."

When Thelonious repeated the name, hope flickered inside me.

"Do you know who that is?" I asked, keeping my voice neutral.

"I've just heard echoes. This *Sefu* is being talked about."

So far I hadn't shared anything that wasn't already out there, but now I had to be careful. Thelonious might have been an incubus, "a connoisseur of the sensual," but he was also demonic. And no matter how he presented himself, he was just as power hungry as the rest of them. If selling me out meant getting his mojo back, he'd do it in a heartbeat. Meaning, he couldn't know I was after Sefu too.

"Well, the demons seem to think I know something about him. To be clear, I don't—in fact, I want nothing to do with whatever they're involved in. But I think the demons are using the bond between us to track me."

"That so?" The heaviness in Thelonious's voice told me he was losing interest in the conversation.

"I want to make a new deal," I said.

"Already told you, young blood. I'm in no condition to help you."

"And you're in no condition to possess me, either. Let's face it —I'm getting stronger while you're getting weaker. If things keep going this way, there's zero chance of you ever inhabiting me again."

That got his attention. "What are you saying?"

"That there's no point in the bond anymore."

He waved a hand. "I don't dissolve my agreements."

Many demons' pacts were like trophies to them, even after the pacts had outlived their usefulness. It appeared Thelonious was no exception. I'd been right to lump him in with the rest of demonkind.

I tested him anyway. "What would it take?"

"I don't dissolve my agreements," he repeated.

"Let's not talk dissolution, then. Not yet. How about a suspension?"

"A suspension? How long we talking?"

"One year."

That was nothing in demon time, but he gave a doubtful grunt.

"And what do I get in exchange?" he asked.

The image of the old man in a nursing home came back to me. "Monthly visits," I answered. "I'll come here. I'll spend time with you. I'll tell you all about my experiences in the world, anything you want to hear."

Thelonious appeared to chew on that. "Even the juicy stuff?"

"Yeah, sure, the juicy stuff too." I could always lie.

"Well, let's see what we've got." He motioned, and a form appeared in the space in front of us. It looked like a thorny tangle of roots in the shape of a thin tree. I grimaced as I realized it was our bond. Damn, the thing was ugly. But at least it was exclusive to me and Thelonious. No other demon could buy or otherwise claim it.

Thelonious made a few contemplative sounds. "You weren't wrong about the demons. Looks like we've got an infestation."

It took me a moment to see what he meant, but the bond's

root structure was writhing with dark energy. It looked like a swarm of black ants. Small columns were winding their way up to what I understood was my end, where another tangle of roots clutched my immortal soul. The demon I'd encountered earlier must have been the first to arrive—but others weren't too far behind.

"Well?" I said urgently.

"Well, what?" Thelonious rumbled.

"Will you agree to suspend the bond that connects us?"

He made some more thinking noises. I looked from him to the bond, where the demonic energy continued to ascend. If he said no, I was going to have a lot of visitors in short order. I could call the Upholders, sure, find sanctuary in one of their safe houses. But then I'd be forfeiting this Sefu to the demons.

"Six months," Thelonious said at last.

"Nine," I countered, knowing that if I agreed immediately to six, he would try to get me down to two or three.

"Six months," he said again.

I made some noises of my own. "Fine," I said. "Six."

Thelonious regarded me for a moment, then turned back to our bond. He made another feeble gesture with a hand. Like high-tension bands suddenly being released, the bond began to snap and unwrap itself before dispersing into the ether. I wanted to cheer and pump a fist as I watched the swarm-like energy of the demons fall in a scatter.

When it was done, all that remained was a single twisted thread.

"Demons won't be able to see that," Thelonious said. "But it's sturdy enough to support your visits. Once a month," he reminded me. "And you'll come bearing the juicy bits."

"That's right," I said.

"Here's the thing, though." He leaned toward me, carrying with him a stale fog of old age. "You don't keep up your end, or I feel you trying to break the bond, not only will I restore it like that"—he snapped his fingers—"I'll help all those demons back up. They'll find you faster than you can ask, 'Is that a pitchfork in my behind?' You understand me?"

"Ouch, but yes."

"Ouch is right," he warned.

I stood. "I'm glad we came to terms."

I extended my right hand, which he clasped in a kind of soul shake. When he finished, I surprised myself by leaning in and giving him a hug. I think it was the joy at being paroled from a bond that had staked my soul for the last twelve years. I was even more surprised when Thelonious patted my back.

"See you in a month," I said.

"I'll be here, young blood."

I ARRIVED BACK IN MY LAB AND DISPELLED THE SHIELDS FROM MY ears. My right leg tingled with sleep as I put my shoes back on and stood. I stomped the leg back to life as I circled the lab. From the library, I pulled down a couple reference books, swapping them for two others in my interplanar cubbyhole. I then squatted in front of the bins beneath my table, restocking my coat pockets with starter potions.

I was still carrying the sealed vial with the frog-beast goo, but sometime after leaving the hotel the substance had gone inert, leaving me zip to cast from. Something told me to hold onto the vial anyway.

With the demons off my scent, I had bought myself some time. But Arianna's warning from last night echoed through my thoughts: *The being is concealed now, but that will change.* Which suggested a clock was ticking down to the moment the demons would be able to locate Sefu without me.

With a full coat, I lunged for the ladder to get a move on, then made myself stop. At what point today had I quieted my thinking mind and really listened to my magic? It was the number one thing Gretchen had been drilling into me. Arianna had also alluded to it last night: *The same magic that speaks to me also speaks to you.*

I sighed and closed my eyes again, cleared my thoughts.

And there was my magic, shifting around in seemingly random patterns. As if catching me watching it, my magic stopped suddenly and started into a new motion, one that took a moment to gain rhythm and momentum. It was the nodding I'd felt earlier. My magic seemed to be assuring me that I was on the right path, that I was gathering what I needed. It didn't feel like head-shaking anyway.

I waited for more, but that was it. Just a slow nodding: *Keep going. Keep going.* By now, though, the sound of my watch's second hand was intruding. A peek told me an hour had passed while I was in Thelonious's realm, and that felt like an hour too long. Especially with Arnaud in the city.

I needed to get up to the Bronx to check on Vega's son.

I found my two teammates downstairs, plates and bowls lying around them. Tabitha was sacked out on her divan while Bree-Yark sawed logs from the sofa. He'd kicked off his work boots, crossed his large feet at the ankles, and pulled an afghan across his belly. When I shook one of his toes, he snorted awake.

"You ready?" I asked.

He ground his fists into his eye sockets and squinted up at me. "I'm gonna let that one fly 'cause you didn't know," he growled. "But never touch a goblin's feet." A snarl curled his scarred lower lip.

"Noted," I said, showing my hands.

As Bree-Yark put on his shoes, Tabitha lifted her head from the divan. "Are we leaving already? I *just* nodded off."

"Yeah, c'mon," Bree-Yark said, swatting her divan in a gesture of comraderie I found touching. "Let's move it." Even though I could use Tabitha in the demon-detecting department, she'd put in a long day. She looked too exhausted to harm herself, and I could give her more elixir to ensure she slept until I returned.

"Listen," I told her. "If you'd rather stay, I understand."

She rose, arched her back, and let out a tremendous yawn. I thought she was going to settle back into her depression, but she surprised me by thudding to the floor. "If I stay here, I'll never hear the end of it."

"You're coming?" I asked in surprise.

"Keep asking, and I might change my mind."

Though she was trying to affect a look of irritation, it struck me that somewhere during the course of the morning, she had gotten hooked on our team adventure. She wanted to see what happened next.

I suppressed a smile. "Alrighty, then."

20

"Your Laphroaig," the bartender said, setting the shot glass on the oak bar.

Arnaud smiled beneath the brim of his fedora and pushed a bill toward him. "Keep the change, my friend."

The bartender in a tuxedo shirt and black bowtie tried to maintain his staid demeanor, but he picked up the money a little too quickly. "Thank you, sir. That's very kind." He moved down to the register, where he deposited a one-dollar bill that he believed to be a hundred and pocketed the balance as a generous tip.

Someone was going to have to answer for the short count at the end of the shift, but that was hardly Arnaud's concern. He lifted his glass, inhaled the rich texture of his drink, then sipped just enough to sting his tongue.

"Ah, I'd nearly forgotten the pleasure of a good whiskey, Zarko."

There were few pleasures in the Below. The struggle for control and domination was constant. That competition burned in Arnaud too, yes, but it was tempered by his vampiric side. He had used that to his advantage in the Below. Just as he would use it up here.

Already, he had two slaves in his service, their blood and souls still swimming inside him. And as he sat, enjoying a fine drink in a setting far more agreeable than his underground lair, his slaves were combing the streets, their preternatural senses attuned to the scent of the human who had looted the scepter. Manhattan was not a large island. Arnaud would have his scepter within a week, he estimated, if not much sooner.

In the meantime, he would remain discreet, even enjoy himself a little.

He was raising his glass again when the infernal hooks inside him yanked taut. Hot pain exploded through his gut. He pitched forward onto the oak bar, the expensive whiskey splashing across his face as he lost his grip on his glass. His fedora tumbled after the fallen shot glass, which shattered on the far side of the bar.

Arnaud lay there in the aftershock, panting for breath.

"Sir, are you all right?" the bartender asked, rushing over and stooping for his hat.

The bartender rose, extending the fedora toward Arnaud, then stopped suddenly. He stammered something nonsensical as the blood left his face. Past his shoulder, Arnaud caught a look at himself in the mirror backing the glass shelves of bottled liquor. A hideous gray head with yellow-flecked eyes stared back at him.

The Dread Council, Malphas's voice sounded in his head. *Now.*

Another tug of the hooks tore through him. "Yes, yes, all right!" Arnaud screamed.

He snatched his hat before the bartender could flinch back further, pulled it low over his face, and staggered from his stool.

Outside, the dull light stung his eyes as he looked this way and that. Another sharp tug.

Damn you! Arnaud hissed in his head.

He stumbled into an alley and found a secluded spot on the far side of a Dumpster. The next tug brought him to his knees. Arnaud tore a jagged line across his wrist and used the blood to smear out a hasty symbol for the Dread Council. When he was done, he fell to his forearms and gargled out Malphas's true name.

He felt the air above the circle thicken with his liege's arrival.

"Where are you?" Malphas demanded. "What are you doing?"

"I am faithfully following your command," he answered in a forced whimper. "I looked for the scepter, but someone has taken it. I had no choice but to commandeer two mortals to assist me in the search."

"Two mortals whose souls belonged to *me*," Malphas thundered.

"Y-yes, Great One, but it was necessary. Without them I—"

"Without them you wouldn't be sitting on your ass, enjoying a drink?"

Curse it all! His bond to Malphas was such that he could hide practically nothing when his master came spying. Instead of denying the charge, he fell into deeper groveling. "It was just a short respite, Master. I am not strong like you. Claim the souls from me if you must. I will search for the scepter myself."

He knew Malphas wasn't dumb. The faster Arnaud could find the scepter and dispatch the bastard wizard, the faster he would be able to claim souls for Malphas's army. And if other demons *had* come through, time was of the essence. His master's forces would soon be outnumbered.

"Keep your souls," Malphas spat. "I have a more urgent task for you."

"Yes, Master?"

"Find Everson Croft."

"E-Everson Croft?" Arnaud's fear of the city from that morning had been looking more and more trivial in hindsight, but now fresh panic leapt inside him. "But he is the wizard I've told you about, the one who can destroy me. Without the protection of the scepter, I have no defense against his power."

"Shut up!" Malphas roared. "You needn't fight him. Find and follow him. It is rumored he knows the location of a powerful vessel named Sefu. Possess the vessel for me, and we won't *need* the scepter."

A contingency plan. Arnaud liked that, but it would still mean getting dangerously close to Croft.

"Should you fail," Malphas continued, "one of our rivals will claim the vessel, and they will destroy us. You told me you once lorded over this city, that you knew it more intimately than anything living or unliving. Now is your chance to prove your boast."

"Yes, Master."

"Now go!"

He expected Malphas to issue a final threat, or at least give their bond a violent tug, but the stakes were threat enough. Fail and they would both perish horribly.

The pressure over Arnaud's bowed head released. He peeked to ensure Malphas had left before wiping away the symbol with his hand and pushing himself up.

As he walked toward the mouth of the alley, he considered his task. He thought about calling his slaves to him. Were Croft to spot him, they would make good shields for an escape. Indeed, he could have used them in East River Park the night before. He went so far now as to access their hollow minds. He'd sent the man to the north of the island, and he was working his way down through Harlem. The woman was presently only a few blocks away, snaking north. But Arnaud stopped himself. Withdrew.

"Better they keep searching," he told Zarko. "If they manage to find the scepter before we locate Croft, we will have the advantage after all." At Liberty Street, where his wall had once stood, he hailed a cab.

"Where to?" the driver asked.

"We're going to the West Village," Arnaud said. "Tenth Street."

As Arnaud closed the door behind him, he ignored the perplexed look of the driver, whose eyes were searching the backseat for a second passenger.

"We're checking in on an old friend."

ARNAUD PEERED UP. FROM HIS POSITION IN THE ALLEYWAY, HE could just make out the top of the four-story building. In his last life, he had sent his slaves here many times to keep tabs on Croft. He had even visited the apartment himself once when he'd duped the young wizard into issuing an invitation.

Now his gaze traced the upper ledge for the large feline who occasionally acted as sentry, but there were only pigeons. He circled to the front of the apartment, sniffing carefully. On the street, he stopped as he caught Croft's scent.

"He's been here recently," he whispered to Zarko.

He could smell the large feline too, as well as a third party he couldn't place. A musky cologne covered a vaguely leathery scent. It could have been a passerby, but the threads of their scents seemed to intertwine. Yes, the medley ended at an empty space on the street, suggesting they'd departed together in a vehicle.

Arnaud turned to the building. The invitation Croft had

extended him was almost two years old, but perhaps it still held power over his wards. While waiting for Croft that night, Arnaud had perused his loft. Behind a veiling spell, he had discovered a journal in which the wizard recorded almost everything.

"The whereabouts of Sefu might be in there," Arnaud whispered. "In which case, we won't need to chance an encounter with the wizard."

At the door to the building, Arnaud hovered a finger over the lock. Infernal magic explored inside. A moment later, the bolt thunked back, and he drew the door open. He climbed the three flights, backtracking along Croft's scent trail, which was already going stale.

At the top floor he had only gone a few steps down the corridor when he observed the forcefield pulsing over Croft's door. Arnaud shied back as if the sun had broken from a bank of clouds right in front of him. Even from here the field made his insides squirm.

Like Croft's power, the wards were much stronger than he remembered.

He retreated, not realizing he'd fallen to his hands, until he was back in the stairwell. He straightened quickly. With the apartment too well defended, he would have to do what Malphas had said:

Find and follow him.

"But where has he gone?" he asked aloud.

"Perhaps to his detective friend's," Zarko answered.

Arnaud nodded. "Yesss, I was thinking the same."

21

Shit, I thought as we pulled up in front of the Vegas' house and I spotted Carlos's car.

"Everything good?" Bree-Yark asked as he engaged the brake on his Hummer. His legs were too short to reach the pedals, so he'd had his ride modified to operate gas and brake with his oversized hands. He was actually a good driver, and I wondered if Gretchen was using him as a chauffeur too.

"Super," I said. "Would you guys mind waiting out here? This could get thorny."

I braced for flak from Bree-Yark about not wanting to introduce a goblin to Vega's family, but he only nodded and turned on the sound system. I wasn't sure what I was expecting but definitely not the New Age music that piped from the speakers. "It's world music," he said preemptively. "It relaxes me."

I craned my neck around to find Tabitha asleep in the backseat.

"Could you keep an eye on her?"

"No problem," Bree-Yark said. "Just jiggle the blinds or something if you need backup."

I could see by his face he wasn't joking. It was a shame he hadn't been here last night.

I got out and made my way up the walk, already scanning the wards I'd placed over the doors and windows. They were still working, but they could stand more power. The problem was Carlos. Having to explain what I was doing and why was only going to reinforce his belief I was a danger to his sister and nephew.

The gutless course of action was for me to stay outside, charge up the wards, and then check on Tony last—which was the course I chose. At least I didn't drink a stealth potion, which I'd considered. Moving to one side of the porch, I began to incant. Naturally, the front door opened a moment later.

Just please don't be...

Carlos's head peered around the corner of the porch.

"Everson," he said in a kind of stern surprise. "Can I ask what you're doing?"

I stopped incanting and followed his gaze down to my shoes. I was standing in a flower bed. Making an awkward sound, I stepped back until I was on grass. "Just reinforcing some protections," I said. There was no point in lying. Though I'd only met Carlos the night before, I anticipated the exact shape of his frown.

"I see."

"Everyone okay in there?" I asked.

"We're fine."

"All right, I won't be long."

"Actually, we were just discussing you."

I couldn't imagine that was good. "Oh yeah?"

"In fact, why don't you come in when you're done."

Before I could respond, Carlos disappeared back into the house. A knock sounded from the Hummer. Through the passenger window, Bree-Yark was asking with gestures if I needed him to come straighten Carlos out. He must have picked up the tension in our exchange. I shook my head and signaled for him to stay put.

As I circled the house incanting, I managed to block out the annoyance of having to sit down with Carlos afterwards. A couple of times, I caught him watching me through a window. When I was done, I stood back and looked over the energy that encompassed the house. Satisfied that no vampires, demons, or vampire-demons would be getting in, I drew a breath and entered the house through the front door.

"Back here," Carlos called.

I followed the corridor to the living room, where Vega's four brothers were sitting around the room. A kind of somberness hung over a space that looked more cluttered and less inviting in the light of day. And unlike last night, no one was joking or wrestling. Not a smile to be seen, either, not even on big Teddy.

"Have a seat, Everson," Carlos said.

He gestured to an isolated chair in the center of the room. I could hear the kids behind a door in a back room, playing a video game from the sounds of it. The wives were absent too.

"Is this where you teach me the secret handshake?" I asked, sitting down.

Teddy allowed a small smile. Weaks, who was wearing the same white warmups as yesterday, averted his eyes. The Rock pretended to become interested in the football he was tossing up into a little spiral and catching with the same hand.

Man, even that line would have earned me a chuckle last night.

"I've been talking with my brothers about what we discussed at dinner," Carlos said. The sleeves of his shirt were rolled up and he was leaning forward, elbows on his knees. He had that look like he was warming up for a lengthy deposition.

"Look, I've been doing a lot of thinking about that too," I said before he could get going. "The fact is, your concern for Ricki and Tony is not only fair, it's a concern of mine too. You're right. Over the past couple years, I've introduced Ricki to a dimension of the city—a dimension of this *world*—that multiplies the dangers she already faces. But that was because she insisted. You know how she is. She takes her oath to serve and protect as seriously as anyone I've ever known."

When Weaks made a sound of agreement, Carlos shot him a stern look.

"The thing to know about your sister is that while the danger has gone up in the last two years, she's also helped save thousands of lives. Something she wouldn't have been able to do going straight by the police academy handbook." I knew I was taking a risk with what I was about to say, but I forged on anyway. "I didn't know your father, but Ricki's told me a lot about him. I think he'd be really proud of her."

"You're right," Carlos snapped. "You didn't know our father."

The Rock looked over at his younger brother. "Damn, man."

"Yeah, c'mon," Teddy added in his mellow voice.

But Carlos closed his eyes and shook his head. "No, you guys *c'mon*. We talked about this. Everson's association with Ricki is a danger to her and to Tony." He raised his eyes to mine. "On the surface, it looks like you've been good to them, and we're aware they both think highly of you."

"What do you mean *on the surface*?" I asked.

"I did some looking around. Last year, Ricki initiated an investigation into one Arnaud Thorne for kidnapping and child endangerment. The victim's name was redacted, but Ricki works homicide, not kidnappings. I had some suspicions, so I talked with Camila this morning, Tony's sitter. She told me everything."

He was referring to Arnaud taking Tony hostage in a gambit to pit me against City Hall. I hadn't realized Vega had actually started an investigation into the vampire, though. She'd probably done so during the period we weren't talking. Arnaud's death—or believed death—would have made it moot.

Still, I wondered why she'd never mentioned it. Maybe she just wanted to forget the whole chapter.

"I followed up with a search of the news archives," Carlos continued, "and guess what I found? A story about how the mayor used you as a double agent to take down the same Arnaud Thorne. Are we supposed to believe it was just a coincidence that during the time period you were trying to get close to this man, he also happened to kidnap your girlfriend's son?"

"It wasn't like that," I said, my face growing hot.

He sat back and crossed his arms. "We're listening."

The story about me being a double agent had been a fiction to make the mayor look like he'd known what he was doing and to get me back in the city's good graces. In fact, I had been a pawn in Arnaud's scheme, almost realizing it too late. But that episode with Arnaud was so convoluted, not to mention fantastical, I wasn't going to try to explain it in Carlos's living room court of law. I mean, hell, it would fill two novel-length books.

"It was an isolated incident," I said. "Tony was unharmed, and I destroyed Arnaud."

"Oh, did you?" Carlos's eyes widened in mock surprise. "That's funny, because I heard Ricki on the phone with her department when she came home last night. Thin walls," he said, rapping a knuckle against the one behind him. "I made out a name: Arnaud Thorne. Only she was speaking about this person in the present tense. Are we to believe this is a different Arnaud Thorne? One who's still alive?"

The answer was yes and no—the same Arnaud Thorne, but in a different form.

I gave the next best answer. "He was *presumed* dead."

"Oh, okay, so it *is* the same person," Carlos said with a kind of callous satisfaction. "And from Ricki's side of the conversation, it sounded like you two engaged him last night?"

"We had an encounter, yes," I said.

"And this Arnaud Thorne escaped that encounter?"

I held Carlos's prosecutorial stare, but I could feel the weight of the other brothers' gazes on me.

"We have people looking for him," I replied.

"You see where I'm going with this, don't you? If he took Tony once, what's to stop him from doing it again?" He gestured toward his brothers. "Or taking any of the other kids for that matter?"

The fact was, I couldn't give him any assurances. He was asking the same questions I'd been wrestling with myself.

"That's what I was doing outside," I said.

"Putting up protections?" Carlos asked thinly.

"It's nothing personal against you, Everson," Teddy cut in.

"Yeah, man," Weaks added. "You seem like a cool dude. It's just that we've got families to look out for."

The Rock stopped tossing the football and held it to his chest. "And the thing about Ricki... Well, she has this way of bending in her relationships. We've all seen it. She starts out tough, but before long, she starts making one compromise after another..."

I'd been willing to absorb the accusations and insinuations against me, but when I felt the blame shifting to Vega, rage bloomed hot inside me. "If you're suggesting Ricki would endanger Tony or your children, you're way, *way* out of line." Though I was jabbing my finger at the Rock, I looked around to include all of them, my eyes falling on Carlos last. "Let's keep the focus on me, all right?"

"Did you know Tony's father is a convicted felon?" Carlos asked coolly.

The words arrived like a slap. Vega had said little about

Tony's father other than he was no longer in their lives, and I had never pried. Now I lowered my finger—or rather let it fall like a flaccid balloon.

"No," I admitted. "But that's her business, not mine."

Even as I said it, I caught my mind shuffling through the possible scenarios in which Ricki Vega of the NYPD would knowingly have a child with a felon. I couldn't come up with any. My mouth burned with the acid bite of adrenaline.

"In a close family like this one," Carlos said, "we make it our business. The bottom line is she's too wrapped up in whatever the two of you have going to see the threat you pose. Like Gabe said, it's a pattern."

There it was, more fucking insinuations against their sister.

"If that's all," I managed as I stood, "I have to get back to work."

I was too enraged to trust whatever I might say if I stayed.

"That's *not* all," Carlos said, his eyes cutting over to Teddy.

The oldest brother shifted his large mass on the couch uncomfortably. "Like we said, it's nothing personal against you, Everson. But we'd appreciate it if you stopped seeing our sister. We all agree it's for the best."

I stared at him, feeling like he'd just plowed one of his meaty fists into my gut. He was reading off Carlos's script, of that I had zero doubt, but still ... Had he actually said I was to stop seeing Ricki?

At that moment, a door to a back room opened, releasing a burst of video game sounds. I could hear Tony's voice as he ran down the hallway toward us. "Mr. Croft's here," he panted. "I heard him!"

Heavier footsteps raced after him, one of the wives probably, and then both sets of footfalls stopped suddenly. A woman's whispering voice was followed by Tony shouting, "Let go! I just want to say hi!"

"Not now, Tony," I called past the lump in my throat. "We're in the middle of a meeting."

There was a silence followed by Tony being led in a grumble back to the room he'd emerged from. The door closed again. When I turned back to the brothers, three of them were visibly uncomfortable. But Carlos watched me with keen eyes, as if trying to guess my next move.

"Keep Tony inside until Ricki gets back," I reminded them. I started to turn, then stopped. I needed the last word on this.

"Ricki's a big girl. She can decide who she wants to see."

22

I got into the Hummer and slammed the door. Bree-Yark had reclined his seat back a little and laced his fingers behind his head, but now he levered himself upright.

"Let's head back to the hotel," I said.

He'd left the motor idling, so he had only to slot the gearstick into drive to get us rolling.

"And no offense," I added, "but I can't handle this right now." I leaned toward the stereo and twisted the volume knob until the swirly, mystical sounds of Bree-Yark's *world music* snapped off.

"Went that well, huh?" the goblin asked.

"Ever had four brothers hold an intervention to make you quit their sister?" I still couldn't believe what had happened. It was like a ridiculous stress dream except that I hadn't been sleeping.

"No, but I had a goblin chieftain sic his tribe on me for trying to court his daughter," Bree-Yark said. "I escaped, but barely. He had a reputation for cutting off her suitors' ears and wearing them on a leather thong around his neck." He ran a hand over his notched right ear and shook his head. "Probably just as well things didn't work out."

"If we were dumb teenagers it would be one thing," I went on, "but we're both in our frigging thirties."

Bree-Yark tilted his head as if to say, *Well...*

"What?" I asked.

"From where I'm sitting, that's still pretty young."

"Yeah, because goblins live like five-hundred years."

"*Can* live up to five-hundred years," he corrected me, "but that's if we make it out of our first century, and most don't." He waved a hand. "But look, I'm the last goblin you should be talking to about this sort of thing. I haven't exactly got it figured out myself. I mean, look at me. I play caretaker for Gretchen."

"What's that all about anyway?"

"Mostly me being an incurable fool."

Ever since seeing Bree-Yark at her house the night before, my mind had been struggling for an explanation. I wondered if Gretchen had placed the goblin in her servitude. It wasn't an uncommon practice among the fae, and Gretchen revered them. "Are you paying off some sort of debt?" I asked.

"Debt?" He snorted a laugh. "Maybe for my own stupidity. Naw, this thing with Gretchen has been going on for a while. If not here, then in Faerie. She shows just enough interest to keep stringing you along, but that's all it is. Meantime, she's getting you to watch her houses, scythe her fields, feed her winged ponies—and those suckers will take a bite outta you if you're not careful, stomp your head in too. After ten years, you start catching on to her game, but by then it's too late. You're hooked on whatever messed up thing you think you've got going with the woman. I don't think she has any brothers, but if she did, I'd give anything for them to tell *me* to take a hike."

"Yeah?"

"It would mean we actually had something," he said sullenly.

I thought about his disappointment last night when he learned Gretchen had never mentioned him to me, and then how lonely he'd looked as I was leaving. "Well, can't you just tell her no?" I asked.

"That's what I'm saying. I missed that turn."

"There are other women, you know."

"Who are into goblins?" He gave a humorless laugh. "That's the thing. I can't shake this idea in my stupid goblin brain that if I hang in there long enough, do enough of the right things, she'll come around."

"She won't," I said.

Since meeting Gretchen, I'd been adding mental descriptors: *blunt, unsocialized, powerful, disgusting*. To that list, I now added *manipulative*. I bristled at the thought she'd been using this poor goblin.

"Yeah, I know," Bree-Yark conceded. "That's why I flipped out when the robot guy called me a house elf. Pretty sure that's all I am to her." We fell silent as traffic going the other direction shot past. I could hear Tabitha still sleeping in the back.

"So, what are you gonna do?" he asked at last.

"Huh?"

"About your situation with your girl and her brothers?"

"Oh, that." I'd gotten so absorbed in his dilemma, my own relationship problems had taken a momentary backseat. "Well, I'm not breaking up with her," I said. "That's absurd."

I didn't believe it would make Tony or her family safer, either. Vega couldn't unlearn what I'd taught and shown her, and she wasn't going to stop pursuing the supernatural angle just because I was out of her life. To put it in Bree-Yark's terms, she'd missed that turn. Plus, I still had my ace in the hole: holy sanctuary. I caught my fingers tracing the outline of the Upholder's card in my shirt pocket.

"You going to say anything to her?" Bree-Yark asked.

I dropped my hand from the pocket and shook my head. "No."

"Don't want to pit her against the family, huh?" he said. "Smart move. And it's not like you have to worry about losing an ear."

My phone rang, the display showing Vega's number.

"It's her," I said to Bree-Yark as I flipped the phone open. "Hey, how's it going?" I asked.

Vega's voice was urgent. "We've got a major situation at the hotel."

I stiffened upright in the seat. "What kind of situation?"

"There was an attack on the parade. These creatures came out of nowhere. An army of them. A lot of the con-goers fled back to the hotel, but the creatures are inside too. My ammo barely did anything. I'm with a group inside one of the conference rooms, the Magenta Room. Mae's in here too." Above the shouting, I could hear Buster squealing. "We've barricaded the door, but they're trying to come through."

"Can you describe the creatures?" I asked, my heart slamming through the question. I signaled for Bree-Yark to speed up. The engine rose an octave as he began weaving the Hummer in and out of traffic.

I heard Tabitha stir in the backseat. "What in the hell is going on?"

"They're big," Vega said. "Some look like animals, others like giant trees. I saw one creature that was like the thing we faced in Central Park the night it was napalmed. Hairy creature, but with the mouth of an owl."

"An owlbear?" I asked out loud.

Bree-Yark looked over at me. Owlbears were creatures of the Fae Wilds.

"What about your iron rounds?" I asked.

"Didn't even slow them down. God, it sounds like they're ripping the place apart."

I peered around, my mind scrambling furiously. We'd crossed the Harlem River back into Manhattan, but we were still in the One-twenties. I waved for Bree-Yark to get onto FDR Drive. Even under the best traffic conditions, we were still more than ten minutes out.

Need to stay calm, I thought. *If only for her.*

"Listen to me," I said. "I want your hands free. Put your phone on speaker and slide it into your jacket pocket."

"All right." A moment later, the volume went up on the panicked voices around her. I focused on controlling my breaths. The voices muted slightly as Vega pocketed the phone. When she spoke next, she sounded far away. "Done."

"The coin pendant I gave you has protective powers." I was all but shouting into the phone so she could hear me. Plus, static had started to break over our connection. "If the creatures come through, I want you to hold it toward them. I'll access the coin and crank up the juice until we get there." In other words, I would *try* to access the coin. I'd never attempted from this distance and in a moving vehicle. "Hold it toward anything that comes close until you've gotten yourselves to safety, okay?"

"Did you check on Tony?" she asked. "How is he?"

With everything going on, she was thinking of her son.

"He's fine," I assured her. "Well protected."

The screams around her rose suddenly.

"What's happening?" I shouted.

"They're coming in."

A series of shots sounded.

"Your pendant!" I called.

Another prolonged burst of static seized our connection, and then the line beeped to signal the end of the call. *No, no, no!* I tried to call her back, but it went straight to her voicemail. When I looked over at Bree-Yark, he held up a hand.

"I'll get us there. Do what you need to do."

Though I'd managed to slow my breathing, my heart still felt like a fist punching a concrete wall. The world beyond the windshield wavered, not quite real. I caught my mind urging us faster, but that had been Bree-Yark's point: he would take care of the driving. I needed to get to Vega. I nodded at him and closed my eyes.

I pictured the coin my grandfather had given me: the family symbol, the silvery gray metal, every scratch and taint. I imagined it in my right hand until I could feel the cool weight in my palm. I extended the arm in front of me, aligning my mind to the imagined object. A resident hum took up in my being.

I had it.

Now to unleash a little hell...

But the pendant wasn't in Vega's hand. It wasn't anywhere near her.

When I understood what she'd done, my eyes shot open in a sickening flash of light.

"Go!" I shouted, pushing both hands toward the parkway. "Go, goddammit!"

23

"Right here will be fine," Arnaud told the cabbie.

The driver rolled to a stop at the edge of a sandlot in the Bronx. Arnaud remained preternaturally still for a moment, his eyes watching the simple house across the street and up one lot. Even from here, he could see the wards pulsing like small novas over the access points, creating an impenetrable barrier over the entire home.

Like at the West Village and Brooklyn apartments, the wards bore Croft's signature.

A tightness came over the vampire-demon's body. It still burned him to know that Croft's powers exceeded his own right now. Had Arnaud arrived in the world as planned, on the tempest of fifty thousand souls, the wizard would have fled him like a puny mouse. Arnaud could have incinerated him without a thought. Now he had to dance around his maddening enchantments and spells.

When something bit into his palms, Arnaud saw he'd drawn his hands into mean little fists. His talons were gouging his gray flesh. He forced his hands back open and waited for the wounds to close before handing the driver a one-dollar bill.

"Another fifty if you'll wait again, my friend."

The driver took the money eagerly. "Sure, sure, take your time."

Arnaud opened the back door. "Come, Zarko," he said and stepped out.

An icy wind hit him, but he didn't suffer cold. A beat-up car chugged past as he walked up the street. Detective Vega's apartment had appeared a dead end—he hadn't even picked up Croft's scent—until a familiar face turned up: the housekeeper who had been watching Vega's son the night his blood slaves had absconded with the boy. With a little suggestion, the woman told him mother and son were spending the weekend here, at a family home in the Bronx. She believed Croft was with them too.

Now, as Arnaud passed the house, he opened his senses.

"Yes, Zarko," he whispered. "The wizard *has* been here." But the freshest scent was leaving the house, not moving toward it. As at Croft's apartment, Arnaud picked up traces of the feline and a third party too.

Meaning he'd just missed the cursed wizard again.

Arnaud paused to look the house over. Several cars sat parked in the driveway and yard. Perhaps he could convince someone inside to tell him where to find Croft. But he hadn't a way to approach the house, much less rap on the door, without being harmed. He couldn't even perceive past the wards to know who was inside. He was circling back, pondering his next move, when the door to the house opened.

Or perhaps someone can come out to us, he thought with a grin.

A man and a boy emerged. The curly-headed lad was upset over not getting to see someone. The man was saying they would discuss it over lunch, and did he want to go to McDonalds or somewhere different?

They were walking toward the street, where a burgundy sedan sat curbside.

Arnaud picked up his pace to head them off. It wasn't until the wind shifted that Arnaud recognized the boy's scent. He was older by almost two years, a little leaner in the face, and taller by three or four inches, but it was the detective's son. The same one he'd had the pleasure of passing an evening with, much to the detective's and Everson Croft's anguish. The memory manifested a small smile.

Such incredible leverage that boy provided. Perhaps he could be of use again.

Neither man nor boy saw Arnaud as he reached the car. They had just arrived at the end of the walkway, a journey slowed by the boy's obstinance. The trim, well-dressed man wasn't very good with children, Arnaud saw. He hadn't the patience or the artifice. He was talking to the child as a stuffy adult.

"Lovely day," Arnaud called as the two turned toward him.

The man looked up and stepped in front of the boy, suspicion taking immediate hold of his body. "Do you live around here?"

"Oh, I'm not far," Arnaud replied. "I'm never far. Just out for a stroll."

The man relaxed slightly and gave a curt nod, uninterested in conversation.

"And who's this with you?" Arnaud asked, craning his neck around to see the boy.

In the next moment the vampire-demon was doubled over and clutching his chest. For a moment he thought Malphas was calling him to another Council, but the pain detonating through him was familiar in a different way. It was the same pain he'd felt immediately before being cast down to the Pits.

And it was coming from the boy.

The man approached him carefully. "Are you all right?"

Even through the blinding pain, Arnaud had had the presence to palm his fedora to keep his grotesque head from being exposed.

Arnaud pointed past the man. "Get him back," he hissed.

"He's right," the man said over a shoulder. "Go back inside, Tony."

Whether it was reflexive, the boy touched his chest. Something shifted underneath his sweatshirt. A round pendant, Arnaud realized. The same one the boy's mother had been wearing the night before.

And curses did it hurt!

Much more, it seemed, for the pact having cast him down once already. Arnaud was about to hiss the boy back again when Tony retreated on his own, eyes round with fear and curiosity. Under different circumstances, it was a look Arnaud might have savored. But with the latent power of the pendant skewering him on a thousand white-hot blades, he could only gnash his sharp teeth.

At last, the boy turned and beat it down the walkway. Arnaud recovered his breath but remained on one knee, panting, as the pain subsided by degrees. It wasn't until the boy entered the house and slammed the door behind him that the pain left him entirely. He was shaky as he rose again, depleted.

"I apologize for the scare," Arnaud said breathlessly. "I get these terrible attacks of reflux, and I didn't want to frighten the child."

The man had come closer, the eyes beyond his gold-rimmed glasses firm with concern. "Do you need a doctor?"

"No, no, nothing like that. A baking soda tonic, and I'll be good as new."

He affected as much cheeriness as his still-raspy voice would allow, but the man seemed determined. "Do you live nearby? Do you need someone to pick you up?" The man began reaching into his pocket for a phone.

Arnaud shot a hand forward and gripped the man's wrist. For a moment, he was only aware of the rhythmic squeezing of warm blood through the man's vessels. And beneath it, the power of the man's soul. An insane hunger spiked inside Arnaud, obliterating all thoughts of Croft, of his mission.

And the man was handsome. Arnaud's gaze roamed his angular face with its dark, intelligent eyes. Arnaud yearned to feed, to bond this man to him for all time. Eyes cutting to the man's neck, he drew him nearer.

Then stopped.

With a grunt, the man wrenched his hand free. "Who the hell are you? What are you doing here?"

Arnaud recovered himself—and his sensibilities. Right now, the man was his best lead to Croft. Disappearing him would raise alarm bells. Croft would grow more careful than ever, thinning Arnaud's chances of locating this Sefu. And the consequences of failure, as Malphas had pointed out, would be a terrible death.

"I asked you a question," the man said. "Answer me, or I'm calling the police."

Arnaud steadied himself and peered into the man's eyes. "I'm looking for someone. Perhaps you can help me."

The hardness in the man's gaze took on a slight angle of puzzlement. He was more intelligent than most, though, more determined to hold onto his rationality, where he obviously lived and wrote his own checks. Arnaud could feel the man steeling against the mesmerizing effect of his voice. The vampire-demon smiled sweetly. It was the ones who fought back —futilely, of course—who most endeared themselves to him. This man would have made a wonderful slave. Perhaps he still would one day.

"Yes," Arnaud continued, slipping more power into his words. "I'm looking for a man."

At last his opponent's grip on his mind slipped. The focus in his eyes dissolved. "A man?" he repeated.

"Yes, and what is your name?"

"Carlos."

"I believe it's someone you know, Carlos. A Mr. *Everson Croft*."

"Everson," the man repeated, and began to nod.

THE CAB DRIVER, WHO HAD DOZED OFF, JERKED WHEN ARNAUD slammed the door and slid to the center of the backseat.

"I have another address for you," Arnaud said eagerly. "A hotel in Midtown."

The driver nodded, coughed the sleep from his throat, and put the cab into drive. As they rolled past the house, Arnaud saw that Carlos had started back down the walkway to the front door, but now he stopped and turned around. Perhaps for the man's high intelligence, clarity was already returning to his eyes.

The eyes had been so reminiscent to Arnaud, and then he had it. They were the same eyes as the detective's.

Like brother, like sister, Zarko.

According to Carlos, both his sister and Croft were at the Centre Hotel, on some sort of work assignment. At last he would have tabs on Croft, who, according to Malphas, would lead him to the powerful vessel. If things turned thorny, he could use the detective as leverage. After all, she'd given her protection to her son.

Arnaud smiled and raised a hand to Carlos in thanks.

After a moment's hesitation, Carlos waved back.

24

A light snow had begun to fall by the time we reached Midtown. Bree-Yark smashed the Hummer through an unmanned police barricade that had been blocking off the parade route and peeled onto Forty-sixth Street.

The Centre Hotel rose ahead. We blew through a low wall of smoke and into a fiery scene of chaos: overturned cars, flashing police lights, strewn costume parts, and occasional conference-goers fleeing whatever temporary refuge they'd taken, terror stretching their faces.

"Watch out!" I cried.

Someone in a lizard-man costume wearing red heels stumbled into our path.

Bree-Yark veered, narrowly missing him, but we had bigger problems. Emerging from the smoke ahead was what appeared to be an army of trees. They looked fearsome, even in silhouette, several rising three and four stories tall. They stalked toward us on massive rooted feet that tore up sections of asphalt. Their bowed arms and knotted fingers looked capable of twisting human heads off like bottle caps. Some of the trees fisted chunks of masonry—ripped from God knew where—which they began to hurl at us.

"Aren't those—?"

"Shamblers," Bree-Yark finished for me as he steered deftly, the masonry flying and tumbling past. "Straight from the Birnam Forest from the looks of them. Lost a battalion in there once." He shook his head. "Cranky bastards."

Indeed, as they began to clear the smoke, I could see their craggy faces. They all looked like they'd sucked on the same giant lemon.

It seemed that whoever had conjured the lizards and frog-beast had decided to throw open the gates. And judging by the new arrivals, our perp was someone with access to the faerie realm. Possibly the lunar fae Bree-Yark had been tailing before they shook him. I still didn't know their objective, but terror seemed to play a role.

I flinched as another stone projectile narrowly missed us.

My plan for us had been to enter the hotel through the front and beeline to the conference room where Vega and the others were trapped. But the shamblers were almost to the promenade. We weren't going to get past them without a fight. As fun as it would have been to tell my grandkids about the time I took on a gang of trees, it wasn't time we could afford.

"Has to be a loading entrance..." I muttered, squinting through the smoke. "There!"

Tires squealed as Bree-Yark followed my pointed finger toward a side street and throttled the hand accelerator. The lead shambler kicked an overturned car. I spun around. The busted vehicle came within inches of the rear bumper as it rocketed past.

My gaze dropped to Tabitha. She was wide awake, claws buried in the leather upholstery as she tried to peer out both windows simultaneously. She stopped long enough to shoot me a panicked *what the fuck?* look.

"Hold on, we're almost there," I said.

"Can you do anything about that?" Bree-Yark asked.

I turned back around as he bounced the Hummer onto a down ramp for service vehicles. He'd asked so casually I was shocked to find an accordion steel door rushing up on us.

"Vigore!" I shouted.

My force invocation seized the side of the door with more power than I'd intended and slammed it to the side, leaving behind a scattering of lock pieces. The Hummer plunged through the dark opening barely having slowed.

"Bit of a gamble I'd get it open in time," I said in a trembling voice.

Bree-Yark snapped on the headlights. "I had this baby modified with an off-road steel bumper over the summer. Figured we'd get through one way or another."

The ramp deposited us into the hotel's loading area, an enormous space with boxes stacked along the walls. A few fluorescent lights flickered overhead. I noticed that the smoke had spread down here, washing out everything in a thin gray mist. Bree-Yark steered past several parked cargo vans and came to a stop in front of a service elevator.

"Do you want to stay in the car?" I asked Tabitha.

"And wait for one of those tree things to punt it like a football?" she asked.

"Good point. But you're going to have to keep close."

I got out, helped Tabitha from the backseat, and hustled to the closed elevator door. It had been almost fifteen minutes since Vega's call, and I hadn't been able to reach her since. Anything could have happened in that time.

The service elevator was key operated. Thankfully, someone's elevator key was already in the panel, the rest of the keychain hanging beneath it. I twisted the key and hit the button, setting the elevator's mechanisms into motion. When I looked back, the Hummer's rear door was open, and Bree-Yark was rifling through the trunk.

"What are you doing?" I called.

"Grabbing a couple weapons."

I saw him fasten a sheath to his belt into which he slid a nasty-looking blade.

"Hurry up, elevator's almost here." The words were barely out of my mouth when the elevator stopped and the door rattled open. I staggered back. Tabitha grunted in disgust. It took me a moment to fully understand what I was looking at, but they were rats. Giant ones, the size of fattened pigs. With piercing screeches, the dozen-odd rats wriggled from the elevator car.

"Protezione!" I managed. The shield crackled to life around us moments before the first rats arrived, heads butting into our protection. In a flash, they were crawling over one another to get to us, yellow teeth scraping at the hardened air inches from my face.

"Get them *off*," Tabitha insisted.

"Respingere!" I cried.

With a flashing pulse from the shield, the rats were hurled every which way. But before they'd even come to a rest, they were kicking themselves upright and coming in again. I pointed my sword at the lead one. Before I could shout another invocation, gunfire cracked. The rat screeched as it was knocked into a side skid.

Bree-Yark moved in front of us, an M16 rifle at his shoulder.

"Into the elevator," he barked. "I've got you covered."

Tabitha and I backed into the elevator as Bree-Yark released another series of shots. The charging rats flipped off as if they were being flicked. Good thing, because I didn't want to expend magic that could short our ride up.

I hammered the button for the first floor. Nothing moved.

Or had my magic *already* shorted our ride up?

No, I needed the elevator key that was still outside. Bree-Yark stepped forward and waved a hand behind him: a signal for me to go. As I ducked out of the elevator, the loading level shook. Something was lumbering down the ramp at a run. I grabbed the keys from the panel and pulled them free, not peeking back until I was in the elevator again.

Beyond the giant rats, an ogre was descending into view. The minor giant slowed to a stop, then looked around to orient himself. It didn't take him long to spot the three of us. The fluorescent lights flickered over a dull gray eye in the center of the creature's forehead. Not an ogre, I realized. A cyclops.

Yeah, time to go.

It wasn't just that the thing was unclothed and every time it took a step its gargantuan appendage jiggled in a way that made it impossible *not* to look at. Cyclopes were just plain violent.

I struggled to insert the key into the panel.

Bree-Yark adjusted his aim and opened fire on the cyclops. Shots flashed off the monster's hairy body and head, sending him into a stagger. When he gained his footing, he released a savage roar and charged.

At last the key slotted home.

I turned it and punched the button for the first floor again. The door closed off our view of the looming cyclops and all of his parts. As we lifted off, a heavy pounding sounded, sending shockwaves through the car.

Soon, though, the sound fell beneath us.

"Good God," Tabitha breathed. "Why did I *ever* decide to come?"

I pulled in my power as tightly as I could to preclude any mechanical mishaps.

Bree-Yark lifted his M16 and swapped out his spent mag for a fresh one.

"What kind of ammo are you using?" I asked.

"Iron. What else?"

"Shouldn't that have taken him down?"

"Must be protected."

Great, so not only were we dealing with a fae strong enough to summon shamblers, giant rats, owlbears, cyclops, and who knew what else, we were dealing with one who could cover them in defensive magic. And once we got Vega and everyone to safety, it was going to be my job to find and neutralize that fae.

Anger broke through my fear. Where in the hell was Gretchen?

Gathering myself, I pulled the conference program from my pocket and showed Bree-Yark the hotel map. "The elevator will drop us here. We're heading to here, the Magenta Room. That's where Vega called from." I traced the route with a finger. "I'll wrap us in a one-way shield so we can still attack, but we'll need to stay close. That goes for you too," I told Tabitha.

But she didn't need reminding. Still traumatized from the action in the loading area, she was pressing all forty pounds of her body into my legs. The battle-hardened goblin only sniffed and nodded.

As I returned the program to my pocket, I patted my other pockets to double-check the location of my iron amulet and all my potions.

My thoughts jagged to Grandpa's coin pendant. When I'd accessed it on the drive here, I hadn't felt its aura around Vega, but her son. Meaning Vega was now defenseless against Arnaud and much of faedom.

The elevator rattled to a stop. When the door opened, I poked my head out. The plain corridor was empty. Isolated shouts and screams sounded from the hotel. I waved Bree-Yark and Tabitha out. The air shimmered into a shield around us as we ran down the corridor, Tabitha loping to keep up. I hit a locked door with a force invocation, and we burst onto the second floor's large hall. I pulled up hard.

"Fuck, darling," Tabitha said, taking in the scene from floor level.

The convention had become a horror show. Trolls, owl bears, and large humanoid creatures whose forms were composed of writhing vines lumbered through the smoky mist that had reached the hall. But more horrible were the victims littering the floor. There had to be hundreds, many torn to pieces.

I swallowed hard. *No.*

My eyes moved to the Magenta Room. The doors were flung wide.

I ran toward it, my mind already screaming at what I was going to find. With grunts and low moans, the monstrosities began swinging themselves toward us, several dropping the bloodied bodies they'd been dragging—or gnawing.

"Vigore!" I shouted, nailing them with one explosive force invocation after another. Bree-Yark came up to my side squeezing off bursts of automatic fire. Though the monsters staggered from our attack, we didn't seem to be dealing much damage. But my goal right now was to clear a path to the conference room, and in that we were succeeding. I planned to save my iron amulet attacks and potions for getting us out.

And for dealing with the person behind this.

I reached the door, hoping beyond all reason that somehow, someway...

But among the dispersion of mangled bodies, I couldn't see any survivors.

As though pulled by a magnetic force, my gaze moved to a victim on her side, facing away from me. Her midnight hair was plastered to the back of a black jacket. Where the jacket's right side had hiked up, I recognized the holster at her waist. Her bloodied sidearm was several feet away, knocked from her grip during the massacre.

Even as Bree-Yark's M16 popped behind me, a roaring silence filled my head.

It can't be her, I started repeating, despite all evidence to the contrary. *It can't be her.*

I felt myself move forward. Felt my knees on the floor behind her. Felt my arm reach forward, my hand grip her stiff shoulder.

It was her.

I stopped, unable to roll Vega toward me.

I could already feel her absence, and the thought of seeing an empty pair of eyes...

I straightened the side of her jacket instead, barely aware Tabitha had come up beside me. I had dropped her leash at some point. My cat's breath caught as she realized who I was kneeling beside. She looked from Vega's body to me.

"Can't hold them off much longer," Bree-Yark barked behind us.

I drew out a neutralizing potion, activated it in a monotone, and chugged it down my raw throat.

It was time to find the dead bastard responsible.

25

I pressed my hand to the familiar curve of Vega's back before rising on hollow legs and turning. My shocked mind cast everything in an aura of unreality: the dead around me, the monsters crowding the doorway, the rounds exploding into them, the misty drift of smoke, the fallen woman behind me.

I stood for a moment unable to command a body I felt so detached from.

It was the potion's movement through me that brought me back to myself. Identical to the potion I'd used the night before against Seay the Fae, it would protect me from direct attacks by a fae caster.

A fae caster I would stop at nothing to track down and kill.

I aimed my sword at the host of screeching, snarling faces crowding the doorway.

"Keep 'em back," Bree-Yark barked at me. "I've gotta reload."

The popping of his M16 stopped as he ejected the magazine. But instead of invoking, I slowly lowered my sword.

"The hell are you doing?" the goblin demanded, working double time now to slot his new mag. "They're coming in!"

"No," I said. "They're not."

He looked from the doorway to me in alarm. "You enchanted or something?"

"Past tense," I replied, reality and reason rushing back into me. "We all were. See the smoke? We drove through a wall of it to reach the hotel, remember? But it's not smoke. It's an enchantment mist."

I followed Bree-Yark's eyes back to the door. The door was indeed open, but for me, the monsters were thinning and disappearing as the elaborate multi-sensory illusion lost its grip on my mind. Bree-Yark swore as he fumbled his mag to the floor. When he tried to retrieve it, I stepped on it.

"What are you doing?" he barked.

"Drink about three quarters," I said, activating another neutralizing potion and holding it toward him. "Give the rest to Tabitha."

I could see his mind resisting, but a lifetime in the goblin army had taught him to follow orders. Flinching from the illusory monsters, he snatched the vial and jammed it to his lips. While he sucked it down, I turned, a part of me terrified that everything would prove to have been an illusion *except* for Vega's death.

But the body I'd knelt beside in agony just moments before was gone.

They all were. I spotted their living, breathing counterparts hunkered in a corner beside the stage. With the illusion releasing my ears, the grunts and growls of monsters were being replaced by sobbing and wails. Mae's voice rose in prayer above the others. She was in a prostrate position, her pet carrier hugged to her side.

The only one standing was Vega. She had positioned herself between the group and the imagined monsters, eyes wide, the sidearm she gripped in both hands pivoting from one imagined creature to the next. She must have spent her ammo, because she wasn't firing. But I kept my shield up anyway.

"Stay back," she warned in her take-no-crap voice.

Relief and love dumped through me as I ran toward her.

"Ricki!" I shouted. "There are no monsters! It's an illusion!"

"Croft!" she shouted back, but hers was a call of alarm. "Watch out!"

I looked around, heart in my throat. The room was just as it had been, though. No danger. When Vega grimaced, I understood she'd just seen me meet a terrible end. She began moving forward, maybe to try to reach me.

"Stay the fuck back!" she warned, thrusting her pistol toward my left, then my right.

"Ricki, I'm fine!" I shouted, but she didn't even blink.

I stopped when we reached each other. If I touched her, chances were she'd either feel nothing, or the illusion would distort the sensation such that she would believe one of the monsters was attacking her.

In her fractured eyes, I was dead or dying, just as she'd been in mine moments before. The enchantment was as adaptive as it was powerful, playing on individual and collective fears. I hadn't been able to pierce the enchantment with my wizard's senses. Meaning even if Vega could hear me, I wouldn't be able to talk her out of experiencing what wasn't there. I needed to get my final neutralizing potion into her.

But how?

As quickly and painlessly as possible.

Touching my staff to her head, I uttered a precursor to a healing spell. The fluttering of her eyelids told me her endorphins were releasing. I caught her around the waist as her legs gave out and her sidearm thudded to the floor. I lowered her until she was propped against my thigh. She moaned in protest, but semi-consciously.

I drew the neutralizing potion from my pocket, activated it, and squeezed Vega's cheeks to open her mouth. With another invocation, I created a shield in the shape of a funnel. I inserted it into her mouth until I was as certain as I could be that it was down her throat and not her windpipe. Taking a deep breath, I tipped the potion over the funnel.

"Down the hatch," I whispered.

Her gag reflex kicked in at first contact, then relaxed. When the entire potion had gone in, I tossed the vial aside, dissolved the funnel, and slowly sat her up all the way. In my wizard's senses, I could feel the magic working on her.

"Destare," I whispered.

With the gentle awakening invocation, Vega opened her eyes. She looked at me perplexed, then shot her gaze past my shoulder. Behind me, Bree-Yark had secured Tabitha to one of the conference room chairs. Tabitha stood with her back arched, trying to gag up the potion he had apparently forced into her— the sides of her mouth were green with it—but Bree-Yark himself was nowhere to be seen.

When Vega tried to talk, she coughed. She hacked into her fist and tried again.

"What the fuck is going on?" she rasped. "You're not...? Where are the creatures?"

"I'm fine," I said. "The creatures, everything you saw—it was all an illusion."

"An illusion?"

She peered back at the group still cowering in the corner.

"A powerful fae illusion," I explained. "There was no attack."

Her next cough cleared her voice. "So, everyone's all right?"

"That remains to be seen, but there was no monster massacre."

Vega's dilated eyes cut around again, some primitive corner of her brain still convinced the danger remained and the monsters could reappear at any moment. When none did, she looked back at me.

I didn't know what she thought she'd seen happen to me, and I didn't ask. Judging by her eyes, it was horrible. She pulled me forward by the lapels of my coat and wrapped her arms around my neck, the side of her head pressed firmly to mine. It wasn't a tender embrace. It was to ensure I was as material, as *real*, as I could be. I squeezed and pressed back, a part of me still needing the same reassurance.

Our private celebration of the other's return didn't last long, though. The neutralizing potions might have restored *our* senses, but there were still thousands of people inside the enchantment's misty embrace who were seeing monsters. And the only way to end their nightmare was to find the caster.

When Vega and I separated, she began looking for her sidearm. I retrieved it from the floor and handed it to her. She smiled and wiped her eyes as she accepted it. While she checked the chamber I considered saying something about how she had left the coin pendant with Tony, but now wasn't the time.

A look of surprise came over Vega's face as she patted her jacket pockets. "I thought I was out of ammo, but I have all my spare mags." She ejected the magazine from her sidearm. "And this is still half full."

"Such an optimist," I joked. The fact I *could* joke with someone who I had believed gone only minutes earlier felt amazingly surreal. So much so that I had to suppress a stupid grin. "No, that's how a lot of these enchantments work. They not only make you believe what you're seeing, but what you're touching, hearing, doing." I began digging into a coat pocket. "In fact..." I was wondering whether my two encounters in the hotel that day had been actual encounters or just precursors to this grand finale. I pulled out the vial into which I'd scooped the frog-beast's gunk. It was still full, telling me that sucker, and probably the lizards, had been real.

"You mentioned fae," Vega said, slotting a fresh mag into her pistol.

Before I could answer, Bree-Yark rushed back into the room.

"I saw one of 'em!" he shouted.

"The lunar fae?" I asked.

"Yeah, looking down from one level up. He took off when he saw I'd spotted him. Must've been acting as sentry."

"Let's go," I said, moving toward the door. "Tabitha, hang tight."

"Seriously?" she said above the screams.

"Are we just going to leave them here?" Vega asked, gesturing to the group of a hundred-odd, who still thought they were under attack. Mae's prayerful voice continued to weave in and out of the din.

"I don't like it, but yeah," I said.

Before Vega could offer to stay behind, I waved her on.

I wasn't going to leave her alone again, especially without the coin pendant.

Not after seeing what could happen.

As we left the conference room at a run, I cast a shield around everyone and reinforced my own.

"He was right up there," Bree-Yark panted, pointing with his M16. "Then he bugged off that way."

"You two take the stairs," I said. "If you see him, take a shot. But stay together," I stressed.

"Where are you going?" Vega asked.

"Short cut."

Aiming my staff at the ground, I shouted, *"Forza dura!"*

The explosive force sent me airborne and through the opening to the second floor, where Bree-Yark had seen the fae a moment before. I'd calibrated the invocation just right, my left foot landing on the three-foot-tall railing that ran around the opening. Momentum carried me down to a stone planter and then to the carpeted floor. I noted the improvement in my control. A few months ago I would have fallen on my face.

I jogged to a stop and peered around. No sign of the fae. I switched to my wizard's senses. Fae used glamours to alter their appearances as well as to hide their auras, but with the neutralizing spell in my system, maybe…

Bingo!

A misty plum-colored trail led to a women's bathroom. I ran toward it, noticing a piece of paper taped to the door. It read "Out of Order," the fae likely having glamoured the handwritten sign to appear more official. I pulled up a mental map of the hotel. The bathroom was smack dab in the middle of the second floor, making it the perfect place from which to cast a circumferential enchantment.

Dollars to donuts, the caster's inside.

Behind me, I could hear Bree-Yark and Vega arriving on the floor.

Still running, I waved them toward the bathroom. Ten feet from the door, I aimed my cane and shouted, *"Vigore!"* The force invocation smashed the lock. I took the same invocation, wrapped it around the door, and pulled it open.

The fae were good at concealing their emotions, which made the surprise on this one's face that much sweeter. He was standing in the center of the bathroom as I broke in, a line of stalls to his left and sinks to his right. My arrival sent him stumbling into a backpedal across the tiles on a pair of pointy leather shoes.

"Wh-what are you doing?" he demanded.

"Didn't you see the sign? Bathroom's out of order."

Eyes wide, he threw his delicate hands forward and spoke a fae enchantment. Unfortunately for him, the potion still warming my stomach negated its effect. As I stalked nearer, his words became a frenetic babble.

"What was that?" I asked.

Even without a glamour, the fae appeared immaculate in his slender white pants, silver buckle, and designer jacket. And he was handsome in a starved runway model kind of way. Which made what I was about to do even more of a shame. My right fist caught him in the porcelain-looking jaw. Like porcelain, it broke cleanly.

The fae grunted and fell against the far wall. Before I could land a follow-up blow, he covered his head and shrank to the floor.

"Don't hurt me!"

"Who's casting the enchantments?" I demanded.

I expected a lengthy back and forth, but with his arms still shielding his head, he pointed a finger toward the handicap stall. Vega and Bree-Yark entered the bathroom behind me, their footfalls slowing to a stop. A part of me wanted to toss dragon sand into the stall the fae had indicated and be done with it—I was still that pissed for being made to believe Vega had been slain—but if the caster was Sefu, I would need to get the son of a bitch to safety. When a third set of footsteps entered the bathroom, we all turned.

It was the other male lunar fae, who had probably been on lookout too.

"You're not supposed to be in here!" he cried, clearly perplexed that we weren't under the influence of the enchantment. "Get out!"

Vega answered him with a gunshot. The iron round nailed him in the shoulder, spinning him halfway around and dropping him to the floor. Vega met my surprised look with a stiff expression that suggested the shot had been payback for the twenty minutes of hell the fae had put *her* through. Not to mention that she was the only one who was really supposed to be in the women's bathroom, anatomically speaking.

I gave her a thumb's up.

Using a force invocation, I dragged the wounded fae beside the other one and bound them with magic.

Now for the caster...

I summoned a shield around the inside of the stall, shrinking it until I felt a fae's aura. I tried the door, but the latch was down. I signaled for Vega to cover the two male fae, then pointed to Bree-Yark's foot and the door in turn. He got the message. I drew the iron amulet from my pocket and positioned myself for the breach. With a grunt, Bree-Yark drove his foot into the door. It banged open, and I thrust myself inside.

The female fae was sitting cross-legged in the center of the bathroom. I was half amused to see she'd papered the floor with toilet seat covers so she wouldn't have to come into direct contact with the tiles. The fae were notorious germaphobes.

She was staring straight ahead, eyes the same color as the mist that surrounded and permeated the hotel. The power emanating from her in waves stirred her preternaturally straight hair. She was so absorbed in weaving the enchantment, she hadn't even flinched at the sound of the door smashing open. Evidently, her accomplices' job had been to keep anyone from finding her. Her accomplices had screwed the pooch.

Aiming the amulet, I bellowed, *"Disfare!"*

Whether this was Sefu or not, I didn't hold back. Not after what she'd put us through. The beam that shot from the cold iron smashed through her enchantment and flung her against the stall wall. Toilet-seat covers fluttered in every direction. She landed hard on her right shoulder, then flopped onto her back.

The mist dissolved from her eyes, and she looked around in startlement until her gaze fixed on mine.

"Yeah, sorry to break up your little monster mash," I said. "But it ends here."

When her brow tensed and her irises began to do strange things, I cast through the amulet again, this time trapping her in a cone of blue light. The fae grimaced and writhed under the projection from the cold iron.

I started with the obvious question. "Are you Sefu?"

I hadn't been expecting a woman, but that was the problem with assumptions.

Despite her obvious pain, she spat back, "I am no one of your concern."

"Yeah, well, when you mind-hump my friends and me, it sort of makes it my concern. Now I'll ask you again, are you Sefu?"

I upped the power until she was really writhing. Unlike the runway twins, who had folded like a pair of cheap suits, she showed impressive resistance. The muscles in her temples strained, as if trying to keep her secrets locked inside her, but at last she raised a hand to tell me she was ready to talk.

I backed off the power.

"I am not Sefu," she gasped, steam rising from her body. "My name is Lialla."

I looked over at Bree-Yark, who had entered the stall too. He was holding his M16 on her. "It's a common enough name among the lunar fae," he said. "She's not court level, though, or I'd've recognized her."

That would explain how I had been able to negate her magic and take her down with relative ease. I *was* becoming a stronger wizard—I wanted to think that was part of it—but she also wasn't anything approaching a fae lord. Which made it unlikely she was the vessel in question.

"But she's telling the truth?" I asked anyway.

Bree-Yark's squat nose flared a few times. "Far as I can tell."

"Why the enchantment?" I asked her. "What are you guys up to?"

I remembered what Stan had said when he banned me from the conference. He'd asked if I was in league with the fae, suggesting there might be bad blood between them. But I didn't want to tip Lialla off. Fae were good at picking up on what you wanted to hear and then giving you more of the same. I caught Lialla searching my face as if for some tell, but I maintained a poker-stiff expression.

"It's not your concern," she said finally.

"Oh, so we're back to that?" I was raising the amulet again when someone else came running into the bathroom.

Who now? I thought in exasperation.

"What the hell is going on in here?"

Well, speak of the devil—the voice belonged to Stan Burke, the conference organizer.

Lialla got my attention and looked at me meaningfully.

"We're working for him," she whispered.

26

"Working for Stan Burke?" I whispered back, to make sure we were talking about the same person.

Lialla nodded.

Though the fae rarely told outright lies, they were master manipulators, often using the nuances of language for the very purpose. Lialla could have meant one thing, and I could have heard another—which was exactly how they operated. Getting to the actual meaning was a skill in itself, and even then it could take hours.

More likely, Lialla was trying to save their skin.

"Hey, you're that detective," Stan said to Vega. "What the hell's happening in here?"

I signaled for Bree-Yark to keep his weapon on Lialla, who was still suffering the effects of the cold iron, and stepped from the stall. Stan had stopped in the middle of the bathroom, hands clenched into fists. He was looking from Vega to the two fae on the floor, his gray hair tossed everywhere as if he'd arrived in a sprint. When I stepped into his field of view, his eyes cut over sharply.

"I thought I told you to stay the hell out of my con!"

"I called him back," Vega said sternly. "Your con was under attack, or did you miss that?"

"No, I didn't *miss that*. And the first person I thought of was this joker."

"Watch your tone," Vega said.

"Oh, you're the tenor police now? I have an order." He reached into the pocket of his jeans and pulled out the piece of paper—a faxed copy from the looks of it—with my temporary restraining order. "See?" He flapped it a few times. "Now get him out of here!"

For someone who had seemed so stoner chill when I'd first seen him, Stan was proving to be a hysterical ass.

"No one's going anywhere," Vega said. "Do you know them?"

Using a force invocation, I dragged Lialla from the stall and set her beside the other two fae.

"Should I?" Stan said after looking them over. "I mean, I might have seen them around the con. Wait a minute—they're fae aren't they?" He looked sharply back at me. "See, I knew you were in cahoots!"

I gave him a dry stare. "Does this really look to you like the picture of two parties in cahoots?"

A lump stuck out from the left side of Fae One's jaw where I'd punched him, while Fae Two lay curled on his side, a hand pressed to his gunshot wound. For her part, Lialla looked vaguely ill from the effects of the amulet. She was staring down at her knees, which she'd pulled in to her chest.

I was eyeing Stan for his reaction, but he just looked agitated.

"They were the ones behind the attack," Bree-Yark barked as he emerged from the stall, M16 propped against his shoulder. "Or *imaginary* attack. They cast an illusion around the whole show. Everson stopped them. You should be kissing his feet."

"I thought I ordered you out of here too!" Stan said, craning his neck to see if anyone else was going to emerge from the stall.

"Forget about them for a second," Vega said. "Why would the fae want to attack your con?"

Stan gathered his hair like he was going to secure it in a ponytail, then shook it loose again. "Because we banned them back in '05. Yeah, a group of them showed up with their little enchantments and glamours. Next thing we know, the convention's descending into a bacchanal of drinking, stripping, and costumed orgies."

I raised an eyebrow. Sounded like the darker side of faedom all right. Might have also explained why Stan was so on edge. He had a lot riding on this con.

"You want to know where that whole furry thing went mainstream?" Stan asked, jabbing a finger toward the floor. "Right here. And that's *not* what Epic Con is about. The fae tried to bribe us to let them back in—oh, they'd thought the whole thing was a riot—but we didn't budge. They even offered to fund the con the years we had to go dark. When we said no, *that's* when they turned nasty. Threatened to get even with us. At first I thought they'd sent Everson in to do their dirty work. But if they're here…"

Vega sidled up to me and muttered, "What do you think?"

"Actually makes sense," I whispered back. "And it won't be hard to learn whether his story about '05 checks out."

Vega nodded, drew out her phone, and called the officer in charge. While she spoke with him, Stan came over. "Hey, sorry for jumping to conclusions," he said, his attitude completely changed from just a moment before. He sounded like an aging stoner again. "I didn't think they'd just show up like that."

"It happens," I said.

"Can the police even do anything to them?" he asked.

"I guess it depends on the fall-out from their stunt and if

anyone decides to press charges." I saw what he was getting at, though. Something like this would be hard to prove in court, especially if the fae hired attorneys. While the NYPD had come around to the supernatural reality in the last couple years, the court system had been much slower to adapt, which was to say they hadn't.

Vega ended her call and joined us. "No deaths, which is a small miracle," she said, looking pointedly at the culprits. "Most of the attendees were at the parade when the enchantment started, and they fled the scene. The rest hid in conference rooms. It looks like we have a few sprains and bruises, some faintings, and one case of heart palpitations. Recovering from the psychological shock will take longer," she said, her face darkening. "I have an officer getting the iron cuffs from my car."

In addition to her arsenal, Vega and I had been complementing her forms of restraint to better handle any supernaturals she might encounter. I had even helped her modify a couple of retaining cells back at One Police Plaza to hold them. And it looked like that was exactly what Vega intended to do.

She tilted her phone toward me, showing an article she'd brought up regarding Epic Con '05. The first paragraph confirmed Stan's account. There was a photo below. Even though it was covered with black boxes to disguise the participants and their personal effects, it left little to the imagination.

I nodded and showed her a hand to say I'd seen enough.

When my eyes fell back to the fae, Lialla was giving me that meaningful look again.

We were working for him, the look insisted.

A last-ditch attempt to save herself? Or was there actually something to her claim? I repeated her words in my mind. How many ways were there to interpret that besides how it sounded on the surface? But that was the thing about the fae. You couldn't know what they were working at. Besides, Stan's story was credible. Lialla's? I couldn't come up with any reason for why Stan would sabotage his own conference.

"Let them go," Stan said.

We all looked over at him in surprise. "Come again?" I said.

"They carried out their threat. They ruined the con." He directed his voice to them. "That's how it works, isn't it? We did you an 'injustice,'" he said, air-quoting the word, "so you do us one back. But now we're even. You can't do anything more without cause. It's part of their code or something," he said, turning back to us.

"So you don't want me to hold them?" Vega asked.

"I'm afraid that will just give them a reason to come at us again."

Vega gave a reluctant nod. I think she was seeing the same difficulty as me in making any charges stick.

"Can I get a promise that the fae will never interfere again if we release you?" Stan asked them.

Lialla and the fae with the broken jaw nodded. The other fae just continued to moan on the floor.

"I'm going to have our lawyers write up something they won't be able to squirm their way out of," Stan muttered.

Once more, it all sounded sensible on the surface, but suspicion squirmed inside me. If Stan *had* hired them, he would want to get rid of them before they said something they shouldn't—such as "We were working for him."

"Hey, Stan?" I said.

"What's up?"

"How did you know we were in the women's bathroom?"

"What do you mean?"

"You came in here at a full-on run. I was just wondering how you knew we were in here."

"Well, I didn't know *you* were in here. I just knew something was going on. I heard a commotion."

Vega caught on. "You heard a commotion above the one out there?"

"Well, all that stopped—you said it was an enchantment, right?—and then I heard, I don't know, a scream or something." He looked around at us, a slight wildness in his eyes. "What's this about? Why am I being interrogated all of a sudden?"

"Where did you go when you thought the con was under attack?" Vega followed up.

"I was in the suite we're using as an office."

"Fifth floor, right?" Vega asked. "And you're claiming you heard this commotion in the second-floor women's bathroom from three levels up?"

"Well, I came down to see what was going on."

"No, you didn't," she said. "As far as you knew, the hotel was overrun with monsters. People were getting ripped apart left and right. The best I could do was secure a conference room, and I'm a trained officer. But you're going to tell me you navigated that scene all the way down to the second floor?"

"I found a back stairwell," he stammered.

Like his voice, his story was getting more and more rickety.

"Or maybe you weren't under the influence of the enchantment," I said.

"Man, I don't have to listen to this bullshit at my own con." He turned to leave.

Bree-Yark cut in front of him and jabbed his M16 into the center of his goblin T-shirt. "You're not going anywhere, funny man," he snarled.

"Hey, whoa!" Stan threw up his hands. "Police!" he called.

Vega came up behind him. She drew his left arm down, cuffed the wrist, then did the same to the right.

"You're detaining me?" Stan asked in disbelief as she patted him down.

Vega perp-walked him over to the wall where the fae were

and sat him beside them. "No one's leaving until we get to the bottom of this," she said.

Two officers arrived with the cuffs Vega had requested. The fae shifted uncomfortably as, under Vega's direction, the officers snapped the cuffs around their wrists. In my wizard's senses, the cold iron cast a metallic blue aura around them, preventing them from casting. Vega ordered the officers to return outside the bathroom and watch the door.

She strode back toward Stan and the fae, arms crossed while Bree-Yark covered them. This was going to be good. But before Vega could begin her questioning, her phone rang. She drew it from her jacket, brow furrowed in irritation.

"Vega," she answered.

As she listened, her lines let out slowly before contracting sharply again. "Where again? Okay, stay clear." She hung up and put her phone away. "Ready for this one?" she said to me. "There are reports of a large creature flying down Forty-sixth Street."

I turned on the fae. "How many of you are there?"

"Just us," Lialla said.

"That's not an answer," I growled. "I want a number."

"Three."

"Do you have someone else casting enchantments. A backup team?"

Lialla shook her head. "We're the only fae here."

"Who's responsible for the flying creature, then?"

"We don't know."

Dammit. I didn't have time to dissect her responses.

"It's Brian Lutz," Stan blurted out. "He's behind it."

I looked at him closely. "I thought you said you didn't know him."

"Well..." Stan's eyes shifted around. "I lied."

I moved up beside Vega and lowered my voice. "I don't know whether this is another illusion or what, but I need to check it out. Think you can get some answers out of them while I'm gone?"

"Oh, they'll talk."

"Good. I'll have Bree-Yark stay with you."

At the same time, Vega said, "Take Bree-Yark with you."

Bree-Yark, who had overheard, asked, "How did I get so popular suddenly?"

"No, I want him here," I said to Vega. "I'll radio if I need him."

Before Vega could argue, I turned and ran from the bathroom.

27

The hotel was in chaos as I made my way to the front doors. I looked for Mae among those pouring from the conference rooms, everyone still trying to figure out what had happened. NYPD officers were shouting for the conference attendees to go to their hotel rooms, but it was a futile effort. A thousand frantic conversations collided in the lobby: Were they attacked? Were they not attacked? Had that all been a part of Epic Con?

As I pushed my way through the throng, I tried the radio. "Mae, can you hear me?"

"I hear you, baby," she answered. *"Whew. I thought for sure the good Lord was coming to spirit this old soul away."* When I told her about the fae enchantment, she said, *"Well, that explains it."*

"But you're all right?" I asked.

"Probably lost a year or two off the end of my life. Otherwise, Buster and I are fine."

"Good, can you make it down to our meeting room?" It was the safest place I could think of.

"Don't see why not, but is there something I can help with? You have that sound like you're on a mission."

I didn't know what I was about to walk out into, but if the reported creature proved to be the actual thing and not another illusion, it was probably going to be beyond Mae's abilities to tame.

"I'm just going to check something out," I told her. "If you can get yourself and Buster to the meeting room, great. Whatever you do, stay inside the hotel."

"Okay," she said reluctantly. *"But call if you need us."*

I was almost to the doors when screams rang out. Beyond the glass, a winged creature the size of a school bus swept low down Forty-sixth Street, passing right in front of the hotel. Those in front of me who had seen it began pushing their way back into the hotel, while those behind me who had only caught a glimpse tried to shove forward for a better look. The result was a mosh pit with me right in the middle.

Using a shield invocation, I created a wedge to act as a lead blocker and ran in the wake of parting bodies until I was bursting through the doors. By the time I reached the sidewalk, the creature was nearly a block away.

I squinted at it. Another enchantment?

No, I could still feel the neutralizing spell humming inside me. And a glance around showed that, except for the pieces of costume littering the closed-off parade route, the destruction I'd believed I'd seen earlier was nonexistent.

The creature flapping its giant bat-like wings down the street was an actual wyvern.

Smaller than dragons, wyverns were distinguished by having wings in the place of front legs, versus the four legs of their draconic cousins. They were also less intelligent, and only a rare few could cast magic.

The thing was, pure wyverns, like dragons, hadn't lived on Earth for hundreds of years. They'd been hunted and wiped out. Meaning the wyvern was either a shifter, or someone had summoned it from another plane. Going by the day to this point, I was betting on the second.

The solution, then, was to overcome the forces holding it together. Hit it with everything I had. The problem was my magic had barely been effective against the frog-beast, and we were dealing with something on an order considerably larger and more complex. The assault would need to be physical, then. I eyed the material on hand, from the parked police cruisers to the construction material on the hotel's rooftop.

It would have to do.

Pulling my cane into sword and staff, I summoned a ball of light and slung it at the creature. The light zipped down Forty-sixth like a small comet and exploded into the creature's backside, just above its tail. With an angry cry, the creature reared up and craned its serpentine neck around until a pair of reptilian eyes glared into mine.

Yup, called it right. Wyvern.

The wyvern rose and made a tight turn. With three powerful flaps, it was speeding toward me. The last time I'd seen something in the same family was when I'd helped the Blue Wolf battle a dragon shifter out on Long Island. Like that creature, there was a certain majesty to the wyvern's elaborate scales and the spiny crest that adorned its head. I got why some people worshipped these things.

But they were also deadly as fuck.

The wyvern opened its mouth of oversized teeth. Though every instinct was telling me to flee, I held my ground, forced myself to wait another second...

Now!

With a bellowed Word, I aimed my sword at the police cruiser parked across the street and pulled the sword back in front of me. The force invocation grabbed the car and heaved it into the wyvern's path.

Fixated on me, the creature only saw the two-ton missile at the last moment. It arced its neck and tried to rear from its path, but it was a second too slow. The cruiser plowed into the wyvern's side, driving the creature against the Centre Hotel between the first and second floors. The impact crushed its right wing, and wyvern and cruiser crashed to the street, glass and pieces of siren light raining over them.

That's what the police chief gets for siding with Stan, I thought.

As the wyvern thrashed to its feet, I spoke a second invocation, this one directed at the rooftop. With a hop, the wyvern tried to take to the air, where most dragons preferred to attack from, but its right wing looked like a balled-up piece of wax paper. With a hiss, the wyvern shook out the wing, which was already repairing.

The cruiser stunt had required a sizeable quotient of my power, but the point had been to position the wyvern where I wanted it. I made a subtle adjustment to my just-cast invocation as I moved back. A second later, the loaded construction dumpster on the rooftop completed its twenty-story plunge and landed on the creature with a boom. The wyvern's legs splayed into a split as its head slammed into asphalt. Discarded roofing material flew everywhere.

When cheers sounded, I realized I had an audience. Every available foot of glass at the front of the conference hotel seemed to have a face pressed to it. I waved them back, but no one budged. Even NYPD officers were engrossed in the action.

The wyvern might have been down, but it wasn't out. And I wasn't sure how many more invocations on that scale I could channel. I attempted a shield around the wyvern, but like with the frog-beast, it barely held. I then directed an attack through my iron amulet. The blue cone broke apart when it reached the wyvern, seeming to confirm this wasn't a fae creation. I considered a sword attack, but even if I could penetrate the creature's armor, I wasn't confident I could summon the power to blast it apart.

That left my spell implements.

I reached into a coat pocket and palmed a vial of dragon sand briefly. While fire had the power to destroy, it could also rejuvenate a creature in whom the fire essence was strong. Though this one wasn't spouting flames, wyverns belonged to the draconic class, and many of their lines originated from fire.

I released the vial of dragon sand and dug until my fingers encountered the cool breath of ice crystals against glass. Thumbing the lid from the vial, I drew it from my pocket and aimed it at the wyvern. The creature was rising to its legs with ungainly flaps.

"*Ghioccio!*" I shouted.

A blast of cold shot from the vial and enveloped the wyvern in a hoary white cone. Through it, I could see icicles growing from the creature's spines and off the ends of its wings. Its strength already depleted from the bashing, the wyvern staggered. Unable to flap itself upright, it fell to its chest. But its legs continued to move. The wyvern gave a shove, inching itself toward me. Then another.

Just need to keep this up, I thought. *Weaken the forces holding the damned thing together, then shatter it with a blow from my sword.*

Who had created the forces in the first place? Not the fae punks who'd been responsible for the enchantment. Stan? He was playing at something, but this? And what about him claiming Brian Lutz was the perp? The guy did have an unhealthy fascination with dragons, but summoning a wyvern?

All the time I was thinking, I was pushing more power into the invocation. With each shove of its legs, the wyvern was having to overcome additional cold and ice. Its progress slowed until its fiery essence began to gutter.

"Stand aside!" someone shouted.

What the—?

I turned to find Brian hustling from the hotel, one hand clutching his pathetic wand, the other balling up the lap of his robe so he wouldn't trip over the hem.

Oh, you're frigging kidding me.

"Stand aside, Croft!" he repeated. "Let me handle this!"

"This isn't a goddamned game!" I roared. "Go back inside!"

Even though I used my wizard's voice, he ignored me and kept coming. I held the frost blast on the wyvern for as long as I dared, but Brian was getting too damned close. In another few steps he'd be a popsicle.

I broke off the blast long enough to hit Brian with a force invocation. In my frustration, I nailed him harder than I'd meant to. The invocation threw him from his feet and into the plexiglass siding of a bus shelter. He rebounded and fell onto hands and knees. With a second invocation, I shoved him back toward the front of the hotel, where I hoped the officers would have the sense to pull him inside.

I wheeled back toward the wyvern—in time to see its tail incoming. The thick appendage broke through my shield and slammed into my side. I went tumbling, coming to a bruising rest at the end of a trail of potion vials. The wyvern had shaken off the ice, and now it reared up with a furious scream, wings batting.

Had the sonofabitch reeling, I thought as I staggered up and grabbed my fallen sword. *How in the hell did it recover so quickly?*

I dug into my pockets for another vial of ice crystals, but I'd lost them in the tumble. With a scream, the wyvern thrust its open mouth toward me. I threw up a shield invocation. It shattered on contact as I suspected it might, but the bright shower of sparks gave me the second of cover I needed to dive from the wyvern's path. The creature's teeth scraped sidewalk as they snapped closed around empty air.

I made a dash for a fallen vial of ice crystals, throwing it up with a minor force invocation. I snatched the vial from the air, popped off the lid, and wheeled on the wyvern only to find that Brian had lumbered between us again.

"Dude!" I shouted.

Facing the wyvern, he threw his robed arms out to the side. "You are a being of the Drago," he announced, "and for that we honor you. But you have entered this world unbidden."

The wyvern, which had risen up again, watched Brian with malevolent eyes.

I trained the vial of ice crystals on the creature, but the idiot was right in my path.

"Brian, get out of the way!"

He flapped a hand behind his back for me to shut it. "Yes," he said, directing his voice back to the wyvern. "You are here unbidden. But be not wrathful. Return to your realm, and do so in peace, or I will send you there myself!"

He thinks this is a frigging D&D campaign.

Brian aimed his wand at the wyvern. I was preparing to blast Brian aside with another force invocation when the wyvern's eyes rolled back and its serpentine neck began to undulate—in time to Brian's subtle wand movements.

I hesitated. *Huh?*

"So, begone!" Brian made a diagonal slashing gesture with the wand.

Flames broke from under the wyvern's scales and licked up around the creature. I couldn't believe what I was seeing.

"Begone!" Brian repeated, slashing the wand along the opposite diagonal now.

I threw a forearm to my eyes as a ball of fire burst up from the wyvern. The creature released a fading scream. When I peeked, the once-solid creature was a silhouette of smoke, head reared skyward, massive wings stretched to the sides. Then the wind broke through it and scattered it down the canyon of Forty-sixth Street.

Brian gave a nod and turned back toward the hotel.

"Hold on a sec," I said, running up to him. "Let me see that."

Before he could pull the wand back, I snatched it from his grip. It was the same sorry thing he'd tried to cast through during his session, electrical tape holding the two pieces together now. I scanned it anyway.

"How did you do that?" I demanded. "There's not an ounce of damned power in this thing or you." I tossed the wand back to him. He bobbled it a few times, an indignant frown puckering his lips, before securing the wand against his chest.

"What's the matter, Croft? Feeling your celebrity threatened?"

"I want to know how in the hell you dispersed a wyvern."

"It's called magic."

"Bullshit."

Brian cocked his head toward the hotel. "Do you hear that?"

It was only when he asked that I realized the cheers had risen in pitch. Now conference-goers began to break past the officers along the front of the hotel trying to hold them back. They came streaming into the street, running toward us.

"Excuse me," Brian said. "My fans await."

As he strode off to meet them, he looked over a shoulder as if to ensure I wasn't trying to cut in front of him. The conference-goers surrounded him, talking all at once. Had that been a real dragon? they wanted to know. How had he defeated it? Brian started into his spiel from that morning's session about becoming a wizard, blah, blah, blah. I couldn't believe he was still trying to sell that garbage.

But the crowd was hanging onto every flipping word.

A few who had been approaching me stopped and returned to Brian. And then I caught the mass of dark electrical energy I'd seen that morning. Like in the conference room, it was hovering over the crowd, shifting toward Brian every time he paused to inhale. He was so caught up in his own story, though, I wasn't sure he was even aware that the phenomenon was happening.

Could it be that he was a natural charismatic? Someone with the power to influence people under the right circumstances? I remembered how I'd been drawn to him at the start of his presentation that morning. It could also explain why my wizard's voice hadn't fazed him. And like with Mae's ability to control nether creatures, it wouldn't have been an ability I could necessarily observe.

It still didn't explain him sending the wyvern up in smoke.

Or maybe it wasn't him, I thought. *Maybe someone's working from behind the scenes.*

I scanned the crowd for the other members of his entourage, then switched my gaze to the hotel, but his red-robed brigade was nowhere to be seen. I was thinking in particular of the man wearing the metal gauntlet on his hand. It'd had draconic features. I shoved my way toward Brian.

"Where's the rest of your Military Federation?" I called toward him.

"Keep it down, man," one of the crowd shouted back. "He's talking."

Other voices chimed in basically telling me to shut the fuck up.

"As I was saying before I was so *rudely* interrupted..." Brian looked pointedly at me before continuing. "I received an invitation to attend a secret wizard's school..." I considered yanking him to me with a force invocation, but the throng of people around him was ten deep now and growing.

"Brian, we need to talk!" I shouted.

This time, the crowd response was more vigorous. Everywhere I looked were shouting, angry faces. The Smurfs I'd spotted during the parade were especially PO'd. Hands began to grab my coat.

I radioed Vega. "I need officers out front for crowd control."

"I'll send them, but what's going on?" she asked in concern.

"A mob scene."

"Carry him from my sight," Brian ordered his crowd.

"Stay back," I warned in my wizard's voice, but the crowd was too much in his thrall.

As a group descended on me, I summoned a form-fitting shield. I had to remember they weren't themselves. They seized my protected body and lifted me off the ground. Brian watched with arms crossed, a smug smile on his face. He was obviously relishing the payback from that morning's duel.

A good dozen of the con-goers had a hold of me now. To avoid hurting anyone, I decided to let them carry me off a short distance to drop me or toss me or do whatever they had in mind while the officers came out to disperse them. Then I'd get to Brian. But when someone dressed as an Elf on the Shelf ran up and tried to kick me between the legs, I'd had enough.

"Respingere!" I shouted.

My shield pulsed, scattering everyone who'd placed a hand on me. The elf went spinning off somewhere, his pointed hat flying from his head. I hit the street and quickly regained my feet, this time reaching for a sleeping potion.

At Brian's order, more of the crowd, which had to number in the hundreds now, rushed toward me. There were zombies, pirates, stormtroopers, vampires, characters I recognized from superhero comics, and a whole lot I didn't. Basically, it was like everything in some teenager's bedroom coming to life and deciding they didn't like me. Several police officers were running toward me too. So much for crowd control.

I activated the sleeping potion, uncapped it, and aimed it outward. As vapors began issuing from the vial, I invoked a force invocation to spew the potion into the onrushing crowd. People staggered and began thudding to the ground—individually at first, then in waves as the pink vapors enveloped them.

I moved forward, stepping over their sleeping bodies while squinting through the mist for Brian. When the last of the potion left the vial, I moved it around the few still standing before blowing it away with another invocation.

Through the clearing mist, the front of the hotel looked like the world's largest outdoor slumber party.

But Brian had skipped out.

28

I pushed my way back into the hotel. The crowd that greeted me didn't appear to be under Brian's charismatic control. They weren't attacking me anyway. I jumped up to see past them into the lobby, but there was no sign of him.

"Where is he?" I shouted. "Where did he go?"

But no one seemed to understand who I was talking about.

"Whoa, what happened out there?" someone asked.

I looked over to find a guy in a muscle costume, wearing a leather war skirt and bearing a big-ass sword. In his wig and eye shadow, I almost didn't recognize him, but the eruption of pimples on his cheeks gave him away. This was the young man who had summoned a demon the day before.

"Nathan?" I asked.

His eyes started. "Oh, hey, you're that wizard! Was that you out there?"

"Did you see the guy I was with? Big fellow in a red robe?"

"Naw, the front of the lobby was packed. I couldn't get close enough to see anything."

I looked around. That was probably true of everyone here.

"But did a guy with a red robe come back inside?" I asked.

"A big crowd came back in. Some police with them. They ran that way."

The ones my potion didn't reach, I guessed. I imagined Brian ordering them to conceal him from me while he made his escape. And Nathan was pointing toward the back staircase. I took off in that direction.

"Hey! You going to be doing any spells later?" he called after me.

But I was already fumbling with the radio to contact Vega. "I need you to put an APB out on Brian Lutz. Last seen with a group fleeing toward the back of the first floor. Get officers on the security cameras. Cover the exits. Have them use caution, though. Sounds like he has armed NYPD with him."

"I'm on it," she said and cut out.

I ran until I reached the door to the stairwell Vega and I had checked out earlier, the one we suspected the conjurer had been using to move between floors.

Would he have gone upstairs to his room or down to try to escape through the loading bay?

But when I burst through the door and reached the landing, I had my answer. The casting circle on the wall was similar to the other two I'd encountered that day, but this one had sigils I recognized. The circle wasn't for summoning; it was a portal. And the energies in the room suggested it had just been used.

"Crap," I spat. "Any sightings?" I radioed Vega hopelessly.

"No, I just put the word out."

"Well, I think he and his newest fans just left here through an interplanar portal."

There was a slight lag on Vega's end as she interpreted what I was saying. *"Do you know where they went?"*

I eyed the circle. Like with the others, I had no doubt this one was warded in a language I didn't understand. Attempting a reveal spell on it could shoot me to a plane with acid for an atmosphere and swamps full of tentacled creatures.

"No idea," I admitted.

"Not to change the subject, but that spell book you wanted us to look into? The reverse P.O. box check came back for Brian Lutz."

"You're kidding."

"Not only that, but someone got in touch with the magazine. Brian had been advertising that book for more than a year. He called a couple months back to increase the price, boasted that he'd added another section." The section with the spells Nathan had cast from, I realized. *"But then he pulled the ad abruptly. Said something about mortals not being able to handle it. The ad team had a good laugh over that."*

"Yeah, well, unfortunately I don't think he was joking."

"Background check just came back too. They're sending it over."

"While that comes up, I'm going to see if I can find any clues in his room, something to cast from, maybe."

"I'd hold off," Vega said.

"Why?"

"Stan's already been in his room. It was cleaned out."

"Cleaned out?"

"He has some information about Brian you should hear."

Vega and Bree-Yark had moved the show from the women's bathroom to Stan's office suite. I retrieved Tabitha en route—who was none too happy about having been left in the conference room and let me know it—and arrived to find two officers guarding the door. They recognized me and allowed me past.

Inside, Stan was sitting at a table, Vega standing across from him with her arms folded. The fae had been seated on the couch. Bree-Yark was holding his weapon on them, even though the cold-iron cuffs were doing their job. The three were cast in sickly shades of blue, in no condition to do anything.

Tabitha peered around the room. "I feel like I missed something."

As I walked up to the table, Stan looked over with a harrowed face. "Did you find him?"

He'd obviously been listening while Vega put out the APB on Brian Lutz.

"No," I said. "When I left the bathroom earlier, you said Brian was behind the conjurings. What did you mean?"

"Exactly that," he said, his voice rising. "He's behind them. We need to find him."

Was *Stan* the one who'd had me called that morning, insisting I come to the hotel?

When he tried to stand, Vega pushed him back down. "Why don't you tell Everson what you were doing in Brian's room," she said.

"I was looking for a bone."

"A bone?" I repeated.

"A dragon bone." He sighed. "Brian is going to try to summon an ancient dragon called Drage the Wise."

"That name's on their manifesto," I said, pulling out the envelope the member of the Military Federation of the Dragon had given to me at the parade. I removed the sheet of paper and skimmed it. "'Drage ruled with ultimate Wisdom, Power, and Justice. Indeed, He was the purest expression of Leadership this World has ever known. But rejoice. His Return has been foretold. He will rise to cleanse the Earth in Fire. He will commence the Red Era—a New Dawn. A Second Golden Age will follow.'"

"That's the one," Stan said. "And Brian intends to do it."

I lowered the piece of paper. "Are you saying there's something to this?"

Stan took a deep breath and released it through his nose.

"Ever since I can remember, I've been a dragon nut. Probably started the first time I heard the song *Puff the Magic Dragon*. The whole idea of being friends with a dragon just blew my mind. When Dungeons and Dragons first hit the shelves, I didn't want to be a fighter or a magic-user—no offense. I wanted to be a dragon. You can imagine how stoked I was when they came out with the half-dragon player in the DMG three-point-five edition."

I had no idea what he was talking about but nodded to keep him going.

"When I helped organize the first Epic Con back in 2000, I met a number of others who shared my passion. Together, we started an online forum: Dragon Com. Get it? The forum was a place to pool our knowledge and resources. Through hired sages, we built a comprehensive history of dragonkind across the ages. It was the most awesome thing I've ever been a part of." The joy left his face. "Then Brian Lutz joined the forum."

"When was this?" I asked.

"About a year ago. Man, he was the kind of member you hope *doesn't* end up on your forum. Rude, delusional, arrogant—just an all-around jerk. He claimed to be a high-level magic-user and dragon master. He'd pick fights over this or that in the history, saying he had forgotten more about dragons than the rest of us would ever know. Guy wasn't quite put together. But he never crossed the line into ban-able territory, and all the high-and-mighty aside, he was basically harmless. Or so we thought."

"What changed?" I asked.

"Well, it seemed the guy had money, because he was buying artifacts with supposedly magical properties, posting images of them on the forum. It was obvious the stuff was crap. He took a lot of ridicule for it too. When he went silent for a month, we thought we were finally rid of the guy. But then he comes back with a photo of a new artifact—a 'game-changer' he calls it. We wrote him off, but then he starts posting videos of himself manipulating fire. The tricks were small at first, dancing flames between his fingers, that sort of thing, but they started getting bigger, more complex. One of our forum administrators is a video editor. She said Brian wasn't doctoring the footage. The demonstrations finally reached a point where he'd either hired a special-effects expert, or he was actually manipulating fire."

I thought about the kinds of items that would be able to instill a non-magic-user with flame-controlling abilities but couldn't come up with any off the top of my head.

"He said he was working up to conjuring a dragon," Stan continued. "About that time, his videos caught the interest of another user, someone who posted as 'Cameo.' He argued that Brian lacked the power to control a dragon."

"That's true enough," I remarked.

"They went back and forth. Finally, Cameo said if Brian was serious about conjuring a dragon, he had something Brian could use. Then both of them went silent. After a while, curiosity and this sick feeling in the pit of my gut got the better of me. I used my administrator access to check out their private inboxes. Sure enough, they'd had a lengthy exchange that they later deleted, but it remained in the administrative archives. Cameo started out claiming he had a magic gauntlet that could control dragons."

I thought about the guy in the parade flanking Brian, wearing the ornate gauntlet.

"Brian was doubtful," Stan went on, "but it looked like they got together, ran some tests, summoned some lesser draconic creatures. Over the course of their exchanges, they started opening up about their personal lives. Brian was a software developer who had been forced to sell his share of his company over 'creative differences,' he called them. His wife left him around the same time. "

"That's on his background check," Vega said, consulting her phone. "He was arrested for harassing his ex-wife and threatening to blow up his former company. Judge ordered a psych eval. He did six months at a mental hospital in lieu of jail time."

"Sounds about right," Stan said. "Cameo was in pretty bad shape himself. He graduated college right before the Crash and never found work. Been drowning in debt ever since. They both sounded isolated, angry. They talked more and more about the Lucero Millennium, the Golden Age of Dragons, and in particular about Drage the Wise. They were convinced that the kind of injustices they'd suffered would never have happened under Drage's rule."

"And thus was born the Military Federation of the Dragon," I said.

"Yeah, they wrote their manifesto, put up a website, and started recruiting. Harmless stuff until the discussion turned to trying to summon Drage. Thanks to our work at Dragon Com, they knew Drage the Wise had been murdered by a cabal of dragons in what's now Glogow, Poland. They planned an excavation to recover a bone to conjure from. That's when they deleted their exchange on the forum. Not long after, they claimed on their website that the excavation had been a success. They then began organizing a meetup here at Epic Con, where they would summon Drage, ushering in the Red Era and the second Golden Age."

"You sure it wasn't just talk?" I asked.

"There's one company within fifty miles of Glogow that leases excavation equipment," Stan said. "I called them, and they confirmed that Brian had hired equipment and a crew and spent time at the site. I couldn't get a clear answer as to whether they'd found anything. But, look, we're talking about a conjuring of one of the most powerful dragons that ever lived. I wasn't willing to take any chances, because I don't care what kind of gauntlet Cameo has ... he won't be able to control something like Drage."

Especially with Drage having been dead for thousands of years, I thought. Like forgotten gods, there was no telling what kind of condition he would return in. Probably more zombie than dragon.

"Is that why you hired the lunar fae?" I asked. "To create a distraction while you searched for the bone in Brian's room?"

Stan looked over at the three fae with narrowed eyes and nodded. "I got them passes to the con and put them on standby. I made a few attempts to get into Brian's room, but he had a sentry on his door twenty-four seven. Tried again before his session this morning, but it was another no go. That's when I gave the fae the green light. They went overboard, but that's what happens when you deal with their kind," he snarled.

"Can we go now?" Lialla spoke up from the couch.

Stan looked from them to Vega. "I don't have a problem with that if you guys don't."

"Wait a minute," I said, showing him a hand. "Why did you kick me out of the con?"

"Heh. I thought that thing you took care of on the third floor was one of the fae illusions and that you were going to blow my chance to get into Brian's room. I also needed some, ah, plausible deniability."

"For what?" I asked.

"For bringing down Epic Con. That's why I accused you of working with the fae. So if everything went to shit, no one would suspect I'd had a hand in it."

"The conference's other organizer didn't know what he was planning," Vega explained.

"So, you didn't have someone call me this morning to tell me to come to the con?" I asked Stan.

"No, I don't even know your number. Look, Sherri, my co-organizer is bigtime into sci-fi and fantasy, but she doesn't believe any of it's real. There was no way she was going to buy the whole thing about Brian and Cameo summoning a dragon." He lowered his voice and looked around as if this Sherri might burst in at any moment. "I have a responsibility to act on what I know. If they do manage to summon Drage, a lost con is the least of our worries. But the damned thing backfired. Brian and his crew cleared out."

"Everyone?" I asked. "What about the rest of the Military Federation?"

"Their rooms are empty too. Like they'd been beamed out of time and space."

I directed my next question to Lialla. "Is Stan's account of your involvement accurate?"

She met my gaze and nodded. I looked over at Vega. "I have no problem letting them go."

"Me neither," she said with a sigh. "The fewer we have to deal with right now, the better."

"We'll release you," I told Lialla, "but on the condition you go straight back to your realm."

"Agreed," she said.

Vega unlocked their cuffs and, with Bree-Yark and me covering them, walked them out the door. When they'd left, I cocked my head toward Stan to tell Vega she could uncuff him too. While she did that, I paced the suite, trying to reconcile everything Stan had told me with what I'd seen and learned.

"Can you pull up the image of the artifact Brian posted?" I asked Stan.

"Yeah, might take me a couple minutes to find." He rubbed his wrists, then pulled his phone from his pocket.

I started thinking out loud. "All right, let's go back to the beginning. Brian is a know-it-all magic-user, who doesn't actually know any magic. Dragon obsessed too. He gets ahold of an enchanted object, and he's suddenly able to manipulate fire. Goes from publishing a crap spell book to one with a new section in the back with spells that actually do something." In Nathan's case, he had ended up with a demon, but the fact he'd ended up with a demon of an incendiary strain might have been telling. "Shortly after, he pulls the book from sale. Decides he doesn't want to share his powers with others, maybe. About the same time, this Cameo got into his ear, and they start experimenting with draconic creatures. They found this group, the Military Federation of the Dragon, and start recruiting members."

"Just to feel high and mighty?" Vega asked.

"Maybe," I said. "But I'm thinking it's more than that. To call up a god, which is essentially what they're attempting, you need several things. One of them is a strong belief in the being. And another is a tribute, an offering to the god."

"Human sacrifice?" Bree-Yark asked.

"That's why I think he had them all meet here, at the con," Stan said.

"That and recruiting more members," I agreed. "Making that belief and tribute as powerful as possible."

The door to the suite opened, and Mae came in carrying Buster's pet carrier. I had radioed to inform her of the change in meeting place before arriving here myself. "Sorry it took me so long," she said, a little out of breath. "Got turned around."

"Have a seat," I said. "Bree-Yark will help fill you in."

The goblin rushed over, took the pet carrier, and escorted Mae to the couch where the fae had been.

"We have a main suspect in the conjurings now," I told her. "His name is Brian Lutz, and he's working with someone named Cameo." I directed my voice to everyone now. "So, let's go over the events at the con. This morning, Brian and Cameo gathered with the other members of his Military Federation. They took them to the basement, where Brian summoned a pair of fire-breathing lizards. Beings from the same space as Drage. That would have bolstered the group's belief in Drage. He left the lizards in the casting circles to expire on their own, sealing and warding the doors so no one would find them."

Tabitha snickered, no doubt at the memory of the warded door blasting me off my feet.

I ignored her. "Then Brian held his session on wizardry. This time to create converts to the Military Federation of the Dragon. He packs the room with promises of free-drink tickets and an introduction by Stan the Man over here."

Stan paused in his search to give a sheepish wave.

"Why *did* you do that?" Vega asked.

"Like I said, Brian paid for it. I didn't want to stoke his suspicions by refusing. I admit, I got a little carried away up there with all of this—" He pumped his fists like he'd done on stage that morning.

Vega rolled her eyes.

"When Brian spotted me," I went on, "he not only saw someone he considered a rival, but a chance to make a real impression on his audience. The guy's got charisma in spades. So much so, that I could see its effect on the crowd. But when our duel got underway, he couldn't cast for some reason."

"Yeah, dude," Stan said with a little snort. "I admit, I thought you were gonna be toast."

"Having lost his audience, Brian leaves the session in a huff. But the faith of his Military Federation is threatened now too, so he conjures the second creature, the frog-beast that Buster sensed behind the door." Buster chirped at hearing his name. "Only this time, Brian creates a break in the casting circle so the creature can get out."

"To terrorize everyone?" Mae asked.

"Actually, I think Brian was waiting somewhere nearby to

put it down. You know, be the hero. But we interfered and put it down ourselves. He and Cameo go ahead with their plans to attend the parade, because..." I thought of the way Brian had been marching at the head of his Order, chest thrust out, face beaming with arrogance. "Well, because I think Brian couldn't resist. But they had to be concerned about having enough faith and tributes. When the fae broke up the con, they may have decided to cut their losses, start clearing out—that's why you found the rooms empty—but Brian was determined. The wyvern summoning may have been a last-ditch effort." I gave a dry laugh. "Ambitious as hell, yeah, but it went off beautifully. Brian dispersed the wyvern publicly and very spectacularly, getting him the followers he'd needed. When I tried to interfere, he turned half of them against me and took the other half with him. Question is where in the hell he took them."

"Oh, hey, I found the photo!" Stan said, holding up his device.

I walked over and peered down at the image of the item Brian had acquired.

"Oh, fuck," I said.

29

"What?" Vega said, coming around so she could see the image on Stan's phone too.

Bree-Yark and Mae came up as well. Even Tabitha plodded over and leapt onto the table, craning her thick neck while trying to maintain an expression of barest interest. I dragged a hand through my hair.

"Brian's not performing any magic," I said.

"Then how was he doing all that stuff with the fire?" Stan asked. "And the conjurings?"

"This is a phylactery for holding elementals," I said, tapping the screen. "He used it to summon an efreet. That's what's been doing the heavy lifting."

"An efreet?" Vega asked.

"I should have put it together," I muttered. "Efreets are a kind of genie."

"Like Aladdin and his magic lamp?" Mae asked.

"Very similar, actually. They're powerful elemental beings. Ages ago, dark sorcerers would conjure them, then bind a part of their essences to objects like this one. It was a way to claim ownership, but it was also a faster, more economical way to call them up. Over time, most of the genies broke their bonds to the objects, murdered their owners, and returned to their realm. A few genies remained, their objects either passing hands so many times no one knew what they were anymore or becoming lost altogether. I'm not sure how Brian ended up with this one, luck maybe, but see the inscription here?" The bronze phylactery on the phone was shaped like an oblong crystal. I tightened my aura so I could zoom in on one of the phylactery's faces, where an incantation was inscribed. "That's how he called it up. And this particular genie is an efreet. Their element is fire."

"But I thought you said he had no magical ability," Stan said.

"He doesn't," I replied. "Probably a combination of his charisma, a large enough quotient of the efreet's essence already inside the object, and timing."

"The rips around our world," Vega said, understanding the third factor.

"In fact, I think I know why I couldn't sense the being." I opened a portal to my cubbyhole and withdrew the book with the maps of the layers around our world. Stan watched the whole process wide-eyed, but this was no time to be discreet. "The efreet's realm is here." I displayed one of the maps, even though none of the others could have known what in the hell they were looking at. "It's not far from the Below. When Brian called the efreet, the balance of its essence would have come up through the path of least resistance—the Harkless Rift. Like with the demons, that passage cloaked the efreet's aura and magic."

"So, every time Brian cast, it was actually the efreet?" Stan asked.

"Had to be." I thought about the casting circles, an amalgam of old sorcerer magic and the efreet's protections, which is why I hadn't recognized them. Good thing I hadn't attempted to cast on them. "As an elemental force, it's invisible to everyone but Brian. I doubt he even told Cameo about it."

"Nothing in their exchange," Stan confirmed.

"And with Brian's charisma, he's able to control it," I said. "For now, anyway."

"Then why wasn't Brian able to cast against you this morning?" Vega asked.

I stopped to consider that. "You know, that's a really good question."

"The important question is where Brian went," Stan said. "According to the website, they were going to try to summon Drage tomorrow night, but I've got a feeling they've moved everything up."

"Right," I agreed. "Might not have wanted to take a chance on losing their support."

"But how many people did they recruit?" Mae asked. She knew a thing or two about magic from her year of research on the subject. "If it was just a hundred or so, is that going to be enough belief?"

"Well, they have the most important components: the bone, the efreet, and the tribute. The efreet just might have to work a little harder to call up..." My voice trailed off as another piece of understanding snapped into place.

"What is it?" Vega asked.

"The efreet is the vessel the demons are after," I said. "Sefu is the name Brian gave it—a made-up name, probably after a D&D character he created. That's why it didn't register with me or anyone in the Order. But demons could easily have heard the name as the efreet was being summoned through the Harkless Rift. The race was on then to find and possess it."

"They can do that?" Mae asked. "I mean, possess an elemental?"

"With the kind of energy Brian is asking the efreet to call up, the phylactery won't be a sufficient channel. The efreet will need to take physical form, become a channel itself. That's the one case where a demon can possess an efreet."

"Why don't the demons just take the phylactery?" Vega asked.

"They could, but it wouldn't do them any good." I reached into my cubbyhole again and produced another reference book. "Once an owner becomes master of an efreet, they're its master for life." I flipped between a couple sections as I spoke, a skill I'd picked up during my ten years as a professor. "And it says here that the efreet can't be relinquished by the owner or stolen away. Indeed, it requires powerful and highly specialized magic to undo that bond, something the demons don't possess."

I could see Bree-Yark trying to think like a demon. "So, why not just kill Brian?"

"That would terminate the contract, yeah, but the efreet would then sleep for a hundred years—or longer—before it could be called up again. And the demons want its power *now*. That's where the form becomes important. Because demons are from the same general area"—I gestured to the strange map again—"they can possess that form. For the same reason, demons are immune to the efreet's power, which puts them in super-exclusive company. With the possession, the demon doesn't just inhabit the efreet, but fuses with it, creating another being entirely. One with advanced demonic powers and an inexhaustible supply of elemental energy." I remembered what the pump-house demon had said about his master smiting their competition. "One that can even kill other demons."

I didn't want to think about the *human* destruction a being like that could wreak.

"So do you think that's what Arianna meant by Sefu being concealed now but the situation changing?" Vega asked.

"I do. The manifestation of the efreet's form will send shockwaves through the ether, calling all demons within a hundred-mile radius. They'll stop at nothing to claim that kind of power." I read a little more. "Oh, great."

"What?" Vega asked.

I paused to finish the section. "It would also mean we'd have to handle Brian with extreme care. I mean, like literally swaddle him in bubble wrap and stick him in a padded cell. The efreet's form carries a ton of energy that it needs to burn off before it can return to the phylactery. That can take weeks. If Brian were killed, though, the efreet's form would be pulled back to the phylactery, ready or not. Meaning that energy would discharge all at once. We'd be talking a massive explosion."

"How massive?" Vega asked.

"According to this, massive enough to level mountains, rattle the tectonic plates, and send up a plume of dust so thick it could kick off the next Ice Age. Of course, none of us would be around to enjoy the cooler summers."

Mae shook her head and made a *tsk*ing sound.

"Can we get back to the dragon?" Stan asked nervously.

As I'd been talking, the prospect of a resurrected dragon, even one as powerful as Drage, was paling in comparison to the literal hell that could follow with the efreet and demons. And *that* was saying something.

"Don't worry," I told him. "To prevent the efreet from taking form, we'll definitely need to stop the conjuring. Do we know where they were planning to summon Drage? Was there any info on their website?"

Stan shook his head. "It said everything would be revealed at the con."

"Dammit." I checked my phone to see if I had any new messages. "Someone called me this morning and told me to come to the hotel. Said there was going to be a conjuring in the basement and that I was the only one who could stop it. If it wasn't you," I said, nodding at Stan, "then I'm thinking there's a defector in their ranks."

"Have they been back in contact?" Vega asked.

"No, and that's bothering me. Someone walked in at the end of their call this morning. If it was Brian or Cameo and they caught on to what this person was doing, they might have taken care of them."

"And no one's come up to you at the con?" Vega pressed.

I started to shake my head, then stopped, remembering the young man at the back of the Military Federation of the Dragon's formation, the one who had pushed the envelope into my hands.

Had he been trying to give me a message?

I pulled out the envelope again and looked it and the manifesto over. No other writing besides what I'd already read. My gaze fell to the red ticket sitting at the bottom of the envelope, good for a free drink.

"Someone did give me this," I said lifting out the ticket.

When I turned it over, I noticed a faint thumb print staining the reverse side. Whether or not the print was intentional, I could use it.

I showed the print to the others.

"Human oil," I said. "It makes a strong agent for a hunting spell."

I PREPARED THE SPELL IN THE LARGER OF THE SUITE'S TWO bathrooms. It featured a jacuzzi tub and enough counter space for a small village. Plenty of floor space too. That's where I sprinkled out two casting circles, one for the drink ticket and another for my own protection, featuring powerful protective sigils.

As I worked, I caught myself wondering about the young

man who had given me the envelope. The same person who had called me that morning? That voice had belonged to a woman—unless he'd disguised his own. If so, who was he? How had he gotten my number? And why hadn't he contacted me directly again?

Something about it didn't add up, which put me on guard.

I stood within my protective circle and incanted until I felt power coursing through it. I then aimed the opal end of my cane at the ticket in the circle opposite me and spoke a second incantation. White light swelled from the gem. A moment later, a thin mist began to rise from the oil of the thumb print. It moved in a twisting path toward my gem, becoming absorbed into the hunting spell.

Now for your location, I thought.

Without warning, the ticket burst into flames—and then the entire bathroom.

I instinctively threw up a shield, but nothing manifested. Panicked, I looked down to make sure my protective circle was still intact. But I was standing on a black precipice, swollen rivers of fire leaping and thrashing on all sides.

Everything was fire. The land, the sky, the air crackling in and out of my lungs.

The power was violent and immense. For a dizzying moment, I hungered to control it, to bend it to my will. The magic I would be able to manifest ... The people I would be able to protect ... Vega, Tony, her family. The idea set off every nerve ending in my body as I burned with the need. It was reminiscent of my encounter with Sathanas two years before. I actually began pulling the fire into me before reason took hold.

Who in the hell am I kidding? The fire would eat me alive.

At that thought, the precipice began to crumble. I staggered back, but I was too slow. The ground disappeared, and I plummeted toward the raging rivers of molten.

"Disfare!" I shouted.

Energy detonated out in all directions, and I landed hard.

The bathroom took form around me, the tile floor hard and cool beneath my cheek. I pushed myself up to sitting. Sweat ran from my hair and soaked through my shirt. I stripped off my coat and sat panting, arms hugging my knees. I'd fallen out of the casting circle. My cane lay beside the jacuzzi, smoke drifting from the opal. In the other casting circle, the ticket had been reduced to ashes.

Crap.

Whether the defector had intended for me to use the ticket to track him or not, the efreet had built a literal firewall around their location. Oil, sweat, hair, a severed hand—it wouldn't matter. No matter how potent the target material, nothing in my spell arsenal was going to be able to punch through that wall.

Hell, I'd barely made it back here.

I stood and paced the room on shaky legs. Brian and his Military Federation could be well into the ceremony to conjure Drage, and here I was in another bathroom.

I stopped and tried to listen to my magic. But it was still doing that head-nodding thing, telling me I was on the right track, that I had what I needed.

The hell I do, I shot back.

I pulled out my phone and dialed Claudius, but the call went immediately to voicemail. I left a message and then pulled the Upholders' card from my shirt pocket. Arianna had said my *first* action shouldn't be with them, but we were well beyond that. I looked at the card for another moment before dialing the phone number, Malachi's I assumed. The line rang several times, but no one answered.

I clapped the phone closed.

"Fuck!" I shouted, sending the obscenity ringing off the walls.

Outside, I heard the murmurs of a conversation go quiet. A moment later, a soft knock sounded on the door. I turned to find Vega looking in. Her gaze went from the ashes in the casting circle to me.

"Everything all right?" she asked.

I waved her inside, and she closed the door behind her. "The hunting spell was a bust," I confessed, dropping my phone back into a pocket. "The efreet set up a perimeter that I can't get through. Just trying to figure out if there's another way to know where they are. The Order's still AWOL."

Vega walked past me, brow furrowed in thought, and took a seat on the edge of the jacuzzi.

"I noticed you're not wearing the pendant," I said, unable to stop myself. The manic burst of relief at her being alive was tempering now, exposing an underlying annoyance at her for not holding onto the powerful protection.

She looked down at the place where the pendant would have been sitting. "I gave it to Tony last night."

"Why?"

"A mother's intuition," she said, voice tight with defiance.

A part of me wanted to give her an earful. Instead, I sighed and took a seat beside her.

"Look, I get it," I said. "You wanted more protection for Tony. But you left yourself vulnerable. What if that enchantment had been real? I wouldn't have been able to do a damned thing. There's no way I would have gotten back here in time."

Her shoulder stiffened when I began to massage it, but it softened again. She leaned against me. "I didn't mean to scare you, but as long as Arnaud's out there, the pendant's staying with Tony."

"Fair enough. But what about you?"

"I have a 9mm duty weapon armed with silver rounds."

Something told me that wouldn't be enough, not against whatever Arnaud was becoming. I didn't say that, though.

"What is that?" Vega asked.

I realized I was still holding the card from the Upholders, turning it over in my fingers, flipping between the phone number and the sigil. I thought about my meeting with Vega's brothers, their demand that I quit seeing her.

I stopped turning the card. "An opportunity to protect you and Tony."

Vega peered up at me, the skin between her eyebrows folding in question.

"I met with a group last night. They're dealing with demon incursions and want to form a sort of mutual-protection organization. I help them, and they help me. Malachi's involved. He was the acolyte at St. Martin's when the demon lord possessed the vicar." Vega nodded that she remembered. "His involvement gives the organization the backing of the interfaith community, and that means a spot in their safehouses. There are no more secure places in the cities. If I join, I can get you and Tony in."

"What's the catch?" Vega asked.

"Like I said, I help them, and they help me. But in that order."

"So, you'd have to, what, bail on this thing with Brian and the efreet?"

"Not necessarily." I remembered the face Malachi had made when Jordan spelled out the terms of the agreement, as if the druid were being unreasonable. It was something I had been revisiting a lot that day. "The others in the group may not like it, but I think I can convince Malachi to give us those spaces *and* let me complete my work here." That was what I'd been hoping to talk to him about when I called him just now.

"I know that doubtful look in your eyes," Vega said.

"Well, the agreement would be bonded by magic." I indicated the sigil on the card with my thumb. "And if I'm wrong..."

"You could be pulled off this," Vega concluded.

"Yeah."

"Then forget it," she said.

"Even if means protecting—?"

"We have a powerful instinct to protect our loved ones," she cut in. "That's natural. But so does everyone, Everson. If we start putting our priorities first, we're abusing our positions. Me as a sworn NYPD officer, and you as a member of the Order. Look, I want Tony to be safe more than anyone. But if there's even a *chance* that getting him a place in a safehouse jeopardizes what we discussed in the other room, forget it. Could you live with that? The death, the destruction, the rampant *fear*? All because we put something of ours first? I couldn't. And that's something my brothers will never understand."

I cracked a smile.

"What?"

I kissed her and slipped the Upholder's card back into my shirt pocket. "I think that's exactly what I needed to hear. But now comes the hard part. Figuring out where Brian and the efreet went." I could feel the clock ticking on the dragon conjuring, the efreet taking form, the demonic race to reach it...

"Doesn't your teacher keep telling you to listen to your magic?" Vega asked. "What's it saying?"

I tuned in to it again. "That I have everything I need."

"Then I'll get the others ready," Vega said, standing.

"But I don't know what in the hell it's talking about."

"You will," she said simply, and closed the door behind her.

I stood, wishing I had Vega's confidence in me. But she was also telling me I needed space to think, something I'd had precious little of since being awakened by the anonymous caller that morning.

Still on the edge of the jacuzzi, I bowed my head and replayed the call in my mind, listened to the voice. It belonged to a woman, not a man disguising his voice. I was sure of that now. There were women in Brian's Military Federation, but the person who had given me the envelope had been a man. A different person, in other words.

I replayed that moment, watching the flicker behind the young man's vacant eyes. I then considered Vega's question about why Brian hadn't been able to cast against me that morning.

"Unless they *were* the same," I whispered.

My magic stopped moving and gave a pair of hard nods.

I stood suddenly, grabbed my coat from the floor, and dug in the pocket until I was holding the envelope again. What if the point of giving me the envelope hadn't been the drink ticket, but the manifesto?

I unfolded the single sheet of paper and turned it over to the blank back.

I drew a lighter from my pants pocket. Holding my breath, I thumbed the wheel.

The flame glowed through the paper. Several seconds passed before something began to happen.

"Well, I'll be damned," I said.

30

I emerged from the bathroom, holding up the manifesto triumphantly. Vega, Mae, Bree-Yark, and Stan met me at the table in the center of the suite, where I set the manifesto down to display the writing on the back. Tabitha, who had turned half the table into her personal lounging area, sauntered over for a closer look.

"What is this?" Stan asked.

"The Military Federation of the Dragon's schedule for the con," I replied. "But made invisible to the uninitiated. Brian used the same technique in the final section of his spell book. It can only be revealed by fire. They had events scheduled for both days—meetings and 'validations,' they called them—all of it culminating in this." I tapped the last item on the schedule.

"'The New Dawn,'" Vega read.

Stan nodded fervently. "That's the summoning of Drage."

I moved my finger down the page. "And we have an address."

"That's an old quarry up in West Nyack," Vega said. "About thirty miles from here."

"How fast can the NYPD get us there?" I asked.

"I'll call in some helos," she said, pulling out her phone. "They can have us up there in ten."

While Vega made the call, I considered the location. "Quarry makes sense," I remarked. "Concealed, but plenty of room."

"And they're going to need it," Stan put in. "Do you know how big Drage was? We're talking the size of a city block."

"Well, the idea is not to let them get that far," I said.

Mae shifted uncomfortably. "What about the efreet? If it's working for Brian…"

"Actually, I'm pretty sure we're on the same side."

The others looked at me quizzically. Even Tabitha tilted her head.

"The person who called me this morning and the person who gave me this"—I indicated the schedule—"were different. But I believe they were both under the control of the efreet. Though efreets can't challenge their masters outright, they're constantly looking for ways to undermine them. Powerful sorcerers knew this and put fail safes in place before summoning the efreet. But even if he'd had that kind of foresight, Brian didn't have the power. Just his charisma. I think he realized the efreet had phoned someone," I said, remembering the second voice I'd heard in the background of that morning's call. "I think he put stricter controls on its contact with people. The efreet could no longer communicate with me, but it was able to give me the program with the secret schedule."

"What do you mean by being on the same side?" Bree-Yark asked.

"More an overlapping of interests. If the efreet kills Brian, it will go to sleep, but still be bonded to the phylactery. The efreet wants to be permanently freed, and it sees me as the best path. It probably tapped into Brian's mind to learn about me in the first place, then used his computer skills to find my number."

Vega ended her call, but had had an ear on our conversation, apparently. "Even so, what's to stop Brian from ordering it to attack you?"

"It ignored Brian's order to attack me at the session this morning," I pointed out.

"And you don't think Brian made sure that wouldn't happen again?"

"It's a risk I've considered, but with the efreet seeing me as an asset, it's going to pull every stop to help me help it. And again, Brian's no sorcerer."

Vega's expression told me she was only half reassured. "The helos will be here in five. Because there are officers involved, the NYPD wants in. I've already told them this is a supernatural case," she quickly added, before I could argue about their inclusion. "I'll keep them out of your way."

That relaxed my shoulders a little. The last thing I needed was for the NYPD to try to take the lead on this. I looked over my team. My mind was already coming up with reasons for why I didn't need them on the final push—until I remembered what Vega had said about my habit of going it alone.

One person—or wizard—can only shoulder so much.

She seemed to have been following my train of thought, because she looked at me pointedly and cocked her head toward my teammates.

"All right," I said to the group. "Who else is in?"

Bree-Yark raised a hand. "Just need to stop off at the Hummer for some more ordnance."

Mae's hands wrung the handle of her carrier. It was the having to fly part.

"Look, Mae, I'll understand if—"

"No," she said, looking up. "I don't know what I can do to help, but I didn't know what I'd be able to do at Yankee Stadium either. And like I said then, I'm an old woman who's only going to get older sitting around. I'm in too."

"Good," I said. "Tabitha? I could use you on demon watch."

She responded to the sudden attention with her irritated face.

"You've come this far," Mae pointed out.

"Yeah, and I still owe you a dinner for doing lunch today," Bree-Yark put in.

"Fine," Tabitha huffed, then turned to me. "But I'm off ledge duty for the next month."

"Fair enough." I gathered my things. "Let's move out."

"Hey, what about me?" Stan asked.

I stopped near the doorway and waved the others past. Stan had stood from the table. Even though he had to be pushing sixty, he wore the expression of a child who hadn't been picked to play kickball.

"It's going to be a scene," I said.

"And I'll just be one more person in the way."

There was no point sugar-coating it. "Yeah. But you got us to this point. The info on Brian, Cameo, the gauntlet, Drage, the Military Federation of the Dragon. Vital, vital stuff. The fae enchantment was kind of screwed up..."

He snorted. "I guess that *was* kind of screwed up. Probably not worth the five years off my life either."

"You gave them five years?"

"Each. So, actually fifteen."

I whistled.

"Yeah," he agreed.

At that moment, a stocky woman pushed past me, her face red as a ham. "I leave the con for thirty minutes, and I come back to this?" she screamed. "The sessions are derailed! The hotel's a mess! There's talk of monsters and murder and mass illusions! Attendees are leaving! What in the hell have you been doing?

I raised a hand to Stan. "Hey, ah, it sounds like you have some things to take care of here."

He gave me an aggrieved look but waved for me to go ahead. I closed the door on more screaming. No wonder he'd wanted plausible deniability.

I was hustling to catch up to the others when my phone rang. I fished it out of a pocket.

"Claudius," I answered, recognizing the number. "Just the person I was hoping to talk to."

"Yes, Everson, I'm so sorry. I received your message, but I've been getting so many. I think it all caught up to me, and I, well, I fell asleep."

"Any word from the Order?"

"Nothing lately. I'm starting to get a little worried, Everson. I—"

"All right, don't worry about them right now," I cut in. "I need you for something."

He stopped suddenly, as if I'd smacked the top of his head. "You mean, you'd like me to pass on a message?"

"No, Claudius, I need *you*."

"Me? Whatever for?"

"Just listen."

"What do you want me to do?" the cabbie asked.

Arnaud shifted in the backseat for a better look. Something was happening. Two blocks ahead, beyond a police barricade, helicopters were setting down on the street in front of the Centre Hotel. This must have been what the wizard and detective were involved in. Arnaud stiffened.

A person had just stepped from the hotel and was moving

toward the lead helicopter. Arnaud recognized the tall figure and batting coat.

Everson Croft.

The wizard's cat was with him, trailing from a leash. The detective followed. Behind them appeared a stout figure—a goblin, Arnaud realized. No doubt the one whose leathery scent he'd picked up earlier. The goblin was helping a large woman, whom Arnaud recognized from Yankee Stadium. His sharp teeth scraped together. She had taken control of the imps and devils who were to have helped feed his return to the world.

"Well?" the cabbie said.

"Silence!" Arnaud snapped. "I'm not paying you for your boorish talk!"

If he hadn't needed the man, he might have ended him right there. Arnaud ordered him to remain, not even bothering with the pretense of payment this time. He stepped from the cab and walked toward the barricade, his stride no longer a shuffling hobble. He was growing stronger, more fluid, but what good was it if he lost the wizard again? If he forfeited his chance to claim this Sefu before the others?

Arnaud reached one of the officers managing the cordon as the helicopters began to lift off.

"What's happening here?" Arnaud asked pleasantly. "Where are they headed to in those whirligigs?"

The officer remained staring past him, his thick arms crossed at his chest. The man's insolence coupled with the sound of the helicopters batting away sent a spike of rage through Arnaud. He seized the officer's throat and drew the man's face to his.

"*Tell me where they're going,*" he demanded in a demonic voice.

As the officer's eyes found his, Arnaud could all but see the surge of irrational fear short-circuiting the man's training to light up his reptilian brain. There was charming, and then there was horrifying.

"R-Russell Quarries, up in West Nyack," he stammered. "Some sort of hostage situation."

Arnaud squeezed until the man gargled, then shoved him away. Though he had the location, a red-hot anger continued to thrash inside him. Part way into his turn from the officer, Arnaud stopped and looked back.

"I want you to go to your car," he told him quietly, "count to thirty, insert your service weapon into your mouth, as far as it will go—yes, until you're positively choking on it—and pull the trigger."

Back in the cab, Arnaud gave the location to the driver.

"I know where that is," the driver said, executing a three-point turn. "I can have you there in forty."

"I do need you to hurry," Arnaud said calmly. "I apologize for erupting at you earlier. Zarko and I have had a trying day."

"No prob. Hey, what did you say to that officer back there?"

"Officer?" Arnaud had all but forgotten about him. "Oh, I just gave the man a little life advice."

"Huh," the cabbie grunted and turned a corner.

Behind them, a gun banged.

31

I pushed through the undergrowth that had taken root in the berm of earth surrounding Russell Quarry, swearing silently as brambles snagged my coat. I crawled the final feet to the top and parked on my forearms beside a bush. A few seconds later, Vega arrived next to me. I whispered an invocation to deepen the shadows that concealed us.

"Anything we missed from the air?" she asked, taking in the massive stone quarry below.

We had done one pass at high altitude to make sure we had the right place. We did. The scene now looked much as it had through binoculars from 5,000 feet. About a half dozen NYPD officers were positioned around the berm to act as lookout for Brian. Farther below, beyond small mountains of earth and stone, lizards patrolled the roads that switch-backed down. I didn't need to go closer to know they burped fire.

At the very bottom, standing around a large basalt-colored pond were the robed figures of Brian and the rest of the Military Federation of the Dragon. Their unwitting tributes stood behind them, numbering well over a hundred. Strange draconic chants echoed off the steep, excavated walls. The sound alone raked me with chills. In my wizard's senses, I could see the power building in the pool.

"Looks like we accounted for everyone," I replied. "And every*thing*. But we're going to need to hurry."

Vega nodded. She had donned a SWAT vest and helmet, and now she spoke in a low voice into the second. The NYPD had wanted to swarm the quarry and subdue Brian and his group with force in order to get their officers to safety. Fortunately, we were able to convince them of the awfulness of the idea.

When Vega finished, she said, "Everyone's in position. They're awaiting your word."

I looked around the berm again. Though spaced over a hundred yards apart, the enthralled officers were in sight of one another. The timing needed to be exact to take them out without alerting anyone in the quarry. I didn't want to hurt them, either. The NYPD officers weren't themselves.

I took a deep breath, pulling in as much ley energy as I could contain while forming a Word in my mind. Even with the chanting echoing from below, and the power continuing to build from the pool, I let my eyelids slide close. I locked in on the officer's positions, then on the officers themselves. It wasn't until I felt everything align—energy, breath, magic—that I released the Word.

"*Vigore.*"

The force from my cane split in six different directions, homing in on their targets.

As the force invocation ripped six guns from the officers' grips, I spoke a second Word. The air around the officers' heads hardened, muting their surprised shouts and making their available oxygen very, very finite. I arrested their arms and legs before they could begin thrashing—attention we didn't need.

I gave Vega a thumb's up.

"Now," she said into her radio.

Moments later, SWAT team members broke through the brush behind the officers and pulled them out of sight. I dropped my eyes to the pool, but there was no sign the Military Federation of the Dragon was aware they had just lost their upper sentry.

The officers would be okay. I had calibrated my shield invocations to dissolve in about ninety seconds, the time it would take for them to lose consciousness, taking into account exertion. By the time they came to, the officers would be safely away from the quarry and no longer under Brian's control.

That took care of the NYPD's biggest concern—getting their personnel back.

Now, thanks to Vega digging in her heels with her department, we had carte blanche to stop the summoning and free the tributes. The remaining NYPD on the scene would serve in a backup capacity. Already, snipers were taking positions around the berm. I couldn't see them, but that was the point.

"The officers are safely away," Vega whispered. "How are you doing?"

"That took a bit of power, but I still have plenty in the tank." I pulled a stealth potion from a coat pocket and activated it. I could see Vega's concern in my peripheral vision as I drank the sludgy potion down.

"Be careful," she said.

"If we execute like we discussed, we'll be fine," I said, drawing a sleeve across my mouth.

I rose, secured my coat, and moved to the edge of what must have been a two-hundred-foot drop. The plummet would land me behind a small range of heaped-up earth, well below the lizard sentry and only a short run to the summoning ceremony. Vega and I had discussed knocking Brian out from a distance, but it was too risky. The efreet could repel the attack and help Brian escape through another portal. Getting close was my best chance to get the phylactery from Brian. Maybe my *only* chance.

Vega reached up and squeezed my arm. The X factor remained the efreet, and we both knew it. If I'd guessed wrong about it being the one to have reached out to me—and why—I'd have a major fight on my hands. One I probably wouldn't win.

On that question, my magic didn't have much to say.

"I'll be all right," I reassured Vega, my voice already becoming insubstantial. When Vega pawed up and down my arm, unsure whether she was still holding it, I knew the stealth potion had taken effect.

She withdrew her hand, and I stepped off the edge of the precipice.

The force of the drop peeled my coat up to my belt. My potions and spell items had to be rattling, if not smashing together, but wrapped in an aura of stealth, they didn't make a sound. I struggled against my coat while trying to keep my cane aimed between my feet. Wind blasted past my ears.

With the ground coming up fast, I began pulsing out a series of force invocations to stall my descent. The Words boomed inside my head as if I were shouting them with my ears plugged. Small craters appeared behind the mounds below. The final invocation gave me a fresh fall from ten feet up. Even so, my legs collapsed on impact, and I landed hard on my side. But all without a sound.

When I looked up through the dust, the quarry spun several times.

It took me a moment to make out Vega's head. I'm not sure what, if anything, *she* could make out. That was the main drawback to the stealth plan: no one could see whether I was in trouble. To call for help, I would have to dispel the potion first, forfeiting the element of surprise.

"He's here," Vega radioed me.

Good, I thought, *everything's on track. Just need to get my hands on the phylactery.*

I stood and straightened my pockets, then crept around the mounds until I had a view of the quarry. The lizards were still patrolling the levels above, smoke snorting from their nostrils. One level below me, the ceremony continued. Brian was facing the vast pool of water, chanting with his face reared skyward, arms held out to the sides. A section of petrified bone, the size of a loaf of bread, lay at his feet.

Behind and to one side stood Cameo, the fist with the dragon gauntlet braced across his chest. The rest of the Military Federation, several in headdresses, and the hundred-odd tributes repeated each chant from the bottoms of their diaphragms, unaware they were calling up something that would devour them.

The pool eddied with strange energies and spawned occasional bubbles.

My gaze shifted back to Brian. There were several ways to disrupt the ceremony, but the key to stopping the summoning *and* preventing the demons from possessing the efreet was the phylactery. Problem was, I couldn't see it. I couldn't sense it, either, thanks to the cloaking effect of the efreet passing through the Harkless Rift. But there was a small mound beneath Brian's robe at his chest.

That has to be it.

I tuned into my magic for a second opinion, but the cloaking effect seemed to be confounding it too. Steeling my breath, I drew my cane apart and aimed my sword at Brian's chest. Though I'd had recent experience with this very maneuver, my hand trembled. I was taking a big chance here.

"*Vigore!*" I called.

The force invocation snagged the chain around his neck. I drew back on the sword. Brian's chant broke off as the force yanked him forward. The chain snapped, saving him from plunging headfirst into the pool. The necklace whipped through the air. I caught it and brought it down to inspect.

Oh, c'mon!

This wasn't the phylactery in the photo Stan had shown me. From a sterling chain that had been sculpted to look like little branches and leaves hung a twenty-sided die. Probably something Brian wore while presiding over D&D games as the Dungeon Master.

When I looked back up, Brian had regained his footing. He peered wildly around. Still wrapped in my stealth potion, I remained invisible to him. I then witnessed the difference between an accomplished sorcerer and an amateur: instead of using the efreet's powers to reveal his attacker, Brian panicked.

"Abandon the conjuring!" he cried.

Tucking the bone into the crook of his arm like a football, he balled up his robe at the waist and hustled toward a portal. From above, I hadn't seen the symbol in the vertical rock wall, but it was pulsing now, growing.

I aimed my sword at Brian, but the rest of the crowd closed in behind him, blocking my shot.

Dammit. I dug through my pockets—I had to close the portal, prevent his escape—before remembering I was out of neutralizing potions. Realizing something, I switched to my pants pocket and emerged with my flip phone. The neutralizing spell continued to hum around it, protecting its circuitry from energy spikes. A part of me hated what I was about to do. I'd become attached to the little phone.

"*Vigore!*" I shouted.

The force invocation ripped the phone from my grip and slung it toward the portal. As it shot over the tributes' heads, I followed up with an invocation to release the phone's neutralizing spell. White light exploded from the device and into the portal. The portal fell apart with a sound like shattering glass. An instant later, the phone bounced off the rock in pieces, and Brian nearly ran face first into a solid wall.

His escape thwarted, he spun around, searching wildly again. My invocations must have burned through the potion, because this time, his eyes locked on mine. When he thrust his wand at me, I braced myself. But like at the morning's session, nothing happened. I'd made a good gamble. The efreet wasn't attacking.

I wasn't out of the woods yet, though. The lizards had noticed the commotion and, with low grunts and plumes of fire, began scrambling down the sides of the quarry. Meanwhile, Brian was waving his followers toward me.

"Stop him!" he shrieked. "Stop the imposter wizard!"

"Plan B," I called into my radio, my voice more substantial now. "Commence plan B."

"Roger that," Vega answered.

I would have to trust my teammates now. Willing a shield around me, I ignored the descending lizards and mob scene and focused on Brian. He was staying low, trying to use his followers as a human shield. With an invocation, I parted them like the Red Sea.

Exposed, Brian cowered back and jabbed his wand ineffectually. Though I was itching to blast him into next week, I couldn't chance getting fancy.

"Protezione," I uttered.

An orb, like the ones I'd used for the officers, formed around his head. When my magic spiked in warning, I spun to find Cameo running in from my blind side, his hood blown back. He was younger than Brian and thinner. Nothing in his appearance suggested the handle 'Cameo,' though I wasn't sure what would. With determined eyes, he reared back the fist bearing the heavy gauntlet.

In what was becoming a favorite counter attack, I met his intent to cold-cock me with a staff shot to the gut, a force invocation crackling down the length of wood. The blast sent him through the air and splashing into the pool. His robe immediately took on water, and he began to thrash.

"Help!" he cried.

From the sides of the berm, dull thuds sounded. Tear gas canisters arced through the air and began tumbling around us. The gases they spewed sent Brian's followers running and gagging in all directions.

Brian fell to his knees. He might have been protected from the gas, thanks to my shield invocation, but he was also short on oxygen. And damned if he wasn't still thrusting his wand at me, determined for something—*anything*—to happen.

A grunt sounded, and hot fire broke over my shield. But it hadn't come from Brian.

I spun toward the source and swore. The first of the lizards had reached me. Clinging to the side of a wall, its throat leapt as it prepared for another blast. I beat the lizard to it, hitting the creature with a force blast that knocked it from its perch. I then spun and nailed two more incoming lizards, sending them flying off.

I'm wasting power, dammit. Where's the rest of Plan B?

At that moment, a helicopter appeared over the rim of the quarry and dipped down, batting the tear gas around. *Better late than never,* I thought. A voice boomed from the chopper's sound system.

"Stop going after that man!" Mae called. *"Leave him alone!"*

The lizards that had been scrambling toward me halted in their tracks and craned their necks around. They were on the lower end of the spectrum of what Brian and the efreet could conjure—certainly not on the order of the frog-beast—but would Mae's abilities have power over them?

"*I want you to go into that cave over there,*" she ordered them. "*Right where that light's shining.*" The helicopter's search light was centering over a deep opening in the side of one of the rock walls, where it looked like a hydraulic shovel had gone digging. The lizards' necks craned from Mae toward the cave.

"*Go on!*" she shouted.

The lizard that had been closest to me turned and scrambled in the direction of the cave, stopped, then scrambled again. Miraculously, the others followed. Before long, the twenty-odd lizards were crammed into the back of the deep recess, their flickering eyes peering out like chastised children.

"Well done, Mae!" I radioed.

"*Anytime, honey. You got it from here?*"

"Yes, ma'am."

Thrusting my sword above the lizards, I shouted, "*Forza Dura!*"

The force invocation plowed into the rock wall like a 747 jet. The cave collapsed, along with half the rock face.

"*Goodness, I guess you do,*" Mae radioed as the helicopter lifted away from the great plume of dust.

With the lizards buried and the Military Federation of the Dragon and its tributes in disarray, I turned back to Brian. He had stopped trying to wand-attack me and was pawing at the orb around his head, mouthing something. I hustled toward him through the loose sand and gravel, determined to find the phylactery. But in a burst of flames, the orb vanished from Brian's head. The dispersed magic returned to me in a hot blast.

Brian took a heaving breath and shouted, "Protect me!"

A wall of fire burst up around him and the pond, the force of its heat knocking me backwards. I regained my footing and cast a force invocation to grab Brian. But the fire incinerated my magic before it could penetrate the wall. With another invocation, I attempted to enclose the fire in a shield and squeeze it out of existence. But no sooner than I'd manifested the shield, a sensation like molten lava ripped through me.

I dispersed the shield with a cry, surprised to find I wasn't a charred husk.

"What's happening down there?" Vega asked.

It took me a moment to get my breath. "Brian just realized he can't use the efreet to attack me, so he's using it defensively." I started digging through my coat pockets. "He's encased himself in a wall of fire."

"Looks like a dome from up here," Vega said. *"Should we take a shot?"*

She was referring to the police snipers. The ideal scenario was to keep Brian alive, but we had also agreed that if he endangered lives, we would drop him. I didn't like the current setup, though. Even if the snipers' bullets could penetrate the fire barrier, they would be shooting blindly, and there were tributes inside.

I seized a vial of ice crystals and pulled it out.

"Hold off," I said. "I'm going to try something."

As I removed the lid, I heard Brian take up his chanting again. Incredibly, he was trying to finish the dragon-summoning ceremony.

"Ghioccio!" I called, aiming the vial at the fire barrier.

The cone of sub-zero frost that blasted out met the barrier with a loud hiss and billowing plume of steam. But unlike with the wyvern, the cold spell had no real effect. As the vial petered out and the steam lifted off, the manifested fire remained. Hell, what did I expect? I was going up against a powerful efreet.

Brian continued to chant, the flames and heat seeming to excite his voice and give it more power. I dug desperately through my pockets, but nothing I encountered was going to do a damned thing.

I was gathering power for another force invocation, a

stronger one, when the fire barrier dropped suddenly. Brian was standing at the edge of the pool, a water-logged Cameo slouched beside him. The tributes and members of the Military Federation of the Dragon were scattered, still recovering from the effects of the tear gas. But Brian had an expression on his face like he was somehow back in control.

Had he completed the summoning?

I looked down, but nothing stirred in the pool.

"*Vigore!*" I shouted, releasing the gathered invocation at Brian.

From nowhere, a tall woman appeared in front of him. She was black skinned with radiant auburn hair and flames set back in her dark eyes. My invocation broke around her in a flash of fire. The woman strode forward, but I knew it was no woman.

This was Sefu, the efreet.

32

For a moment, I could only stare at the efreet, the embodiment of elemental fire. Though she wore no clothes, her female form appeared as if it had been molded from obsidian and then smoothed over to remove the anatomical details. Looking at her was like looking on the face of a god, and she was beautiful. Not in any human way, but in the way a full-spectrum sunset or the majesty of the Milky Way on a cold, moonless night deep in the woods can steal your breath. She was that kind of beautiful.

But she had taken form in our world, and that scared the shit out of me.

"Is that who I think it is?" Vega radioed.

"Yes," I said. "The snipers need to back off. Now."

With the efreet out, a bullet through Brian's head would result in one of the biggest detonations since the impact of the Chicxulub asteroid that wiped out the dinosaurs. Naturally, Brian had no clue he'd just made himself the detonator.

"I told you I was the superior wizard," he taunted.

"Listen to me," I said, my eyes still on the efreet, who looked back at me without expression. "You're dealing with something you know nothing about and that you haven't the power to control."

"Then what do you call what I'm doing?" he shot back, still hiding behind the efreet.

"Shut up and listen. That phylactery in your possession. What do you think happened to the sorcerers who owned it before you? When the efreet got tired of doing their bidding, she found ways to kill them."

I heard him swallow. "Well, then they were weak."

"They were sorcerers, Brian. They commanded real magic. She'll do the same to you, but in a fraction of the time." I was exaggerating a little. She would wait until she was back in the phylactery first.

"No, she won't."

"Give me the phylactery," I said.

"Oh, so *you* can control her?" He snorted a derisive laugh. "Not a chance."

"No, so I can return her to her realm where she belongs."

By unbonding the efreet from the phylactery, the being could go straight home, bypassing the need to discharge energy. Everyone would be happy, including, I assumed, the efreet. But she showed no reaction to what I'd said.

Beyond her, I caught Brian's hand balling up the lap of his robe. He'd done that a few times, but now the gesture looked protective. For the first time I realized it was where he was keeping the phylactery. Probably tucked away in an inner pocket. If I could just snag it...

"Vigore!" I shouted, flicking my sword.

But the efreet moved more quickly, dispersing the invocation in another flash of fire.

"Nice try, *Croft*," Brian sneered.

Dammit. Though the efreet was counting on me to help her —I was pretty sure of that now—she was still under Brian's orders to protect him. I was going to have to somehow convince him to voluntarily give up the artifact.

"The snipers have switched to rubber rounds," Vega radioed. *"Two of them have a clear shot."*

That hadn't been part of the plan, but Vega, who was still watching from the berm, was no doubt growing worried. She'd already watched me die once today.

"Stand by," I radioed back, then returned my attention to Brian. "I understand why you got into this. You wanted power, respect, recognition. That's perfectly normal, perfectly understandable. Even I crave those. But you have to listen to me. Holding onto the efreet will kill you. One way or another."

"Ah-ha!" Brian cried. "You admit it!"

"Admit what?"

"That you crave the power I wield!"

"Go ahead," I radioed Vega.

With the efreet taking form, the signal had gone out. The demons would be on their way. Though we still needed to handle Brian with kid gloves, we also needed to get the phylactery before the demons arrived.

Brian's face appeared from behind the efreet, and he glared at me defiantly.

Shots cracked from the berm. Brian flinched. But feet from him, blinding white flares hissed in the air. The rubber rounds went up in twists of smoke. More cracks sounded, only to result in more flares. The efreet wasn't letting anything get to her master.

Wonderful.

"Hold fire," I radioed Vega.

When the shots stopped, I appealed to the efreet. "I can free you, but I need the phylactery that binds you." She gave no indication she understood or even heard what I was saying. Not that I knew how to read a being as old as the cosmos.

Brian hustled around to the front of her now, his face red. "Shut up! She listens to no one but me! She does what *I* say!"

That was generally true of genie-master relationships, and yet somehow the efreet had been ignoring his order to attack me. And then it hit me. Genies would execute any order except ones that resulted in their own destruction. Somehow, the efreet knew that harming me would harm her own survivability. Whether it was from the summoning of Drage or the demon apocalypse, the efreet could sense an immediate future where, without my intervention, she would be destroyed. That must have been why Brian was freaking out. He knew he didn't have complete control over her.

I decided to press that button.

"But you can't make her attack me," I said, stepping forward.

He barked a laugh. "I could have you incinerated right here."

"Do it."

"I don't want to."

"Then I challenge you to another duel," I said.

Brian glanced around. Cameo, who had recovered from his near drowning, was watching, as was the rest of the Military Federation of the Dragon. The tributes who hadn't fled were watching too. Though most appeared mesmerized by the manifestation of the efreet, Brian no doubt believed their attention to be entirely on him. Further, he believed their continued allegiance to him depended on what he did next. He seemed to gather himself before straightening and puffing his chest out.

"I accept."

"Good." I had him where I wanted him. "But this has to be a *true* wizard's duel."

"What's that supposed to mean?" he demanded.

"Offense only. I disperse my shield, and you order the efreet not to defend you."

Red smudges grew over Brian's cheeks as he glanced around at his audience.

"A true wizard wouldn't hesitate," I said loud enough for everyone to hear—and for Brian to know they'd heard.

"Yes, fine," he said quickly. He turned to the efreet. "You're not to protect me during the duel. In fact, you're not to do anything." He then whispered an addendum that, thanks to the acoustics in the quarry, I picked up: *"But you will hit Croft with everything you have when I give the word."* He glared at her as though challenging the efreet to defy him. That's when I knew just how delusional he was.

The efreet didn't respond.

"Back to back," Brian ordered me. "Move aside, everyone."

"What's happening down there?" Vega radioed nervously.

"Another duel," I whispered. "If anyone besides Brian pulls a weapon, take them out."

I dissolved my shield and turned so our backs were touching. It was the same position we'd been in just that morning. If only I'd known then what I knew now... I tuned into Brian's muscle tone, an invocation on the tip of my tongue in the event he tried to get cute and drive a knife into my back.

"Five steps," he said. "Cameo, give us the count."

"One..." Cameo began.

"Protezione!" I shouted and spun.

My shield invocation covered Brian's mouth, muting him. Another invocation bound his wrists and ankles. Brian implored the efreet with panicked eyes, but per his own orders, she wasn't to protect him. When I moved toward him, he tried to hop-step away, but he lost his balance and fell to the ground for the second time that day.

Cameo took a step forward, but I warned him off with a look. Deciding he didn't want to be blasted into the pool again, he stopped and showed his hands, including the right one bearing the dragon gauntlet. The others seemed to follow his lead and remained back.

I manifested a form-fitting shield around myself anyway and knelt beside Brian. He kicked and thrashed as I dug a hand into his robe, found the secret pocket, and drew the phylactery free.

Gotcha!

It was the same one as in the photo—the real artifact.

I looked over at the efreet, but she was following Brian's order to the letter: *you're not to do anything*. She returned my look with the same passive expression. For the first time, though, I thought I caught a flicker of passion in her eyes.

"Is he still with you?" I radioed Vega.

"He was until just a second ago…"

I was about to ask where he went when someone appeared beside me.

"Oh, Everson!" the man said. "I couldn't remember if I was supposed to wait or come down here."

The man was stooped forward, his face sagging in a confused sort of way—that much I had pictured correctly. But instead of white or gray hair, his was dark and parted in the middle, sending it down the sides of his face in two lanky curtains. He also wore a pair of glasses whose round lenses were tinted. The hair and glasses alone conspired to give him the appearance of an aging rock star, but his all-black getup completed the look.

And that wasn't *at all* what I had pictured.

"Claudius," I said, just relieved he'd come. It had been a challenge getting him to leave his phones and pile of messages, but I convinced him that this job made all of the others gnat-sized in comparison, which might not have been a stretch.

"Is that it?" he asked, walking over to me.

I nodded and dropped the phylactery into his hand.

This man who had told me just last night that his job had

once been to work with complex bondings poked the phylactery around his palm. He hmm'd and grunted for several moments as he looked it over. The magical aura that bent the air around him was powerful but also disorganized. That worried me.

At last, though, he nodded.

"I've worked with something like this before."

"Great," I exhaled in relief. "How long do you need?"

"Oh, a couple hours. Maybe three."

"Three hours?" I scanned the berm. "I'm not sure we have that much time."

"Me neither," Claudius said. "Oh? What's happening over here?"

I thought he'd spotted a demon, but when I followed his gaze, he was staring at the body of water. It had started to froth. The cobalt color was shifting, turning an oily black, and the vapors drifting from it carried a scent of death. The members of the Military Federation of the Dragon moved closer. Even Brian, who was still on the ground, stared at the pool in a kind of trance. For the first time, I noticed the dragon bone was no longer on him. He must have dropped it into the pool at the completion of the ceremony.

At the edge of the pool, Cameo adjusted the gauntlet on his hand.

"The time is nigh!" he announced. "The return of Drage the Wise is upon us!"

33

I wheeled toward Claudius. "Can you stop the summoning?"

The senior member of the Order wrung his curtains of hair as he watched the water. "I'm afraid not, Everson. I mean, not without blowing up the lower half of New York state. There's too much energy at the interface—"

"There's no way to contain that energy?" I interrupted.

Claudius looked at me like I was crazy. "Between us? Heavens, no."

I felt the same immense buildup of energy he did. It might not have been on the order of the efreet's, but I understood the challenge of attempting to disperse that energy while at the same time preventing it from blowing out into our world. I had just been hoping an insight from Claudius's vast years of experience might flash-bulb in his muddled mind, because I had nothing.

"We'll have to wait for it to come through," he said.

"And then what?" I was having to shout above the boiling pool now.

But instead of answering, he stared slack-faced at the water, where strange lights played under the surface now. He seemed to have forgotten all about the phylactery. I turned to the efreet. It was by her power the dragon was being called up. Could she put it back down? Brian would have to give the order.

My gaze shifted to the former software developer who had done time in a psych ward and was no doubt off his meds. From his knees, he stared, watching his plans come to fruition. A wonderstruck glow came over his face.

I've done it! I could practically hear him thinking. *I've ushered in the new era!*

There was no way I was going to be able to convince him to reverse the conjuring. And if I unmuzzled him, who knew what he'd command the efreet to do. Reclaim the phylactery? Transport them elsewhere? She was presently under orders to do nothing, and under the circumstances, that was probably the best-case scenario.

"What's happening now?" Vega asked through our crackling connection.

"Drage is coming," I said. "Get yourself and everyone back. Far back."

The last part was buried in a burst of static. Black bands of energy were arcing from the water now, leaving harsh ozone trails. The atmosphere inside the entire quarry was turning brooding and electric, as if a massive storm were coming. More and more of Drage's realm was spilling into the world.

Worse, this wasn't going to be the wise and just dragon the sages had seen. Judging from the stench, whatever was emerging would be a monster whose ideal form had spent thousands of years in an underworld where forgotten beings went to die.

I hated being right sometimes.

A horned head broke the water's surface and thrashed into full view. The Military Federation and its tributes drew back with gasps. I felt the air go out of me as well. It was the enormity of the head—I'd seen smaller houses—but it was also the grotesqueness. A vast disorganization of dark scales clung to rotting flesh. Hollow eyes peered out, black flames flickering in the massive cave-like openings. Drage released his first roar, a ragged sound that filled the quarry and vibrated to the depths of my bones.

Taloned hands clawed into view next, followed by tattered wings the size of ship sails. The dragon strained and twisted as though being birthed from Hell's womb, his gigantic black teeth crashing together.

I turned to Claudius, who continued to stare.

"The phylactery!" I shouted. "Start working on the unbonding! I'll deal with the dragon!"

When he didn't answer, I shook him hard enough to skew his glasses. He straightened them and blinked at me. "Yes, yes," he stammered. "The phylactery."

"And watch the efreet!" I said. "If anything comes for her, get her and Brian the hell out of here!"

Back at the pool, Drage's wings cleared the water. He beat them furiously, generating putrid cyclones throughout the lower quarry. I lowered my head, pushing my way toward Cameo. I needed to get control of the damned dragon.

The rest of Drage's rotting body appeared from the pool, half scaly flesh, half skeleton. At last he whipped his tail free, water pouring off him as he rose. We all craned our necks back. Stan had said he would be the size of a city block, and he wasn't too far off. As it was, the dragon blocked out much of the sky.

Cameo, who wore the dragon gauntlet, backed into me. Instead of commanding Drage, he was gibbering like a fool. When I seized his arm, he screamed and rounded on me, his eyes gaping with fear.

"Give me the gauntlet!" I shouted.

He pulled the armored fist across his chest. I drove a forearm into his chin.

Cameo's legs crumpled. I grabbed the gauntlet as he went down—it slid off his limp hand with ease—and put it on my own. The warm metal gripped my forearm and hand. I hadn't sensed its power before because it had been cloaked in the aura of the efreet, but now it pulsed down the length of my arm.

The dragon released another roar and cocked his head to the scene below. Tributes had begun to flee, many trying to scramble or scale their way up the steep rock walls. Even members of the Military Federation of the Dragon were looking at one another worriedly.

But not Brian. Though he was bound and muzzled, his face shone with a kind of messianic joy. Something told me he wasn't seeing the same thing the rest of us were. His fanatical mind was spinning visions of majestic gold scales and heavenly choirs.

For her part, the efreet watched the dragon with a neutral face.

I aimed my armored fist at Drage until a thin resonance, mediated by the gauntlet's enchantment, took up between me and the creature. Though the gauntlet was potent, someone like Cameo wouldn't have been able to compel Drage to blink, much less take control of him. Even with my ability to channel and shape energy, I was struggling just to hold the connection.

Images cascaded through my mind of ruthless rule, death, a world engulfed in black fire. I needed to bend his will to mine, but the energy coming off him! It was like trying to land a hurricane with a fishing rod.

Drage dipped down and scooped several tributes into his mouth.

Through our connection, I experienced the horrible sensation of bones crunching between his teeth, of blood and bodies sliding down his gullet. But the meal only seemed to stoke Drage's maddening hunger.

He cut around and sighted on a pack of tributes running up an earthen ramp.

C'mon, dammit, I thought as I urged more power through me. I reached toward the currents of ley energy circling the quarry, willed them toward me until new energy was storming through the gauntlet, strengthening my connection to Drage. When I felt myself gain a fingerhold in the dragon's mind, I drew my fist back—hard.

Feet from the tributes, the dragon reared up as if he'd been lassoed.

Got you, you son of a bitch, I thought in triumph. *But what to do with you?*

I had an idea, but it was going to be the ballsiest thing I'd ever attempted.

Straining to hold onto the connection to Drage, I brought my fist around. Drage roared in protest and tried to climb away, but I managed to break up the timing of his wing flaps. He crashed into a rock wall and fell to the ground a safe distance from us. As he thrashed to get up, I ran toward him and shouted a force invocation.

The pulse from my cane launched me like a mortar. As I plummeted toward his batting wings, I summoned a shield invocation that funneled me, knocking back and forth, toward the crest running down the back of his neck. I came to a jarring rest between a pair of broken spines. More invocations secured me to the massive being.

Can't believe I'm doing this, I thought, choking on his putrid stench.

As Drage rose into flight, I focused into the gauntlet again. It was easier to reestablish the connection this time—the proximity and contact no doubt helped—but it took everything I had. Not just to maintain the connection, but to reform the shaky invocations holding me in place. The dragon's aura was having a disrupting effect on my magic, which was only going to get worse as he gained strength.

Drage veered back toward the tributes, his entire body shuddering with hunger. He dipped his head toward Brian, but seeming to recognize him as the one responsible for bringing him into the world, he changed course.

My heart resuming after the close call, I seized one of his spines in my gauntlet and pulled back. Drage bucked several times before going skyward. In two powerful wing thrusts, he cleared the berm. Through the snow that had begun falling again, I could see the parking lot behind the large building where we'd made our initial approach. Dozens of police vehicles were amassed there, the helicopters parked farther back.

I squinted but couldn't tell whether Vega and my teammates were among the personnel.

I refocused on the ley lines, steering Drage toward one running in the direction I wanted to go. The dragon fought with everything he had, but for now, the energy I channeled through the gauntlet was doing its job.

When we hit the ley line, that energy jumped.

I ducked my head to the frigid wind as we picked up speed.

Before long, I could see the Hudson River where it widened to lake-like proportions. My target was a power station on the west bank, farther north. I didn't have the capacity to disperse a being as large and powerful as Drage, but a million-odd watts of electricity might. I only knew about the Hudson power station because our class had toured it when I was a kid, and it had been in the news recently in a story about increasing its capacity to avoid the rolling blackouts that had plagued the city that summer.

There!

I spotted the power station with its large cooling units and complex arrangement of transformers and cables. Getting there meant separating from the main ley line and using a network of smaller ones, but I didn't have a choice.

I pulled on the dragon's spine, banking us hard left. As we broke from the line, the power through the gauntlet faltered. Below, suburban neighborhoods scrolled past, one of them arranged around a sprawling golf course.

Drage dove toward it.

No! I yanked back on the spine.

But Drage didn't change course this time. With a bellow, he spewed a long, noxious jet of vapor over the golf community. Trees withered and toppled, while rooftops burst into corrosive black flames that imploded entire homes. The dragon dipped lower until his lashing tail was knocking over vehicles parked in driveways and smashing through garages and porches.

"Stop it!" I shouted futilely against the blasting wind.

Like any summoned creature, Drage's first job was to build his energy, and something his size was going to need a lot of fuel. Though he couldn't see them, his hungry mind sensed humans nearby. His head pivoted from side to side, black flames roaring in the pits of his eyes. I tried to regain control, this time channeling as many currents of ley energy as I could. When I drew back on his spine, he reared up.

I had him again, but barely.

The power station wobbled back into view ahead. In my wizard's senses, I could see its buzzing, crackling dome of energy.

Drage lurched this way and that, trying to break from my control. Teeth gritting with effort, I drove him on, aiming him toward the football field-sized array of transformers. The steel and coil configurations seemed to rush up on us. I waited until the last moment before dispersing the invocations that bound me to Drage. With a force blast, I shot myself from his neck. I sailed back, just clearing the dragon's thrashing tail.

But even as I fell, I continued to will my control through the gauntlet, driving Drage down, down toward the massive reservoir of energy. It wasn't until he hit the first transformer in an eruption of sparks that I looked groundward.

I was plummeting toward a clump of trees, and there was no time to activate the feather potion I was carrying. Dammit.

Pivoting my cane down, I shouted an invocation. The force blasted through leaves and split open a trunk with a loud crack. Though my descent stalled, branches whacked my shielded body, and I rag-dolled the rest of the way down. I discharged a second invocation, managing to land on my feet.

Meanwhile, great booms were sounding. I limp-ran from the trees and into view of the station.

Drage had come to a crashing stop in the middle of the field of transformers, his body entangled in a mess of thick conductor cables. Thudding explosions went off around him while streams of sparks whipped from severed wires. Through our connection, I could feel Drage straining to hold himself together against the thousands upon thousands of watts coursing through him, threatening to undo his form.

C'mon, baby, I thought toward the station. *Take that fucker apart.*

The thuds began to peter out. The wires stopped hosing electricity. The power station was going dark—and along with it, my hopes.

Aside from some dislodged scales and missing chunks of flesh, Drage was still intact. He rose to his thick legs, wings batting, until he was free of the cables. Smoking black lines seared his body. Rearing his head back, he released a roar that must have resounded for miles. I shrank from the deafening sound and covered my ears.

Drage bit off his roar and angled his head toward me. The black flames of his eyes flashed with malevolent recognition.

Here we go, I thought.

34

A gulping sounded from deep in Drage's chest, and in the next moment a jet of corrosive vapors spewed toward me. I threw up a shield invocation and braced against it with everything I had. The poison slammed into it, disintegrating the grass around me. Behind me, trees groaned and toppled. Miraculously, my shield held. The wattage had taken its toll, I realized. The dragon wasn't nearly as powerful.

"*Respingere!*" I shouted.

Energy pulsed from my shield, blowing the poison aside. When the dragon gulped again, I bound his jaws in an invocation. Definitely easier. Drage struggled against it, then gave a hard flap of his wings to clear the power station's outer fencing. The earth shook when he landed, the momentum carrying the aircraft carrier-sized dragon into a run toward me. Yeah, just a little intimidating.

But I'd locked onto a healthy ley line, and I still wore the dragon gauntlet.

I thrust the gauntlet toward him, palm out. The dragon heaved to a sudden stop. The tail that had been whipping toward me fell, pushing up a mound of earth that was almost my height by the time it stopped a few feet away.

I rotated my palm down until it was parallel with the ground. Drage responded by flattening his neck. Beneath the electrical burns that seared his rotting flesh, I could feel his hatred at being commanded.

I could also feel his strength returning in popping flares.

The power station might not have destroyed him, but I knew what would.

Climbing back onto Drage's neck, I strapped myself in with invocations and willed the dragon into flight. In his weakened state, it took him longer to gain altitude, and for the first mile, his tail hung like a dowsing rod, smashing through trees and the occasional rooftop. Once I accessed the ley line running back to the quarry, I pushed Drage higher. His wings responded with great, heaving strokes.

I was too focused on the objective—destroying Drage—to appreciate the fact I was riding and commanding a frigging dragon, even if it was one that smelled like a Dumpster full of meat in midsummer.

Before long, we were bearing down on the quarry. A line of police vans was jouncing their way back out, probably after having picked up the scattered tributes. A couple of helicopters lifted out as well.

Good, I thought. *The fewer innocents to navigate, the better.*

When the bottom of the quarry came into view, my heart leapt into my throat. Claudius was still down there, fussing over the phylactery, but Vega must not have gotten my message, because she and the rest of my teammates had gone down to the pool. Vega and Bree-Yark were watching over Brian and the efreet, weapons drawn in case demons turned up. Not a bad idea, considering Claudius's current state of distraction, but they were in my flight path. Mae was down there too—no doubt because she'd insisted. She was holding Buster's carrier in one hand and Tabitha's leash in the other.

I tried the radio. "Vega, can you hear me? I need you to clear out!"

Silence in response. Dammit.

Beyond the quarry, I made Drage bank around, but he was getting harder to control. I didn't know how long I'd be able to keep him in a holding pattern. I was about to try Vega again when static burst through my headset.

I caught a snatch of her voice: *"...verson."*

"Vega, can you hear me?"

"Barely ... go ahead."

"Get everyone back but Brian and the efreet."

"Copy that," she said, her voice coming in clearer. *"Where are you?"*

"Look up," I answered.

When I saw her cock her head, I waved.

"Holy ... Is that you?"

"Yeah, I'll explain later. Just get yourselves safely back. Not sure how much longer I can control this thing."

Vega gestured to the others, and they began to climb towards the mounds of earth I'd landed behind earlier. I really had to grit my teeth to bring Drage around this time. When I had him in position, I forced him into a stomach-plunging dive. My target was Brian. In his broken mind, he believed this rotting dragon was the second coming, that Drage would bring on another Golden Age.

I had about five seconds to convince him otherwise.

As we plummeted, I tried to will Drage's jaws apart. I could feel the dragon resisting, something in his makeup reluctant to threaten his creator. But I finally overcame him, even managing to squeeze a roar from his throat.

Below, I watched Brian's face go from rapturous to horrified.

His mouth was moving as he tried to wriggle himself back behind the efreet, evidence his self-preservation instinct was overriding his crazy. With a Word, I dispersed the invocation that muzzled him.

"H-help me!" he cried. "Protect me!"

Hot damn! That was my cue. As fast as I could shout invocations, I released myself from Drage's neck and blasted myself clear. A moment later, the efreet's fire slammed into the dragon, enveloping him.

I covered my teammates with a shield and threw a spherical one around myself. Flames blasted past me as I splashed into the pool.

When my body stopped bouncing, I squinted into the supernova overhead. In its center, Drage screamed and batted wings that were being reduced to skeletal appendages. Scales plummeted, erupting into geysers of steam around me.

I followed the stream of fire back to the efreet. It shot from her arms in a relentless storm. The light that glistened over her smooth, serene face was almost too much to look at, so I switched my gaze back to Drage.

It was hard to believe that something so colossal could be overcome so quickly, but it was happening. Drage released a final scream as the elemental heat that had given him life overwhelmed the final bonds holding him together, and he erupted in dust. The efreet lowered her arms. As suddenly as the spectacle had begun, it ended.

I bobbed in my sphere for several moments, Drage's black ashes mingling with the snow that fell around me.

My radio crackled.

"Are you all right?"

I turned to find Vega and the others emerging from behind the mounds.

I let out a relieved laugh. "I'm fine," I said and used a small invocation to push myself to shore. "Just exhausted. How about everyone up there?"

"We're good," she said. *"So that takes care of the dragon?"*

"Amazingly, yes." I'd only been about fifty percent sure my second plan would work. "But there's still the efreet," I said. "And Brian."

As I arrived on solid ground, I invoked to cover Brian's mouth again. I wasn't sure I needed to, though. He had curled onto his side and was sobbing—in fear, disappointment, shame? Probably some combination of the three.

As my teammates came down to meet me, I scanned the berm.

Bree-Yark clapped my low back. "That was some kick-ass dragon riding."

Mae arrived beside me. "Yes," she said sternly. "You and I are going to need to have a talk about that."

"Well, it's not something I plan to do very often. How's the unbonding going?" I asked Claudius. He had shuffled down behind the others but become preoccupied with the phylactery in his hand and was now wandering toward a random corner of the quarry.

"Hey, Claudius? Over here."

He blinked up, looked around, and jogged toward us. "Oh, ah, yes," he said. "It's proving to be rather tricky. With so many owners, there are a riot of bonds to untangle to reach the root connection."

"Then we need to get everyone out of here," I said. We'd been there much longer than I'd intended, and my magic was talking to me, telling me we were going to have company—and lots of it—if we didn't make tracks.

"I requested a helo," Vega said.

"Good."

"Um, Everson," Tabitha said.

When I looked down, she was pointing a paw at the berm. I followed it above and to our left. A silhouette had appeared, and it wasn't alone. Everywhere I looked along the berm now, another one seemed to take form.

"Demons?" I asked, even though they looked like normal men and women.

As though a starting gun had sounded, they began scrambling down the sides of the quarry.

"Demons, darling," Tabitha confirmed.

Well, crap, I thought, my heart pounding the back of my sternum. As team leader, my priority was getting us out of there. Now. But until that happened, we needed to keep the demons from the efreet and Brian, and after my dragon-flying stunt, I was low on power. I gauged the progress of the lead demons. The helicopter, which I couldn't even hear yet, wasn't going to reach us before they did.

"Claudius!" I shouted.

He had gone back to working on the phylactery, and he looked up distractedly.

"We've got demons incoming. You translocated yourself down here, right? Can you carry eight of us out?"

He looked from us to the descending demons, then gnawed at the end of a finger in thought. He paused to spit out a piece of nail.

"Well?" I shouted.

"Yes, yes, I think so. Just trying to remember the right incantation. It's a little different when you're not going solo. One wrong word, and you'll end up where you want, but with someone else's arm or head."

I swore inwardly. "All right, keep working on it. Let us know when you have something. Vega?"

She anticipated my question and already had an answer. "We'll do better up there," she said, pointing to a plateau of earth and stone with a sheer wall above. There were also a couple of mounds to use as cover.

"Agreed," Bree-Yark barked.

"Get everyone up there," I said. "I'll work on Brian and the efreet."

Brian continued to sob on the ground beside the pool while the efreet stood over him protectively. She was still operating under his last command, but unlike with the dragon, her powers wouldn't destroy, much less fend off, the demons coming to claim her.

While Vega and Bree-Yark urged everyone up to the staging area, I scrambled toward the pool. The lead demons were only a few football fields away now. With their preternatural speed, that was nothing. Our best chance was for the efreet to transport us out. But for that, I needed Brian again.

I grabbed him and hauled him to his feet. His red face was tear streaked and snot ran freely into his goatee.

"Brian, listen to me," I said, pushing power into my wizard's voice. "Demons are coming for your efreet. I need you to order her to take us someplace safe."

Brian squinted away like a child and sobbed harder.

For fear of how the efreet would react, I had to stop myself from slapping him. "Brian!"

This time he tried to jam a thumb into his mouth, but it ran into the shield I'd gagged him with. He screamed silently.

Dammit, it was no use. He was regressing, becoming more and more infantile. And I didn't trust what he'd say if I ungagged him. Probably cry for his mother, whom the efreet would then be compelled to summon. And the last thing we needed was more people to have to carry out of here.

Shots cracked and popped. I looked over to find Vega and Bree-Yark firing from their new position. Across from us, the lead demon—a middle-aged woman in a green pea coat—

recoiled with a sharp hiss, smoke bursting from the bullet wounds. It was an encouraging sight, but the silver rounds were only going to slow them. It would take banishment to end them, and there were too many for me to handle. Thirty if I had to guess, and more arriving.

I needed to get Brian and the efreet up to the others. There we could better defend them until Claudius got us the hell out of there. I could carry Brian, but I had no power to order the efreet. *Do I risk an invocation to move her?*

Then something occurred to me. Still holding Brian up, I faced her.

"You'll be best able to protect Brian by staying close to him."

She looked back at me with that same placid expression. I wasn't ordering her, but expanding the scope of what protecting him meant. Of course, the test would be whether she complied. I began jog-dragging Brian toward the others. When I looked back, I found the efreet following in powerful strides.

Thank God, I breathed, surrounding us in a crackling shield.

But we had to hurry. Several of the demons had managed to avoid the worst of Vega's and Bree-Yark's fusillade and were now only one level above us in the quarry. I turned and nailed one with a force invocation, throwing him backwards.

When we hit the incline to where the rest of my team was, Brian decided to become dead weight. I wasted needed energy on an invocation to haul him along. If he hadn't been the trigger to a world-shattering being, I would have dropped his ass. By the time we reached the others my lungs were on fire.

I pulled Brian behind Vega and Bree-Yark, who were still shooting out into the quarry.

"We're holding them off, but that's about it," Vega said.

Bree-Yark snarled. "If they want to come closer, they can have a taste of goblin steel." He paused firing his M16 to slap the belted scabbard that held the blade I'd seen him pull from the Hummer earlier.

Mae emerged from behind cover. When she saw the sobbing mess in my grasp, she hustled over and together we helped Brian behind the mounds. The efreet followed.

I found Claudius and Tabitha back there, but they couldn't have been a starker study in contrast. While Tabitha stared around with puffed hair and pupils the size of dessert plates—a reaction to the gunfire as well as her proximity to so many demons—Claudius paced slowly, a fist propping his chin as he muttered variations of the same words, only to stop and shake his head. He could have been at home in his study for all the concern he showed.

I was afraid to ask. "How's the translocation coming?"

"Well, I've eliminated a few incantations it's *not*," he said.

Yeah, that sounds promising, I thought dismally.

"The helo's coming in," Vega shouted above the gunfire. "They're going to try to land it here."

That would have to be our ticket out, but the pilot was going to need help. I looked around a mound in time to see a boulder flying toward the chopper. Aiming my staff, I shouted a shield invocation. I grunted as the boulder smashed into the hardened air and plummeted. More demons hurled rocks and small boulders at the descending chopper. Though I blocked them, each impact took a further toll on me.

"Everson!" Mae shouted.

I turned to find her pointing up the sheer rock wall above us. Three demons were crawling down it face first: two men and a woman.

Shit.

Holding the invocation around the helicopter with the staff. I used a force invocation through my sword to drag Brian away from the wall. Mae and the efreet followed him, but Claudius continued to pace, muttering to himself.

"Forget the incantation!" I shouted. "We have demons!"

Claudius looked up. The demons were swiping at each other now, competing to be the first to reach the efreet. I looked back at the chopper. The projectiles had tapered off as the demons converged into the lower quarry and fights began breaking out there too, every demon for him- or herself.

I turned back to find the demons on the wall in a tangle of hair-pulling and limb-twisting. They fell as a group, plunging the remaining thirty feet. They quickly disentangled themselves upon slamming to earth and raced for the efreet.

I was halfway through a shouted invocation to stop them when a black void appeared in front of them. The void seemed to buckle as it swallowed them whole and closed again.

"That's the thing about a translocation spell," Claudius said, lowering a trembling hand. "Getting it right doesn't matter so much when you're casting it on an enemy." He had a point. I imagined the demons popping into a parallel plane with each other's arms and legs sticking out of their sides.

"Take care of any more that come down!" I called.

Claudius was probably the last one here I wanted covering our rear, but I didn't have a choice. I needed to land the chopper.

Seizing Brian's arm, I dragged him around to the front of the mounds, behind Vega and Bree-Yark. Once more, the efreet followed. The hovering chopper blasted sand and grit around us.

I prevented another rock from smashing through the chopper's blades, but the quarry was a full-fledged demon brawl now, the creatures' proximity to the efreet stoking their power-hunger and violence. Stronger demons battered and tore apart weaker ones, then raced down, eager, it seemed, for the next encounter.

Survival of the most hellish.

Finally, the helicopter set down, and a side door opened.

I waved Mae forward. She hustled toward the chopper with her head bowed, one hand holding Buster's carrier and Tabitha's leash while she fought futilely to keep her hair in place with the other. Bree-Yark covered her and then helped her aboard.

I gestured for Vega to go next. I wanted to bring in Brian and the efreet while Claudius watched our backs. Vega nodded and ran ahead, pausing to take final shots at the nearest demons.

I pulled Brian behind her and, running, shouted for Claudius.

After several heart-pounding moments, he appeared from behind the mounds. He gave an embarrassed wave, as if I'd caught him in the act of taking a leak, and hustled to catch up. He had no idea four demons were behind him.

"Turn around!" I shouted.

Claudius craned his neck, did a double-take, then incanted to summon another portal. This time, I saw something massive and slug-like humping around in the depths of the void before it closed again, taking the demons with it. Probably a good thing he hadn't attempted to translocate the eight of us earlier.

Sparks spilled over me as a force broke through my shield.

I brought my sword around, but a demon had already seized the efreet and pulled her into his embrace.

35

The demon holding the efreet had assumed the guise of a street tough you might find hanging out under the elevated tracks in Spanish Harlem. His face was a tapestry of black ink that matched his slicked-back hair, his plaid shirt fastened with a single button around the throat. He pinned the efreet around the neck with one arm, while with his other hand he aimed a Dirty Harry revolver at Brian.

But his malevolent eyes were locked on mine.

"You know how this works, *cabron*," he said through a grin that revealed a flash of silver teeth. "You so much as flinch, and I'm putting a bullet through fatso's head and blowing this entire show to shit."

Dammit. He understood Brian's connection to the efreet.

My gaze flicked past him to the demon hosts that lay in his wake, the demons themselves scattered into the ether like smoke until they could reconstitute themselves. Of the first wave, the Chicano was the lone survivor. Late arrivals hung back on the upper levels of the quarry, knowing the minute the Chicano's master possessed the efreet, they wouldn't be scattered, but destroyed. And judging by the way the efreet wasn't reacting to

Brian's danger—or indeed, her own—the demon master was partway there, already infusing her form with his evil essence.

But how in the hell did the Chicano get to us without anyone seeing?

I spotted a hole in the ground at his back. The son of a bitch had used his demonic strength to burrow his way under, then up, the dust storm from the chopper concealing him. And he'd managed to emerge from under that tonnage of rock and dirt looking immaculate.

"Call off your posse," he said with a smirk, his reedy voice somehow penetrating the noise of the rotary blades.

Up ahead, Bree-Yark and Vega were aiming their weapons from the chopper. Behind me, Claudius had a hand raised as if he was going to incant another portal into being. He wore a look of deliberation on his face, weighing the odds of success. I was cycling through my own options, but with the demon's preternatural speed, we wouldn't be able to do anything he couldn't beat us to. And the sadistic glint in his eyes told me he would absolutely put a bullet through Brian's head, even if it meant erasing himself from existence.

Fuck.

I gestured for Vega and Bree-Yark to lower their weapons and for Claudius to do the same with his casting arm.

"Where are you taking her?" I shouted.

"I don't need to take her anywhere. I'll take her right here," he said lewdly.

He flicked his tongue out and ran the tip up and down the side of her black, burnished neck. The gesture spoke to the horror of what he was doing—taking a godlike elemental against her will and making her not just a servant, but a demonic host. Fusing her to his master for her inexhaustible energy.

I watched an emptiness spread over the demon's face as he

acted as the channel between master and efreet. Meanwhile, malevolent flames I'd not seen before were taking hold in the efreet's eyes.

"Do you think your master is going to keep you around once he has her?" I shouted in a last-ditch attempt to get the demon to reconsider what he was doing. But the demon only laughed in the lazy way of someone who had just taken a hit of morphine.

"Does it look like I care?" he said. "I serve at master's pleasure." He shuddered as if he'd just been given another dose.

His demon master's sedating him to make sure he completes the task, I realized. *But will that also slow his reflexes?*

Either I stood there and did nothing, and once the possession was complete the demon-efreet hybrid would destroy us. Or I risked an invocation.

Even in the demon's euphoric state, I could still be too slow. That would mean a bullet through Brian's head and an explosion that would take out the entire Northeast, but at least the second option gave us a chance.

I glanced over at Vega. She met my gaze and nodded.

I turned back to the demon and drew a shaky breath.

God, forgive me if I bone this up.

But I hesitated. Something was happening behind him.

The demon hosts he had wasted, or who had wasted each other, were rising to their feet. *So soon?* They began moving toward us in a lurching run. Within moments they were scrambling up the plateau. The demon must have seen my reaction because life flashed back into his emptying eyes, and he spun his head around.

My chance, I thought, adrenaline surging through me.

I couldn't risk a spoken invocation—the demon's gun was still aimed at Brian—so I made a quick sign in the air. The efreet's eyes flickered as the portion of demon master that had infused her caught the movement.

The gun banged three times.

The demon master was willing to sacrifice the efreet and his servant to prevent anything else from claiming her. But in the time it had taken him to communicate my action to his underling, I'd opened my interplanar cubbyhole in front of Brian's head. Bits of paper and binding burst out like confetti as the rounds impacted the books I'd stored inside. A small price to pay to be able to invoke.

"*Protezione!*" I shouted, willing a shield around us.

The ensuing gunshots flashed off our protection.

"*Vigore!*"

The force invocation smashed the weapon from the demon's grip and twisted it apart. I wasn't sure the Chicano demon even noticed. He was more concerned now with keeping the arriving demon horde from stealing his prize. And he was no longer acting as a channel, I saw. The demon master's essence was draining from the efreet's eyes.

The Chicano cast an infernal invocation through his hand, torching the first arriving demons in black flames. But still they came. And they weren't behaving like the demons of earlier. They weren't tearing each other apart. If anything, they seemed to be acting cooperatively, closing in on the Chicano from three sides. Some even shambled right past the landed chopper, which also struck me as strange.

When the Chicano saw he was about to be overrun, he clutched the efreet tighter and turned.

And my father's sword was there to meet him. The demon's eyes popped wide as I drove the blade through his gut.

"*Disfare!*" I shouted.

The blade's topmost rune glowed white, and then the entire blade flashed with holy light. The enchantment broke through the demon, reducing him to a burst of black smoke that dispersed a moment later—banished. Unlike the demon in the pump house, there was no host to land in my arms. The Chicano had been the demon's form.

Instead, I caught the efreet.

Have you ever held the power of the Earth's molten core in human form? Me neither, and it overwhelmed my magic and mind. My body short-circuited until all I was aware of was a primal flicker of white flame that existed at the heart of all flames.

I stared at the flame for lifetimes, it seemed, and then I realized someone was catching me and that only the briefest moment had passed. I expected to find Bree-Yark or even Claudius holding me, but it was the efreet.

The demon master was gone from her eyes, and in the backs of them I glimpsed the same white flames I'd seen a moment before. The efreet's eyes were impossible to read, but the being seemed to be ensuring I was all right.

As she placed me on my feet, reality rushed back to my senses.

And it was frigging chaos. Firing had taken up from the helicopter again, and bodies were falling around us as demon heads exploded. I hauled Brian up from the ground and waved Claudius toward the chopper. He was busy opening and closing dysfunctional portals on more demons, a skill which had proven useful after all.

As we boarded the chopper, the rock-hurling resumed from a new wave of demons. I invoked a shield to deflect the projectiles. Following her order to protect Brian, the efreet took out any that got past me with bursts of fire. Vega gave the pilot the liftoff sign. My stomach lurched as we rose straight up in a powerful thrust, the pilot no doubt as anxious as anyone to escape the hell she'd found herself in.

I peered around the inside of the chopper, not quite able to believe we had all made it. I had placed a still-sobbing Brian beside me, the efreet taking up a position on his other side. Bree-Yark was perched halfway out the door, firing down on the demons with barked threats and promises, most of them not very nice. Mae was sitting across from us, mouthing a prayer with closed eyes, while Tabitha, who was no fan of flying either, had managed to wedge herself between Mae's right hip and Buster's carrier.

Claudius, who had taken a seat beside them, leaned toward me. "Anyone going to miss this quarry?"

"Probably," I replied. "Why?"

He gave me a sheepish look as though to say, *too late*.

I looked out the window in time to see the sides of the quarry sliding down toward an enormous portal he'd opened at its bottom. The pool Drage had been summoned from dropped out, and five and ten-story rock faces cascaded down. The hordes of demons were caught in the sinkhole too. They had barely enough time to scream before they were crushed and buried. The sheer volume of material disappearing was incomprehensible. Moments later, the portal closed, and all that remained was a massive moonlike crater.

"Just rocks and dirt, right?" Claudius said.

"And demons," I added, staring at the settling cavity. "How does the crew seem to you?"

He looked the pilot and copilot over and shrugged. "Fine."

"Everson?" Vega asked.

When I looked over, she was peering into my eyes, trying to read them. I'd been thinking about the demons who had attacked the Chicano. Only they hadn't been demons, I understood now. They had been zombies. Someone had resurrected the dead hosts. I had a strong suspicion who that was, and an even stronger one that we were playing into his hands somehow. Arnaud was as cunning as they came. He was also a survivor, and I knew for certain he had not been sucked into the abyss just now.

But there was too much noise to attempt to explain all of that to Vega.

The pilot, who Claudius had just cleared, craned her neck. "Where to?" she asked.

"Downtown," I shouted back. We were clear of the quarry. Far to the south, the Manhattan skyline appeared as a ghost through the snowy haze. A pair of NYPD helicopters joined us in flanking positions.

"Who are they?" I demanded.

"Escorts," the pilot replied.

"Tell them to drop off." My mind was jumping with paranoia. "And kill all radio contact until we're about to land."

The pilot looked at Vega, who nodded for her to comply. When the pilot turned back to the front, Vega gave me a questioning look. I waited for the flanking helicopters to turn and thump away before addressing her.

"I need you to call a number for me. I lost my phone."

I reached into my shirt pocket and handed her Malachi's card.

While she read the number, I got the pilot's attention. "St. Martin's Cathedral," I shouted.

It would be the safest place for the efreet, I decided.

36

From a dark street corner in the heart of his old district, Arnaud watched the helicopter touch down through the lightly falling snow.

He hadn't anticipated Everson ordering away the ride in which he, Arnaud, had been a passenger, the pilot under his thrall. So, a point to Mr. Croft. But the moment Arnaud saw that they were returning to Manhattan, he had a strong suspicion where they were going. He suggested that the pilot parallel their helicopter from a distance until he was sure, then ordered him to come around from the south of the island and land in Battery Park, a brisk ten-minute walk from the cathedral.

Now Arnaud smiled.

Croft may have become a more capable wizard, but his thinking remained transparent, predictable.

Arnaud remembered the case Croft had pursued years before at St. Martin's. Croft had even come to his office for information, the reckless fool. In any event, that experience would have reinforced in Croft's mind the soundness of the cathedral's defenses, with its faith-based protections and mighty fount of ley energy.

Following the very close call at the quarry, and the knowledge that more demons remained—demons like Arnaud—Croft would have cycled through all the safe places he knew in and around New York City.

But none, in his mind, would have rivaled St. Martin's for security.

"And here we are, Zarko," the vampire-demon whispered. "And not a moment too late."

He'd known it would take time for the police to clear the street in front of the cathedral before the helicopter could land. In fact, upon arriving, Arnaud had had to wait a couple of minutes himself. But he didn't mind. It gave him a chance to meditate on the rightness of him reclaiming his power, and then some, in the very place he had lost it.

The goblin hopped down from the helicopter first, pointing his automatic rifle around like a toy soldier, Arnaud thought. The woman detective appeared next, covering the other side of the street, the side closer to Arnaud. He was too well concealed for her to see him, but that would change shortly.

And now it was Everson Croft's turn to make an entrance. A worm of hatred wriggled through Arnaud as he watched the wizard step from the helicopter, holding onto the large, sobbing man—the efreet's master. Arnaud clenched his fists at the idea so pitiful a fool should have been allowed to control something that would soon enter into a fiery amalgam with his own vampiric and demonic nature.

Had there ever been such a being? Arnaud wasn't sure, but he doubted so. Zarko did too.

A moment later, the efreet appeared behind Croft, power radiating from her in tremendous waves, power he would soon claim. Arnaud had no doubt of this. He could already feel the changes coming over him, as though worlds had decreed it should be so. And perhaps he *would* rule worlds one day.

But for now, the efreet.

Arnaud had admired her from the rim of the quarry, but he'd had no plans to confront Croft and his ring to claim her. And he refused to reduce himself to the barbaric mindlessness shown by the other demons. No strategy, no finesse—just racing headlong toward the efreet and hoping for the best. Arnaud shook his head. No, not for him. So, he had improvised with mind control, animations, and simple calculations.

And where were the other demons now? he thought with swelling conceit.

But he needed to focus. The group of Croft, the large man, and the efreet were moving toward the cathedral now. A second wizard took up the rear, but Arnaud wasn't concerned about him, even despite his impressive feats at the quarry. He had seen the old man freeze when the demon seized the efreet. The old man would respond in the exact same way when Arnaud seized the detective.

And it was time.

He crossed the street and sidled up to a police officer managing the scene.

"Walk with me," he told the officer, pushing power into the words. "And kindly loan me your weapon."

The officer complied on both counts, unfastening his service pistol and slipping its cool grip into Arnaud's hand. They paced toward the detective, Arnaud careful to keep a police cruiser that had been parked away from the helicopter between them. When they arrived at the cruiser, Arnaud had the officer stop.

At the door to the powerful cathedral, a young man met Croft and his group. Following a short exchange, he allowed them inside. The efreet joined them, passing through the cathedral's defenses, but this would only be temporary. Here again, Arnaud knew Everson Croft's mind. Using the wizard's most sensitive pressure point, he would compel him to send the efreet out again. To send the being to him.

As the cathedral door closed, Arnaud's gaze cut back to Detective Vega.

"Now," Arnaud said to the officer. "Bring the detective over here and be quick about it. Tell her it's to do with her son."

The officer nodded and trotted toward Vega. Meanwhile, the goblin had shouldered his weapon to help the older black woman from the helicopter. Together with the large feline, they walked toward the cathedral.

The detective had begun to follow when the approaching officer caught up to her. She brought her weapon around—*so suspicious*, Arnaud thought with a grin—but when the officer began to speak, she lowered her weapon and angled her head. When he turned, she followed him.

And so predictable.

Arnaud was already anticipating the trade with Croft: the efreet for the detective. If the wizard delayed, Arnaud would hurt her. If he balked, he would kill her. He would lose the efreet, but so would the other demons. The power game would be a wash. Arnaud would accrue power some other way, but the torture he had envisioned for his adversary would be underway. For was there any greater pain than losing one's beloved to senseless violence?

Perhaps he would kill the detective anyway, just for that pleasure.

Arnaud was contemplating the very idea when a hot spike seared his chest.

He seized the front of his shirt in a fist and fell against the cruiser. Through the windows, he could see the officer and detective approaching. With each step, the white-hot pain became more intense, more blinding.

And he knew the pain!

Arnaud spotted the chain around Vega's neck. The pendant it held had ridden up above her tactical vest, appearing as a small lump beneath the fabric of her shirt. Underneath his pain, Arnaud's confidence fell out.

Croft had given her the cursed ring, and it was stealing his power!

Arnaud's legs trembled, and he fell to his hands and knees, dropping the gun. The pain was positively ripping through him. Smoke began to drift from his flesh. The detective still couldn't see him, but at this rate, the energy of the ring would reduce him to ashes before she even arrived. And if there was still life in him, she would end it with a series of silver rounds to his head at point-blank range.

Too weak to cast toward the ring-bearing detective, Arnaud summoned his final reserves and thrust his arm at a police cruiser coming in from a side street. The force caught the front of the vehicle and veered it into a parked car. Vega and the officer wheeled toward the clapping bang, giving Arnaud a sudden respite from the pain. He gained his feet and began limping in the other direction, harsh lights flashing in his vision.

Vega shouted, but she was calling for assistance for the accident.

Arnaud turned down a street and then into an alleyway, where he found refuge behind a stack of crates. He collapsed against the wall, then slid down to the filthy asphalt, nothing left in him, his insides cored out. When a large rat waddled up and sniffed his shoe, he hadn't even the strength to kick it away.

"We failed, Zarko," he rasped, not believing he was saying it.

The bastard wizard had won again. By the time Arnaud recovered his power, the efreet would be gone. He knew this. Worse, Malphas would call him to a Dread Council, wanting to know what had happened. When his master found him in this pathetic state, having failed to claim the efreet, he would cast him back to the Pits. And this time, Arnaud would have no shadow demon to fend off the most vicious devils.

The rat began gnawing on his rubber sole.

Arnaud watched in resignation, dumb to the sensation taking hold in his mind—a scent, he realized dimly. A human scent. Arnaud straightened as the scent resonated with one he'd stored earlier in the day.

"The blood slave has found the one who has taken the scepter," Zarko whispered.

Arnaud strained to tune into the security guard. It was the woman. She had covered a good bit of ground, and now she was standing before an apartment building in a neighborhood he knew. That was where the scent led.

"Indeed, she has, Zarko," Arnaud said.

His eyes remained on the rat, which had already worked through a sizeable chunk of sole.

"Very good," he told the female blood slave, a resurrected hope filling the words. With the scepter, he would be immune to Croft's cursed objects. He would never know this kind of pain or defeat again. "Keep a low profile. I'll meet you there."

The rat squealed and kicked as Arnaud seized it and brought it to his mouth.

He was going to need his strength after all.

37

As I crossed the threshold into St. Martin's Cathedral, a familiar wave of energy rippled through me, taking with it a quotient of my wizarding powers. That was all right. I wasn't going to need them in here.

At last.

With Brian still in my grasp, I turned to ensure the efreet made it across as well. Claudius came up behind her.

Malachi, whose invitation had given us all safe passage, closed the door. He had been uneasy about providing refuge before I had committed to the Upholders. I was right, though—that had been the druid's position more than the others'. When I explained the situation as well as the catastrophic implications over the phone, Malachi relented.

I looked around now, breathing hard with exertion and relief, not quite believing we had actually made it. My gaze stopped at the cavernous nave, where I used to attend services with Nana. I even picked out the pew where we would sit. The same stained-glass window presided above the apse. Among the depicted angels and hallowed saints, glowed the image of Michael, the forebearer of my magic-using line.

A good reminder of my work's purpose.

"This way," Malachi said. "I've cleared a room for you."

He led us down a corridor and into an office with a desk and several places to sit. I brought Brian to the couch, where he promptly curled onto his side facing the back, knees tucked to his belly. The efreet took a sentry position beside him while Claudius settled behind the desk and produced the phylactery from a pocket. As I placed the dragon gauntlet on a corner of the desk, Malachi asked to speak with me outside.

"Jordan is insisting you invoke the bonding spell," he said.

"I will once the efreet is free, and this is done," I promised.

Malachi pressed his lips together. "You're putting me in a difficult position. It makes it look like I'm playing favorites, and we decided from the start that the Upholders needed to be egalitarian."

"Why is he so damned adamant I be a part of this?"

"He..." Malachi squinted past my right shoulder as though considering how much to reveal. I remembered the tension I'd felt during last night's meeting when I'd asked Jordan about his story. At last Malachi sighed. "The Stranger who infiltrated his druid community took possession of his wife."

All right, that explained it.

"Sorry," I said, "but holy shit."

"Yeah, right?"

Sudden sympathy for Jordan cascaded through me. What lengths would I go to if something like that ever happened to Vega? I looked down at the cane that concealed my father's blade with the banishment rune.

"Reassure him that it *will* happen tonight," I said, "once the efreet is free."

Malachi nodded. "We'll complete your induction tomorrow, then."

"And I want places for Vega and her son."

"It will be arranged." He waved toward the front of the cathedral. "I'll let the others in," he said, referring to Vega and Bree-Yark, who had covered our approach, as well as the rest of the team still in the chopper.

I considered joining Malachi to ensure they got inside safely, but the cathedral's aura would ward away any demon who attempted to get close. Plus, I had given Vega my ring to wear, topping it off with protective power. Arnaud wouldn't be able to come within two hundred feet of her without seriously regretting that decision.

But I didn't think he would. Assuming he had been behind the animation spell at the quarry, there was no way he could have beaten us here—or even known where we were going.

I returned to the room to check on Claudius's progress. I was anxious for this to be done, for the efreet to be freed and returned to her realm. To his credit, Claudius was hard at work. Strange lights glistened in the phylactery's metal faces as the magic-user's fingers trembled over the artifact.

"Ah!" he said suddenly. He pinched something invisible and drew it back, then smiled in satisfaction as the phylactery glowed warmly for a moment. "There went an especially nasty knot. The rest should be easier. Won't take much longer."

"Great," I said, stepping back to let him work.

He seemed much calmer and more in his element here than over the phone.

A moment later, Mae, Tabitha, and Bree-Yark came through the door.

"Your girl's behind us," Bree-Yark said, anticipating my question.

Mae sat down in a chair, propped Buster's carrier on her thighs, and released a weary sigh. "I should have known better than to wear brand new shoes," she said, clapping the toes of her white tennis shoes together a few times. Buster replicated the sound with a series of clicks. "I'm pretty sure my bunions have grown bunions, God bless 'em."

"Well, take a load off," I said. "We made it."

"I'll believe it when I'm back home on my own cushion," Tabitha muttered, hopping onto the chair beside Mae.

The same cushion you were so down on last night? I thought.

But that reminded me... "Hey, Mae. I have a cat question for you."

"Sure, honey," she replied with closed eyes, her words going slack with fatigue.

"Not any cats we know," I added quickly, remembering what I'd promised Tabitha—though I could tell by my cat's breathing, she was already asleep. "The feline in question is about seven or so, and she fell into this sudden funk."

"What kind of a funk?" Mae asked.

"Well, if she could talk, I think she would've said her life had lost all meaning, that she saw no reason to go on."

"House cat?"

"For the most part, yeah."

"That's not uncommon." Mae paused to stifle a strenuous yawn. "At that age, cats are getting on in years. Their bodies are changing. The treatment is to get them outside now and again. Shake things up. Let them have some adventures. After a good night's sleep, they're right as rain."

"Yeah?"

"The bigger the adventure, the better."

When Tabitha began to snore, Mae opened her eyes long enough to wink at me.

Well, how about that? I thought. *I've been treating Tabitha without even knowing it.*

Bree-Yark coughed in the exaggerated way of a goblin trying to get someone's attention. I turned to find him in the far corner of the room, M16 strapped across his back. When he cocked his head, I walked over.

"Hey," he said in a lowered voice. "I've been thinking about our Gretchen talk. You're right. I'm ready to cut the string she's been using to dangle me along. No more house-sitting. No more pony-watching. When she gets back, I'm going to tell her all that's over. I can't keep doing this to myself."

I nodded proudly and clapped his shoulder. "Welcome to the first day of the rest of your life."

"Tell you the truth, a lot of it came from watching you and your girl today. The way you treat each other. The way you listen. 'Might be kids,' I kept thinking, 'but what they've got is the way it should be.'" For the first time since I'd met him, Bree-Yark smiled. And if you've never seen a goblin smile, it's terrifying.

"Wow," I said. "That's really flattering."

"Oh, one more thing." He lowered his voice further. "What do you think about Mae?"

"Mae?" I followed his squash-colored eyes to where the nether whisperer was slumped in the chair. "Well, I mean, you've spent time with her. She's kind, loving, about as motherly as they come." Actually, she was the anti-Gretchen, now that I thought about it.

When I caught Bree-Yark nodding, I wondered if he was thinking the same thing.

I was about to add my hunch that Mae might have been interested in him too when she snorted and startled upright. "Everson, honey," she called. "I am falling right off. Afraid I'm going to have to call it a night."

I caught Bree-Yark's eyes with mine and jerked them toward Mae.

The goblin jumped into action. "Oh, ah, I'll go with you. Make sure you get home safe."

Mae giggled as he took Buster's carrier and helped her to her feet. "And I thought chivalry was dead."

I met them at the door, where I gave Mae a hug and we exchanged cheek kisses. "Thank you so much for your help," I told her. "Buster too." Mention of his name sent Buster scrambling around the carrier.

"I may have to sit out the next few," Mae said. "But don't forget about this old woman."

"I definitely won't. How about you, Bree-Yark? I can always use your tactical knowledge and muscle. And you've been solid company."

He looked from me to Mae and back. "Count this goblin in."

I gave him a thumb's up and then a wink after Mae had turned away. As they made their way down the corridor, Mae said something about searching for those guillotine clippers back at her apartment, if Bree-Yark still wanted them.

"I do," Bree-Yark said. "For my talons."

Such a player.

I was about to check on Vega when she passed the two coming from the other direction. She removed her SWAT helmet wearily, walked straight into my open arms, and nestled against me. I held her for several moments.

"Everything all right?" I asked.

"Just an accident out front. Police officer lost control of his vehicle, but everyone's fine."

We entered the room and moved to the far end so as not to disturb Claudius. The efreet remained statue still at the end of the couch where Brian continued his marathon sobbing session. Still unable to believe we were sharing space with an ancient fire elemental, I caught myself staring at her. I expected to find Vega doing the same, but she was looking at the floor, her gaze sharp with concern.

"Is there something else?" I asked.

"Oh, one of the officers at the scene seemed to think he'd picked up a communication about my son. But when I called home, everything was fine. False alarm that I'm still coming down from." She patted her chest and forced a smile.

Something about that troubled me, though I couldn't say why. All the more reason to get her and Tony spots in the safehouse. I was about to tell Vega what I'd discussed with Malachi when Claudius exclaimed from the desk. We turned to find him standing, fingers pinched above the phylactery as he drew away what I guessed was the final binding knot. He pulled slowly, slowly, then gave a final tug.

"Done!" he announced.

The phylactery glowed, then went permanently dull.

All of our gazes turned to the efreet. The being's dark form shimmered with fire as the quotient bonded to the phylactery flowed back into her. I had believed that upon being freed, she would disappear back to her realm in an instant, that there would be nothing more to hold her here. But she didn't appear in a hurry to go anywhere.

She looked around at the three of us and Tabitha, then peered down at Brian, her final master. I tried to read her face. What could a being like that be thinking? I didn't know, but I wasn't going to wait until she had incinerated him to find out.

I cleared my throat. "We'll see that he's punished."

More likely he would be sent back into psychiatric care, but regardless, I didn't want the efreet exacting justice here. She had no doubt slain masters before.

She turned toward me. Where she had appeared mannequin-like just moments ago, her face was now aflame with something resembling passion. She strode forward.

I moved Vega behind me, cast a shield around us, and readied my sword. But thanks to the cathedral's threshold, I was hurting for power. In my peripheral vision, I could see Claudius poised to open another portal.

"Do not fear me," the efreet said, her voice deep and strangely harmonic.

Just in case the situation wasn't clear to her, I said, "You're free now."

She stopped in front of us and looked down at me for an uncomfortably long moment. Though I couldn't see the white flames in her eyes from earlier, I could feel them penetrating me, exploring my entire being.

"Hand me your blade," she said at last.

I glanced over at Claudius, who nodded in an ardent way that said, *Don't piss her off.*

I extended my father's sword, handle out. Fire shimmered along the beveled blade as the efreet accepted it and looked it up and down.

Why did she want it? I feared now that she would take it with her or reduce it to slag. While the sword would be meaningless to a being like her, it was everything to me.

But she held the sword up in front of her almost ceremonially and caressed the second rune, the one just below the banishment enchantment. Fire burst along the symbol's grooves. A moment later, the blade glowed orange in her grip, and flames licked along the edges, but I was no longer worried for it.

She waited for the flames and glow to recede before handing the sword back.

The handle I gripped was cool, but I felt new power coursing along the blade. She had activated the second rune, I realized, one that held a fire enchantment. I would no longer need to carry dragon sand. Was this a payment for saving her from demon possession? For helping free her from bondage? Or was it a gift?

I bowed slightly. "Thank you."

"More will come," she said in her strange voice, and I understood she meant the demons. "Prepare yourself, Everson Croft." Was she seeing what Malachi had when he'd referred to a demon apocalypse?

"Are you saying—?" I started to ask.

But the efreet's eyes flashed white, and she was gone. Not even a wisp of smoke remained.

"Well," Claudius said, dusting off his hands and tucking his curtains of hair behind his ears. "Guess I should get back to the phones. Ah, the Order will want these too." He picked up the phylactery and gauntlet. He was already starting to incant for a portal when I signaled for him to hold on.

"Doesn't what the efreet said concern you?" I asked.

"I didn't catch it all, actually. My hearing's starting to go. Think you can write something up and send it?"

I could have told him right there, but odds were he'd forget.

"Yeah, sure," I said wearily. "And, hey, thanks for coming."

He chuckled. "I actually enjoyed that. Reminded me of the good old days." Claudius opened a portal beside the desk, told me we would talk soon, and disappeared.

Vega looked around the room. It was just the two of us and Tabitha, who had slept through everything.

"So, is that it?" she asked.

We had thwarted a major dragon summoning, denied the demons a weapon of mass destruction, and returned the efreet to her realm. But after what the efreet had said, it all felt like the opening salvo in a much larger war. I didn't mention that, though. Instead, I took the Upholders card from my pocket and held it up.

"There's just one more thing."

38

The next evening

The induction into the Upholders took most of the day. It was held in their townhouse basement and involved oaths and strategy and going over what the four had already mapped out, using Malachi's visions and their collective intel. The level of organization impressed me.

Despite our bad start two nights earlier, the four struck me as good people—or beings, anyway. Seay the Fae and Gorgantha the mermaid treated me civilly. And Jordan, who had been the most pissed about me jumping in line for sanctuary, had made a point of shaking my hand. His forceful personality all but ensured we would butt heads, but at least I understood where his passion came from. That understanding would help.

Plus, we have matching tattoos now, I thought dryly.

As I walked down East Fourteenth, headlights flashing past, I pulled my right hand from my coat pocket and studied the white sigil that had appeared following last night's invocation. The sigil sat below the webbing between my thumb and first finger on the outside of my hand. A cool little design, actually. I just didn't like the idea of it.

The aversion came in part from what Vega had alluded to the day before—me not being comfortable yet working with others—even despite yesterday's success. And part of it was the feeling I'd been branded.

But getting sanctuary for Vega and Tony had been worth it, I thought as I returned the hand to my pocket. There was an interfaith house in Brooklyn we planned to check out in the morning. A place they could stay for as long as they needed. They could come and go, too. The enchanted objects I'd given them would absorb the power of the safe house, providing them extra protection when they were out. Demons would steer clear of them, and that included vampire-demons.

Vega still had mixed feelings about the arrangement, part of it coming from the guilt of receiving special treatment when so many would be left vulnerable. But her relief last night in the cathedral room had been apparent when I'd revealed my decision.

My decision, I emphasized. Arnaud was after me, and I would be damned if I was going to leave the two closest to my heart exposed. Not only that, but knowing they were safe would allow me to be more aggressive in my hunt for Arnaud. That street ran both ways.

Vega remained by my side as I spoke the invocation and took on the bonding.

Who knows? I'd caught myself thinking. *Maybe Carlos will back off a little.*

Yeah, and maybe pigs would fly.

When I reached the East Village apartment building, I ducked through the boarded-over doorway and hurried up the steps. I hadn't been in touch with the vampire hunters that day, and I needed to update them. Arnaud was more demon now than vampire, and his zombie feat at the quarry meant he was even more powerful somehow than he'd been the other night at Container City. I wanted the hunters to keep their eyes on the streets, but to back off the hunt.

I couldn't ask them to engage him now, not even for thirty thousand.

As I neared their floor, I listened for the rumbling of a generator and the sounds of screaming guitars and vocals, but all was silent in the condemned building. The second I stepped onto the corridor, my stomach clenched from the unmistakable scent of blood. My gaze followed a line of rust-colored footprints backwards to the apartment at the corridor's end, where the vampire hunters' door stood ajar.

A minute later, I was on my reserve flip phone.

"Who's this?" a gruff voice answered.

"Hoffman, it's Everson Croft."

"What's up?" the detective asked. "You okay?"

My mouth was so dry, I could barely form the words.

"Triple homicide," I said faintly, then fought to swallow.

"And Hoffman ... It's bad."

An hour later, Hoffman emerged from the apartment in one of his polyester suits. He peeled off a pair of latex gloves and joined me at the other end of the corridor, where I'd remained rooted. Behind him, officers and techs continued to work the inhuman scene where I'd discovered the bodies of Blade, Bullet, and Dr. Z.

Or what remained of them.

Hoffman released a heavy sigh and dragged a hand around his wreath of curls. "You weren't kidding. That might be the worst I've ever seen, and in this city, that's saying a lot." He gestured to the line of footprints he'd been careful to step around. "You were right about those, too. The vic pulled from the East River yesterday morning was wearing the same size and brand when he left the house."

"What did you find inside?" I asked, my throat still raw.

"The perp tossed the place pretty good. He was looking for something, but not valuables. There was a wad of cash on one of the beds he didn't touch." Probably my first payment to them, I thought. "Some other things. No telling if he found what he was looking for."

But I knew he had. The way he'd displayed the bodies spoke to a man—or creature—celebrating. Given the hunters' work, the object of his pursuit could have been something that had belonged to a vampire or vampire spawn. Something that would further his cause. What that was, though, I could only guess.

"You think it's this Arnaud Thorne, huh?" Hoffman said.

On that question, I didn't have to guess. "I know it's him."

"That why you called me and not Vega?"

I nodded. There was no way I could have let her walk in on that with her knowing the same creature had held her son captive. "If you don't mind," I said, "I'd like to be the one to tell her."

"Then you better get a move on. Once the reports start going out, she's gonna know."

Vega had spent the day making sure Brian and Cameo were processed while helping the department sort out exactly what had happened at Epic Con and the quarry, not to mention the Hudson power station and the surrounding neighborhoods.

I looked from the bloody footprints to the portly detective. We'd had our battles, but ever since teaming up at Yankee Stadium, we'd developed a grudging acceptance of the other.

"Thanks, Hoffman," I said.

He grunted and slapped my shoulder. "Sorry about your friends."

Without waiting for a response, he returned to the crime scene.

WHEN I CALLED VEGA, I ASKED THAT WE SPEAK IN THE CORRIDOR, where Tony couldn't overhear us. I arrived to find her waiting outside her door in a pair of faded jeans and one of her thick white turtlenecks.

"What is it?" she asked, the corridor amplifying her whispered voice.

I took a moment to gather myself. "The vampire hunters are dead. Happened sometime last night."

"Arnaud?" she asked.

I nodded. Vega clasped my hands tightly in hers and waited for me to explain. I didn't describe what I'd seen when I pushed open their apartment door, what Arnaud had reduced the three of them to—I couldn't. Only that it had been brutal.

Unimaginably brutal.

"What we need to understand," I went on, "is that Arnaud is a different creature than the one I sent down. His time in the Pits ... It changed him. Not that he wasn't already a monster, but the scene he left at the apartment ... Whether he intended it or not, it was a message. If he ever gets his hands on us, he won't play the kinds of games he did as a vampire. He's going to do much, much worse."

Vega absorbed the information solemnly.

"And I think Arnaud found something at their place."

"What?" she asked, her voice gone husky.

"I'm not sure, maybe something that protects him. The detectives found gray salt in the apartment, which can be used for storing enchanted objects. I didn't pick up anything like that inside, though."

I'd forced myself to return to the crime scene and do my part before coming here.

Vega released one of my hands to touch the ring hanging from her neck. I doubted she was even aware she was doing it. She rotated the ring back and forth a few times through her turtleneck. When she tried to return it to me last night, I refused to take it. And I damned sure wasn't going to take it now.

But a sinister whisper took up in the back of my mind: *What if he's protected against the Brasov Pact? What if the coin pendant and ring do nothing now?* Was that my magic talking, or my own fears?

"I have some news too," Vega said, breaking up the thought.

I lifted my gaze from the ring. "Oh yeah? What is it?"

Her eyes turned moist as she tried to smile.

"I think I'm pregnant."

DRUID BOND
PROF CROFT BOOK 7

When the deal you need isn't the one you want

To protect Vega and her son from the demon-vampire Arnaud, I've secured spots for them in a powerful safehouse. The price? Pledging my services to the Upholders, a group searching for stolen loved ones.

My new teammates are a young minister, a snarky half-fae, a hulking mermaid, and a druid with major control issues. Bonded by said druid's magic, I couldn't wriggle out of this deal if I were coated in wizard's oil.

Now we're hunting demons in a past version of New York City that's on the bad side of strange. But I can't stop thinking about Arnaud. He's too close to the ones I cherish, and growing more lethal by the hour. He's also gotten his talons on an enchanted item that could undo their protection.

I need to fulfill my contract to the Upholders and race home. But dangers here are mounting, verging on biblical. If I don't crank my magic to eleven and become the leader this team needs, I may never see Vega again...

Or hold our future child.

AVAILABLE NOW!

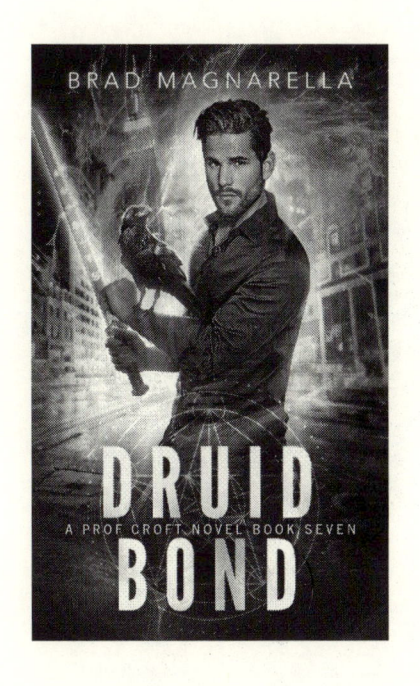

Druid Bond
(Prof Croft, Book 7)

AUTHOR'S NOTES

Power Game is my love letter to urban fantasy. In what other genre can you feature an efreet, demons, a zombie dragon, and a character inspired by the Comic Book Guy from *The Simpsons* in the same story?

The correct answer is either none or a really trippy Tom Robbins memoir.

We also got the series' first sci-fi and fantasy convention. Knowing the con might end in disaster, I worked furiously to squeeze in all the genre nods and Easter eggs I could reasonably get away with. Writing a cameo for myself was definitely pushing the envelope and yeah, self-indulgent as sin. But Stan Burke organizing another Epic Con *and* inviting me back seemed like a long shot. So I grabbed my fifteen minutes while I could.

Fun and cons aside, this installment is what I kept thinking of as Everson's "Big Leap Forward." That goes for his improved casting abilities, his deeper commitment to Vega, and thus adulthood, and his first stab at leading a team.

His was an odd team, granted: a depressed cat, a lovelorn goblin, a geriatric nether whisperer (and her tentacle-lipped pet), an NYPD detective, and a senile magic-user who'd apparently raided Ozzy Osbourne's dressing room.

All things considered, I think Everson did a commendable job. And the rescued efreet apparently agrees, having leveled him up a rune on his sword. I wonder what the other seven runes do…

Now for the bad news. Vega's brothers have aligned against him. The vampire hunters are dead. Arnaud is clearly back, armed with a bond-negating scepter. And we've met a new, and perhaps even bigger, threat in his master, Malphas.

We do see Everson taking steps at the end to balance his need to go after Arnaud with his growing responsibility to protect Vega and her son. That has meant a commitment to a more powerful team, but whose objectives might not align with his own. This challenge will very much be the focus of the next book, *Druid Bond*.

Oh, and of course Vega's little revelation there at the end.

A quick note on that, lest you call me wicked names for ending things on a cliffhanger. I had no idea Vega was going to say those final four words until right before she actually did. I was as stunned as anyone and had to squint at her announcement from a few different angles before deciding that, yes, of course she does.

Some will say that's a sign of a weak writer. Me? I say it's a sign of a character who knows her own biology.

There are many people to thank for *Power Game*, so let's get cracking. A big thanks to the very talented team at damonza.com for designing another in a series of exemplary covers; beta and advanced readers Linda Ash, Danny Barron, Mark Denman, and Erin Halbmaier for their invaluable comments and feedback; proofreaders Sharlene Magnarella and Donna Rich for final proofing; and Akha Ama Coffee in Chiang Mai, Thailand for fueling me with green tea and award-worthy café lattes while I sat at my corner table logging daily words.

I also want to thank James Patrick Cronin, who brings all the books in the Croftverse to life through his gifted narration on the audio editions. Those books, including samples, can be found on my Audible.com author page.

Finally, thank you, incredible reader, for inhabiting this very special world with me.

Till next time…

Best Wishes,
Brad Magnarella

P.S. Be sure to check out my website to learn more about the Croftverse, download a pair of free prequels, and find out what's coming! That's all at bradmagnarella.com

CROFTVERSE CATALOGUE

PROF CROFT PREQUELS
Book of Souls

Siren Call

MAIN SERIES
Demon Moon

Blood Deal

Purge City

Death Mage

Black Luck

Power Game

Druid Bond

Night Rune

Shadow Duel

Shadow Deep

Godly Wars

Angel Doom

SPIN-OFFS
Croft & Tabby

Croft & Wesson

BLUE WOLF
Blue Curse

Blue Shadow

Blue Howl

Blue Venom

Blue Blood

Blue Storm

SPIN-OFF

Legion Files

For the entire chronology go to bradmagnarella.com

ABOUT THE AUTHOR

Brad Magnarella writes urban fantasy for the same reason most read it…

To explore worlds where magic crackles from fingertips, vampires and shifters walk city streets, cats talk (some excessively), and good prevails against all odds. It's shamelessly fun.

His two main series, Prof Croft and Blue Wolf, make up the growing Croftverse, with over a quarter-million books sold to date and an Independent Audiobook Award nomination.

Hopelessly nomadic, Brad can be found in a rented room overseas or hiking America's backcountry.

Or just go to www.bradmagnarella.com

Made in the USA
Columbia, SC
23 April 2025